OUT

OUT

A NOVEL BY JOHN SMOLENS

Michigan State University Press | *East Lansing*

Michigan State University Press
East Lansing, Michigan 48823-5245

Printed and bound in the United States of America.

28 27 26 25 24 23 22 21 20 19   1 2 3 4 5 6 7 8 9 10

LIBRARY OF CONGRESS CATALOGING-IN-PUBLICATION DATA
Names: Smolens, John, author.
Title: Out : a novel / John Smolens.
Description: East Lansing : Michigan State University Press, [2019]
Identifiers: LCCN 2018016027| ISBN 9781611863123 (cloth : alk. paper) | ISBN 9781609175917
(pdf) | ISBN 9781628953541 (epub) | ISBN 9781628963540 (kindle)
Classification: LCC PS3569.M646 O88 2019 | DDC 813/.54—dc23
LC record available at https://lccn.loc.gov/2018016027

Book design by Charlie Sharp, Sharp Designs, East Lansing, MI
Cover design by David Drummond
Cover art is *Deep forest*, by sandsun, and is used under license
from iStock, by Getty Images.

Michigan State University Press is a member of the Green Press Initiative and is
committed to developing and encouraging ecologically responsible publishing
practices. For more information about the Green Press Initiative and the use of
recycled paper in book publishing, please visit *www.greenpressinitiative.org*.

Visit Michigan State University Press at *www.msupress.org*

Something gnaws inside my head. It asks forgiveness.

—*Yellow Dog Journal*, Judith Minty

Oh, the trouble soon be over, sorrow will have an end.

—"Trouble Soon Be Over," Blind Willie Johnson

FOR DAVID RAYMOND, *Artist / Educator*

There is no perfect thing
until even the shadows,
as darkest forms,
unfurl in constant, shining revelation.

—"Chiaroscuro," D. R.

In order to find one's way during a blizzard, particularly in whiteout conditions, one must rely upon memory, an innate sense of direction, and dumb luck. Writing this novel, and its companion, *Cold*, necessitated these same attributes. The geography in *Out* does not strictly adhere to any map of Michigan's Upper Peninsula. Though the Yellow Dog River is in the U.P., you won't find Yellow Dog Township, at least not until you stop looking.

ACKNOWLEDGMENTS

Grateful is one of those words that, like hero, we toss around too often and far too easily. They are words we should employ sparingly, so that when we do use them the true meaning of the word and the real measure of the person upon which it is bestowed comes through. In this instance, to say that I am grateful to the people who have helped me while writing this book is an understatement.

John Beck
Julie Harrison
Walt Lindala
Julie Loehr
& the Staff at Michigan State University Press
Ellen Longsworth

OUT

He lived out.

In Michigan's Upper Peninsula the term often means to reside not just outside of town but in the woods with little or no reliance on the usual modern conveniences. He had electricity, propane, a septic tank, and well water. Out but not entirely off the grid.

They bought the house five years ago. It had been a hunting camp on forty acres, built by a logging baron before World War I. For three years they remained in their house in Marquette, renovating the camp on weekends and during the summer. They did most of the work themselves, with the help of friends. The house had exposed timbers and an enormous fireplace constructed with stones gathered from the Lake Superior shore.

Since his second surgery, he spent much of the day on the couch, staring at the fire, at the stones. The Percocet helped the ache in his left hip, and periodically he drifted into a distant place he thought of as three-quarter-sleep. Once the pills took effect, he liked listening to music and throughout the afternoon he'd been playing Bach cello suites on the stereo. With the heat from the fireplace, with his eyes closed, the somber notes surrounded him like warm water. He was in the Cello State, nothing but the bow working back and forth across the strings, horsehair on gut, and when he would revive from this state, it would take a moment to remember who and where he was, to realize that he was waiting.

When they had moved here, the idea was that they no longer would have to wait. For anything. But after less than two years of living out, it happened to Liesl. Then all they seemed to do was wait. Whether you lived in town or out, there was always the waiting. After she died nine months later, he wondered if he was through waiting. He thought he might be there.

———————————

The best thing to do is to do what you're supposed to do.

So she drove out County Road 644, where the snowbanks were higher than her Ford Escort. Instead of numbers, she wished they'd give all these roads names, real names, the names of people. If not that, then the names of places or animals. Some ten miles out 644 the snow was heavier here in the woods, big flakes drifting down toward the windshield, a Nordic meteor shower. Everything was white except the trees, which were the blackest black.

When she turned into the drive, she could tell it had been plowed earlier that day, but there was already another foot of new snow. No fresh tracks. The drive went up and around to the left, where it leveled off and widened before the house. The shingles had that new cedar color she liked because the wood still looked alive. There was a good two feet of snow on the roof and no lights in the windows. She wondered if there was no electricity to the house or if there was a power outage. Out here, you never knew.

To get out of the car she had to grab hold of the top of the door and pull herself up. She got her shoulder bag from the rear seat and climbed the steps to the porch. By way of knocking, she stamped the snow off her boots. From inside the house she could hear music, a solitary instrument, and at the moment she couldn't remember the name of it, though she liked its resonant, mournful sound. There was no doorbell, and she was about to rap her gloved fist on the wooden door when a man's voice inside said, "It's open."

He watched her close the front door as she gazed up at the pitched ceiling crisscrossed by exposed timbers. After removing her wool hat, coat, and scarf, she took from her shoulder bag a pair of worn moccasins decorated with blue, white, and red beads, which she placed on the pine floor just beyond the doormat.

"What happened to Jennifer?" he asked.

While pulling off her boots and stepping into the moccasins, she kept one hand on the doorframe for balance. "Called in sick, I guess. Or maybe she quit?" She came over to the sofa that faced the large stone fireplace. "This place is, um, big. Open."

"There were too many walls, too many rooms, so we ripped out what wasn't necessary." He looked at the tag pinned to her sweatshirt. *M. Fournier.* "What's the M stand for?"

"Marcia." She decided to sit on the large slab of pine that served as a coffee table between the sofa and the fireplace. With one hand she pulled her dark blond hair away from her eyes, while with the other she removed a laptop from her bag.

He glanced at her sweatshirt, her belly. "How far along are you?"

"More than a baby bump, eh?" Her smile formed dimples in her full cheeks. "Into the ninth month now."

"And still working."

"I'm on call. Just filling in here and there. Can't really afford to stop working. I'll have to eventually, I guess." She was concentrating on opening her computer, which was perched on her knees.

"First?"

"Hm-hm." Again, she swept hair off her forehead as she squinted at the screen. "So, you are Delbert Maki."

"Just Del is fine."

"Okay. And what's your birthdate, Mr. Maki?"

"Eight, twenty-one, forty-nine. Think you might have the wrong guy lying on his couch way out here in the woods?"

Del could see she wanted to smile but was uncertain. He supposed someone her age might not be sure when someone his age was making a joke. Instead, she tucked her lower lip under her front teeth as she leaned closer to the screen. Somehow he felt in that moment he knew her entire life. This happened more and more often. He'd look at someone and just felt he knew them. Sometimes he was wrong, but often he was quite on the money. He suspected he knew what seemed to be confusing her.

"Which hip are you here to work on?" he asked.

"Well, your right one was replaced last January, and your left this January." Still she seemed uncertain. "They were done a year apart. To the day. Let me guess: hockey player."

"Very good. Does it say that in your computer?"

"No. It's a game that results in knee and hip replacement later in life."

"I like the way you say that, later in life."

She didn't smile, though he could see that she was tempted. "Last year I was in on a consultation between a man who wasn't fifty and his doctor. They were looking at the X-rays, and the doctor said, 'You have the hips of a seventy-year-old woman.' The guy took it as a compliment. He was a goalie. They're nuts. You weren't one of those?"

"No. I was a defenseman. You might say I was sane."

She placed the laptop on the table next to his stack of books and magazines, what he considered his active pile. "So what kind of exercises has Jennifer had you doing?"

"You know, simple stuff. Lifting the leg repeatedly. Standing up and sitting down. Maybe she thinks I'm a seventy-year-old woman?"

Marcia smiled this time, but then there was a sound and she looked alert and worried as something began scraping the roof toward the back of the house.

"Tree," he said. "I should have trimmed that branch before winter, but with my hip I let it go. With the weight of the snow there's this one that's been hitting the house. Next summer that whole tree'll have to come down."

"Why?"

"It's dying is why. Norway maple. Hardly any leaves this past year." She was silent. "You don't like the idea of cutting down trees, do you?"

"Well, no, but if it's, you know, dying." Marcia ventured a look at Del, and he thought he saw something; he wasn't sure what, but it wasn't what he expected. "Everything dies," she said. "It's just a question of when and how."

Connor Tyne couldn't really think.

Too much adrenaline.

He had left Barr lying in the snow, and in the failing winter light the blood appeared to be black. Connor didn't even know his first name. Nobody ever called him anything but Barr.

So Connor just drove around Marquette, for how long he wasn't sure. Slowly, his hands on the steering wheel began to feel like his hands again and as he calmed down he tried to figure out what to do next. Marcia would say, *Think of your options. What are your options?* If he said he didn't know, she'd get angry. If he said it didn't matter because either way he was fucked, she wouldn't speak to him. For days sometimes. When she did that, he would just about lose it, imagining that she was with Barr, her other option. But now Barr was lying in the snow. Dead, he was no longer an option. If he wasn't dead, that part of it wasn't over. Either way, Connor was still fucked.

One option was to go back and see how bad he was, see if Barr was still alive. If he was, Connor could get him in his truck and take him to the hospital. Eventually he'd be caught and maybe that would be in his favor, the fact that he'd taken Barr to the hospital. If Barr was dead, then it really didn't matter.

No one would buy that this wasn't Connor's fault. Except Marcia. She would know that she was partially to blame. She had been there, and when she saw the way it was going, she ran off. She could see the truth in things, which made it harder for him to understand why she couldn't see the truth in Barr.

Connor called her cell phone, but he pressed *End Call* before he heard her phone ring. Not a minute later, as he was driving along Lake Shore Boulevard, he hit redial, and this time he got her voicemail and said, "Where'd you go? Call me."

He pulled into the lot at Picnic Rocks, which was empty, and parked so he could look north across the water toward Presque Isle. The waves breaking along the shore were six feet at least, and the wind caused his truck to shiver and rattle. It occurred to him that, dead or alive, Barr would soon be buried in snow. Earlier in the day, Connor had heard on the radio that this blizzard could last two or three days and they might get up to four feet of snow. The windchill could drop to fifty below zero. Route 28, where it ran along the lake, was closed as far as Munising, fifty miles to the east. It was going to be that kind of a storm. No one would be able to get out of Marquette. Nothing would be able to get in. Ordinarily Connor liked these storms. Since he was a kid, he thought they were something to survive, something to endure. They were adventures. This one he wanted to escape.

After trying Marcia's phone once more, he called Lindy, her supervisor. He wasn't supposed to do that—Marcia was clear about it, saying that Lindy could be a real bitch when it came to taking personal calls.

Lindy picked up after the first ring. "Up North Physical Therapy and Rehabilitation."

"I'm trying to reach Marcia Fournier, and I'm only getting her voicemail." There was a pause over the line. He suspected she knew who he was—or she might not be sure which *one* he was. "This storm," he said. "It's gonna get worse, and I want to make sure she gets in all right."

Still Lindy didn't respond immediately. He heard a series of clicks as she tapped on a computer keyboard. "Yeah, this is going to be a good one," she said. She sounded distracted, and he suspected she was peering at the computer screen while she spoke. "You tried to reach her recently?"

"Just a minute ago."

"Well, according to the schedule—here it is—she's out 644."

"If she doesn't get on the road soon, she'll never make it back into Marquette."

"Hm." She wasn't disagreeing.

"Where on 644?"

"Let's see. Del Maki. He's at 2387. Yellow Dog Township. That's a ways."

"Okay, thanks. I'll keep trying her."

Lindy didn't say anything else but just hung up.

———

While she took Del Maki through his exercises, Marcia wanted to check her cell phone, but she couldn't find it anywhere, not in her bag or her pockets, not in her coat.

"I think I've lost my phone," she said. "I need to check in my car while you do your squats."

"Fine," he said. "Jennifer has me do them in the kitchen, where I can keep a hand on the counter for balance."

"No cheating."

She pulled on her coat and boots and went outside, carefully retracing her steps down to the car, where she looked on the floor and under the driver's seat.

When she got back inside the house, he said, "I didn't cheat." He slowly lowered himself until she could only see his head above the counter that separated the kitchen from the living room. "Find your phone?"

"No," she said as she shrugged off her coat. "I don't think you're the cheatin' kind."

He smiled as he came up slowly and exhaled. "Try my phone—it's there on the coffee table, but good luck getting a signal."

After stepping into her moccasins, she found the phone amid the pile of magazines and books. After fidgeting with buttons, she said. "Nothing. You ever get a phone signal out here?"

"Depends."

"Depends on what?"

"Who knows? The miles of hills and woods between here and the signal towers? Or maybe it's the satellite? Or there's eagle shit on the dish?" He grabbed his cane and worked his way around the counter and came to the sofa. "Why, you got a hot date?"

"It's a bit late for that."

She expected him to smile, or even laugh, but he didn't. There was an unusual concentration that came into his face as he carefully lowered himself into the sofa. He wore glasses, which somehow made his eyes seem brighter, his gaze more piercing, and as he stared straight ahead toward the fireplace, she wondered if he was one of those people who meditated. That sort of thing frightened her a bit, but it also intrigued her. Where do they go when they meditate? Don't you really just meditate—think—all day long? Or when you meditate do you really *empty* your mind; do you really change the way your mind works? It seemed the idea was to think of nothing, and she didn't know if that was possible, for her, at least. To think of nothing you had to be dead.

"The thing is," she said, "I'm actually relieved that there's no phone signal out here."

Now he turned those eyes on her. They were curious and perhaps sympathetic, but he didn't ask, didn't say anything.

"Next, we want to do the exercises on the bed."

Nothing seemed to change in his expression. "It's a bit late for that."

She smiled. She couldn't help it.

Getting in and out of bed was the hardest part, same as after the first hip replacement last year.

"My left leg is pathetic." He was sitting on the edge of the mattress. "Very little strength to lift itself at all."

"It'll come. You know that from last year. You've done eight. Just do two more."

He turned his upper body and then there was the moment where he wanted to lie back on the mattress but his left foot remained on the floor. "I just can't tell my leg to lift itself up on to the bed. I have to use the loop—I hate this part."

"That's what it's for."

He sat upright again. The loop—he didn't know what its real name was and if the therapists had ever told him he didn't remember—was in his left hand. It was made out of material that reminded him of a dog leash, yet it was stiff, though not rigid; stiff but flexible. It was about a yard long and one end formed a loop, which he placed around his left foot. Even that took some doing since he had difficulty lifting his foot off the floor, but finally he had the loop under his instep, which made him think of the stirrup on a horse's saddle. He held still for a moment, and then turned his upper body again, and this time with his left arm he lifted the inert, dead weight of his left leg up and deposited it on the mattress next to his other leg. It took complete concentration and he was exhausted.

"That was very good," she said.

"Liar."

"Rest a moment and do one more."

"Number ten." He closed his eyes. He could fall asleep right now. It was the pills, he supposed. They made you not want to do anything but lie still. He tried not to take them—his doctor said he could take up to two every four hours. He seldom took two at a time, and often he went much longer than four hours before taking another dose, but there were moments when the throbbing ache in his new hip, and the total weariness everywhere else, just became so much that he realized it didn't make sense to hold out any longer, and he would give in and take another pill. They called it *Keeping ahead of the pain.* An absurd but practical notion.

With one more leg lift to do, he wondered if he could distract her so she might forget about it. Sometimes with his regular therapist, Jennifer, he could get her talking and she'd just go on and on, and she'd lose count of the exercise he was doing and finally just simply tell him he'd done enough.

"You mind my asking?" He kept his eyes closed. "Do you know if it's a boy or a girl?"

"Don't want to know."

"I like that."

"I like surprises."

"You'd better."

"I have been thinking of names."

"And?"

"Nothing yet. Guess I have to see him or her first."

"Sounds like this is all your decision."

"It is. It's my baby."

He opened his eyes because he knew she was looking at him.

"You're out here all alone," she said. "Your wife, how did she die?"

"Did I tell you I had a wife who died?"

She shook her head.

"But you knew."

"Kinda."

"How'd you know?"

"Wild guess?"

"I'm not buying that."

"It's this house. Something about it." Now she hesitated, and he suspected she didn't want to pursue it, the notion that a man living alone wouldn't be this neat. "What happened?" she asked.

"She died of a brain tumor. About a year and a half ago. She was fine, then one day she wasn't. Nine months later she was dead."

"Nine months." Marcia seemed reluctant to take it further, but he knew she would—somehow he was certain that she couldn't help it. "Seems like a long time. For me, that is. For this." She placed a hand on her belly. "I guess it depends."

"Most everything depends."

"Really?"

"Yes, really. It's something I've learned later in life."

After a moment she said, "You've done nine lifts. Ready for number ten?"

"Damn. Never thought you'd ask."

Barr heard a phone ringing.

It didn't sound right, didn't sound like his phone, and it was muffled. On the third ring he turned his head slightly, causing pain to surge from his neck up into his skull. The left side of his face was numb. Cold. But the cold couldn't get to the ache in his teeth. His jaw felt out of whack. It occurred to him that he was lying in snow. It occurred to him that it was snowing because the right side of his face was covered with snow. It occurred to him that the ringing was coming from his pocket.

He moved his right arm, and the snow covering his shoulder slid onto his neck. It was a different kind of cold from the numbness on the left side of his face. The snow on his neck felt clean and the cold made him more alert. He put his right hand inside his coat pocket and found his cell phone. Slowly, he took it out and held it up in front of his face. His right eye was nearly swollen shut. With his good eye he could see his phone, a black oblong in his hand. It wasn't lit up; it wasn't ringing. Yet the ringing continued, muffled, somewhere beneath him.

Until the ringing stopped and he could hear the wind, he could hear the snow pelting his coat. Then he heard a voice. Though it too was muffled, he knew that voice.

"Where'd you go? Call me."

———————————

Marcia remembered now: it was a cello, a single, solitary, so solitary cello, and when the CD ended she became aware of the wind. Driving through the woods on 644, there hadn't been much wind, but now it was building in massive, extended gusts. The house, its pine ceiling and thick timbers, which made her feel like she was staring up at the underside of a bridge, creaked and groaned. The wind was a hand, cradling the house, and that branch was its fingers, clawing at the roof.

She followed him as he worked his way from the bedroom back to the living room. Many patients would still be using a walker this soon after surgery, but he was doing quite well with the cane. When he sat and then stretched out on the couch, she said, "I'd like to use the bathroom."

He nodded toward the kitchen. She went around the counter, through the kitchen, and into the bathroom, and after closing the door, she moved the handicap seat with armrests and sat on the toilet.

The light above the sink went dark. Just like that. As though by design. Light to dark. She peed for a long time, wondering if the relief after giving birth could match this, be anything like this. When she was finished she put the handicap seat back in place over the toilet and looked out the window. The snow was horizontal. She could barely see the woods, not thirty yards from the house. Whiteout conditions—people sometimes described it as like being inside one of those glass snow globes they had as kids, but it wasn't like that at all. It was far more intense. And more beautiful.

"Power go out often?" she asked when she returned to the living room.

"Depends," he said from the couch. "What do you consider often?"

"Like the phone signal."

"It occurs frequently. Some might say with considerable frequency."

"Particularly during a blizzard."

"You don't think this stuff happens on a sunny day in August, do you?"

Marcia stared out the window next to the front door. She could barely see her tracks leading from the car up to the house. "On the radio they said this could be a good one. Don't suppose you have one of those backup generators?"

"We talked about getting one but never got around to it. I got a radio with batteries, if I want to listen to the weather forecast. But I think yours is pretty accurate. It'll be dark soon. You should get going."

"You'll be all right?"

He turned his head toward the corner of the room, where logs were stacked. "Long as I have fire, I'm fine."

The flames gave his face a deep gold color, and she thought she could detect the young man he had been. His beard was white and the whiskers looked prickly, but they seemed like something she would like to stroke with her fingers, like the pelt of an animal.

"Seriously," he said. "You need to get on your way."

"No phone, no electricity. This is why you live here, right?"

"Apparently."

Once Connor got out of Marquette on 644 he realized how bad it was, and it was only going to get worse. His pickup was able to push through a foot of new snow because of the three sand sausages in the bed, adding several hundred pounds over the rear axle. He hoped, wherever she was, that Marcia wouldn't even try to get back into town, not in that little piece of shit for a car.

He had her Ford Escort to thank for all of this. They had known each other for years, sort of. That all changed one night two years ago last summer. The car was pulled off the road on the west side of Presque Isle.

Though it was after eleven o'clock, there was still light in the western sky—it was less than a week before Fourth of July, and Marquette was drunk on sunlight, the days impossibly long, the sun rising before six and setting minutes before ten. It was that brief time of year when everyone wanted to be outdoors all the time, when you wore clothes that seemed inconceivable during the long winters. She was wearing a T-shirt over a two-piece bathing suit. Her hair and the T-shirt were wet. The T-shirt clung to her breasts, and its logo was so faded he couldn't read it. He tried not to stare too long. She was barefoot, standing next to the front of her car, the hood raised. He'd been out on Presque Isle, drinking beer with Barr and his cousin Zack. They'd gone out to Black Rocks, where they had a clear view of the northern horizon on Lake Superior. There were no lights, no moon. They had a six-pack while they waited, watching. The air was humid and still, the lake flat, only the faintest lapping of water against the rocks. Zack struck up a joint, passed it to Barr, and when he held it out Connor shook his head. *Pussy*, Barr said. *Not unless we see them*, Connor said. *Pussy*, Barr and Zack said together.

By the time they killed the six-pack, the sky above the horizon was as black as the lake itself. So they climbed off the rock, but when Zack got in Barr's car Connor said he was going to stay a little longer. They both chided him, saying you weren't going to see shit tonight, but finally they took off, leaving Connor alone to watch for the northern lights. He leaned against the front grill of his truck for maybe another twenty minutes, staring toward the horizon. Nothing. So black that he could barely see the line where water met sky. But that was all right. He liked it out here, always did. And finally, he climbed in the cab, put a CD on, and left Presque Isle. Funny, he was listening to an old Dire Straits song called "Fade to Black."

And then, cruising around Presque Isle to the west side, he saw her standing by the front of her car. At first, he couldn't tell who it was, couldn't see her face in the dark, but he saw her bare legs, and that the hood of her car was raised. When he got out and realized that it was

Marcia Fournier, he had a moment when he regretted pulling over, something that he thought about later, when it was too late. A little part of him always said, *Don't get involved*, but it seemed he never listened to it. As he walked toward her, she said, *Battery's dead. I could use a jump.* A moment's hesitation, suggesting that she realized how what she had said might be taken. *You don't have battery cables?*

He did.

———————————

"Before I go," she said as she shoved her laptop in her bag. "What can I do?"

"Add a couple of logs to the fire," he said. "And I think I could use one of the pills in the bathroom cabinet."

He closed his eyes and listened to her in the kitchen. He used to lie here sometimes and listen to Liesl, able to see everything she was doing, opening drawers, the refrigerator, turning on the gas stove, the burners clicking several times before igniting the flame. If there was music on—they listened to music much of the time—and if it was stuff they grew up with, called oldies now, she often sang along softly. Frequently she would harmonize with Roy Orbison, Aretha Franklin, or Bonnie Raitt. Secretly, he knew, she had always wanted to be a singer. She was too shy for such things. But at home she sang. No one else ever got to hear her sing. A privilege. She must have felt safe. When she sang, something, some concealed part of her, opened up. She had a good voice, but he never said anything, never said, *You have a good voice*, because he knew that a compliment would only shut her up.

When Marcia brought him the pill and a glass of water, he opened his eyes and sat up a bit. He took the pill and stared into the fire while she put on her boots and coat.

"All right, I'm off," she said as she went to the front door.

He didn't turn to look at her.

"You going to be all right?" she asked.

"Soon as that pill kicks in."

"Your next physical therapy visit is Friday."

"It gonna be you?"

She didn't answer immediately. "Depends."

He turned his head and looked across the room at her. "Good luck with that, Marcia."

Again, she didn't answer immediately, and then she said, "Thanks. Bye."

She opened the front door, allowing the howl of the wind, snow, and a cold gust of air to stream into the house until she closed the first door behind her. He stared at the fire again. The heat on his face was good, and he thought of their last dog, Lucky, who loved to lie in front of the fire with his head only inches from the crackling logs. His snout would get so hot they didn't know how he could stand it. But he did. He was a lab-shepherd mix, and they'd had him for a dozen years. When they moved out here from Marquette, they realized it was the best thing that had ever happened to Lucky. He never needed to be walked on a leash; here, they just let him outside, and he could come and go as he pleased. After he died they buried him behind the house, just beyond where the garden was going to be. There were a lot of things they were going to do—backup generator, a garden, build a shed, maybe even a garage—and they thought they had plenty of time. Liesl's brain tumor was discovered only a few months after Lucky died. They talked about him a lot, in waiting rooms, in hospital rooms. Del supposed that's what most couples without kids did, have pets and talk about them a lot. During the ten weeks Liesl was in hospice care here in the house, he gave her morphine often, first drops under the tongue, but toward the end he gave her injections. When she was spaced out he needed to believe there wasn't any pain. Between the morphine and the growth in her left frontal lobe, she became more distracted, more detached, more adrift. She said things that didn't make sense. She saw things that weren't there. The hospice aides told him it was common for people with brain tumors to hallucinate. He didn't like the word and insisted on the word *visions*, on saying that she was having *visions*. But there was no question that the tumor was killing her. Worse, it was killing who she was, slowly. Sometimes she asked about Lucky as though he were there, sleeping by the fireplace. He couldn't bring himself to tell her Lucky was dead.

Hinges creaked, and Marcia came back in the house, yanking the front door shut against the wind and cold. He turned his head, which was a bit of an effort—the pill was beginning to do its thing—and he saw that her left side was completely covered with snow.

He already knew but said, "This mean it's Friday already?"

She stomped her boots on the mat. "Car won't start. I turned the key several times, but there was nothing."

Barr managed to sit up.

There was blood in the snow. Overhead he heard that sound that could be made by strong wind in pines, and in the distance the roar of the lake. He got to his knees and tried to stand, but he was so dizzy he fell over on his side. Something was desperately wrong with him—he didn't know what.

He lay still for a minute. Or ten minutes. He had no idea.

When he began shivering, he realized that if he didn't get up and out of this he could freeze to death. It was that kind of weather, that kind of storm.

Again, he got to his knees and this time crawled to the nearest tree trunk. The bark was rough and cold on his bare palms but he was able to pull himself up until he was standing. Both hands on the tree, he leaned forward and puked into the snow. It came out of him in great heaves until he was gasping, and the burning stuff was backed up in his sinuses. A long strand of snot hung from his nose, swaying in the wind, until it finally let go. He wiped his nose and mouth on the sleeve of his coat and straightened up.

There was nothing but woods. His car must be nearby. The sound of the lake was to his right, which was the direction the wind was coming from, so he began to walk in the other direction. There was much deadfall, and he had to go over and around downed branches. He was moving downhill, and then he saw the road. It was just a white band of open space in the woods, but clearly it was a road, and suddenly he knew where he was: Presque Isle. He made his way down to the road, sometimes on all fours as the grade steepened, and looking to his left he saw his car fifty yards away.

And then some of it came back to him.

Presque Isle: it had been Marcia's idea.

Marcia removed her hat and shook out her hair. She was so cold she was reluctant to take off her coat, but she did, and then her boots. Once she had slipped her moccasins on, she went over to the couch. Del had covered himself with a blanket.

"You look cold," he said.

She folded her arms. "I am."

"It's a gas stove. Why don't you heat something up? I have lots of soup. Also, there are kerosene storm lanterns on the bookshelf. We should get a couple of those fired up before dark."

"Okay." She picked up his cell phone from the coffee table and saw that it still wasn't receiving a signal. "This is getting strange. The phone. The electricity. The car."

"Try to keep the rustic charm in mind."

She put the phone back on the table and went to the bookshelf. When she had the lanterns out on the counter, he said, "Is someone expecting you back in Marquette?" When she didn't answer right away, he said,

"What about the agency, don't they expect you to report back to them?" When she still didn't answer, he said, "Expecting, but not expected, eh?"

"Ha-ha, very funny. No, it's after five," she said. "My supervisor's probably gone for the day. I'd only call in if there's a problem, some emergency. Otherwise, I check in first thing in the morning. The schedule, it changes all the time."

After she had the lanterns lighted, she looked in the cabinets. He had a lot of canned goods. Single people, old people, often do. "What kind of soup? Or chowder. And there's chili."

"Nothing right now," he said.

"Coffee? Tea?"

"Tea, maybe later. You go ahead." After a moment, he said, "There's a bottle of Irish whiskey. I'll have a wee drop, lass."

"You just took one of those pills."

"I promise I won't drive." He turned on the couch, rearranging the blanket. "I hope you're not afraid that I'm going to chase you around the house."

She laughed then, and it took a while to stop. Laughter caused her belly to shift about. Finally, she said, "You have Earl Grey. I'm going to make myself tea, and later I'll heat up some soup. How's that sound?"

"Sounds like a pajama party. You also might get a blanket from the bedroom for yourself."

"Right." After she put the kettle on, she took one of the lanterns and went into the bedroom. There was a wool blanket folded at the end of the bed. The bed was made, and there was not one article of clothing lying about. There were two kinds of old people, single people: those who made the bed every morning and those who didn't. She wasn't surprised he was one of the bed-makers. As she draped the blanket over her shoulder, she turned toward the bureau and saw the framed photographs, mostly of a woman who must have been his wife, and a few of him when he was younger. She was slender, with some gray, and Marcia guessed she was the kind of woman who refused to color her hair. There were no pictures of children, though there were three of a big dog.

She went back into the kitchen and poured her tea. When she returned to the living room with her mug and a small glass of Irish whiskey, his eyes were closed. She thought he was asleep. But then he moved his feet slightly and said, "Why don't you help me with my legs so you can sit down at that end and then put the blankets over you and them."

She was accustomed to touching people. Old people. Sick people. People who were often considered infirm. It was her job. At first, she had to convince herself that she could do it, touch a stranger, but now she just did it. Every day she worked, she handled limbs, touched backs and shoulders. There were times, particularly with the elderly and the post-ops, when she could feel them strain with the effort of performing some simple exercise, standing up, lifting an arm or a leg, and often she tried to will some of her youth and strength to pass from her to the body of the person she was touching. She didn't believe in that New Age stuff, but this she did because it seemed an extension of herself, her concentration, her effort to help someone who was recuperating from illness or surgery. She never knew whether they actually felt her energy pass into their bodies—it wasn't something she dared ask—but occasionally she detected in their struggle some sudden surge of effort, some heightened determination. She doubted she was responsible, but with some of them she suspected that they would not have been able to lift an arm or a leg that high if she hadn't been there, hadn't been guiding their movement with her hands.

When she took hold of his feet, he inhaled as he lifted his legs. It took effort but he did it, lifted his legs enough so she could turn and sit on the couch, and then, exhaling, he let his feet ease down on her lap, his right foot resting gently against her belly.

"If I feel it kicking, I'm going to kick back, understand?" he said.

She arranged the blankets over herself and his legs. "I feel like a soccer ball."

He picked up the glass of whiskey, took a sip, and then laid his head back on the pillow and closed his eyes again. "Pelé's a nice name."

"What's Pelé?"

He smiled, though he kept his eyes closed. "Famous soccer player. Brazilian."

"Before I was born, huh?"

A smile. "Yes. Decades."

"That's what interests you?" she asked. "History?"

He opened his eyes. She could see he was impressed. She was too, really, though she pretended not to be.

"I was thinking." He took another sip of whiskey. "You could take my truck. It's out back."

"I don't know."

"What don't you know?"

"Leaving you out here without your truck."

"It hasn't been started in a few days, but I'm sure the battery's good. It ought to be run."

"And leave you out here, with no phone, no power, no vehicle?"

"And no Bach cello suites. No Duke Robillard, Aretha Franklin, Buddy Guy, or the Reverend Al Green."

"I don't know." She sipped her tea. "Maybe my car will start in a while. Or maybe I could pull the truck around and jump the battery."

He kept his eyes closed. "What're you driving?"

"Ford Escort."

"The way it looks out there I doubt you'd make it down to the road."

This was true. More than being stuck here, she feared the car getting stuck when she was still miles from Marquette. Occasionally, there were news stories about people who got trapped in blizzards, usually out on some remote stretch of county road. They'd spend the night in the car and run out of gas. Often it was a snowplow driver who would find the bodies. It would be in the news, the pregnant woman, frozen to death on County Road 644. Some people would see the story and say, *That poor child.* Some might ask, *What the hell was she doing out there, nine months pregnant?* She wouldn't be able to say, *I was working, you idiot.*

"Getting a jump from the truck's a good idea," she said. "Even if it's just to get the battery charged up. After this cup of tea, I'll make something to eat, something hot, and then I'll go out and bring the truck around."

He didn't open his eyes. "Deal."

They didn't speak and Marcia watched the flames in the fireplace. After a few minutes she wondered if he had fallen asleep. He lay perfectly still with his eyes closed. It must be the medication because with the wind howling outside, the fire crackling, and that branch raking the side and roof of the house she didn't know how he could sleep. But this was not uncommon, her clients falling asleep, particularly during or after a massage. They were like babies, and they seemed to sleep better for having her near them.

She drank her tea, trying not to move any more than necessary. She liked the feeling, the weight of his lower legs lying across her lap, his heels pressing into her right thigh and one foot leaning against her hard, round belly. She was tempted to give him a foot massage, but that might wake him, if he was actually asleep. She gave great massages; her clients often told her so. She had strong hands, sensitive hands, and she liked to feel their muscles respond, the tension being kneaded out of the tissue, the skin, lightly glazed with shea oil, becoming warm and supple beneath her fingers. Elderly clients often apologized for the fact that their skin was aged, for the warts and the moles and the liver spots, but she told them there was nothing to apologize for, and after such assurances she could feel their bodies go soft and pliant beneath her hands.

The problem was people touching her. Boys and now men. Before the pregnancy put the weight on her hips, her thighs, her butt, before she developed what people affectionately called her baby bump, which eventually swelled to an enormity that she couldn't believe, as though it were a separate being, glommed onto the front of her, they wanted to touch her. They wanted to get their hands on her breasts, their fingers up her skirt or down her pants, they wanted to press their flesh against her skin; they wanted to fuck her in the worst way. She used to like being touched, but she wanted to make love, wanted to be in love, wanted her flesh to be a source of connection with another human being in a way that would go beyond or rise above sex. And now, when she thought of being touched, she felt much the way she imagined her older clients felt when she began to give them massages, embarrassed, even ashamed.

"Marcia, you mind if I ask about Pelé's father?"

"I didn't think you were awake."

"I might not have been. I tend to drift off and I don't know if it's for a minute or an hour. I've decided that it doesn't really matter because when you sleep time is different. It isn't *time*, that thing measured by a clock."

"Then what is it?"

"That is a very good question. I don't know if anyone really knows for sure. Where are we when we dream? Or is this the dream? In mythology there's a god called Hypnos, which is where we get the word hypnotism from, and he's the god of sleep. His brother is Thanatos, the god of death. Sometimes I think that that's it, we go halfway to death when we sleep. Sometimes it's a pleasant dream, sometimes a harrowing nightmare. It's kind of a crapshoot. Do you suppose eternity is as well?"

"A crapshoot?" She sipped her tea. "I don't know. If it is, then I guess it doesn't really matter what we do in this life."

"No eternal reward or damnation based on your behavior. No descent into the rings of Dante's inferno." He opened his eyes enough that he could reach out for his glass of whiskey, which he then held on his chest.

"Are you Catholic?"

"Raised." He kept his eyes closed. "You weren't."

"No. I guess my mother was Episcopalian, and I don't know what my father was. I was pretty much raised as nothing, religion-wise. I had friends who were, you know, Catholic, or their parents were really into some church or other, and there would be crosses all over the place, a picture of Jesus in the kitchen, that sort of thing. I just thought it was weird. But sometimes now I wonder if I missed something." She glanced down at her belly. "When you're expecting you begin to wonder how you'll handle it all. I now understand why my mother always seemed worried. I mean at some point Pelé's going to come home from a friend's house and ask 'What's a crucifix?'"

"What are you going to say?"

"I don't know. You can't ignore all that. You can't tell a kid it's just stuff people believe in. It's more than that, I suppose." One of the logs collapsed, rejuvenating the flames, causing the heat from the fire to suddenly become intense. "My dad, when he was around, he would just say something like 'Most people deserve to be nailed to a cross; Jesus was just unlucky' or 'Don't ask so many questions unless you know the answers.' He was usually working on a car or a truck and his hands had that 10W-30 smell, with the engine grime down under the fingernails. But he was the handsomest man in the world. I believed that—still do—and though Mom had plenty to blame him for, she never denied that he was one good-looking man. More than once she said that was the problem."

Del finished the remaining whiskey in his glass and tried to move his legs.

"I guess I'm avoiding your question," she said, "about Pelé's father. I didn't mean to."

"It's all right. I was being too nosy." He was attempting to sit up more and she looked at him, trying to think about where to begin. Connor. Barr. It was impossibly tangled. It was kind of the chicken and the egg. But before she could speak, he said, "Can you hold that thought? Because I can't, you know, hold it much longer."

"Oh, sure."

She helped him ease his legs off of her lap and on to the floor. It was an effort, but he got up from the couch and, using the cane, began what seemed a slow, tedious journey into the kitchen.

"After the operation, didn't they give you a walker?"

"They did," he said as he reached the bathroom door. "But after seven days I put it away, same as last year. From here on it's a cane until I'm a biped again. Hated the walker. Being a triped is the preferred mode of transportation." He shuffled into the bathroom and shut the door.

———————————————

As Del came out of the bathroom, there was a series of loud cracks, followed by a moment of silence and then an enormous percussive thud accompanied by the sound of metal buckling and glass breaking. A great shudder ran through the frame of the house.

Marcia came into the kitchen, her face curious and alert but, he thought, not frightened.

"Tree limb, a big one," he said. The scraping overhead had stopped. "Probably that one on the roof."

He crossed the kitchen to the back door and she followed. They looked out the window and could see the limb lying across the dented hood of his pickup, which was parked behind the house. The windshield was broken and branches filled the cab.

"It'll take a saw to cut that beast up. Not a job for a guy who just had surgery. Or a pregnant woman."

She put her face up closer to the glass. "So much for charging my battery."

He couldn't tell whether there was despair or relief in her voice. Maybe it was acceptance. He gathered that for such a young woman she'd had to accept a great deal. "You mentioned heating something up," he said. "Now that I'm standing, let me help."

As she looked through the cabinets she seemed grateful for the activity.

He shuffled into the living room and brought back one of the kerosene lanterns. "We have plenty of wood, which is the important thing."

"And lots of soup. You have a preference?"

"Not really."

She opened two cans of beef barley soup and emptied them into a pot. He leaned against the counter, where he could feel the heat from the stove.

"What do you think the temperature is here in the kitchen?" she said.

"It's in the fifties."

"I was thinking of the water pipes."

"I know. With the fireplace going it shouldn't get too cold in here. Plus the pipes are well insulated, but we can always drip the faucet, if necessary." He reached up to the basket on top of the refrigerator and took down a loaf of bread. "Pumpernickel okay?"

"It's fine." Marcia continued to stare into the pot as she stirred the soup. "Pelé's father. I'm not sure who it is." She made a little sound, pushing air out her nose, and seemed to have come to a decision. "There are these two guys, Connor and Barr. Connor, I guess you'd say he's a handyman. Does a little of everything, carpentry, roofing, painting, hauls stuff in his truck, you name it. Always working. Barr, he's another story. Never seems to work, not so's you'd notice. And . . . well, let's just say there are these two guys and now I'm going to have Pelé." She turned off the flame under the pot of soup.

Del was silent for a moment, and then he turned slowly and opened the cabinet behind him. He said, "Bowls."

About a half dozen miles out County

Road 644, Connor rounded a long, descending curve and saw a dented SUV perched on top of the snowbank. He assumed that after going into a skid it had rolled over completely, before ending up on top of the six-foot wall of plowed snow.

He pulled over, got out of his truck, and walked back toward the vehicle. He couldn't see anyone inside as he clawed his way up the snowbank. In the back there was one of those wire fences designed to keep dogs from jumping up into the seats, and behind it a dog lay in a tangled blanket. It was a German Shepherd, female, with a white snout. At first Connor thought she might be dead, but then she raised her head and stared at him.

Connor went to the back of the SUV and took hold of the door handle. He thought about it a moment. The door might be locked, and if it wasn't the dog could attack. Injured dogs were unpredictable, but this one continued to lie on her side and Connor could see plumes of vapor puff from her nostrils.

He lifted the handle and the door opened. The dog remained on her side, watching him.

Connor didn't look the dog in the eye, turning his head to the side. "How you doing?" He kept his voice low, calm. The dog's front legs moved with effort. "Can you get out?"

He realized that the dog's breathing was shallow and labored. When he ventured to look the dog in the eye, she released the faintest whine.

He stepped back from the open door. "Come on, now. Let's see if you can get out." The dog gazed at him and didn't move. "Come on."

The dog struggled to get up. There was something wrong with her right front leg, but finally her managed to jump out of the open door. When she landed in the snow, she released a pained yelp, and then stood, holding her right paw up out of the snow. With difficulty, she squatted down on her three good legs and peed.

Connor sat down in the snow about three yards from her. He looked up and down the road. There was one set of tracks in the snow, continuing on toward Yellow Dog Township, which was maybe another five miles up 644. The wind was gusting high in the trees and the snow made it impossible to see much more than fifty yards.

The dog moved slowly, hobbled by her front leg. Connor didn't turn his head toward the dog as she approached. She sat next to him, and then leaned heavily against him, placing her head on his shoulder. With his bare hand he stroked her between the ears.

"The first few months, I couldn't keep much down," Marcia said as she put her empty bowl on the table. "Now it's thirty pounds later and I feel like I'm eating for two. Which, I guess, is what I'm doing."

"Want to finish mine? Since the surgery I don't eat much." When she shook her head, Del put his bowl on the table next to hers.

She stared into the fire because it was bothering her—she wasn't sure why she should offer an explanation, but she realized that she wanted to; she wanted this man living out to understand, because she believed he could understand. It had to do with the fact that he was intelligent, she supposed, but more so because he'd been through things that either ruin a person or make them stronger. She sensed that he and his wife truly loved each other, and she believed that her death coupled with his surgeries had forced him to look at life, his life, differently. For some reason the word *resources* came to mind. He was a man whose circumstances had been a true test of his resources. And he had passed that test. Not necessarily that he was stronger now, but he knew himself better, accepted his limitations, which in some way gave him a rare kind of freedom. Maybe she just needed him to understand, to say it's all right, you're doing the best you can. It's not a matter of fault. It's not your fault. Most of all, there was that, the desire to have someone simply say, *It's not your fault.*

"I've known who Connor was for a long time. Hard not to in a town the size of Marquette. He was a few years ahead of me in school, but I didn't really *know* him until the summer before last. Then one night—it was during this heat wave, the kind we don't often have this far north—I was out on Presque Isle, cooling off in the lake, and when I came out of the water my battery was dead." She turned and looked at Del. One side of his face was illuminated by the fire. His eyes were closed now, but she knew he was awake, knew he was listening. She stared at the fire again—it was easier to talk to the fire. "Weird, huh? I got a new battery after that night and it worked fine until today. Anyway, this guy Connor stops, and he has jumper cables in his truck. Tools, equipment—he usually has what you need for the job. We get my car running and, you know how it goes, he seems like a pretty nice guy."

"Seems." He didn't open his eyes. "Seems is one of those words."

She put her hands under the blanket that was covering her, not because they were cold but because the heat from the fire was so intense since she'd put new logs on. She placed her hands on his feet gently. "I'll bet you'd like a little foot massage."

"Seems like a good idea."

She smiled as she began to work on his arches. "I shouldn't use 'seem' with Connor. Big shoulders, strong back, and still something of the boy in his face. He *is* a nice guy. Usually. He does mean well. Really, I was in love with him. We were in love, and it seemed—*oops*—it was like nothing else I'd ever known with a guy. We were in love."

"And now?"

She shrugged. "How's this feel?"

"You have no idea," he said without opening his eyes.

His socks were wool, but the soft kind, not scratchy, and they felt good in her hands. She applied more pressure with her fingers, working along the bottom of his right foot out to the toes. Then she began working on each toe. "When I first started doing physical therapy I learned that you can't really get to a person unless you do their feet. There's all these pressure points that most people don't even know about. You just put on your socks and shoes and walk around all day and your feet never get the attention they deserve."

"My feet have been starved for attention." He opened his eyes. "There's a *but* coming, isn't there?"

"Were there buts with your wife, Liesl?"

His eyes were closed again, and he appeared to be smiling slightly—it was difficult to tell in this light and with his three-day beard. "There are always things—buts. You come to love them because they're a part of someone."

"I believe that," Marcia said. "In theory, I do believe that."

"There's really not much theory to it," he said. "Love is or it isn't. Like this fire or the storm outside. There's nothing theoretical about love."

Barr sat hunched over and shivering, his forehead resting on the steering wheel, while he waited for the engine to warm up so he could turn on the heater. He had his hands in the pockets of his jacket, and after a few minutes it occurred to him that he was holding a cell phone in each hand. He removed his right hand from his coat and looked at the phone, his phone, and then he returned it to his pocket. The phone in his left hand was smaller, more rounded in his palm, the kind that flipped open. He took it out of his pocket—he couldn't remember where the phone came from, how he had gotten it. But he knew this: Marcia had suggested they go out to Presque Isle. That was it. That was all he remembered.

Maybe not quite all. The other thing he remembered was from last night. Or was it early this morning? It was dark. Marcia was crying. She was pissed off.

He looked at the phone in his hand. It had to be her phone. He didn't know how it came to be in his pocket, didn't have a clue. He would call her, if he could—but, no, he couldn't do that, because he had her phone.

But the phone had rung. That must have been what he'd heard while he was lying in the snow. It was Marcia's phone that was ringing, muffled because it was beneath him in his coat pocket.

He flipped the phone open. One of these old ones. The screen lit up and after a moment he tapped the button for *Messages*, and then held the phone to his ear and listened: "Where'd you go? Call me."

Connor.

But what caught him by surprise was how Connor's voice sounded: as though he was in an ongoing conversation, as though he and Marcia were on the same wavelength, always, the connection always there, always open, even when they're apart, when there's silence and distance between them, the connection was never broken.

Where'd you go? Call me.

The dog wanted to jump but couldn't because of her sore leg, but she didn't mind that Connor picked her up and laid her on the seat of his truck. Once he got going on the snowbound road again, he stayed in second gear. The dog rested her jaw on his lap.

For the next two or three miles there was just the snow angling through the headlight beams and the gusts of wind that rocked the truck. No other vehicles. The trail weaving up the middle of the road was quickly filling in with snow.

Then he saw her. She was walking on the right side of the road, so small between the high snowbanks. Though she had a hood up, he was certain it was a woman, leaning into every step. The snow was up to her knees, sometimes higher.

She turned around, and when he stopped the truck she came to the passenger side and opened the door. "Thank you," she yelled over the wind. As the dog tried to sit up, she cried, "*Ilo!*" And then she climbed in, and the dog worked her way around on the seat so that she could lick the woman's face. "I wasn't going to just leave you out there, you know," she said to the dog. And then to Connor: "You saw my car. I was lucky I had my seatbelt on, but Ilo, she got banged up bad. She couldn't have walked this far with me. Thank you so much." He couldn't see her face clearly in the dark.

"No problem," Connor said. "Sorry about your car."

Gently, she moved Ilo so she had enough room to pull her door shut. As Ilo began to settle down, the woman pushed the hood back off her head. She had fine, straight, blonde hair and a small, lean face, a face that seemed timeless. She was over thirty, but he couldn't tell beyond that—she could be in her forties or even fifties.

"I tried to use my phone," she said, "but there's no reception out here."

"Where are you going?"

To his surprise, she laughed. "I think I am there. Don't you?" He stared at her, and she laughed again. "We are in the storm, no? Where else is there?"

Connor nodded and decided to concentrate on the road. He put his truck in gear and let out the clutch slowly. It was difficult getting traction, and the rear wheels spun for a moment before the truck began to move forward through the snow. "I'm going to Yellow Dog Township," he said. "Where are you headed?"

"Into the storm, I told you," she said, though now, rather than laughing, she seemed distressed that he had failed to understand her.

"Yes, but before you rolled your car. What was your, you know, destination?"

"My you-know-destination?" She rubbed Ilo's head. "Must I have a destination? Or maybe the question should be, if I have a destination, will I know when I've reached it?"

"Well, no, I suppose—"

"My destination is the storm."

He shifted into second gear. "You drove out here just to be in the storm."

She looked down at her dog. "Ilo, I think he's starting to get it."

Connor couldn't tell whether or not she was mocking him. She spoke with an accent, yet her English was good, her pronunciation slow and precise. He suspected she was better educated than he was and that she had truly studied English, whereas he had always hated English class. He was certain she was the kind of person who read books because she wanted to, and he often had difficulty understanding such people. It seemed the more they read, the less they made sense. Perhaps the best thing was to just remain silent, so he concentrated on the road ahead.

After a minute, she said, "You think you can actually know your destination?"

"Yes."

"Interesting. Why?"

"Because I need to find someone."

"*Ah.* Me? You found me. And Ilo. But maybe you were looking for someone else?"

"I was looking for someone in particular."

"As opposed to what, in general? Or maybe just here, in the woods? In the storm in the woods." Her laugh. It came easily, and Connor suspected that she was the kind of person who laughed to herself. Often. "Finding someone in particular—that is very hard to do," she said. "What is your name?"

"Connor."

"I'm Essi. E-S-S-I. People here often ask me to spell it, and still they mispronounce it. It's *Essi*." She laughed as she put a hand in her coat pocket and pulled out something that she held toward him. For a moment her outthrust arm startled him and he was afraid to look, but then he saw that her palm was filled with small brown nuggets of some kind. "Chocolate-covered raisins," she said. "Have some."

"No, I'm fine."

"You're fine. Right." In disbelief, perhaps even disgust, she withdrew her hand. She put a few raisins in her mouth and chewed, and the heated cab of the truck was filled with the sweet scent of chocolate and raisins. "Life is too short, Connor," she muttered, chewing noisily, "to turn down chocolate-covered raisins."

He decided that she was at least in her forties, late forties, though he wasn't sure how he knew this. It was the smell that made him change his mind and want to ask her for a few chocolate raisins, but she only stared out the windshield, chewing, and he was afraid to ask her. She might laugh again. She might chastise him. She might even refuse him.

Del's half-sleep receded,

and when he finally admitted to himself that there was no going back he opened his eyes. Marcia was sitting at the opposite end of the couch, gazing at the fire.

"We're going to need another log soon," he said. "Let me do it, and I want you to lie on the couch for a while."

"I'm fine."

"Sure you are. But I need to stand for a bit."

He pulled the blankets off his legs and concentrated on lowering his feet to the floor. With his hands on the armrest, he pushed himself up off the couch. Taking his cane, he went to the stack of firewood. He'd always liked the way the round and flat sides of split logs fit together as though by design.

"Can I ask you a question about your wife?"

He selected a log, and after placing it on the fire, he sat on the stool next to the hearth. "Sure."

"You think about where she is, I mean now?"

"I do."

"You have any ideas?"

He leaned back against the large, round chimney stones. "I doubt I can find the language to describe it. I don't think we're supposed to understand it. I don't have the usual notions of heaven, if that's what you mean."

"You think there is an afterlife?"

"I don't know. Nobody does. Does someone's consciousness continue in some way after they die? I think that's what we're really asking. 'Will I be aware of anything after I die?' I tend to think not, at least not in the way we think of 'consciousness.'"

Marcia considered the new log crackling in the fire. "But we're part of something big. Bigger than we can imagine."

"Something makes all this work. Call it Nature, God, whatever you want."

"But you don't feel as though you can, you know, communicate with your wife?"

He shook his head. "After she died there were times when I'd wander around the house, or sometimes outside in the woods, usually after a few drinks, and I'd try talking to her. I'd tell her to give me something, anything: a sign. Even if it scared me to death. I meant it. I said, 'Give me a heart attack right here and now.' Never happened. Nothing." He picked up the poker leaning against the chimney and pushed the logs around on the andirons. "I don't believe she's out there watching over me, or anything like that. But is her spirit—or whatever you want to call it—still present? Yes. That I can feel. When I came to that, and it's taken a while, I stopped asking for the heart attack."

"You believe in closure?"

"No such thing." He put the poker down. "But I do believe in living your own life. Going on, as they say." He got up off the stool and made his way back to the couch. "Now it's your turn. You lie down and I sit."

She stretched out on the couch, which took some effort because of her belly. When she seemed settled, she pulled her legs up so he could sit, and then she put her feet in his lap. Together, they spread the blankets over them.

"Can I tell you something?" she asked. "It's strange but I feel like I've known you a long time. Not like you're my father or anything, but you know."

"That's good because I don't think you're going to get out of here soon."

"And the baby. I have these moments when I can feel it. Not just that it's moving. There's plenty of that. I feel like we already know each other. I sometimes wonder if this baby has lived before. It's still a fetus, I know, but it's bearing things from the world, things that I don't understand. It's like it's returning and I'm just the—I don't know."

"The means," he said. "You feel like the means."

"Yes," she said. "The means to an end."

"Which of course is the beginning. Again."

"So." She hesitated. "So, do you think it might be reincarnation, something like that?"

Del studied the rocks embedded in the chimney. Each was different; all rounded by being in the lake, but none the same. Their colors were variations on white, black, and gray. "I'll tell you something I've never told anyone," he said. "Liesl wasn't religious in a conventional sense, not since she was a child, but over the years I knew her, she became truly spiritual. She read about spirituality in different cultures. She sometimes went to these sessions—I don't know what else to call them—with other people who were seeking some kind of a spiritual understanding. Or awareness, I think that's what they would prefer to call it. I didn't go. But she was very serious about this. She once told me that during one of these sessions she became convinced that she'd been alive before, at least once. And she said it with such certainty. You've got to understand that she wasn't into psychic phenomena, or anything like that. She had both feet on the ground. I think she was actually resistant to all this, but she couldn't help being drawn to it, and somehow she came to believe she'd lived before and she had glimpses of it."

"What glimpses?"

"I don't know exactly, but she said they were images, horrible images, and she suspected that she was a woman, or perhaps a girl, who had been in a Nazi concentration camp."

Marcia shifted on the couch, and for a moment Del thought she was going to try and sit up, but then she only folded her arms and stared at the ceiling, her eyes welling up as she released a sob. "I know this, this feeling, I really do," she said. "At first I thought it was just my hormones going nuts during the early stages of pregnancy. But now." She ran a finger under each eye, trying to keep tears from spilling down her cheeks. "Now I think I'm getting glimpses, too. I'm not even sure what they mean. I sometimes doubt that I'm having them, that it's just my mind playing tricks on me. But I keep having them. I'm happy—no, elated, I'm elated—and at the same time I'm just petrified. And it really, *really* scares me."

He put his hands under the blanket, found her right foot, and began massaging the instep.

———————————

As the car began to heat up, Barr lifted his forehead off the steering wheel. He remembered that maybe a week earlier he'd bought a pint of schnapps, and opening the glove compartment he found the bottle, about half full. He took a pull and his head was flushed with intensely cold peppermint, causing him to go weak and slump against the door. But as the warm liquor descended to his chest, he felt revived.

Still, he couldn't recall exactly what had happened earlier in the day. He wasn't sure why he came to be out here on Presque Isle, but he was certain Marcia, and probably Connor, had something to do with it. What was coming back were glimpses of things that had happened last week, last month, last summer. Sitting in this car, for instance, watching a house.

Whose house? How many houses? The names of the occupants didn't matter. But the addresses did. He could remember the first house, up in Shiras Hills. It was a winter's night, high snowbanks lining the street. A little before seven o'clock the automatic garage door rolled up, and a Subaru station wagon backed out into the driveway. As it turned in the street, Barr slid down in the driver's seat so that his head was lower than the top of the steering wheel. The Subaru came slowly toward him, and as it passed by he saw both of them: a couple at least in their seventies, the husband driving, gazing straight ahead. The way he drove, Barr thought, it'll take them forever.

They were going to a concert, the Marquette Symphony, performing at Kaufmann Auditorium in the school on Front Street. Barr knew this because Marcia had gone to the house two days earlier for the wife's physical therapy session. The wife was recovering from shoulder surgery, and while Marcia was working on her, she said that they had four tickets to the symphony Friday night, but her cousin had called that morning to say he and his wife had to cancel their trip from Minneapolis up to Marquette. So she offered the tickets to Marcia. Free, of course. That's the kind of people they were: two extra tickets—don't sell them, give them away. They sure as hell didn't need the money.

So Marcia pulled from her bag a pair of tickets and said, *I've never been to the symphony.*

No shit.

Interested in going?

No way.

Why?

Why? You have to ask me why I don't want to go to the symphony?

But how do you know you won't like it?

He laughed then, and said he had other plans Friday night. When she asked what plans, he said, *Plans.* She knew he hated it when she asked about his every move, so she let it drop.

Maybe you can get a friend to go. Someone from work?

But Marcia just wanted to drop it and got quiet in that hurt, resentful way that pissed him off.

So maybe Marcia was there at the symphony, sitting next to old Mr. and Mrs. Subaru Outback, and their house was empty and dark, except for one light on in the living room window and another over the front door.

Barr gave it another ten minutes. Old folks forgot shit and then they had to come back and get it.

When he got out of the car, he walked down the sidewalk, watching the houses he passed. Some were dark. One had a TV flickering in a front room. He crossed the street and then went up the drive to the Subaru's house. When he reached the side of the garage he was in dark shadow and he stood still. There was nothing, no movement on the street, nor in the neighbor's yard, which had a stand of birch trees. He continued on to the back of the garage and turned the corner. There was a door, and through its window he could see a small light on above the stove. He went around to the back of the house, where there was a sunroom.

From the pocket of his leather jacket he took a roll of duct tape and, as he approached the back door, he tore off a few strips. There were small windowpanes in the door, and he put the tape on the one just above the doorknob, being careful to leave a bit of excess tape hanging free. He took the hammer from his other coat pocket and gave the taped pane one good tap. The glass broke but didn't fall in on the floor. He pulled the tape and the glass out, and then stuck his hand through the jagged opening and unlocked the doorknob. After glancing over his shoulder—Mr. and Mrs. Subaru Outback had a big stone patio in their backyard—he opened the door and entered the house.

Barr took another pull on the schnapps. That was the first house. It got easier. It depended on the neighborhood, places where retired assholes with sunrooms and patios and stands of birch trees lived. Shiras Hills. Doctors on Pill Hill. The East Side, particularly between Ridge and Ohio Streets. He'd do a drive-by for several days and figure out their routine.

If the place looked like it had potential, he'd eventually park down the street at night and wait. These were the kinds of people who went out to dinner often, people who ate broiled whitefish and salads with balsamic vinaigrette dressing. People who wore North Face apparel all winter and bought organic vegetables at the food co-op, and then went to the bakery for a six-dollar loaf of bread.

He did jewelry mostly. It was easy to find—usually in a bedroom bureau. It was easy to pocket. Necklaces, earrings, rings, and watches. Watches were the best: Omega, DeMesy, TAG Heuer, Movado, Philip Stein. The kind Roger Federer wore in commercials. Sometimes, though, there'd be other stuff. Gold. Cups, bowls, dishes, the sort of things that were put on display in a cabinet. Once a set of small vases that looked very old, very Chinese.

He took all this stuff to his cousin in Ishpeming. Zack drove down to Chicago every other week or so, a trip he always referred to as going to see my dying mother, which meant to do business with a fence. When he returned he'd meet Barr someplace in Marquette, Remie's or sometimes the Portside because Zack loved those thick-cut steak fries. They went fifty-fifty with the fence in Chicago, and they split their 50 percent half and half. Early on Barr questioned this arrangement, suggesting that since he was the one who took all the risk he should get a bigger cut, but Zack just pushed another french fry through his massive puddle of ketchup, and as he chewed he said, *That's the deal, Cousin, take it or leave it.* Barr let it drop, but it continued to gnaw on him.

Risks. That was the good part, really, his thick-cut steak fries. A couple of times he set off alarms, and sometimes houses would have dogs that went ballistic before he even got close to entering. He went in through doors mostly, windows sometimes. Often, houses weren't even locked. That's how easy it was, how stupid these people were—just because they lived in Marquette they believed their shit was safe. He was almost doing them a favor, giving them a wakeup call. In those houses he considered doing something, breaking something, crapping on the floor, something that would really send home the message. But that was teenage stuff. He just wanted to get in and out. Clean.

When he stopped massaging her foot and looked at her hands, Marcia said, "I'm doing it, aren't I?" Del tilted his head. "Fidgeting."

"They rarely stop moving," he said. "Why is that?"

"Oh, I may as well tell you. If I do, would you keep doing that a bit longer?"

"This?" His hands beneath the blankets continued to work on her foot.

"That." She moved a bit. Sometimes lying on her back she felt like she was balancing a giant egg on her stomach. "That's better." She closed her eyes as his fingers kneaded her heel. "You'll probably hear about this anyway, eventually. There will be something in the paper and at some point my name will be involved and you'll put two and two together."

"You break the law?"

She gazed down the length of the couch at him. "I don't know."

"You don't know. Well, it's not like I can pick up the phone and call the cops."

"No, I guess not," she said.

"If that phone did have reception, who would you call? Connor? Barr?"

"I'm not sure." She took a deep breath and then exhaled. "Both. But I'm not sure who I'd call first. That's been the problem."

He nodded as he began working on her other foot.

"Do you know what it means to be an accessory?" she asked. "No, I know *you* know what it means, but can you explain what it means to me? In legal terms?"

"I'm not a lawyer. What are the circumstances?"

"They go back a ways." She laced her fingers over her belly and decided to try and keep them there, to hold still for a while.

"But today," he said. "You're fidgety because?"

"Because I called Barr today. I called Barr because Connor asked me to. I knew what it meant, and I said to myself this has to end somehow. I've been pulled between them for too long—long before this started." She patted her belly. "But once I realized I was pregnant it brought things out of both of them. Earlier you said there was a *but.* There was. At first, Connor was too nice to believe. *But* after a while all these things, these insecurities came out. I guess I knew they were there from the beginning, but you tend to ignore things at the start. You only want to see what you want to see. He would apologize for anything, all the time. If it was just that, I might have been able to put up with it, or better, I might have been able to help him through it, change it. In some ways I thought I was doing that. His parents, particularly his father, messed him up some. That's what parents do, usually, isn't it? That's why we are the way we are, because they screw us up. I suppose I'll do a number on Pelé here, but I'm sure going to try not to—but you don't know, it just happens, parents can't help themselves, probably because their parents messed them up, and it just goes on and on and on, one generation after another."

"Cyclical."

"Right," she said. "So at first Connor is this really nice guy but meek. Always apologizing, even for stuff he didn't do. It wears on you after a while. And slowly we went from this good thing we started that night over a dead battery to something that was closed in and needy. That's about the time Barr became part of it. He and Connor have known each other for years. Not real pals but they hung out together sometimes. And Barr, well, he's no Connor. Nothing needy about him and no apologies for anything. I knew he was always watching me. He has these eyes, it's like he's watching you even when he's not looking at you. At some point, when I'd just had too much of Connor, all his neediness, I did this stupid thing. I let Barr get to me. He's a bit older. He carries himself differently. Maybe I'm not saying this very well? But he was a relief after Connor. I felt, I don't know, like I'd broken out. Or away. With Barr there were no rules. Which could make it pretty hot, sexually speaking.

I mean, Connor was good and loving but, well, I'm not going to go into that, not in detail."

Del nodded.

"So. So, when Connor learns about me and Barr, which of course he did eventually, it brings out this whole other side of him. This meek, needy guy turned ugly. He roughed me up a couple of times."

"And Barr?"

"He wasn't happy about it, but Barr isn't the kind of guy who goes around beating on people. I suppose you might think he's dangerous in his way, but physically he's never going to take on Connor. And I came to understand that the way Barr tears you down is by playing with your head."

"So you were caught between both of them."

"I was caught, yes. A very old story, I know. But when you're in the middle, it might as well have never happened before. It fucks you up. Sometimes it gets you knocked up."

Del stopped massaging her foot. "So what happened today?"

Her hands began to fidget, but then to stop them she folded her arms in that place between her belly and her breasts. Her forearms pressed against her ribs, and she realized that most everywhere else now she felt like it was *her* bundled inside another person, a woman with this belly, these swollen breasts, this butt, these thighs, all smothering her. She, Marcia, packed in all this heavy flesh, sharing this tight space, this cocoon, with the fetus, the growing thing, okay, call it Pelé, or whatever, but they were both there, inside this expanding woman, and there were moments when she wanted to break out, to punch, scrape, even cut her way through all this fat and skin, all this excess, and climb out, head first, if necessary, as though being pushed out of the womb, which, when the baby came, she knew was going to hurt like she'd never hurt before. But the ribs, she could still feel her ribs, there, just beneath her breasts, and that, along with a thousand other things, made her want to cry. Again. She cried on and off, all day and all night. No reason, the tears just pooled and spilled out of her eyes. But now, there was a reason. "Today," she said, staring up at the ceiling. They called them cathedral ceilings, and this one was made with knotty pine boards. Each knot was an eye, gazing down at her. "Today I think we might have killed Barr. I didn't do it. But I made it possible. I might have been an accessory."

The second time Essi offered, Connor accepted a few chocolate raisins. Whoever thought of coating raisins in chocolate was a genius, and he was sorry when she tucked the plastic bag in the pocket of her coat. In order to do this, she had to lean forward, giving him a better look at her face in the dim green light from the dashboard. She may have been older than he had first thought, perhaps not even forty but over fifty.

"You have this accent, I can't place it," he said. "You mind if I asked where you're from?"

"Why would I mind?" Her voice was playful. "Everybody wants to know where you're from, when what's important is where you are."

"True. You've already made it clear. We're in the storm."

"But you're just curious." She still sounded amused. "People often are." She stared out at the snow for a long moment. "The wind, the way it causes the snow to rise up in these large swirling clouds, it makes me think of ghosts."

"I never thought of it that way, but you're right."

"You believe in ghosts?"

"I don't know."

"You don't know?"

"I guess I did when I was a kid, but now—I've never seen one, so I guess not."

"How do you know you've never seen one? You think they wear white sheets and go *Boo*?"

Again, he was starting to feel uncomfortable and unsure how he should answer. "No, I don't think that," he said. "I'm not a child anymore."

"I see."

"I'm sorry. I didn't mean to sound . . . I don't know."

"How did you sound? Was I supposed to be offended?"

"No, I just spoke a bit too sharply."

"Could that be because something's on your mind?"

He turned and stared at her, but she wouldn't look at him—she didn't need to, he suspected, because she could see him anyway. He wanted to say something, he wanted to ask her why she was this way, why she was so weird, weird without doing anything really weird, without trying even, which is what most weird people did, but he was certain she'd give him some answer that would only make it worse. No, he was afraid to ask. That was the problem. He was afraid to ask a simple question. Instead he said, "We should reach Yellow Dog Township soon."

"Yellow Dog." She smiled, almost as though she knew that he hadn't said what was really on his mind.

"It gets its name from the Yellow Dog River which runs through here."

"You have interesting names around here. Isn't there a Garlic River?"

"There's two. The Big Garlic and the Little Garlic."

"I love it. You don't usually associate rivers with garlic."

"I suppose not. You're not from around here."

"Evidentially."

He had no idea what she meant. Then she said something in a foreign language. "What's that?"

"My mother used to say it, an old Finnish proverb: *Pessimisti ei pety.* A pessimist will not get disappointed."

"You're from Finland. Interesting."

"Why?"

"In the U.P. there's lots of Finns. Lots of Norwegians and Swedes. You know, their families came from Scandinavia, back a generation or three, usually settled here to work the mines and farm. But I don't think I've ever actually met someone *from* there."

"*That* is interesting."

"So what brings you here? The storm?"

"The storm, yes, definitely."

"Hope you don't mind my asking."

She found this amusing and snorted. "Why would I mind?"

"It's none of my business."

"The point is I'm here now."

"In the storm."

"And you were kind enough to pick me up." She took some more chocolate raisins from the bag in her coat pocket and put them in his waiting palm.

He put two in his mouth and just let the chocolate melt. "I have to say I feel—I feel like we're almost speaking different languages."

"Isn't that true, though?" She seemed pleased. "Isn't that the way it is between all of us? We speak but we seldom hear each other. Do you know what I mean?" She laughed. That laugh. "Tell me you know what I mean!"

"I know what you mean." And he laughed as well.

"But you haven't told me what's on your mind, Connor. Maybe you can't or don't want to, but you could try."

He thought about Barr lying in the snow on Presque Isle. "I don't think I can understand it myself, if you want to know the truth." He knew she was looking at him now, but he continued to stare at the road. The snow was very deep, and there were no tracks of another vehicle. They began to round a tight curve, and he was careful not to allow the truck to fishtail.

She stroked Ilo behind the ears for a moment. "Are you in trouble, Connor?"

"What makes you say that?" There was the slightest edge to his voice, which he immediately regretted. He wanted to apologize for it but didn't. This was what Marcia had done for him—or perhaps *to* him. He apologized for things, a lot, and she'd made him aware of it, she made him realize this about himself to the point where he recognized his desire to do so beforehand, so he often would catch himself and not apologize.

Trouble was, he still felt bad, and it didn't seem to make it any easier for him to get along with people. It certainly hadn't helped with Marcia. She had been this incredibly pretty girl in a bathing suit and T-shirt who had a dead battery, and now it was all screwed up. Often he wished he could go back to that moment when he had first seen her on Presque Isle. If he could go back to that night, he would start over and get it right so that everything wouldn't turn out the way it did. Or he would just drive on by, pretending he hadn't noticed her standing by her car. It's what most people do. They drive by someone in trouble, not because they don't want to help, but because they know it might get them in trouble.

"I can tell you with certainty that I do not believe in ghosts," Essi said.

The side of her face was faintly illuminated by the green dashboard light. He'd never seen a face like hers. It was beautiful but not pretty. Her eyes were fathomless, earnest and mysterious. He had heard people talk about how some people had a presence—Marcia sometimes said this about her clients, mostly old people, that they had this *presence*. He was never sure what she was talking about. A person was a person. But this woman had something that he was not only afraid of but drawn to—it was a presence.

"Yeah, I don't believe in ghosts," he said, relieved, as he ate the rest of the chocolate raisins.

"No ghosts," she said. "But I do believe in spirits."

He wanted to say something. He wanted to say, *When you stop to help someone in trouble, it usually gets you in trouble.* He wanted to ask her why he kept stopping for people if it only led to trouble—he suspected she knew the answer. But he didn't ask. He wanted to look back at the road. He needed to look back at the road, but he couldn't. He stared at her eyes in the green dashboard light, and then he felt it, that sudden sense of weightlessness as the rear tires began to slip sideways to the left. He turned the front tires toward the skid, which usually worked, but not this time. It was too late, and the steering wheel was useless in his hands as the truck went into a spin.

Barr might have dozed off

for a few minutes. It was warm in the car now, so warm that he turned down the heater fan. But the side of his head was cold, and he touched it with his fingers. His hair was matted with drying blood, thick as syrup. He remembered that he was wearing his hoodie underneath his leather coat. Carefully, he pulled the hood up over his head. At least it was warm in there.

He switched on the headlights and watched the snow blow diagonally through the beams. If he didn't get off Presque Isle soon, the one road to Marquette would be impassable, and then his car, a Nissan with over 150,000 miles on it, could be stuck out here for days. The road curled past the marina, the ore dock, the power plant, until he reached Fair Street, where everything was dark. No streetlights, no house lights. In Marquette, blizzards often knocked out the power.

As Barr took another nip of schnapps, that thing Marcia liked to say grazed his memory but he couldn't find it. She said it like it was her mantra. *I do what I do*, but that wasn't it. Sometimes when he told Marcia she took her work too seriously—she more than once said he *chided* her, which was one of those words that sometimes just came out of her—she would repeat it, her mantra, this thing Barr couldn't quite get a handle on.

He drove slowly through town. The only lights were at the hospital, which had emergency generators. His head ached, and he thought his jaw might be dislocated or broken—his teeth didn't line up right. He considered going to the ER and having somebody look at him.

And I'm going to pay the ER with what?

Then it came to him: *The best thing to do is to do what you're supposed to do.*

And he remembered why he was on Presque Isle—Marcia had asked him to meet her there.

She set it up. She set him up.

So, getting me killed was what you were supposed to do?

Well, you missed. My turn now.

———

Del closed his eyes as he listened to Marcia's voice. It quivered, it shook; it was no more than a whisper. She paused often to catch her breath, to sniffle, to wipe the tears away. She wasn't crying; she was weeping. He didn't know why, but weeping was worse. It came from a deeper place. He had learned this with Liesl. She seldom cried, even toward the end, but when she wept the world stopped and he felt utterly helpless. And useless. You cannot keep a woman from weeping. It was an injustice. It was *the* injustice. While Marcia wept, he tried to remain perfectly still. His hands merely held her feet now, the ridges of her metatarsals soft and distinct beneath his fingers.

She kept saying how she wasn't explaining things well, but she was because he felt he understood her perfectly, or as perfectly as any one person can understand another. He seldom talked about Liesl's death for the same reason: he couldn't really explain things well. He didn't like talking about it because it didn't help, and because he felt he was trying to free himself of the thing that he needed to keep. Liesl was his; in death, she was his; he needed to keep it close. He could talk about the circumstances, the discovery of the tumor, the doctors involved in her case, the trips to hospitals and clinics for second opinions, the first surgery, the second surgery, her decision to forego chemotherapy and radiation treatments. He could talk, though seldom, about the last few months, the seizures, the hospice staff that took control of their house, helping them both to arrive at the inevitable place, and he needed to keep that place within himself. He was alone with her when she died on a Saturday night, the sole witness. Sometimes, perhaps to avoid saying that someone died, people called it a passing. It was that, a moment when she stopped breathing and, he knew, he sensed, she wasn't going to begin again. It was a passing, out of the pain, into stillness. She hadn't left; she had arrived. It was the moment he never talked about, the moment when loss and relief and awe become one.

What Marcia was explaining was familiar and oddly welcomed because since Liesl had died most everything felt strange, alien, unfamiliar. Not new. Not even different. Unfamiliar in an unfamiliar way. Marcia was providing some respite, a story: two men and a woman. Their entanglements dark and treacherous and seemingly insoluble. And in the telling Marcia's voice began to change. It became stronger, calmer. It was buoyed by the simple fact that she could tell the story.

Del opened his eyes.

She was no longer weeping.

Marcia paused when she realized he was staring at her. "Listen to me, talking on and on."

"It's all right," he said. "I'm not going anywhere."

Now she closed her eyes. "Do you think it's possible to love two people?" He didn't answer. Of course, he didn't answer. "I didn't think so," she said. "I didn't think you could *really* love two people. So equally. So differently. But you can. I can. This is why it's so hard. It's not just not knowing whether Connor or Barr is the father. For some reason that hasn't seemed important to me—if that makes sense. I made a mistake, a terrible mistake earlier today. I made it while I was angry, really angry. And hurt. Leading up to it I felt this pressure, like I *had* to make some decision, some choice."

"A mistake?"

"Yes," she said, "because I now wonder if I don't know how to live without either of them. I haven't just lost one of them; I've lost that part of me that I am when I'm with him. Or him. That make sense?"

He nodded.

"I didn't want to lose any of it, which I suppose makes me in a way very selfish." She placed her hands over her belly. "And then Pelé here, I can already feel how he, or she, is turning me into someone else, though it's someone I guess I always knew I'd be." Opening her eyes, she asked, "You and Liesl, you didn't have children."

"No." He kept his eyes on the fire. "How did you know?"

"When I was in the bedroom getting the blanket. There were photos of you, Liesl, a dog. No kids."

"We married late. It wasn't that we didn't want kids. It was just too late." She could tell he didn't want to talk about this any longer. "When you reach that age, Pelé will be a teenager."

The way he said it made Marcia giggle.

The truck hit a tree.

It had gained speed as it descended the hill, doing a three-sixty, before it ran up and over the snowbank and slammed head-on into the trunk of a pine. The motor was silent. There was only the howling of the wind overhead. Connor thought he was all right. He had his seatbelt on, and he was afraid to move, fearing he'd discover that he wasn't all right.

He turned his head only slightly to the right. The dog was dead, he was sure. As the truck had gone into its spin, Ilo was hurled against the passenger door, and then against Connor's shoulder, until they hit the tree trunk, and she was thrust into the windshield so hard that she gave one yelp as the glass buckled and burst into a fine web of white cracks. She now lay in Essi's lap, her head hanging down to the floor. Essi was bent forward, her face buried in the dog's fur. She had not been wearing her seatbelt, and thanks to the dog she hadn't gone headfirst through the windshield. But she wasn't moving. His recollection was that when the truck was spinning, when it shot up the snowbank, and when it slammed into the tree, the woman had been absolutely silent. He had the sense that she was fascinated by the whole thing.

Connor unbuckled his seatbelt and tried to open his door. There was some resistance, but when he shoved with his shoulder, the door swung open, creaking loudly. He climbed out into the snow. The cold was somehow a relief after the confined heat in the truck. Slowly, he stood up straight. Mostly he felt numb, but there was stiffness in his lower back.

The hood was buckled from the impact with the tree. The truck wasn't going anywhere. He walked slowly around to the tailgate. His legs sank down in the snow, sometimes almost to his knees. He placed one hand on the tailgate, for balance, for fear that somehow he might drift away and not be able to get back to the truck. When he started up the other side, he was moving into the wind. The snow was a horizontal blast that stung his face. With his free hand he touched his right temple and discovered blood on his fingers.

When he reached the passenger door he yanked on the handle, thinking it would fight him, but it swung open as if pushed by the weight of Essi's body, which leaned out until her shoulder rested against his knees. The truck sat at a severe angle, and she would have fallen out of the cab had it not been for the weight of the dead dog on her.

"Hey," he said.

Nothing. But then one gloved hand moved, turning up in a gesture that suggested she was checking to see if it was raining. It was a small hand and the forefinger trembled.

"*Hey*," he said, louder. "*Essi*."

She didn't answer, didn't move.

He was undecided. The cold wind and the snow made him want to return to the protection of the driver's seat. He considered trying to tuck Essi back inside and slamming the door shut to keep her there. Instead he took her by the shoulders and tried to pull her out of the truck. But her legs were pinned beneath her dog's body. He reached over and took hold of Ilo's front paws, which were still warm. He yanked on the dog until she was out in the snow, and he dragged her away from the truck. After wading back to the open door, he again took Essi by the shoulders and eased her out until she was lying on her back in the snow.

He knelt down and put his face close to hers. "Essi."

Her eyelids moved, but she didn't open them.

In the truck bed there were three sand bags, which were positioned over the rear axle for better traction during the winter. There was his toolbox, behind the cab. He climbed over the rail and into the bed, and after opening the box lid, he examined his tools, trying to determine what might be useful.

He couldn't think, and he sat back in the bed, his head against the high-side wheel well. He was so tired he thought he could go right to sleep. The logical thing was to climb back into the truck, close the doors, and curl up, but he wasn't sure he had the strength to do even that—so he just lay there, his face turned away from the wind-driven snow.

Barr drove to Marcia's apartment

on Baraga Street. She lived on the second floor of the house that had a snowblower chained to the porch railing and a van with *Superior Tiles* stenciled on the side. Her Ford Escort wasn't in the driveway, nor was Connor's pickup anywhere on the street. The second floor windows were dark. Barr drove past the house and parked around the corner where his car wouldn't be obvious while he kept an eye on the place.

It was hot in the car now, and he was sweating. He turned off the engine and after a moment took the key from the ignition. The keychain—that did it. Dangling from his keys was a pair of gold-plated crossed hockey sticks. They'd been on the kitchen counter in the house on Ridge Street. Barr had found not only jewelry but a wooden box filled with old coins. At a quick glance, they were minted in the 1800s, most from other countries. They had weight you didn't find in American coins. He liked the look and feel of them, so he emptied the contents of the box into his leather bag and went back through the house to the kitchen, where he'd found the back door unlocked.

Then he noticed the keys, sitting on the counter. He liked to take something, some insignificant but personal thing, from each house. Often something that was on a nightstand—a clock or once a set of dentures. He liked to remove something people used—nobody really used jewelry, not in Marquette. Stolen jewelry wouldn't change somebody's life. They were *valuables*, covered by insurance, unless people were stupid, as stupid as those who left their doors unlocked. Pocket some small thing and it'll haunt them. Then they'll lock their fucking doors.

So there was the keychain with the crossed hockey sticks. Marcia had mentioned this client. The husband was an insurance broker—certainly *his* shit was covered—and they had a grandson who played hockey for Northern. Barr recognized the name, one of those Finnish names, so common in the Upper Peninsula, that ended in *en*. Pekkanen, something like that. Must have been from the wife's side of the family because this insurance agent guy's name was Warner.

There were three keys. Barr didn't want them, just the keychain. The stove light had been left on, and holding the keys up close to the oven hood, he used his pocket knife to pry open the ring and remove the keys. The first two came off easily, but the third was tight and fought him. He was tempted to just take that key with the chain and go, but that wouldn't be the point. He continued to fidget with the last key, when a band of light swung through the kitchen and he heard a car pull into the driveway. They would need time to get in the house. Marcia said the old man had recently had back surgery, and he was still moving slowly.

Barr continued to work on the third key. He heard the car doors shut. He got the blade of his knife to separate the ring, so the key could be removed, and then he dropped everything, which clattered on the stovetop. The knife fell into one of the front burner wells, and he had to remove the iron grill to retrieve it. Footsteps were coming up the walk to the front of the house. There were voices, a man and woman. Barr picked up the knife. The last key was still on the ring, but it was caught between the coils of the ring. Very tight. The kind of thing that required small hands and long fingernails. Using the knife again, he opened the ring and rotated it until the key came free just as the front door opened—that wasn't locked either. Barr placed the third key on the counter with the other two, went to the back door, and opened it. Lights went on in the living room. The man's footsteps were slow as they came through the dining room toward the kitchen. Barr looked over his shoulder and saw the man's shadow slide across the floor tiles, and then he stepped outside and didn't bother to pull the door shut.

When Zack looked over the jewelry, he seemed impressed, but he found the coins particularly interesting. He knew a guy in Chicago who would appraise them. They were sitting in Remie's—an early afternoon crowd of pensioners and the hardcore. Outside the sky was overcast, and the snowbanks were the color of coffee with cream.

"This is good," Zack said. "I think you've found your calling, Cuz. In fact, my guy in Chicago was asking about you."

"That so?"

"He wanted to make sure you weren't supporting a habit or nothing. These meth addicts, they'll steal anything, but they get sloppy and mess up, and when they mess up they get caught, and when they get caught they get strung out and they talk. You're not sloppy, and you got a good eye for coins and such."

"Uh-huh. But why's this guy in Chicago asking about me. Is he okay?"

"He's fine. In fact, he wants to know if you'd be interested in doing a road trip."

"Road trip where?"

"He mentioned Sarasota. As in Florida." Zack smiled. "Interested?"

"They don't have snowbanks down there, right?"

"Good," Zack said.

Cooling it in Marquette for a while would be a good idea. There'd been a story in the *Mining Journal* that referred to a prowler—a word Barr quite liked—who the police believed had been responsible for a series of breaking and entering jobs over the past half year. *Entering*, yes, but *breaking* was seldom necessary.

The day that Zack called about the job in Florida, Barr had been at Marcia's apartment. She'd gotten back from work and was in the shower, and when she came out of the bathroom, her hair wrapped in a towel, Barr had just shut off his phone and dropped it on the coffee table.

"Who was that?" she asked.

"My cousin."

As she tied her bathrobe he noticed something different about her, though he didn't know what it was. He studied the line of her hips beneath the terrycloth.

"What?" she said.

"You putting on weight?"

"Why?"

He just shook his head, his I-don't-want-to-get-into-it move.

She turned to go into the bedroom but then stopped and came back, gazing down at the coffee table—his can of beer, his wallet, his cell phone, his keys.

Marcia tilted her head, studying these items. When she picked up the keys, the crossed hockey sticks glinting gold as they dangled from her fingers, he knew his mistake right there, before she even said anything.

Connor sat up in the truck bed, snow sifting down inside the collar of his coat. He took out his cell phone and held it close to his face. No bars. No signal. Nothing.

He climbed out on the low side of the truck bed and looked at Essi, lying on her back in the snow. *We have to get out of here because no one's going to come and find us.* He might have said this out loud—he wasn't sure—or he may have hollered it because of the wind. Either way, Essi still didn't move.

He looked in the toolbox and found the canvas tarp he used to cover loose stuff in the truck bed. There were various screwdrivers and hammers and fifty feet of rope, coiled up neat. There was his handsaw, a good Nonpareil.

He removed the saw and waded out into the woods. First, he took an urgent piss, and then he began to cut two low branches from a pine tree. He didn't know exactly where he'd seen this, probably in a movie, but he began to build a contraption—he was trying to think of its name—by tying the tarp to the two branches. After putting the rope through the grommets and tying the knots, his fingers were numb. He wondered what had happened to his gloves. He could have sworn he'd had them on earlier in the day, when he was driving out to Presque Isle.

When he finished building the contraption, he knelt next to Essi and leaned down until his face was close to hers. She opened her eyes, but he could tell she was still out of it.

"I'm going to put you on this thing," he said, and the word came to him. "This litter, and I'll pull you down the road until we find a place to get out of your storm."

He didn't wait for a response and took her by the arms and pulled her onto the litter so she was lying on her back. He wrapped rope around her chest, under her arms, binding her to the branches beneath her. Two wraps, and each time he pushed his arm through the snow behind her he realized his hands couldn't feel the snow or the cold at all. He yanked the rope taut against her chest and then tied a square knot.

Standing with his back to the litter, Connor picked up the ends of the branches, walked over the top of the snowbank, and sidestepped down to the road. He figured it might be a mile to Yellow Dog Township, but it might be two—distance was hard to gauge in the woods. It was slow going, and he wondered if he should have left her in the truck, wrapped in the tarp while he walked to Yellow Dog on his own. He'd get there faster, so he might find someone who would drive him back to his truck.

But he decided that leaving her behind would be too risky, and he kept walking, dragging the litter through the snow.

———————————

Marcia started with her mother. It was where she usually began when she tried to understand things, explain things. Mom always said it was better to tell her what was on her mind, to get it off her chest. And when Marcia did, Mom often said, *Now, don't you feel better?* Marcia did, usually. Mom seldom got mad, provided that Marcia had told her everything. It was when she held something back that caused Mom to get angry. And somehow Mom could tell when Marcia was holding something back. When Mom was angry, Marcia wanted to disappear. She wanted to cease to exist. Nothing was worse than when Mom was angry.

There was just something about Del that made Marcia want to tell him everything. She believed he could understand, but to do so she couldn't hold anything back. Yet she also believed that he was the kind of person who understood things that were left unsaid. When she told him she thought she might be an accessory, he merely continued to stare into the fire, patiently waiting for her to go on. She was certain he knew that there was a difference between being an intentional accessory and being an accessory by circumstance. She suspected there were legal terms for this distinction, but she didn't know what they were, and if Barr was lying dead beneath the snow on Presque Isle, that distinction would probably become a factor when some lawyer tried to plead her case in court.

But then, the problem was intention. What do you intend? When do you know for certain that you intend to do something? When she told Barr to meet her on Presque Isle this afternoon, before the blizzard really started, did she have any idea where it might lead? What was her intention then? Where did she think it might go? Did she really think that Barr and Connor would work things out quietly, rationally, like two grown men? Was that what she wanted? Was that her intention? Or did she just want an end to all this crap?

"Mom was my best friend," she had told Del, "or so she liked to think." But that wasn't the case, really, not once Marcia came to understand that Mom wanted to be friends with her daughter because she didn't want any trouble, because she was lonely, because she really didn't have any friends. She wanted Marcia to be her friend because that would be easier than being her daughter, which would then require her to be a mother.

Mom didn't want to be a mother. She didn't want Marcia. Hadn't wanted Marcia. She was a mistake, though Mom would never, could never, admit it. It was Mom against the world, and having Marcia just made things more difficult, more complicated. She used to say, *I have to take my daughter into consideration.* It was something she told employers, when there was some problem at work, either she was late for her shift or she didn't show up or she didn't do something right—it was always because she had to take her daughter into consideration. How can the bosses and the managers at the bars and restaurants where she worked argue with a woman who was taking her daughter into consideration? Some couldn't, though some finally caught on and they fired Mom, letting her go for reasons that had nothing to do with her being a mother. Talking back to customers. Stealing from the till. Instigating dissension among the staff. That one really got to Mom. She would say to herself, and to Marcia, *I got let go*—she never used the word *fired*—*because I'm not a team player. Honey, promise me you'll put that on my gravestone: Lorraine Fournier, Not a Team Player.*

Taking her daughter into consideration was particularly useful with men. If she didn't want to see a guy, that was her reason. If she needed something from him—a ride, a favor, money—that was her reason. Men passed through their apartments, sleeping in Mom's bed, sitting at the kitchen table, lying on the brown corduroy sofa that accompanied them from one apartment to the next, and at some point they realized they too had to take her daughter into consideration. Most of them tried to be nice to Marcia because that would make it easier for them to get her mother into bed. Some of them took another tack, either ignoring Marcia or acting like she didn't belong there.

Then there was Carl, who came and went over the years. At first, when she was very young, Marcia didn't get why Mom brought him home and took him to bed. But over time she began to understand. Carl could be terribly sweet. He would make Mom sigh and moan when they were in her bedroom. At first, Marcia thought he was doing something that hurt her, but she came to accept that whatever he was doing had a lot to do with Mom allowing him to come and go the way he did. Like Mom, Carl wasn't a team player, and he was also what Mom called a real nomad, which when Marcia was very young she thought meant that he never got angry. But he could get angry, though when he did it wasn't a matter of screaming and shouting like Mom, he just got quiet and his anger was there in the terrible thing that happened to his eyes. Then he wouldn't be sweet, and often Mom asked him not to be so mean. It was at such times that Carl tended to disappear. He'd just stop coming to whatever apartment they were living in, though Mom always seemed to be waiting for him to return. And when he finally did come back it was always sudden, unexpected, usually late at night at the end of a shift, and Marcia would be awakened by the desperate sounds they were making in Mom's bedroom. And then he'd be sitting there at the kitchen table the next morning, drinking coffee, acting like he'd never left.

When Marcia was nearly twelve, Carl began to touch her. The first time was when Mom went down to the corner for a pack of cigarettes and Carl was playing solitaire at the kitchen table. Most of the other men who stayed at the apartment watched TV much of the time and some would read the newspaper, but Carl seldom did either. Usually he'd sit at the kitchen table playing solitaire, or he'd just smoke and gaze out the window, as though he were waiting for something to happen. After Mom left the apartment, he asked Marcia if she knew how to play this card game, and when she said no he let her sit on his leg, which she had done often enough before, but this time, as she was flipping the cards over, his hands seemed to roam, searching her T-shirt. After that, he often touched her briefly when Mom wasn't around, his hands gentle but determined. His fingertips made her nipples stand up, and then he once slid his hand down the front of her pajama bottoms, which caused her to scream. He slapped her and then put his hand over her mouth as they listened to her mother wearily climbing the stairs to the apartment. He looked right into Marcia's eyes, and it was a warning, which sent her running to her room, certain that if she said anything he'd kill her.

After that, when Carl was in the apartment, she stayed in her room much of the time. If Mom needed to run out on an errand, Marcia insisted on going with her. And then, when Marcia was thirteen—it was the week after her birthday, a Thursday night—Mom came home from work early. She was drunk and hysterical, and she went into her bedroom and closed the door. Marcia listened to her in there for hours, crying, sobbing, talking to herself, until she finally fell asleep. In the morning, Mom sat at the kitchen table and told her that Carl was dead. She was trying to break the news without crying. She was trying to help Marcia through it. But when Marcia asked how Carl had died Mom couldn't bring herself to explain it, only saying that they weren't sure, they meaning the police, and there would be an investigation. When Marcia asked if they were sure Carl was dead, Mom looked baffled at first, and then she became resentful and finally angry—the kind of speechless anger that lasted days and made Marcia want to disappear.

"It sounds like I'm making excuses," Marcia said finally, "for being an accessory."

Del tilted his head. He was being noncommittal. She liked that about him. People were too quick to judge, but he seemed content to just listen.

"I suppose I am," she said. "But I think you have to understand that there are circumstances."

"There are always circumstances," he said.

"Isn't there a term they use in the courts—you hear it on TV shows—circumstantial evidence?" Marcia watched his head nod slowly. "But really I suppose you could say everything was circumstantial." He continued to nod. "Life is circumstantial."

Del stopped nodding then. "What are you trying to tell me?"

"I'm trying to tell you about Barr and what happened out on Presque Isle this afternoon. I'm trying to tell you why I may be an accessory to something terrible."

Del didn't say anything, and he continued to stare into the fire.

———————————

The crossed hockey sticks. Marcia was so fucking pissed.

Barr wouldn't look her in the eyes, but concentrated on her white terrycloth bathrobe, the way it swelled at her hips.

"I know I saw this at their house. The Warners'. They both have them on their key chains, in honor of their grandson, who plays hockey for Northern. I don't understand. How did you—"

"I took it," Barr said.

"What do you mean you *took* it?"

So he told her. After a minute, looking like she didn't have the strength to stand any longer, she lowered herself to the edge of the coffee table. She wasn't angry now but something much worse. Tears seeped from the corners of her eyes. She leaned forward, her elbows on her knees, the lapels of her bathrobe opening so that her tits, those remarkable tits, looked like they were about to tumble out in the open. She could be so oblivious about such things, which was part of what got to him about her, the way she would move yet be so completely unaware of the effect it was having on him. On all of them—on any guy with eyes, a dick between his legs, and half a brain in his head. How did that old blues song go? *She could make a blind man see, a lame man walk.* She had that effect on men, even on that jerk, Connor. A piece of her, any piece of her could set this thing off in a guy's brain so that nothing else mattered. This was the reason women like her were called a piece.

And now, while he told her about the crossed hockey sticks, he could see that he was driving her initial anger back inside her. What remained was fear. And remorse. And confusion. She finally wiped her face on the sleeve of her bathrobe, allowing something to clarify in her eyes, and she looked at him as though she'd never seen him before.

"What you're saying," she said, "is you've been doing this—*this*—for some time. You've been following me to my clients' homes. You've been casing their houses, and then you've broken in when they're not home and robbed them. And you also take some little thing, something like this key chain just because—because you want to leave a message, to send them a signal, saying 'You people are dumb fucks because you make it so easy for me to get in and out of here.'"

"You could say that," he said. "But I rarely have to break in."

"You just walk in. You open a door."

"An unlocked door."

"Which makes it all right, that's what you're saying?"

He didn't bother answering.

"And you take stuff that's valuable." She placed her hand on her jaw for a moment, covering her mouth. "What do you do with it? You sell it?"

"Not directly. It gets sent down to a guy in Chicago. A fence. He sells it and I get my cut."

"What do you mean 'sent down to a guy'? You *mail* it?"

"Are you that stupid?"

She dropped her hand, and there was a flare of anger, but it was overwhelmed by hurt. "I don't understand how you get it to Chicago."

"You don't want to know, Marcia. You don't want to know anything about this. You want to forget it, all of it."

"But I do know. And I'm not going to forget it. I *can't* forget it." She moved, as though to push herself up off the coffee table.

"If you can't forget it," he said carefully, "what do you think you can do about it?"

"Do? What can I *do*?"

"Yeah. You think you can stop me? You think you can go to the police?"

"The police?" She might not have heard the word before. Then: "You're breaking the law. I suppose I could do that, go to the police."

"Really. And what would you tell them?"

She was not stupid. In fact, if she had a problem, it was that she was too damned smart. A little slow to catch on sometimes, but once she began to work things through she could see a situation clearly. All of its implications, like those chess masters who can see the consequences of every possible move on the board. He watched this happen now, watched her eyes, the set of her mouth as she figured it all out.

"No," she said quietly. "I guess I can't go to the police."

Connor's hands were a glazed red—

they might have been boiled. He wished they were numb, wished he couldn't feel them.

He'd pulled the litter at least a half mile but still saw no indication of Yellow Dog Township. Up ahead it was just woods, just this narrow road winding through the snowbound forest. No tracks—no one, either on foot or in a vehicle, had come this way in several hours. It was quite beautiful, particularly the way the wind created ghostly swirls that rose up off the snow. In the truck, that had been Essi's word, *ghostly*. It was one thing to appreciate it from inside the warmth of his truck, another to be out here, with the ache in his back and legs, and his hands gone.

He stopped and looked back down the road, a white swath cutting through the black forest. His trail weaved up the center of the road. Essi lay bundled in the litter. He had wrapped her face in her scarf, so only her eyes were visible. They were closed, and her lids looked so peaceful she might have been sleeping. Or meditating.

He turned around, took hold of the two pine branches again, barely feeling them in his frozen hands, but feeling the weight of Essi transmitted up his arms and into his shoulder and back. People often noted how strong he was, which meant that when he was working on a house, framing walls or replacing a roof, he was often given the heaviest lifting tasks, which led people to assume that he never tired, but they were wrong. He was pulling this tiny woman on a litter through a blizzard, and he didn't think he had any strength left, but then he took a step forward, his boots disappearing down into the snow, until he sank almost to his knees, and then he took another step and then another.

And he remembered what happened to his gloves: he'd left them on Presque Isle. When he saw Barr and Marcia there in the woods, he'd walked toward them, pulling off his gloves.

It was a point of honor, really.

Marcia liked to say, *The best thing to do is to do what you're supposed to do.*

This is what I'm supposed to do, Connor had thought as he walked through the woods toward Barr. Just seeing Barr made him angry. All the shit he'd put Marcia through, put him through. Connor was seldom angry, but when it came it came on suddenly, consuming him as though he had just been engulfed in smoke from an unknown source. And that seemed to fuel his anger, the fact that he didn't really know or understand its source. It just was, and there was no controlling it. *Some things you don't do with your gloves on. You use your bare hands.*

When Marcia hesitated, Del decided it would be good for him to get up off the couch. He needed to move his hip, which often began to ache after he remained still for too long. She wanted to tell him something about Presque Isle this afternoon, and the way she'd said it he wondered if he should hear it.

"I need to stand up," he said.

"Can I get something for you?"

Del nodded toward the bathroom, and she curled her legs under her so he could get up off the couch. He wanted to give this girl some time to think about what she was telling him. He wanted to look out at the storm, because if anything the wind was getting stronger. Most of all he wanted to take another one of the pain pills, close his eyes, and just listen to the storm. Bach cello suites would be nice, but he'd settle for this north wind.

What he really wanted was to hear Liesl's voice. Just one more time. She had a deep voice for a woman, and often when she answered the phone and it was a call from someone who didn't know her—some solicitation, usually—the caller would think Liesl was a man. Sometimes she went along with it, and later, when she'd tell Del about the call, she'd laugh, explaining how she'd had this conversation on the phone with someone who kept calling her sir. And sometimes, such as when she talked on the phone with credit card companies or banks—she called them the Menu People—she used their belief that they were dealing with a man to her advantage. She said a woman's logic and a man's voice was a formidable weapon. Controlled outrage. At the end of such conversations she usually told them her name was Liesl. No, Del is my husband, you're talking to Liesl, she'd say, and often she had to explain this several times until the Menu Person understood that the entire conversation had been with a woman. Once, Del overheard one of these conversations, which Liesl ended by saying, "It shouldn't make any difference that you think you're talking to a man when you've been talking to a woman all this time, but unfortunately it does." And then she hung up.

What was missing from the world was her voice. It was not only deep, but he found it reassuring and soothing. What remained was this ache in his hip—last January the right one, and now, a year later, the left one. What remained was shuffling with the aid of a cane, not walking. What remained was this sense of waiting, waiting for *what* was difficult, if not impossible, to determine. He sometimes liked to think he was finished with waiting, that he'd waited long enough, and that he'd somehow gotten beyond waiting. For anything. Ever again. But then five minutes later he'd realized it wasn't true. You never stop waiting. You wait for the next moment, and the next and the next, and this was the real fear of death: *you have nothing left to wait for.* You listen to a young woman like Marcia and part of you thinks you've heard it all before, that it's a kind of déjà vu, and that you know where she's going with what she's saying, but then she talks about being an accessory and about a terrible thing she'd done that afternoon on Presque Isle, and you realize you haven't heard it before, you don't know where it's going, and you're not sure you should hear the rest of it. You wonder at what point *you* become an accessory. She needs to talk to someone, certainly. Really, she'd be better off talking to Liesl. If she could hear Liesl's voice and look into her eyes, she wouldn't hesitate in telling her everything, because she'd know she was talking to someone who wanted to understand, someone who cared.

After he pulled the bathroom door shut, Del stood in the dark, his free hand gripping the edge of the sink. The porcelain was cold and smooth, like an ice cube. Even if there had been power, he might not have turned on the light. He often didn't turn on lights in the house. The dark was comforting. He was so familiar with the house, with where everything was, that he didn't need lights. Sometimes he moved about at night, touching doorjambs, tables, counters, the backs of chairs as though he were blind. The faintest pale glow came through the bathroom window. Outside, the world was the color of a pearl. In the distance, he could see the blackness of the forest. The wind was thrashing the trees, the snowy white space between the house and the edge of the woods strewn with fallen branches. If he were a painter, this is what he would paint: a view from a window of tree limbs lying in the snow. He would call it *Waiting.* A lot of people wouldn't get it. Liesl would, though. Waiting for the next branch to fall. She would have suggested the title. It would just come to her: *Waiting.*

He raised his free hand up from the porcelain sink, and his fingers found the glass knob of the medicine cabinet. After opening the door, he removed the vial from the bottom shelf. He unscrewed the plastic cap and tapped out one pill. Oval-shaped. He knew it was blue, robin's egg blue, though in the dark it had no color. He put the pill in his mouth but didn't swallow, while he returned the vial to the cabinet. As he stood in the dark, he felt the oval-ness of the pill on his tongue. He liked the way it felt, smooth, uniformly manufactured. The ache in his hip was the other thing he felt, and this pill was his only defense. Yet he was reluctant to swallow. Somehow the pain was what kept it all together. Without the pain, what would be left? He'd thought about this several times, more than once standing right here in the dark bathroom, facing the medicine cabinet. During Liesl's illness she was given a wide assortment of pain medications. After she died, the hospice nurse dutifully collected some of them, such as the syringes filled with morphine. She stood at the counter and injected the morphine into a tin of coffee grounds. As Del watched, she said it was required by law. But she failed to collect all the pain medications, all the pills. He still had them, plus what he'd been given after his last hip surgery. There were enough here in the medicine cabinet to take the pain away at any time. Since Liesl had died it had become a source of comfort, knowing that these vials of pills were here in the dark, that they were an option, waiting.

After the crossed hockey sticks, Marcia refused to see Barr. Even when he promised to never again break into the house of one of her clients, she said she didn't want him to call her, didn't want him to come around to her apartment, didn't want to see him, period.

This meant she would go back to that dipshit Connor.

It was all right. Zack had set things up with the guy in Chicago, and soon Barr was on a plane to Sarasota. He was given enough money for the trip, and he rented a car and checked into a motel just two blocks from the Gulf of Mexico. It was February, temperatures in the seventies, the nearest snowbank a thousand miles away.

The next day he got a call on his cell phone from a woman named Veronica. They met at a bar with a deck that looked out on Sarasota Bay. She was in her mid-thirties, a few years older than Barr, and she said people called her V. Her smile revealed a gold tongue stud, but she was all business—the friendly stuff was just for show. He smiled too and adjusted the new shades he'd bought.

"So my friend in Chicago," he said, turning his head as though he were gazing out at the bay, though he kept his eyes on her face, "he says after I arrived I'd get a call from you. And what are you going to do for me?" Her expression didn't change.

"Curb that thought." V had this sexy hoarse voice from all her cigarettes. "In," she whispered. "I'm going to get you in."

"In."

"I run a cleaning agency, you know? I got this fleet of girls in little uniforms who go into condos up and down the bay and they clean people's kitchens, vacuum their carpets, scrub off the shit streaks in their toilet bowls."

"So you know where stuff is, and you can get me in the door."

"Right."

"In where? And what am I taking out?"

"They'll let us know where soon, in a day or so." She leaned a bit closer, and he glanced down at the cleavage that was pushing up between the lapels of her purple satin blouse. "This is not—" She hesitated, for effect. "This is not quite like the jobs you been doing up there in Minnesota."

"Michigan."

"Whatever."

"Okay, so why bring me all the way down to do it? You don't have guys with the right credentials here in Georgia? Sorry, Florida, the Whatever State."

A little smile, just a lift at one corner of that mouth. "Oh, we got plenty of them. Too many. And they all know each other." V's tongue slid out, the gold glinting, and moistened her full lower lip. Her mouth, her tits, her ass, even her terrific calves all had that injected plump look. "For this they want an outside guy is all I can tell you."

It was too easy. But he was here, and he liked the way the breeze off the Gulf moved through the Hawaiian shirt he'd bought to go with the shades. He smiled, and they ordered another drink.

The night after his drinks with V there was a knock on the door of his motel room.

"V sent me." She wasn't Hispanic, not entirely, but she wasn't white either. She wore enormous shades and, like V's, her lips looked like they were about to split open. "She say you need your room cleaned, huh?"

They had a drink, vodka and tonic. She was barely five feet tall, and her black skirt rode way up her thighs when she sat on the bed and crossed her legs. When she removed her sunglasses he saw that she had a small birthmark, a pink blotch beneath her right eye. Her phone vibrated almost constantly, until she shut the thing off.

After she finished her drink, she stood up, and the way she took her blouse off she might have been alone in the room. No bra. He figured she might not be twenty-one. Everything about her was firm, athletic, and her tan lines suggested the kind of bikinis you only dream of in the U.P. With one hand against his chest, she pushed him down on the bed while her other hand hiked up her skirt so she could straddle him. She rubbed against him, slow, patient. When he reached up to her breasts, she leaned back and smiled. "Honey, we need to prioritize."

She climbed off of him, picked up her blouse, and closed the bathroom door behind her.

Barr stared at the ceiling, which was covered with the white clots of stuff that contractors shot out of these guns that were hooked up to air compressors. Stipple guns. Years ago he had a job where he worked with a crew that was remodeling houses, and a few times he'd sprayed a ceiling with a stipple gun. It was kind of fun at first, moving the gun back and forth, trying to get even coverage on the ceiling, but by the time he got the hang of it, he was bored and quit after a couple of weeks. Now, listening to the toilet flush, the anticipation was eating at him, so he concentrated on the ceiling, trying to find where the seams in the Sheetrock were concealed.

When the door opened, he looked at her, upside down. She was wearing her blouse, tucked in, and before leaving the bathroom she leaned over the sink to check her hair in the mirror.

"Got time for another drink?" he asked, sitting up.

"Not right now."

"So what is this?"

She came out of the bathroom. "Maybe I check back in with you after the job's done."

"This is just an appetizer."

"Something like that." She went to the bureau and rummaged through her large purse.

"It's part of the deal. A transaction."

"Something like that."

Who ordered this, who paid for it? V? Or was it some guy in Chicago? It sure as hell wasn't his cousin Zack. It occurred to him again that this seemed all too easy. But what was he going to do, walk away from it? From the warm breezes beneath the palm trees? The drinks overlooking the bay? The tan lines on this girl?

She turned away from the bureau, a folded slip of paper was in one hand while the other slung her purse over her shoulder. After putting on her sunglasses, she dropped the note on the rumpled bedspread and didn't break stride on her way to the door. "Tomorrow," she said. "Be on time." She didn't bother to look at him and pulled the door shut against the blinding sunlight.

Barr lay back on the bed. You don't walk away from something like this. They don't let you.

Yellow Dog Township was a gas station and two old brick buildings facing each other across the road. Not one light. The gas station was dark, and looking in the plateglass window, Connor suspected it had been out of business for some time. He pulled Essi through the snow to the nearest brick building. There was an antique shop on the first floor. Dark. There was also a door that he thought might lead up to the apartment on the second floor. He knocked on the glass, but there was nothing inside, no movement, not a sound.

He pulled Essi across the road to the other building. It looked abandoned. He thought there used to be a constable's office there, but that must have been years ago. Next to the building was a dumpster, and he dragged Essi in the space between it and the brick wall, where they found some protection from the wind. Exhausted, he sat down in the snow, his back against the dumpster. When he looked at Essi, he saw that her eyes were open, and she was staring at him.

"You okay?"

"I don't know," she said. "We had an accident?"

"Yes. We might have to stay here and wait this out."

"That could be a long time."

"I know."

"You were going somewhere, somewhere on the other side of Yellow Dog Township." He nodded. "We should try to get there," she said. "I can't seem to move. I don't know if it's because I'm cold or I've injured my back or what." She gazed up into the snow a moment. "Did Ilo die?"

"She did. But I think it was quick, the way she hit the windshield. She kept you from going right through the glass."

Essi closed her eyes. This only seemed to confirm something she expected. He wanted to say something about Ilo, that he was sorry she'd died. But he wasn't sure. With this woman, he wasn't sure what to say. "What do you do?" he said finally.

When she opened her eyes, he regretted speaking at all. But there was actually a kind of humor in her gaze. "Do? You mean like work?"

He nodded.

"That would be very difficult to explain, and it would take a long time. We'd freeze out here, most likely."

He nodded again.

"It would be easier to tell you the things I *haven't* done. That would be a shorter list."

He was reluctant to show any response and held perfectly still, though it was not easy because he could feel the cold creeping into his shoulders.

"You," she said, "you do something, I'd say, with your hands. Carpentry, maybe? You got the truck, the toolbox in the bed. You look like you climb ladders often."

"Roofing, yeah, lots of roofing, in season. And I've repointed brick chimneys and replaced flashing. I guess I do a little bit of everything. Framing, Sheetrock, painting. Not electricity, though occasionally I'll fish a line through a wall. Or plumbing. You gotta call someone else to get that done."

She glanced down at the litter. "I'm bound up like I'm in a papoose. You built this." She looked at him again, and he nodded. "Nice job."

"Thanks. And we shouldn't stay here much longer. It's better to keep going, I think."

Essi didn't appear to agree or disagree with him. It wasn't that she didn't care but that she accepted whatever he decided to do. She was older than he'd first thought, but even bundled up there was something vigorous about her face, as though she had reserves of energy and strength that she still hadn't tapped. Somehow it had to do with the storm. He didn't understand it, but realized that the storm was feeding something in her. And he wanted to tell her that he also felt different during a blizzard, that ever since he was a kid he felt stronger and alert when the wind was high and the snow got heavy. He wanted to say he felt more like himself in this weather.

Instead, he got to his feet. "We should get moving, I guess."

"I keep hearing this song in my head, an old song that played on the radio when I was young. You probably weren't even born then. I can't remember the words but it goes like this." She hummed a melody.

"Nope," Connor said, standing. "Can't help you." He turned around and took up the pine limbs in his raw hands and pulled Essi out into the road. At least the wind was at his back here.

She continued to sing, and after a moment she said, "The song began just with a guitar, and it went like this."

"That part's familiar," he said. "But I can't think of the name of the song."

Barr's head hurt and it seemed to be getting worse. He figured he'd been in shock or something back on Presque Isle, but now pain was flooding his skull. A heavy pain that made him wonder if his brain was leaking or bleeding or something like that. He drove through snowbound Marquette, thinking about Sarasota, dogged by the notion that if things had gone differently down there, everything would be different now.

Then he pulled over and stopped, the car angled up on the snowbank. *Cell phones.*

It had been a cell phone that that screwed him up in Sarasota. He reached into the pockets of his jacket and pulled out both cell phones.

His. Marcia's.

Her flip phone. The keypad lit up, and then there was a screensaver photo, a selfie: Connor's arm extended so he's holding the phone away from them and Marcia has her arms around his waist, while he has his other hand on her swollen belly. It's a fall day and they're wearing sweatshirts, his gray with a frayed collar, hers with faded letters: *Say Ya to Da U.P., eh?* They are on the beach in McCarty's Cove with the red brick lighthouse on the rocks behind them.

Something about her cell phone he couldn't quite remember. It was this thing she used to do with it in an absent-minded sort of way. She'd flip it open and start thumbing buttons, until she found something.

Fucking cell phones.

In Sarasota, he was on time the next day. He drove to the address that was on the slip of paper that the girl had dropped on his bed in the motel room, a sports bar in Bradenton Beach, on Anna Maria Island. V was there, sitting in a booth. The place catered to Chicago sports fans, Bears, Cubs, White Sox, Bulls, Blackhawks shit all over the place. It was too dark, so he took off his shades.

"Here I am, on time." He raised his hand to get the waitress's attention. "What's the deal?"

"No time for drinks," V said as she slid out of the booth.

Outside the light was crushingly bright. They got in her car, a BMW convertible. The island was long and narrow, separating the bay from the Gulf, and she drove north slowly. After a couple of miles she turned left and drove down a lane that ended in front of sand dunes. They kicked off their shoes and walked out on the beach of fine white sand. They headed north, the blue-green water to their left and condos and bungalows rising up just beyond the dunes.

V stopped, and when she turned and faced Barr, she put her hands on his shoulders. It was a pose, like the other day in the bar. "See that condo, the pink one?"

"Yeah."

"Third floor. They left today, going back up to Chicago for the weekend. Rikki will be in tomorrow, so the place will be spick-and-span when they return. There's security—it's that kind of place. There's a guy in the lobby, and there's a guy that just kind of patrols the property. He likes to scan the beach with binoculars, checking out bikinis, which is why you don't want to look like you're staring right at the place, you know? That guy is where Rikki comes in."

"She's going to put her cocktease routine on him?"

"She's going to distract him just long enough so you can get in the condo."

"Cameras. A place like that has security cameras all over."

"The kind of people who live there, they don't want any record of who comes and goes. There are cameras, but Rikki says they're fake."

"And how do I get in?"

"There's a service entrance on the north side of the building. Rikki's got the security code and is going to disarm it so you can get in and up the back stairs. After she cleans the condo, she'll close the door but make sure it's not locked. Number Six, third floor."

"Okay." He put his hands on her shoulders, lacing his fingers about the back of her neck, beneath her soft dark hair. He tried to pull her toward him, but her arms on his shoulders were strong, and she held him away.

"That won't be necessary," she said.

"We don't want the binocular guy to think we're fake."

She still held him off.

"You do put in your time at the gym, don't you?" he said.

"Every damn day."

"I'll bet you could bench press me."

"Like a dumbbell."

"Nice. I get in Number Six, what am I looking for?"

She seemed to change her mind and leaned against him, her hands now clasping the back of his neck tightly, perhaps too tightly, as she pressed her cheek against his. "A cell phone."

"They won't have taken it to Chicago?"

"Let's hope not."

"And it would be too easy, too obvious if Rikki grabbed the cell phone."

"They look through her stuff thoroughly before she leaves the building."

"What's so important about this cell phone?"

She stepped out of his arms then and began to walk back toward the car. "You just find the cell phone, that's all, and you bring it to me at that pub where we just met."

Barr closed Marcia's phone and looked out at the snow, swirling on Front Street. A long ways from Anna Maria Island.

He flipped her phone open again and tapped *Calendar*. He remembered that she kept her client appointments in there. She would check it and say something like *I got an appointment in Gwinn in forty-five minutes.*

"There you are," he said. "You're out in Yellow Dog Township at 2387 County Road 644. Working on some old guy named Maki."

Marcia moved her legs

so Del could sit on the couch again. He wouldn't look at her. She thought it odd, like he was concealing something from her. Something had changed. Something had happened in the bathroom. He was further away somehow.

"You okay?" she asked.

"Why do you ask?"

"You just seem—I don't know—different."

He looked at her then. His eyes seemed only faintly there. But curious. Then he appeared to come back, back from wherever he'd gone, and this seemed to her to be an attempt to cover up, to conceal, something he was doing for her benefit. "You were telling me—" But he paused. He couldn't remember, because whatever had happened to him had pushed it, had pushed everything else, aside. He was a man who went places in his mind, places where no one else could go. She was sure it had to do with his wife, with her death, though she suspected it had been happening to him even before her death. Distracted. He looked distracted.

"I just realized that you don't do something most of my clients do."

"What's that?"

"The retired ones. They almost immediately tell you what they used to do. Banker, nurse, whatever. It's as though this is the only way to tell you who they are. Or were. You haven't told me any of that." She waited. "Maybe it's not important?"

"Could be. Or maybe I did so many different things that it would only bore you."

"Ah. But it wouldn't, it wouldn't bore me." She waited again. "You gonna tell me? I'm not going to try and guess."

"I did a lot of things. I was in law enforcement some of the time."

"Christ."

"No, I was just constable here in Yellow Dog. People sometimes called me sheriff, because I actually worked for the county. Very little actual police work. Domestic disturbances sometimes. It was mostly traffic violations and the occasional summons. One night this couple, they were in their seventies, came to the office and requested that I marry them then and there."

"Did you?"

"Once I ascertained they were consenting adults."

"What else did you do?"

"You name it. Pounded nails when I was your age. After the constable thing I tried to open a sort of bed and breakfast with Liesl, but after a few years that didn't pan out. When we moved into Marquette I became a parole officer." He looked at her, absolutely noncommittal.

"And here I'm telling you about my maybe being an accessory. You could have me arrested."

"No, I couldn't. I was sort of at the other end of the judicial tunnel."

"The light."

"Some thought so. Most didn't. Listen, you don't have to tell me anything, unless you want to."

She stared into the fire. He was waiting, and she knew he would wait as long as it took. "I'll bet you've heard a lot of things. People tell their parole officers all sorts of stuff. Usually trying to say they're innocent, that they couldn't possibly do something wrong."

"Only about 99 percent of the time."

"All right," she said. "I'm going to tell you. I'm not going to lie."

"I know that."

"Thank you. So. I was telling you about this afternoon. I was an accessory. I think. I was trying to tell you the circumstances, but in the long run they're not important, are they?"

His fingers raked through his beard for a moment. "I suppose it depends."

"Depends. On what? In the cop shows the detective looks for the motive, but once the arrest is made the court judges you for your actions."

"Yes, but they do take circumstances into consideration. You mentioned intent."

"See, that's where I get confused. It's where I'm not sure. I know what I did, but I don't know what my intentions were."

"Do you want to tell me what you did? Just that?" After a moment, he added, "You're not in a courtroom, you know."

Marcia gazed up at the ceiling, at the knot holes that made her think of eyes. "The jury," she said, "is always with you, whether you like it or not."

"Maybe. It's an awful way to live. But maybe."

"I'll tell you what I did, and you be the judge."

Del took a moment. "I can't do that."

He was back, back from wherever he'd gone, and she was glad of it. "No, I suppose you can't, which is why I want to tell you. It was very simple, really. I called Barr this morning and told him I needed to talk to him. I said I wanted to tell him something. But that wasn't my intention. I told him to meet me out at Presque Isle. It's a special place for us. For me, for Barr, and for Connor. Since all this started I've gone out there with both of them. In the summer, just to walk, to climb the rocks, to swim sometimes. Even in the winter, on days like today, just to look out at the cold dark lake. I hadn't talked to Barr in a while. So when I called him and said to meet me on Presque Isle, it meant something."

"You wanted to get back together with him?"

"This is what I don't know. This is where my intentions come in. I need to go back, back to shortly before I realized I was pregnant. I was confused. Both Barr and Connor were—they were both around. I hated the fact that I couldn't make up my mind, but I have to admit I liked it, too. Barr said I was working both of them. Connor just pleaded and apologized a lot, like it was all his fault. Barr was right. He usually is, you know. He sees through people. He's honest in a way that few people are. He saw that I actually liked it, working both of them, that I liked the attention. I liked the fact that they were trying to outdo each other in their own way, you know?"

Del tilted his head slightly.

"But then I discovered something about Barr that really upset me. He was robbing people, breaking into their houses and stealing I don't know what, money maybe, but personal stuff like jewelry. That part really didn't surprise me. If you met him you'd know he was capable of that sort of thing, and you'd know that that was somehow connected to the way he was honest about things. I know that's true, though I can't explain it. He has this thief's sense of justice, or something. When I learned about it, he didn't deny it. But what really got me was he was stealing from some of my clients. He'd watch their houses and figure out when it would be a good time to go in and take stuff. And I realized I couldn't do anything about it. If I went to the police, no one would believe I didn't have something to do with it. I'd lose my job, at the very least. I could get arrested for being an accessory or an accomplice. Even if they couldn't prove it, even if Barr said I had nothing to do with it I'd be connected to it. A town the size of Marquette, who'd hire me? I'd have to leave, and go where? Chicago, the Twin Cities? So I stopped seeing him. Even when he promised not to steal from my clients anymore, but I just said it was too much and don't come around anymore." Marcia ran her hand through her hair, and Del glanced at her. "Know what he did? He did as I asked. Didn't call, didn't come around. He kept away. At first I was glad. It was just me and Connor then, and I thought, I really believed that that's the way it should be. Me and Barr, it would never work, never go anyplace. It was too much like my mother and Carl. Barr would come and go as he pleased, and like my mother I'd just wait for him. With Connor, there was a chance of things turning into something. When you get past all his apologies, Connor is strong in his own way. He apologizes because he's sorry he's flawed. He wants to be perfect. To not make mistakes. And he's willing to work at it. He really tries to do better. It's like he's not fully formed, not quite there yet, but I believe he can be a good man. That's a rare thing, a good man."

"It is."

"It's just a confidence thing with him. He would never *dream* of walking into someone's house and robbing them. So I went to Connor, and I told him it was just him from now on, and nobody else. Then I learned I was pregnant." Marcia had to pause. She inhaled deeply, and when she let the air out, she could hear the quiver rise up in her lungs, as though the very center of her was a gyroscope out of balance. "At first, well, after the shock wore off—I guess I couldn't really be surprised—I thought, *All right, so I'm going to have a baby, and this will be all right.* And I was, I guess, I was reassured when I told Connor about the baby and he was happy. More than that. He was out of his mind happy, and at that point I loved him so much." Marcia tried to sit up. "I can't—I think I have to get a glass of water or something."

"Sure," Del said as he took the blankets off her legs.

The plows were working the streets of Marquette, but going out 644 would be difficult. It pissed Barr off. Nothing was ever easy in the Upper

Peninsula, particularly in winter. He could stay in town and wait out the blizzard and go after Connor and Marcia later. It might be the smart thing to do. But right now he had a pretty good idea where they were. Element of surprise. Later, after the blizzard, Connor and knocked-up Marcia would get in that truck of his and bolt. They would head south. America was below the Mackinac Bridge. Or, if they went west, it was below Green Bay. Down there, they had freeways and the snow didn't come up to your ass. Down there, in America, you could get away. Get lost. You could disappear. Which is why he had agreed to do this job in Florida.

Except Zack just called it the *Thing*.

"This thing," Barr had said a few days before he flew to Sarasota. "What *is* the thing?" They were sitting in the booth at the Portside. Zack was eating french fries. Again. His cousin was pushing two hundred and fifty pounds and he just couldn't get enough of those thick-cut fries. "This deal is fucked. I'm going to Florida, grab some *thing*, but I don't even know what it is yet. Then what?"

"It's simple." Zack took the bottle and squeezed out another enormous puddle of ketchup on his plate. It was Friday night—fish fry night—but he hardly touched the deep-fried beer-battered cod. Just the fries and a bit of the coleslaw. A sliver of carrot was stuck in the corner of his mouth. "It's a matter of small steps. After you take a step, you learn a little more, and then you take another step. After you get to Sarasota, you're going to meet a girl named Veronica. I'm told she likes to be called V. As in vagina. She'll tell you what your next step is going to be."

"This feels blind, Zack."

"It's safe. You don't need to know more than you need to know when you need to know it."

"That's bullshit. That's to protect someone else, not me."

"Listen," Zack said. "It protects everybody. Including us. I don't know much more than you do. I don't *want* to know more than I need."

"What you *want* is to wipe that piece of carrot off your lip."

Zack swiped at his mouth with his fingers. He got the carrot but left a smear of ketchup in his mustache. Barr sat back in his booth and shook his head.

"This isn't like the other stuff," Zack said, "where you bring me shit and I take it down to Chicago. The reason you're being asked to do this is because you've given them good stuff and you don't screw up. You're careful and you're efficient. That's why you're getting this job. Lots of guys could do this, but they want you. Down there, nobody knows who you are, is the way I figure it."

"Well, that can work against me, too."

"You don't want this job you should have said so when I first mentioned it. Too late to back out now."

"Is it?" Barr was drinking Labatt and shots of Irish. He finished his shot and considered getting out of the booth and just walking away, from Zack, from Chicago, from the Thing, all of it.

Zack saw this. "It is," he said. He held a particularly long french fry, loaded with ketchup, in front of him. "It's too late for that, Cuz. For you and for me." He pushed the entire french fry into his mouth. "It's simple and we keep it simple. You take one step at a time and when you deliver you get paid."

"Five grand. All at once. By you."

"Right." Zack worked his fork around the little plastic cup of coleslaw. "There's the twenty-five hundred I'm going to give you tonight for expenses. You get to keep anything left over. Consider it a bonus. As soon as you get the thing you'll give it to V. It'll be out of your hands, less than an hour. You're done. You get on the plane and come back, and I'll have the five grand."

"You don't have it now?"

"No, I don't have it now. They don't work that way. I'll have it when you get back."

"So. V calls them after I give her this thing, I fly back here, and then they send you the money to give to me."

Zack nodded as he pushed his plate away. "It's their idea of trust, Cuz. It's all in the small steps. This way there's no misunderstandings."

"You and your small steps, Zack. I'm a big picture guy. I like to see the whole enchilada."

"I'll show you some enchiladas." Zack took an envelope from inside his jacket and laid it on the table next to the beer bottle. When he smiled his teeth were covered with mashed up potato and ketchup. "What, it's not a lot of money for a plane ride and a few days in the sun?"

Barr glanced about the restaurant. Busy. Everybody eating, nobody paying attention to anything but their plates. He picked up the envelope and opened it just enough to see the wad of bills, hundred dollar bills. Old ones. It was a lot of money. And five thousand at the other end. It would allow him to lay off the house jobs around Marquette for a while.

"Like I said, Cuz. Simple."

Barr tucked the envelope into the pocket inside his jacket.

He took the steps, and they were simple. A few days later, after his brief encounters with V and her little fuck-me cohort, he was sitting in his rented sedan looking at the condo on Anna Maria Island, waiting for five-fifteen, when Rikki would disarm the service entrance door alarm. How she did this, how she got the alarm code, he didn't know, but Barr had no doubt that she could get it. Rikki. Sure. Rikki, don't lose that number. Girls like that got most anything they wanted. Who knows, maybe she would pay him a visit when they were on the other side of this job.

At five-fourteen, he left the car and walked across the parking lot. As he neared the side of the building, a sound startled him—the water sprinkler system around the foundation of the building came on—but he managed not to break stride. None of the shrubs and plants looked real—spiky desert stuff, and it was all too neatly landscaped. But despite the fact that it had rained that morning, one of those swift thunderstorms that come out of nowhere, the sprinklers were on a timer, and he felt the faintest cool mist on his face and forearms as he walked up to the service entrance door.

He put his hand on the doorknob and avoided the temptation to look around to see if anyone was watching him—if he did, it might seem suspicious, like he didn't belong there. He turned the knob, the door opened, and there was no bell, no alarm. He stepped into the stairwell. The building couldn't have been more than a few years old. Even the concrete steps looked like they'd hardly been walked on.

As he climbed the stairs, he took the rubber surgical gloves from his back pocket and worked them on to his hands. At the second floor landing he stopped and listened. Nothing. He proceeded to the third floor and, after pausing again to listen, opened the door and stepped out into a carpeted hallway. There were two doors, and he walked down to the one on the right, Number Six, and saw the card Rikki had wedged between the lock and the frame. He opened the door and the card—a Publix discount card—dropped to the floor. After he picked it up, he closed the door behind him.

He turned around. The place had one of those open floor plans. Kitchen, counter with chrome-frame stools, white leather living room furniture all laid out in front of a bank of windows overlooking the Gulf. There was the smell of lemon oil. The place had just been cleaned and was as tidy as a hotel suite. Houses he entered in Marquette were lived in. Stuff left on counters and tables, clothes hung over the backs of chairs. Once he helped himself to some stew that was simmering in a Crock-Pot. People lived there. Nobody, it seemed, lived here. It was too neat, too clean, and here was this incredible view of the Gulf with enormous clouds that rose up off the pastel horizon.

He started in the master bedroom, going through all the drawers. Then the study. There were framed photographs. Group shots taken in restaurants, bars, one at Wrigley Field. Some of the faces were familiar. That comedian, Bill Murray. The Cubs announcer, Harry Caray. A black guy, a singer whose name Barr couldn't recall. In each group there was a guy, balding, serious gut, a suit with the good sheen, and usually a cigar wedged between his fingers, which were studded with big rings.

He looked like the kind of guy that would have dinner and drinks with celebrities and pick up the check. On the desk there were two photos of him with a woman: one in black and white, taken decades earlier, when he was thinner and had dark hair with sideburns, and she wore a dress that advertised her wares, and the other, when he'd filled out and her plastic surgeon had run out of nip and tuck options. She was still a showcase, with those silicone tits and butterfly eyelashes.

In the lower right-hand desk drawer there was a lacquered wooden box. He opened the lid and found a neat row of cigars. He didn't know cigars, but they had a good scent. Cuban seals. As he closed the lid, he thought he heard something, and he held perfectly still. Footsteps out in the hall, maybe.

He went through the living room, to the front door, which had a peephole. The glass was curved, making it possible to look up and down the hall, and he could see a woman unlocking the other door. At first he didn't recognize her, but then realized it was Rikki, wearing tight black pants and a pullover with lettering on it. She wore a matching blue baseball cap, and her hair was in a ponytail, pulled through the opening in the back of the cap. She looked like a kid who cleaned condos quickly and efficiently, not the tease with tan lines. When she opened the door, she picked up a plastic bucket packed with bottles and rags. Just before going inside, she glanced down the hall toward Barr, and then she was gone, the door closed.

He walked back to the study, looking at bookshelves—no books, just more photos and some pricey crystal vases and bowls. In the study there were shelves lined with sets of books, leather-bound, the kind no one ever actually takes down and reads. He considered taking the books off the shelves, but there were hundreds of them. He decided to look in the guest bedroom first, but as he was leaving the study he realized that he'd left the desk drawer opened.

He shut the drawer.

Then opened it again.

Carefully, he lifted the cigar box out and placed it on the ink blotter. It was perhaps four inches deep. After raising the lid, he took hold of the dividers that kept the cigars in neat groups and lifted the wooden tray out of the box.

In the bottom of the box there was a cell phone, a Nokia.

He slipped it in his pocket. There was also a ring and two passports. Both passports had photos of the Chicago guy. In the Venezuela passport his name was Ricardo Sanchez and in the European Union passport it was Ronaldo Sandoval, with an address in Lisbon. The ring was like nothing Barr had ever seen before—certainly not a school graduation ring. He picked it up and slid it down his ring finger. Large, too large.

He looked at the ring closely and whispered, *"Holy shit."*

It was a 2005 Chicago White Sox World Series Championship ring.

He took it off and held it close to his face, studying its facets, and then he put it back in the box. He fit the tray in the box, hesitated, and then removed one cigar. As he closed the lid, he looked at the photos of the guy and his wife. This guy had never been any ballplayer, certainly not in 2005. Barr opened the box again, removed the tray, and took the ring. Fuck him, it's stolen.

Barr was out of the condo in less than a minute. The hall was empty, quiet. From the other unit he could hear a vacuum cleaner. Rikki, sucking up the dirt.

He went down the back stairs and out the service entrance door, giving the knob a quick wipe as he closed the door. After the air-conditioning, the heat coming off the asphalt in the parking lot was something. He told himself to walk easy, not too fast, and don't look around. Just get in the car and drive.

On the way to the Chicago sports bar, he pulled over in a strip mall parking lot and opened the phone. The address book was filled with names, mostly Italian and Hispanic. Addresses in Chicago, Sarasota, Miami, a few in New York. If some of these guys were important, why wouldn't the guy keep the phone with him? There were dozens of names, too many to copy down. When he reached the Ts he found the name of Gianluca Tessi. Anybody who paid attention to the news knew that name.

Then Barr opened the phone's notebook and found a list of names. Some he recognized—athletes, entertainers, politicians. There were numbers after the names. Though he had the air-conditioning on high, he was sweating. Best thing to do was get this phone out of his hands.

He got back on the road, and when he pulled into the parking lot, he saw V, sitting in her BMW, top down, parked in the shade of a palm tree. She was checking her lipstick in her rearview mirror, so she could watch the parking lot entrance. After Barr pulled into a space, she got out of her car and walked to the bar, never once looking in his direction, and entered by the back door. He waited a few minutes, to give her time to get settled in a booth.

Something kept him in his car. This was more than he'd thought it would be. There was shit on this phone that was valuable. Just walking in and handing it over, maybe it wasn't the best move. Maybe it was. He needed to see the fuller equation. He didn't want to get played cheap. Start with a different venue. Rather than going to her, he should have her come to him.

Barr had memorized V's phone number. He was dialing it but stopped when he saw two guys cross the parking lot and go into the bar. Tight haircuts, sports coats, slacks with the right break. He looked toward the back of the parking lot, where they'd come from, and saw one car parked there. A gray sedan.

He held the phone on his thigh for a minute, probably worth a few hundred dollars. This one was worth a lot more, more than five grand. But how do you get something close to its real value without getting yourself in serious trouble?

Barr began to finish dialing V's number. He just wanted to hear her voice. She had said to just bring the phone into the bar, give it to her, and get himself to the airport. A little thing like calling her from out here in the parking lot, it might throw her off. She might be pissed. But maybe he could make a deal with her, just her. She wouldn't want the people she was collecting the phone for to have any reason to think things didn't go without a hitch. He might get another five out of her. He'd say ten and see what she said. She and Rikki, they cut deals every fucking day.

As he was about to tap in the last number, Barr glanced across the parking lot and saw the back door to the bar open. V came out with the two guys in tight haircuts. She walked between them across the lot. Her walk, something to behold, seemed stiffer than before. She was hemmed in between them as they approached the gray sedan. She was wearing her sunglasses, and she only looked straight ahead. When they reached the sedan, the larger of the two guys opened the back door for her. She climbed in, showing a bit of thigh as she slid across the seat. He got in the back with her. He put his arm around her, easy, like they were sweethearts.

Barr laid down in the front seat of his car and listened to the sedan's engine start up. He kept perfectly still as the car crossed the lot, passed by his car, and pulled out into the street.

Essi would hum the verse,

followed by the chorus, and then she'd stop. Sometimes she'd guess at the title, but then say, "No, that's not it." At first it bothered Connor, her humming while he was dragging the litter through the snow, but when she was silent the damn song would continue to run through his head, so he was relieved when she'd hum it again.

"I can't believe between the two of us we can't figure this out," he said finally.

"I know. It has one of those guitar parts that you recognize immediately."

"Right. Kind of funny," he said, and then he thought it better to let it go.

"What?"

He took a few more steps. She was waiting. "Funny, you trying to come up with the name of an old rock-and-roll song."

"Why is that funny?"

"I don't know, it just is. You just don't strike me as the rock-and-roll type somehow."

"What type do I strike you as?"

"I don't know. More classical."

"Because I can't remember an old song from the radio doesn't mean I don't like classical."

"I suppose."

"You suppose," she said. "I like Mozart."

"Christ."

"What?"

"Mozart, Beethoven—don't know how you can tell the difference."

"I see."

"Music to put your lights out."

"It's called art."

"Right," he said.

"Like Arvo Pärt." She pronounced like *pear*, with a *t* at the end.

"What's that?"

"*Who's* that? He's a composer. Contemporary. Lives in Estonia."

"Estonia. Your accent—that where you're from?"

"No, but you're getting warm."

"Maybe this would be easier if your lights were still out."

"What?"

"Nothing. What about Arvo *Peart*, this guy in Estonia?"

"He composes these pieces that are recorded in old churches, for the acoustics. Lots of voices. Some instrumentation, but mostly a choir. Influenced by Gregorian chants. He's got one called 'Te Deum.' It's a prayer, a mass, all about the glory of God. What's really remarkable about it is the silence, how he uses silence. That's the secret ingredient—to music, to everything." Then she didn't say anything.

She was toying with him. He kept walking, lifting his legs out of the snow, his thigh muscles aching. He knew she wanted him to ask about the silence.

Del watched Marcia go into the kitchen, where she got a glass down from the cabinet. While she ran the faucet, she kept her finger under the stream of water. "This is really cold. You don't think the pipes'll freeze?"

"They might. Why don't you let it drip some?"

"Okay."

She came back as far as the counter that separated the kitchen from the living room. She drank all the water and placed the empty glass on the counter. He could tell by the way she gazed at the glass that she was reluctant to continue, that telling him about whatever had happened out at Presque Isle earlier today was something she needed to reconsider.

"You don't have to go on," he said. "It's none of my business." She continued to stare at the glass. "The years I was a probation officer I heard all kinds of stuff. People in trouble with the law always have a story. Part of my job was getting them to tell me the story, the straight story."

"Why?"

"It helps."

"How they see themselves? And their situation?"

"Something like that, yes."

"The truth," she said. "You had to earn their trust."

"I suppose I did. But I am not your probation officer."

She walked around the counter and, rather than coming back to the couch, sat on the stool next to the fireplace. "I know." She eased her back against the large stones in the chimney. "We only met a little while ago, and here I am, I almost feel like I'm making a confession. You're talking about deception, self-deception, aren't you?"

He nodded.

"So I'm going to tell you the straight story."

"Okay."

"You want a drink or something?"

He thought about a drink and about the pills in the bathroom cabinet. "No, I'm good, thanks."

"All right. So I'm going to have to go back a bit and tell you about a guy named Leon." She glanced at him. "No. This is different. Leon was from Chicago. He came up here because Barr got himself into something serious. I don't know exactly what it was because that's stuff he doesn't like to talk about. But he was in trouble with somebody down there, somebody who was, you know, *somebody.* Remember, Barr has been robbing people around here. Well, I finally get enough out of him to figure out that he'd done something bigger than taking some jewelry from a house in Marquette. He'd gone to Florida to do something for this somebody in Chicago. Steal something. And it went wrong. I don't know the details. He was worried. His cousin Zack, who I learned has been helping him sell stuff he steals down in Chicago, *he's* worried. And then this guy Leon shows up."

"Sent by the somebody in Chicago."

"Right. So what Leon does is he comes to my place. I don't know how he knew about me, but several months after I learn I'm pregnant, and I'm through with Barr, or so I think, Leon shows up one night and says, 'You're coming with me.' And I don't even know who he is, though he's clearly not someone you just say no to. He's got one of those shaved heads and looks like he does serious workouts at a gym. But I tell him I don't know him, and I'm not going anywhere with him, so he grabs me by the arm and the hair and walks me out to his car, a very nice car, and puts me in the front seat. Before he closes the door he says, 'Don't think about getting out of this seat till I tell you or I'll shove my hand up your cunt, rip out that fetus, and eat it right in front of you.'"

Del watched Marcia. She couldn't look at him. She studied her hands, first palms up, then palms down. Then she placed her hands between her knees and leaned forward and stared at the floor.

"So we drive slowly through Marquette, and Leon says he wants me to take him to wherever Barr is—he was under the impression that Barr was staying with me, apparently, and it was a great imposition to have to go and find him. Leon acted like he should have finished his business here half an hour ago. It was all a big waste of his time, you know? Before I can even say anything he tells me not to bother saying I don't know where Barr is. But then he kind of laughs and says he doesn't know why Barr would leave me alone, and he puts his hand on my thigh. Then he stops the car—we were right downtown on Washington Street—and he just pulls over quickly and leans toward me till he's right in my face, and he gives me this line about *I don't like hurting women unless I have to, so tell me how to get to wherever the fuck Barr is.* I'm really scared. I mean I'm shaking and my stomach isn't feeling great. So I tell him. We drive to Barr's apartment, which is in a house on West Bluff. Leon makes me go with him to the door at the back of the house, and though the place is dark, he punches out a pane of glass in the door and lets himself in. No Barr.

"So. We go back to my place. And not five minutes after we get there Connor shows up. I was both relieved but also afraid. Connor is a strong guy, but he's timid, and he doesn't understand who this Leon is, and before he can even ask a question about what this guy is doing here Leon punches him once, knocking him out cold on the floor. Then he smiles at me and says something about my sex life needing to be simplified.

"So. Then Leon gets a beer from the fridge, and he takes my cell phone from my bag and says 'Let's call Barr.' He scrolls through and finds the number, and gives me the phone when it begins to ring, giving me instructions that I need to get Barr to come over. When Barr answers I can tell from the background noise that he's in a bar. I say I need him to come over right now. He's suspicious, and I suppose he'd had a few. I tell him it's about the baby. Now Barr is funny. In so many ways he comes off as this lone wolf, but I know that the baby, the idea of the baby, gets to him. He'd never admit it, but it's not something he can hide—not from me anyway. So he says something like *Are you all right?* When I don't say yes immediately he hangs up. I shut the phone off and tell Leon he'll be over in a few minutes.

"Now at this point I don't know what's what, but I do understand that Barr has something that Leon—meaning the somebody in Chicago—wants. I knew Barr went down to Florida, and I knew that something had gone wrong. I knew this because I ran into his cousin Zack, and he was both pissed off and scared. What I didn't know is that Leon had already visited Zack that night and beaten the crap out of him, put him in the hospital for like ten days. He almost died because of some problem with his throat—they had to do that thing with his windpipe where they cut a hole in his neck and put in a tube so he can breathe? A tracheotomy, that's it. I didn't know any of this stuff about Zack at the time, but Connor was out cold on the floor, and I didn't want to know what was going to happen when Barr walked in the door. I really believed somebody was going to get killed. I was so scared, and my stomach was so bad I went into the kitchen and puked in the sink.

"Leon watches this, and after he gives me a towel to wipe my mouth he says, very sweetly, he says I have nothing to worry about, as long as he gets what he came for from Barr. When I ask what that is, he says, 'You really don't know?' And I tell him I really don't know, and I think he believes me.

"At this point, Connor begins to come around. His jaw is swollen, so I get some ice in another towel and get him on the couch. We're a real pair, there on the couch, you know? So we wait, and after about ten minutes, Leon starts to look unhappy. He opens a second beer, and he says if Barr doesn't show by the time the bottle's empty we're both in deep shit. Connor is still woozy, and he has no idea who this guy is, and he just sits there, holding the towel of ice to his jaw.

"So we wait. Leon drinks his bottle of beer. When he's nearly finished we hear a car out on the street. I know it's Barr because I know the sound of his engine. Leon sees something—my expression gives it away, I'm sure—and he goes to the door and looks out. Barr's car is stopped in the street, but he must have seen Leon's car, which I suppose had Illinois plates, and he takes off. Leon opens the door like he's going to chase Barr, but then he comes back inside and goes on about, *I'm never going to find him, am I? Little fucking town like this, all these woods. No way.* I shake my head and tell him Barr could be anywhere."

Marcia got up off the stool, and, using the poker, she turned the logs and added a new one. Del wanted to tell her he didn't want to know any more. But he couldn't. He was suddenly feeling paralyzed. This was something that happened quite often since he'd been on his own. It was usually inconsequential, and he just let it pass. He'd be doing something, often something around the house. Most recently, a few weeks before his surgery he'd been replacing a couple of boards in the porch steps. He had one board cut, and he fit it in place. He had the first screw and his cordless drill in his hands, when he just put them down. He sat on the step and stared out at the woods. He remained that way for a long time, until it was beginning to get dark and he was getting cold. Finally, he went in the house, leaving his tools and everything on the porch. First, he thought he'd make tea to warm himself up, and then he'd add logs to the fireplace. But he did neither—couldn't do them. He just stood in the kitchen staring at the counter, until it was dark in the house. Then he went into the bedroom, lay down in his clothes, boots and all, and pulled a blanket over himself. He didn't sleep but just laid in the dark. For hours. It seemed time had stopped. He must have had thoughts—mostly about Liesl, he supposed—but he remembered none of it. He remained in bed on his back until sometime in the middle of the night when he had to get up to take a piss. He remained that way, just lying in bed, for nearly an entire day. It wasn't until the following afternoon that he got up, built a fire, and then went out and finished screwing the board in the porch step. He cooked dinner, he carried on as though nothing had happened; but for that spell he'd been more or less paralyzed. It happened too often. He was afraid that one day he wouldn't come out of it; that he wouldn't find a reason to go on and do the things he usually did: eat, build fires, work on the house, sleep. None of it would be necessary any longer. It was at that point that he knew he would go into the bathroom and take the pills. All of them. Then he would lie down on the bed and wait, though sometimes he thought he might walk out into the woods and lie down. Rather than the bedroom ceiling, he could stare up at trees and sky. He imagined animals finding his body out there, eating it, so that there was nothing left, no remains. He imagined people wondering if he really had died. But they'd find some evidence—blood, clothing, a boot—something that made it clear that the coyotes, or even wolves, had eaten him.

Del lay still on the couch, eyes closed. He couldn't move, couldn't even open his eyes. It was like he was all alone. Even though he could hear Marcia shifting the logs in the fireplace, there was no one else there.

As Barr drove out to County Road 644, blacked-out Marquette gave way to the real dark. The woods had always been his refuge. Growing up in Eben, when his father went into one of his drinking rages, Barr would escape to the sanctuary of the night forest. He had places where he'd hide out for days at a time. The best was the abandoned hunting camp on a stream, where he could fish and build a fire. He stashed canned goods out there and a sleeping bag, and at night he'd stare up through the caved in roof at the chimney smoke as it drifted across the stars. He believed he had been a hunter or a trapper in another life. He would go for months without seeing another person, and at the end of the winter, he'd haul a sled loaded with skins into Marquette. But this life was all cockeyed. He had the soul of a trapper, but he was stuck in this small northern hamlet, a prowler, according to the newspaper, who fed off the stupidity of people who didn't know enough to lock their doors and windows.

Marquette wasn't like any place else, which was why it was so hard to leave. It was an island, surrounded on one side by Lake Superior, on the other by the forest primeval. He didn't know where he had first heard that phrase, school probably, but it was on the mark. Here on 644, he was driving through the snowbound forest primeval. About a dozen miles down the road he'd come to a house that belonged to someone named Del Maki, and there he'd find Marcia and Connor. He'd surprise the crap out of them—they probably thought he was dead and buried in the snow on Presque Isle. But Marcia would be relieved that he was alive. Barr remembered now: when Connor was putting the beat on him she began to plead with him to stop. *You'll kill him, Connor! Christ, you're killing him!* It was the last thing Barr remembered, his face down in the cold snow, his mouth and sinuses clotted with blood, and her voice in the wind becoming very distant.

He'd find them—they couldn't hide from him, not in these woods. That was something else buried in his genes, the ability to track down prey. But if they thought he was dead, they were not hiding but running, running from the recognition of what they thought they'd done. He'd surprise them all right. It was his turn.

Death brings a kind of recognition. When his mother found his father on the bathroom floor, dead of a heart attack, there was recognition in her eyes when she came back into the kitchen. She was free of the bastard. She looked across the kitchen at him and said, "You're father's gone," and in that moment he saw it in her eyes, the recognition that her youngest, the only one to still be home with her, was free, too. He was fourteen, and he was gone in a matter of months.

Someone dies, you run. You hide.

That night in Sarasota, after he returned to his motel room, he saw it on the local TV news: the police pulling a woman's body out of Sarasota Bay. A young, unidentified woman. Drowned. Cause unknown. Unidentified. V? Rikki? Didn't matter, really.

What mattered was that Barr had the phone.

He decided to fly back to Marquette. Zack picked him up at the airport.

"You know what's on this phone?" Barr asked once they were in the car. Zack's car was a piece of shit a dozen years old with a timing belt out of whack and a blown muffler.

"No, and I don't want to know. Why do you even have the phone with you? Jesus. I just want to get it to Chicago and be done with it." But Zack already understood something had gone wrong. Whether he'd gotten a call from Chicago or he saw it in Barr eyes when he met him in the terminal, it didn't matter. "You were supposed to pass the phone off down there."

"That didn't work out."

"This is not good, Cuz, bringing the phone up here."

"This phone, it's worth a fuck of a lot more than five grand."

"You don't want to go there."

"Why's that, Zack?"

"You don't want to be thinking that way, not with these guys."

"Who *are* these guys?"

"I don't know. My fence set this up. He's an intermediary. I'm an intermediary. I told you—"

"I *know*, you *told* me you only need to *know* what you need to *know*."

Zack turned and stared at him. Barr realized he'd been shouting. Quietly, he said, "This thing is fucked. One of the girls that set this up down in Florida is dead, and if the other one isn't, she will be soon."

"Who did that?"

"I don't know, and I don't care. You're missing the point. The phone is the point." He could see Zack was having difficulty registering this. "Pull over."

Zack stopped the car on the side of the road. They were on the long, slow descent that took them past the county fairgrounds. It was late afternoon, and the sun was setting behind the hills to the west. November and there was already snow up here in the hills.

"Zack, what exactly do you know about this phone?"

"Nothing. You were supposed to give it to V. But that didn't happen. My guy in Chicago called me. He wants me to call him and let him know when I've got the phone. And then he tells me where and when to deliver it." Zack cracked his window and lit a cigarette.

"You deliver it to your guy, in Chicago?"

"Dunno. Guess so. I got to call him first. Told you, one step at a time."

"You and your fucking steps. How much did your guy give you?"

Zack sucked on his cigarette and exhaled. "You get five, Cuz. That was the deal."

Barr slugged him in the arm. "How much did they promise you, Zack?"

Zack coughed as he rubbed his bicep. "Ten. I gave you some of it toward expenses, and you get five when you give me the phone. I keep the rest."

"You gave me twenty-five hundred, so that leaves like twenty-five hundred—your cut is twenty-five hundred? While I'm the one doing all the work down in Florida, where girls are getting dumped in the bay?"

Zack didn't bother to argue.

"I'm guessing that your guy in Chicago knows what this thing is really worth." Barr waited until his cousin turned and looked at him. He had the dull brown eyes of a cow that grazes in a pasture all day long. "I'm guessing that he'll sell this phone for a fuck of a lot more than ten grand. You should see the shit that's in this phone."

"Nobody said anything about opening the phone."

"*Ya think?*" Barr shouted. Calmer, he said, "You should see the names in here. I don't know what this is. Drugs, gambling, whatever. It's big stuff. L. J. Landis."

"The ballplayer?"

"Ronnie Messoud. Dickie Carr."

"Dickie Carr, the singer?"

"Yeah, it's full of guys like that. With figures—I'm guessing it's money they owe. Whatever, it's information that's worth a lot of money."

"I had no idea."

"I know that, Cuz," Barr said. "Idiots don't have ideas. Impressions, maybe. Ideas, no. You're an idiot who has impressions. Now drive me the fuck back to Marquette."

———————————

Essi stopped humming, right in the middle of the thing she'd been repeating over and over.

"You got it?" he said.

"Well. No, but . . ."

"But, what?"

"I just realized. It's not a guitar."

"It's not?"

"No, the intro to the song, the one you recognize immediately, it's not a guitar."

"You sure?"

"I think so. It's an organ."

"You think so. But you're not entirely sure, and you don't have the name of the song."

"Not yet, but this is getting me closer. It's on the tip of my tongue. It's that close."

"I'm getting close, too."

"Are you?"

"Yeah." He stopped walking. He couldn't feel his hands at all. "I'm getting close to leaving you here. Just dropping you in the snow and going on."

"I'm glad you have a sense of humor."

"Are you?"

"I really am, Connor. Life without a sense of humor is, well, it's really hard, particularly in a northern climate."

He began walking again. "You think I'm joking."

"Of course you are. I know you could leave me out here. I'd freeze to death, and nobody would be the wiser. They'd assume I made this very comfortable litter and pulled it all by myself."

"Sometimes my girlfriend Marcia gives me a hard time about assumptions," Connor said. "She says that when you assume something you make an ass out of you and me. Get it? Ass? U? Me?"

"I get it. I think Confucius said it first."

"Believe me, he didn't say it like Marcia."

"She's sounds like a very smart girl."

"You could say that."

"Of course I'm only making an assumption."

Connor paused and considered putting the pine branches in his hands down in the snow—their weight had created pain that ran up his arms, into his shoulders, and down his back. "You're assuming that I would deny that I left you out here to freeze to death."

"Oh. I didn't mean—"

"Yes, you did. That's what you meant. But that's what Marcia would call a false assumption."

"Really?"

"Really."

"Why?"

"Because I would admit to leaving you." She didn't say anything. "I would admit that I pulled you through the snow as long as I could stand it, that it got to the point where I couldn't feel my hands, which I can't, and my arms, my shoulders, my back, and my legs—everything—were killing me. But I continued to pull you through the snow until I just gave up. And you know why I gave up? Because you're weird. You're just out there. You eat these chocolate-covered raisins, and you talk about stuff that, I don't know, it's just weird. But what finally did it for me—this is what I'd tell them, the police or the judge, if it came to that—is I couldn't stand you humming this song over and over and over again. Not that it was a bad song, but that you couldn't recall the title. I couldn't either. I'd say I didn't really care about the title of the song, but you just wouldn't let it go. And that's what did it for me, your humming this song with no title. So, you either stop humming the song or you come up with the title."

He started walking again. He didn't know what else to do. Essi didn't say anything for about a dozen steps.

"This is a side of you I've not seen, Connor. Very assertive. What's Marcia think of it?"

He didn't answer but kept walking, each step slow and deliberate. The snow here was often above his knees.

"I'll bet Marcia loves it," Essi said. "I'll bet she wishes you'd be like this more often."

"Shut up."

"See? I'm right. Of course, I'm right. And so is Marcia."

"I wouldn't mention her right now, if I were you."

"Okay. Got it. That's good, too."

"It's best that you just shut up."

After a moment, she said, "Can I just say this?"

"What?"

"I think we're close to the house. Very close."

"You sure?"

"I am."

"It's an assumption."

"No, it's a feeling."

"A feeling. See, this is what I'm talking about. A feeling that comes out of thin air."

"That's right, Connor. And I just remembered the name of the song."

He waited. "And?"

"I'm not going to tell you."

"What?"

"If I did, you'd leave me out here, for sure."

"It might cross my mind." He walked a few more steps. "But I wouldn't do that."

"Promise?"

"Yes. Now tell me the name."

"You really promise?"

"I really promise."

Essi hummed the intro to the song again, and before she said anything, he said, "Oh. I got it."

"You see why I was afraid to say its name?"

"Yeah."

"So we're just not going to mention it."

"Right."

"Want me to still hum it?"

"Doesn't matter now," he said. "It's in my head anyway."

After Marcia sat on the end of the couch,

she arranged the blankets so Del's legs were covered. He hoped that she'd massage his feet again, but she didn't. She kept her hands outside the blankets, and he watched how she worried them, the fingers entwined. It made him think of small animals.

Marcia turned and stared at him, uncertain, perhaps even frightened. "Should I go on?"

"It's up to you, really," he said.

"You know since this all happened I think about good and bad a lot. What it means. I don't know that I know anymore, and maybe you never really do. I'm going to have this baby and a lot of what I'll do is try to convey some sense of good and bad. It's not easy."

"No, it isn't," Del said. "That's one reason why you're going to be a good mother."

She showed no reaction to this. None. She was thinking about something else already. Over the years he'd known very few people like her, who exhibited a perspective that was difficult for him to fathom. It had nothing to do with their level of education or what they did for a living. They would say things or ask questions that made him realize that they were bringing to a discussion something that he'd rarely, if ever, encountered before. Like Marcia, he assumed that they'd not had an easy time of it, that life had been difficult; and he didn't know if it was for that reason that they were so perceptive. It's something he'd never know. She seemed to think he was some wise old man, but he wasn't. He was just old.

"So," Marcia said. "Barr sees Leon's car with the Illinois plates in front of my apartment and he takes off. Leon immediately knows that he'll never find him. He just stands in the living room looking at me and Connor, who's half out of it next to me on the couch. Finally, he tells Connor to go after Barr. He's convinced that Connor can find him. Something about our reaction confirms this. And he's right. If anyone could find Barr, it was Connor. At first I think we're all going to get in Leon's car and chase after Barr, but Leon actually helps Connor to his feet and says get going. Connor's confused, I'm confused. Alone? Yes, Leon wants Connor to climb in his truck and go find Barr, and when he finds him to call me. And don't think of calling the police because they won't find me here in my apartment. Leon grabs me by the arm and says, 'And she's coming with me.'

"Connor takes off in his truck. And Leon walks me to his car. We drive out Route 41 to a motel where he's staying. At this point, I'm—I don't know—I figure I'm going to be in this motel room with this guy. I'm going to get raped. Raped and killed. It doesn't start out well. He tells me to take off my clothes and lie down on the bed. When I do, he gathers up my clothes and puts them in his suitcase, which he locks. He's efficient, very businesslike—he didn't just throw the clothes in the suitcase but folded them neatly. I'm lying there naked on the bed. He looks at me, but he's almost wary. I'm just barely showing at this point. 'You don't want to get cold,' he says. It was actually too hot in the room because there was this old radiator clanging away, but he gets a blanket from the closet and puts it over me. He sits on the bed, looking at me, but not the way you'd think. I'm wondering if he's maybe gay or something, or has a problem with women. He just sits there a long time, not saying anything.

"When my phone rings, Leon gets it from my coat. It's Connor. I don't know what he says but Leon calmly tells him to keep looking. He assures him that I'm there with him and that I'm all right. After Connor hangs up, Leon asks me which one is the father. I shake my head. He says, 'I'm hoping it's Connor, because I can tell from his voice on the phone that he's really concerned about you and about the baby.' Now he's looking at me all sincere, and I don't think he's faking it. 'Listen,' he says, 'I don't want to have to do anything to wreck your future, but I was sent up here to get that phone, and that's what I have to do. I get the phone, nobody gets hurt. No phone, I can't make any promises. I have people to answer to in Chicago. I have taken on responsibilities, you understand?'" As Marcia's hand pulled her hair back until it was tucked behind her ear, her fingers trembled. "Leon's this very strong guy, like I told you. Maybe forty, forty-five? But he's hard to read. One minute threatening, the next like he'd do anything for me. Maybe he's bipolar or something? He's sitting next to me on the bed, and he begins to rub his eyes, saying it's been a long day, with the drive up from Chicago and everything. He's tired and needs to get some sleep. So he says he wants to lie down and close his eyes. 'Just promise me you'll lie still,' he says. He turns off the lamp and lies down next to me, fully clothed, jeans and T-shirt. And we lie there in the dark on our backs. I keep expecting something, for him to turn, for his hand to do something, but he just lies there until his breathing changes and I can tell he's asleep. I don't move. Not a muscle.

"I must've dozed off, too. Which is strange, but I'd been so nervous and then I just ran out of energy and everything shut down. When I open my eyes the room is only lit by the bathroom light coming through the door that's cracked a couple of inches. A thin shaft of light. Leon is standing at the end of the bed, naked except for these tight white briefs. His back is to me and he's moving, raising his arms, stepping sideways, pausing in certain positions, and then quickly shifting to another pose—like a dance. He passes in and out of the shaft of light doing these incredible moves, and it's very fluid and graceful. I'm assuming he thinks I'm asleep so I lie perfectly still. This goes on for five minutes or so. And then he stops. He holds the last position for a long moment. The shaft of light runs up his back and left shoulder, and it's like he's a statue and I can see each muscle. He has what you call good definition. Then he turns around, one eye in the light, staring right down at me, and I realize he must have known I was awake, that I'd been watching. 'Tai Chi,' he says, 'It relaxes me.' And he begins to talk about chakras and, I don't know, all this Zen stuff. I hear it now and then because there are physical therapists that take great stock in it, but I'm kind of a by-the-book therapist, you know? I just work a certain muscle group, but he's really into it, and somehow this causes me to become really frightened. It's like he's preparing himself for something, some sacrificial ritual, an offering, and I remember the moments when he said things to me, threatening things, and I'm thinking he's preparing himself for whatever he's going to do to me. And his eye, the eye in the shaft of light, it's looking at me with both love and regret, but hard, too, determined to see things through, and I realize he's come to some decision. So he steps out of the light. I can barely see him. He opens his suitcase, and I hear zippers and Velcro, and then he comes back to the side of the bed and when he steps into the shaft of light I see the knife in his right hand. The blade's got to be a foot long. It's almost a machete.

"I start to move, but he sits on the bed, and his free hand presses me back down. His hand is on my throat, and he's incredibly strong. So after struggling for a moment, I just lie still, and he eases his grip some. 'Americans have this thing about firearms,' he says, 'but I think guns are overrated. They're awkward, noisy, and they require a lot of maintenance. And still they fail too often. They're just not my style. But a good knife, there's nothing like it. It's quiet, it can be quick. In its own way it's clean.

You are a decent person, Marcia. I hold no hostility toward you. You are what they call collateral damage. So I will make it quick.'

"He says this with real regret, and I know he means it. I say, 'I know where Barr is.' Leon stares off into the dark a moment. 'He's out in the woods near where he grew up,' I tell him. 'There's an abandoned cabin, a hunter's camp that he's been going to since he was a kid. He took me there once.' Leon still won't look at me. 'You could have told me this sooner,' he said. 'How far is it?' I tell him about a half hour. 'All right,' he says. He takes his hand off my neck and I sit up. 'If you get the phone back, you'll leave us alone,' I say. 'All of us. You'll go back to Chicago and leave us alone.' The blanket—it's fallen down so Leon looks at me, at my chest. I can't tell what he's thinking. At that moment I suspect he's undecided. So I tell him that if he's going to kill me anyway he might as well do it now. I actually think this guy has a sense of honor, and I say something about killing me—or any of us—after he gets the phone wouldn't be right, and he knows it. He thinks about this for a moment, and then he says that if he gets the phone back nobody has to die. Then he gets my clothes from his suitcase."

Barr nearly got stuck twice on County Road 644. There were no other vehicles, no recent tracks in the snow. About eight miles out he passed an SUV that had skidded off the road. It was empty. He continued on, and another few miles he saw Connor's truck. It had gone out of control on a downhill curve and looked like some monstrous hand had flung it up on the snowbank. Barr stopped in the middle of the road and got out to make sure the cab was empty. There was a trail leading away from the truck, continuing on up the center of the road. Though the trail was softened by new snow, it clearly wasn't just footprints, but a kind of trough, as though something were being dragged through the snow.

Or maybe crawling.

Hurt crawling.

Barr got back in his car and followed the trough. If you come upon Connor, injured, lying in the snow, what do you do? Just leave him be and let him freeze to death? Or kick the shit out of him for good measure? It was a tough call. There was no satisfaction in just leaving him. If you kicked him just right, it could be considered injuries sustained when the truck went off the road.

Barr used first and second gear and rarely went faster than twenty. If he caught up with Connor—and with Marcia, he hoped—and if he gave them what they deserved, the problem then might be getting back to Marquette rather than being trapped out here in the woods. If this snow kept up, nobody would be able to get anywhere on this road. He knew about being stuck out in this shit. It could work for you, and it could work against you.

After a few days back in Marquette, it was like Sarasota had never happened. Sun, warm air, they seemed unreal. You don't quite believe it when you're in a place like Florida, and once you leave you don't believe you were actually there. It was all a fantasy—the only reality was winter, perpetual winter. It had been snowing steadily for a day or so when Zack called and said they needed to meet.

"I'm not interested in watching you stuff your fat face with steak-cut fries."

"We're in deep," Zack said.

"You've heard from Chicago."

"Fuckin-A I heard from Chicago."

"Did you tell them what I want?"

Zack didn't answer right away. Barr listened to him breathe into the phone. It was the breathing of an obese guy who smokes and drinks and eats crap day and night, a guy who goes for days without a shower or a change of clothes, a guy whose social life is confined to jerking off while watching online porn.

It was the breathing of a guy who was scared shitless.

"What did they say?" Barr coaxed.

"I didn't tell them what you want."

Barr inhaled and exhaled slowly, audibly for his cousin's sake. "Why didn't you tell them?" He waited. No response, just more labored breathing. "It's a business transaction, Zack. You're the intermediary. You're only effective if you convey my terms."

"Intermediary?" Like it was a foreign word. Then an attempt at a laugh that came out as a whimper.

"I told you to tell them that I'd return the phone for fifteen." Barr wondered again if that had been a strategic error. He was going to go for ten grand, but then he thought that you want to sell a car for ten, you ask something higher and let the buyer negotiate you down. But then there was also the nagging suspicion that he was simply lowballing this whole thing—that this phone was worth so much to these guys that they'd kill a girl and dump her in Sarasota Bay, which meant he should be asking fifty, maybe even a hundred grand. They'd be pissed off—they'd be pissed no matter what he said—but at least they'd think he was more in their league. With guys like that, style is always important. But it was too late for second thoughts. "Zack," he said. "Pay attention. What did they say?"

"Not much."

"What do you mean 'not much'?"

"I mean this guy—this guy who is taking care of this for them—he asks me one question." Zack's voice was trembling. It reminded Barr of when they were kids, playing games, hide-and-seek, shit like that. Even when he was like ten, Zack couldn't outrun anybody, and he sucked at finding places to hide. He usually ended up crying because a game was unfair or he lost or someone—girls, particularly—made fun of him. He spent much of his childhood walking away in a huff saying, *I'm not playing with you anymore,* and all the other kids laughed and taunted him until he was out of sight.

"What was the one question?" Barr said.

"He said, 'Who has the phone?'"

"And you told him."

"I told him." Zack's voice was total defeat. "And then he hung up."

After a moment, Barr said, "Who? Who is this guy that hung up?"

"Dunno. Leon. I never dealt with him before. He's like the guy they bring in when things don't go as planned."

"Leon. And you told Leon my name."

"I did. I did because I don't have the phone."

Barr hung up.

Not a day later Leon called Barr. It was immediately clear why Zack was scared shitless. Leon's voice over the phone was slow and cigarette-husky, and he spoke with a directness and precision that left no room for ambiguity.

"I understand you have in your possession the property in question."

"I do," Barr said.

"The arrangement was that you would give it to your contact in Florida, and she would convey it to my clients."

Clients. "I have every intention of doing that."

"I'm not interested in your intentions. Why haven't you delivered said property?"

"My contact was in no condition to receive *said* property, thanks to another interested party."

"I'm the only interested party you need to concern yourself with in this matter."

"Then you'll appreciate that the value of said property is such that I wish to renegotiate our arrangement."

"Renegotiate? Did you say *re*-negotiate?"

"Yeah, I did."

Leon didn't speak for a moment. Barr wondered if he was smoking a cigarette. "I appreciate now," he said finally, "what I'm dealing with here."

"You appreciate a lot, don't you? What do you appreciate, Leon?"

"You lack integrity. You are not a man of your word."

"My word? When did I give you my word?"

"You don't even know what I'm talking about, do you?" Leon said. "Integrity, honor, these things mean nothing to you."

"I'm getting a lecture?"

"No, no lecture. But a lesson. You will get a lesson."

"I was through with school a long time ago."

Silence. This was effective. It provided suspense. Barr had to acknowledge the fact that his stomach didn't feel great.

Finally, Leon said, "Prepare yourself."

"What?"

"You heard me."

"Prepare myself for what?"

Leon hung up.

"This is it," Connor said.

"This is what?" Essi sounded sleepy.

"That mailbox," he said. "It says Maki. We're going up to the house."

"I don't see any house."

"It must be back there, in the woods."

"It's dark. I don't see any lights. You think anyone's home?"

"We'll find out."

He trudged up the driveway, which was bordered by high snowbanks. Here, under the trees, the snow wasn't quite so deep. He worked his way up an incline that curved to the left, and after about fifty yards a house came into view. It was dark. Marcia's car was parked in front of the porch.

"I'm guessing the power's out," he said.

Essi didn't answer.

Del never tired of watching logs

burn in the fireplace. Like waves on the lake, no two flames were identical, and their perpetual motion formed a constant, each momentary leap of flame distinct, unique, a part of the whole, the fire. A life in the world, a world in the universe. He gazed into the fire as Marcia began to talk about the abandoned hunting camp. It was better not to look at her. He could hear the tension in her voice, and he suspected staring at her would only make it harder for her.

"I can't believe this all had to do with a cell phone," she said. "I'm still not sure what was on it. Information. Some list of names and money—money they owed? Money owed to them? Who knows? But it was important to these people in Chicago. Important enough for them to send Barr down to Florida to steal it, important enough for them to send someone like Leon up here to get it.

"So Leon and I drive out to Eben. I was scared. My stomach ached, and I was really afraid I would lose the baby right there in his car. Maybe it wasn't the best decision. When you're that frightened it's hard to think straight, to think of what your options are. I just thought that if Leon could get the phone back he'd go away. He'd leave us alone." Del realized that she'd turned her head toward him, so he looked at her. There was something washed out of her eyes, something erased, something that made them much older than they were, something that said, *I've gone over and over this in my mind and haven't found an answer.* "That's all I wanted: Leon to go away."

Del had already told her she didn't have to continue to tell him about all this, and he was tempted to say it again. But he knew that she wanted to tell him—to tell someone. And he knew that he wanted to know what happened. Which seemed curious to him. Perhaps it was just a voyeuristic impulse, the desire to get into someone else's business, something he thought he'd had enough of during his years of handling probation cases. More likely it was because hearing this had pulled him up out of himself. He'd been living in there, inside himself, for so long he didn't think he could ever really listen to another person again. But here, now, he cared about this young woman bearing her first child—he wanted to know why her hands fidgeted nervously, why her voice had the faintest timbre that, more than her words, conveyed her deepest fears. She was afraid. He was afraid for her. He didn't think he could really do anything to alleviate that fear, other than listen to her talk about it. And perhaps, too, he was a bit envious of her fear. It was a clear, well-defined emotion. He couldn't remember the last time he'd been able to (or bothered to) define how he felt about anything. It was safer to live in an emotional void. He had felt nothing for so long, it seemed that even this, this vicarious fear, would be better than nothing. Because when you're afraid you want to live.

He was about to tell her that fear had its purpose in that it helped you identify what was important, what was necessary. But he hesitated—who was he to tell her about fear? What could he know about becoming a parent? Anything he might say she'd probably already thought of, so maybe it was better to just say nothing, to stare into the fire and listen.

But she looked at him in a way that suggested she wanted him to say something. Her eyes had changed, and they were asking him, *What do you think?*

But then she turned her head toward the door. "You hear that?"

"Hear what?"

There was the wind howling around the corners of the house and the higher wind roaring through the trees overhead, causing branches to clatter.

Then he heard it, too. Or felt it.

Something on the porch steps. A fallen branch. A footstep. He wasn't sure.

Then they heard it again.

"Someone's out there," he said. "On the porch."

Barr followed the trough in the snow through Yellow Dog Township, a cluster of small buildings gone dead and dark in the blizzard, but not a quarter mile farther down the road his car plowed through a drift, and its wheels spun in the snow. He tried rocking it a few times, but he was in good.

The trough continued on up the road. It was not as soft with a layer of fresh snow now, so he must be getting close. He shut off the headlights and engine, and then got out of the car. He leaned into the wind and waded through the snow to the rear of the car, where he opened the trunk. There was a wooden crate filled with a car jack, a lug wrench, battery jumper cables, and bottles of oil and gas treatment. Using both hands to move things aside, he fished down in the bottom of the crate until he found the rolled-up beach towel. He unwrapped it and removed his revolver, along with the box of cartridges.

Barr jammed the gun in one coat pocket, the box in the other, each knocking softly against a cell phone, and then he began walking, trudging through the broken snow that meandered up the road between the dark woods. The wind was at his back now, gusting so that at times he had to stop and brace himself by spreading his legs until the wind died down.

Prepare yourself.

That's what Leon from Chicago had said on the phone just before he'd hung up.

Barr took him at his word. Something about the man's voice was genuine and true. He didn't make idle threats. So the night that Barr went to Marcia's apartment and saw the car with the Illinois plates parked out front it was all he needed to know. Barr had prepared himself. The five-shot Smith & Wesson revolver had been in various closets and bureau drawers for years, but after that phone call he stowed it in the trunk. As soon as he saw Leon's car, he understood the thing about Marcia's voice that had baffled him when she called him while he was in the Third Base bar: she was scared.

He didn't stop—he wasn't about to walk into her apartment and confront this guy up from Chicago. He wasn't going to try and save her. She was back with Connor, so let dickhead be the hero.

Best thing to do was get clear. Get out.

Barr drove out to Eben, a half-hour drive on a winter's night. He parked his car in the small lot next to Ted's General Store, got his gun out of the trunk, and began walking. He crossed the field behind the store and entered the woods, woods that he'd known since he was a boy. The snow wasn't that deep, six inches at most. He walked about a half mile, until he reached the abandoned hunting camp, which was just as he'd left it back in the fall. There was a stack of firewood and kindling by the chimney, and in an old metal trunk he found his sleeping bag and some blankets in a plastic trash bag, plus several cans of food—tuna fish and baked beans. In the back corner of the trunk was half a bottle of vodka. He built a fire, and then, wrapping himself in the sleeping bag and blankets, he crawled into the lean-to he'd constructed from the caved-in part of the roof. Lying at the edge of the hearth, the lean-to contained the heat from the logs. The vodka was thickened by the cold.

Mountain men and hunters—what kind of contentment they must have had, lying before a fire on a winter's night. Trappers who survived by thinking like their prey. Who set their traps and waited. Who dreamed of fox and raccoon and beaver, of hauling their pelts into town and trading for glasses of whiskey and hot baths and women, warm women with scented skin.

Barr did not dream. Not that night.

He slept to the rhythm and crackle of the fire, until he was aware of footsteps approaching the camp, chuffing through the snow. He crawled out of the sleeping bag, removed the leather glove from his right hand and tugged his revolver from his coat pocket, the grip cold in his palm. He moved to the south wall and sidestepped to the window until he could peer out. The footsteps were coming closer, plodding but determined. All Barr could see was the black skein of branches against the white snow, until there was movement off to the left. Maybe. After a few more steps, there was silence.

Barr cocked the gun, scanning the woods. His ears pounded with blood surging through his veins. Trappers would never allow themselves to be in this position, hiding in the woods, stalked by another man, a man sent from Chicago.

A twig snapped.

Barr turned to his left and extended his arm, aiming at the sound, but he saw nothing.

"Barr?"

He lowered his arm to his side. "You. Jesus, Connor."

"Thought you'd be out here." Connor began moving through the snow, brushing aside branches.

"You alone?"

"Yeah, I'm alone."

Connor kept coming, and then he emerged from the dark woods, striding toward the camp.

"What the fuck are you doing out here?" Barr said.

"We used to come out here to hunt, or just drink. Seemed like a good hiding place."

"Who says I'm hiding?"

"This guy from Chicago, he's come up to Marquette looking for you." Connor stopped when he was five yards from the dilapidated wall. "Why's this guy here?"

"His name is Leon."

"Yeah, Leon. He sucker punched me. He's got Marcia, and I'm supposed to find you."

"Well, you found me. What're you going to do about it?"

Connor considered this for a moment. He wasn't dense, just slow. "You got a fire going in there, I can hear it. Let me in. Freezing out here."

Barr looked beyond Connor. The woods were silent, still and silent. "All right."

Connor banged his fist on the door—a homemade job constructed with rough oak, the kind of door that didn't require a storm door, a door that tells you something about the owner of the house. He heard footsteps inside the house. Marcia's footsteps. He recognized the shuffle of her slippers on wood floors, which had grown slower, more labored as she'd gotten heavier during the pregnancy, but still there was a rhythm to her step—*step-step-slide, step-step-slide*—sounding as if she were moving to some old-timey music, something people dance to, a fox-trot or a waltz.

She opened the door and the wind blew the hair back off her forehead.

"I need to get her inside," he said.

Marcia looked at the litter and then opened the door wide. He pulled Essi inside and lay the branches in his hands down on the floor. On a bookshelf magazine pages fluttered, until Marcia shut the door, bringing stillness. A man was sitting on a couch before a stone fireplace—it had to be Del Maki. The heat from the burning logs was a relief, though Connor could already feel a terrible stinging sensation emerge in his bare hands like some cold disease.

Maki stood up with the help of a cane. He was in his sixties, gray and grizzled, and he looked at Connor as though he knew him, as though he'd been expecting him. He asked, "How far did you walk, Connor?"

"I don't know. Miles. Her name's Essi. She was in an accident the other side of Yellow Dog. When my truck spun out and hit a tree, her dog died in the crash." He almost wanted to make it sound like a joke, her dog dying before they reached Yellow Dog Township, but instead he buckled over, placed his hands on his knees—he thought he might puke, but just began gasping for air. "I can't breathe. It was so cold out there, and I don't even know if she's still alive."

Marcia was kneeling down over Essi. "She's alive. But we'd better get her over near the fire."

"Blankets," Maki said. "I have plenty."

"Connor," Marcia said as she struggled to untie the frozen knot that bound Essi to the litter. "You've got to get her near the fire. I can't do it."

He was catching his breath, though when he straightened up there was a moment when he felt woozy and he thought he might pass out. But after Marcia managed to get the knot undone, he bent down, put his arms underneath Essi, and lifted her off the litter. Though she was wearing heavy winter clothes, she was a slight woman. For years he'd prided himself on his ability to carry weight—bundles of roofing shingles, stacks of stones or bricks, lumber balanced on a shoulder—so she didn't feel too heavy. But she was limp. Her legs hung over his forearms, and her head rolled against his shoulder as he walked around the couch. There was a worn Indian rug on the floor in front of the fireplace. He laid Essi down carefully and then stood before the fireplace with his hands tucked under his armpits.

Maki picked up one of the blankets on the couch and said something, but it didn't make any sense. Connor stared at him, at the blanket in his hands. Again, he felt dizzy, and this time the room began to list. He took a step sideways, until the floor rose up and hit the side of his head.

Barr shouldn't even have been talking to Connor—Marcia was screwing him now. But they squatted before the chimney fire, passing the bottle of vodka. Actually, Barr was relieved. Relieved not to be out there alone. Connor was clueless. He didn't get what was going on, why this Leon had come all the way up from Chicago.

"All I know," Connor said after a deep pull on the vodka, "is he's got Marcia, and if I don't bring you to him, who knows what he'll do to her. The way she had her hand on her belly—she was hurting."

"Really?" Barr took the bottle from him.

"Like she was about to lose it right there on the living room floor. What's this guy want?"

"None of your business."

Connor looked away from the fire, and Barr saw it in his eyes. Ordinarily he was timid. He'd back off at the first sign of resistance. But with Connor there was this line, and when it was crossed he didn't hold back. "Not my business," he said. Quiet, too quiet. "The guy sucker punched me good, and he's got Marcia. So it is my business."

"You can be such a fucking Mountie."

"You have something of his."

"What if I do?"

"Give it back."

Barr considered this a moment. "It's not that simple."

"Why not?"

"Because you're a dumb fuck is why not."

Connor stared at him.

"What?" Barr said.

"You got her—and me—involved in this thing. You fix it; you make it go away." Connor reached over and yanked the bottle out of his hand. "And do it now."

"All right, take it easy."

"Don't tell me to take it easy." Connor pulled on the vodka and didn't return the bottle. "Something bad happens to her, something happens to that baby, I don't know what I'll do, but it won't be good. It'll be on you. You understand me?"

Barr stood up. "Yeah, I got it." He took his revolver from his coat pocket and held it by his side. Connor stared at it. "That's right, talk tough now, dickhead." Then he walked out the door of the camp. "Bring the bottle."

They moved through the woods, following the path they'd already made in the snow.

"What're you going to do?" Connor said.

"I'm going to make the world a safer place for our newborn." He turned and took the bottle of vodka from Connor and paused to take a swig. "You have any idea whose it is? She say anything?"

Connor shook his head.

"What if it's mine and she stays with you? Then the kid's going to grow up calling you Daddy. You see why I might have an issue with that?"

"It's her choice," Connor said.

"Yeah, choice. Women have all the choices now."

"What're you going to do?"

Barr finished what was in the bottle and tossed it into the snow. "Let's find out."

He led Connor along the path through the woods and stopped when they reached the edge of the field. It was about a hundred yards across the snow to the parking lot behind the general store, which was closed. There was Barr's Nissan, Connor's truck, and another car was just pulling into the lot.

"That must be him," Barr said. "Guess I should never have brought you or her out here. That's the thing. An old deer camp like that is like a favorite fishing spot. Once you tell somebody where it is, the whole thing is ruined."

After the headlights were shut off, the doors opened, and they watched Leon and Marcia get out of the car. Barr and Connor didn't move. It was too dark to be seen standing in the woods. After a good minute of talking next to the car, Leon took Marcia by the arm and pushed her ahead of him. They climbed over the snowbank that bordered the lot and started across the field, walking single file, following the path in the snow.

Barr tapped Connor on the chest with the revolver, and they retreated back into the woods.

"You stay right here," he whispered.

He went off to the left through unbroken snow until he was standing behind a tree trunk. He watched Marcia and Leon cross the field, black figures against the white plane of snow. It was a clear night, no moon, and he could see the vapor of their breath rising above their heads. Connor stood in the path, not moving, not saying anything, while they walked toward the woods.

Marcia felt something was incomplete,

something had been left unsaid, but she welcomed the intrusion, because it pulled her back from the telling of it, the reckoning, again and again, the seeing it happen again, sometimes wondering if she remembered it as it was or as she thought it was or as she wished it was, sometimes wondering if it had really happened at all because it seemed so unreal, because it tore at her mind and her heart, as strong as the thought of having this baby tore at her, but in the other direction, toward a darkness that she'd never known to have existed. She needed activity. Idleness caused her to sink into this worry, worry that would only compound itself until she was paralyzed with regret and doubt.

Not paralyzed, frozen.

This business of helping Connor and the woman, whose name was Essi, had everything to do with the cold. First, Marcia helped Essi out of the damp outer layers of clothing—pants, coat, sweater—until she was down to her thermal underwear, which was dry. Essi could barely move her limbs without assistance. Essi. She was an ageless woman, it seemed, her arms and legs thin but their muscles firm. She must workout, or maybe did yoga or Pilates, something that helped tone the thighs and calves, something to keep the arms sinuous and taut. Even though the woman was in pain, she seemed able to maintain some distance from it, a distance that was the result of experience. There was a disconcerting calmness to her gaze. Marcia guessed she was in her early fifties.

And Connor. He'd passed out on the floor, momentarily. His hands looked bad. Del had asked Marcia to get a bath towel and soak it in warm water—not hot—and then he carefully wrapped Connor's hands together, so that he sat on the couch as though wearing handcuffs. Now he stared into the fire wearily, on the verge of falling asleep sitting upright. Marcia looked into his dull eyes several times, trying to get a response from him, but he was just too exhausted. What had happened earlier in the day out on Presque Isle seemed to have been wiped clean, the ordeal of pulling Essi through the blizzard completely stripping his memory. She envied him that, and she wondered if Barr was lying dead and under the snow.

Del looked at Marcia and said, "Suppose you could heat up a little soup?"

"Sure."

She went into the kitchen and got two cans of chicken noodle down from the cabinet. After she emptied them into a pot on the stove, she looked over her shoulder. Del had eased himself onto the stool next to the fireplace. He leaned forward, his elbows on his knees. Connor on the couch, Essi on the floor, Del on the stool, they were all still while the wind continued to rake the house. Marcia stirred the soup with a spoon.

"Where were you going?" Del asked Essi.

"Where?" Her voice was weak, but it seemed to be tinged with humor, as though to say, *What a silly question.*

"Yes," he said. "Where?"

"I was going into the storm."

"Is someone expecting you? In Marquette, or were you heading elsewhere?"

"I left Marquette."

"Heading where?"

"Into the night. Into the woods. Is there something wrong with that?"

"On a night like this," he said. "Alone?"

"I wasn't alone. My dog was with me."

"Your dog?"

"Ilo. My dog loves blizzards as much as I do. It killed her."

"I'm sorry."

"Don't be. She was meant to die in a blizzard. She's out there."

"We can find her after this passes."

"Her spirit, it's out there. You believe in spirits?"

"I don't know."

"Not ghosts. Spirits. They're everywhere."

Del was silent. There was only the crackle of the logs in the fireplace, the ceaseless wind, and the sound of the first bubbles rising in the pot of soup.

"What happened to you?" Essi asked.

"Hip replacement. Had the other one done a year ago."

"That's not what I meant."

Del didn't answer. Marcia tried to fill the silence by stirring the soup.

"I meant what happened to you?"

Del still didn't answer.

"You think it doesn't show?" she asked.

"What?"

"You think surgery and that cane hide it?"

"Hide what?"

"You think you look like you're recovering?"

Del took a moment. "You're a very perceptive woman, Essi."

"No, just someone who lost her dog. What did you lose? Oh, let me guess. A woman."

They didn't speak.

Just as the soup came to a boil Marcia turned off the gas and got two bowls from the cabinet.

Connor watched Marcia sit next to him on the couch. The bowl was cradled in her palm, which was draped in a dishtowel because of the heat from the soup. She blew on a spoonful of broth and brought it to his mouth. It was hot, almost too hot, but he thought he'd never tasted anything so good. The next spoonful contained some noodles and a piece of chicken. He couldn't wait. The spoon went into his mouth and, as he chewed slowly, he realized that this was who she was to her patients: a young woman who was expert in simple things, necessary things, such as helping you eat soup.

She watched his mouth as she brought each spoonful of soup up to him, but as he chewed she looked him in the eye. It was the same look she'd given him the night he stopped to help her on Presque Isle. There was a problem, and her eyes were saying, *You can help me; we can help each other.* There was something in her eyes that he'd never seen in a woman before, something he'd always wanted, wanted so badly he avoided thinking about it, avoided wishing for it because he never really expected it to happen, never expected someone like her to come his way. But there she was and he saw it immediately. She did too, he was sure. It wasn't just about getting her car started; it was about getting their life started. She wanted to do that with someone and, because he had pulled over to help her, but not *just* because he had done so, she wanted to do that with him. It was like she saw who he was right then, immediately seeing things no one else noticed. The weaknesses, the timidity, sure, but other things, things that were there, that he knew had always been there but didn't really show. Probably because no one ever really looked. His mother saw it, in her own way. His father, never. But this pretty girl, this woman in a T-shirt and bathing suit on a summer night, she saw it all immediately.

So it began. It began with a small problem, a dead battery.

And then it got complicated.

Now the problem was bigger than a dead battery on Presque Isle.

It was a dead body. On Presque Isle.

Maybe.

Her eyes were asking if he thought Barr was dead—the way Connor beat on him he had to be—and her eyes began to fill with a quiet alarm that pleaded, *All I care about is us and this baby growing inside of me.*

But then she seemed to catch herself, and she came back to this moment, and asked, "How are your hands?"

"They're killing me."

Her eyes grew wide, then she busied herself with spooning up more of the good stuff from the bottom of the bowl, noodles and chicken and slices of celery and carrot.

"What are we going to do?" she asked, inserting the spoon in his mouth.

"About what?" he said, chewing.

She made a face, her don't-be-so-dense face. "About your hands."

"They'll thaw out. If not, you'll have to feed me my soup."

"I've had plenty of practice," she said.

"I can see that. You're good at it. My hands don't thaw out, I'd become one of your patients."

"Is that what you want?"

He accepted the last spoonful of soup and shook his head.

"Then you'll just have to heal up." She moved with effort to lift herself off the couch.

"I left something on Presque Isle," he said.

He watched Marcia glance toward the fireplace. Essi, who had said she didn't want any soup yet, was lying on her back in front of the fire, her eyes closed. She might have been praying or meditating. Del Maki sat on the stool with his back against the stones, staring straight ahead. He might have been in a trance.

Marcia was standing in front of Connor, so close he wanted to reach out and place his hands on her belly. He wanted that smooth swelling, that roundness, to give off its warmth and penetrate his fingers. "What did you leave, Connor?"

"My gloves," he said. "That's how my hands got this way."

"That's awful." She exhaled. "But then you stopped for Essi."

"That's different."

"I know, but you carried her all the way here. You saved her life."

She took the empty bowl back into the kitchen. Connor closed his eyes and listened to her at the sink. He thought he could sleep forever. Without dreaming, it would be as good as dead. He'd thought about that, too, since the night he found Barr at his abandoned camp in the woods. Because of that night, today had happened.

But that night in the woods, he wasn't really sure what had happened. He and Barr had finished the bottle of vodka as they trudged through the woods, but when they reached the field they saw this Chicago guy—Leon—and Marcia getting out of his car. As they started across the snowy field, Barr told Connor to stay there in the path, and then he went off ten yards at the most, but in the dark he wasn't visible if he stood still. Barr had a gun. Connor considered turning and running deeper into the woods. He thought about calling out, warning Leon and Marcia. But he just stood there and watched them cross the field. He was scared, scared in a way he'd never been before. Once you're scared like that you never see things quite the same again. Fear drives you. It make you do things you wouldn't have thought of doing before. You beat a guy senseless and leave him in the snow, and then you find a woman who's been in an accident and carry her miles through a blizzard to safety. All this because of fear. Connor's hands were coming out of their numbness, and they were becoming even more painful, a pain he couldn't stop, no more than he could stop this other thing, this fear.

———————

The trough in the snow angled off the road and disappeared up a driveway into the woods. At the head of the drive, there was a mailbox, one of the old galvanized tin boxes perched on top of an off-kilter 4x4 post. The house was not visible from the road, which gave Barr a moment of hesitation. He knew the darkness of the woods—it could provide shelter but also surprises. There were too many possibilities, but he'd come this far, too far to walk back to his car, stuck in the snow. So he started walking up the drive, a narrow path on a shallow incline into the black trees.

And because he was cold, there was the kind of deep chill that made his shoulders and back feel as though they were bare to the wind. It was this damned coat, leather with thin fleece lining. Had to be eight, nine years old and worthless in weather like this. He put his hands in his pockets: a cell phone in each and the revolver in the right pocket and a box of shells in the left. His fingers were numb, but the weight of the pistol grip in his hand was reassuring.

This time it would be different. That's why he was here.

The night in Eben, watching Marcia lead Leon across the field toward the woods, Barr had the gun in his hand, holding it against his thigh. Leon was not tall, but his shoulders were broad. He appeared to be either bald or had a shaved head—Barr guessed it was shaved. There was something substantial, something solid about this guy who drove all the way up from Chicago. Not just muscular but unyielding and impenetrable. Barr watched his arms, his hands. They swung free at his sides as he walked through the snow behind Marcia—they swung in a loose, even fashion because his hands were empty. He wasn't carrying a gun. If he had one— Barr had to assume that he did—it was in a pocket or a shoulder holster, not in his hand. So it was important to let Leon see his gun immediately, to see it in a way that he understood he had to keep his hands in sight.

When they entered the woods, Marcia stopped, and Leon came up and stood next to her. There was a moment when no one moved, and Barr figured that they didn't know what they were looking at in the dark.

Until Marcia said, "Connor?"

And Leon said, "What's this twat doing here?" When Connor didn't say anything, Leon took a step forward and said, "He's here. Right? Barr is here." Still Connor didn't say anything. "So where is he?"

Barr stepped out from behind the tree trunk. "Over here." As Leon turned, Barr held his right arm out away from his side so he could see the revolver. "You wouldn't be armed, would you?"

"A gun?" Leon said. "Never carry one."

"Really?" Barr said. He raised his arm and pointed his revolver at Leon, who held his arms out to his side.

"It's true," Marcia said.

"What?" This pissed Barr off. She would know this? "Just shut up and keep out of this."

"He told me," she said. "'Guns are overrated.'"

"That a fact," Barr said.

"This girl does not lie." Leon's voice, though raspy, was smooth and so calm it made Barr suspicious.

"He prefers a knife." Marcia's voice was anything but calm.

"A knife?" Barr held his arm out, aiming the gun at Leon's chest. "All right, let's see this knife. Slowly. Just drop it in the snow."

Leon didn't move, didn't say anything. Barr wondered if he was going to defy him by simply doing nothing. Call his bluff. But then Leon's right arm moved, slow and careful. His hand came up to his belt, and he unsnapped a sheath and slid a knife out. Though it was dark, there was enough light that Barr could see the faint glint of a blade.

"In the snow." Barr pulled back the hammer until it locked. "Just drop it and take a couple of steps back."

Leon tilted his head, suggesting he didn't believe what he was hearing. But then he let the knife drop into the snow and took two steps backward. "All I want's the phone." He almost sounded apologetic but confident—he might have been the one with the gun. "You have it? With you?"

"I do," Barr said, "and your friends are welcome to it once we come to an understanding."

"They won't be interested in that, as I already told you," Leon said. "They would find . . . they would find it an imposition."

"They would get what they want for a fair price," Barr said. "The fact that they sent you all the way up here makes it clear how valuable it is."

"That's flattering," Leon said. "I do appreciate it."

"So it's easy, then," Barr said.

"Is it?" Leon asked. "And how do we come to this understanding?"

"You call them," Barr said. "You tell them that I will give you what they want when they've met my price."

"Your price?" Leon said. "And how long will that take? Days? And what, I'm going to stay up here in the tundra with you and Dumbo here and the girl of your collective dreams?"

"Sure," Barr said. "I have a nice camp nearby. We'll keep you comfortable." He looked at Connor, who hadn't moved. "Pick up the knife."

"What?"

"Pick up the knife, Dumbo. Then we'll take him back to the camp."

"I don't want any part of this," Connor said. "None."

"Will you pick up the goddamn knife?"

Connor just stood there.

"Jesus." Barr took a few steps toward where the knife had been dropped in the snow. He squatted down and stuck his free hand into the cold powder, but he couldn't feel the knife. Then, leaning forward slightly, he dug his arm deeper in the snow, and that was when he lost his balance. Such a stupid thing. His back foot slipped just enough that he began to lean to his right, causing him to lower the gun as he held his arm out to his side, like an acrobat in a high-wire act keeping his balance.

Leon stepped forward, and his leg came up, the toe of his boot catching Barr on the left side of his jaw. As he fell back in the snow, stars streaked across his vision. And then he was kicked again, this time in the ribs. He tried to curl up to protect the center of him, his gut, his balls, but another kick found his rib cage, knocking the wind out of him. He rolled away from Leon, but it was no good. His boots kicked and stomped, causing Barr to curl up even tighter.

And then there was the crack of a gunshot. Incredibly close and loud. The kicking stopped and no one moved, except for Barr, who lay in the snow, gasping for air.

Leon had backed off and stood with his arms stretched out from his side in a show of surrender.

Marcia held the revolver in both hands, aimed at Leon.

"Good girl." Slowly, Barr got to his knees. He coughed, which brought searing pain up through his chest. "Now give that to me."

She was nervous, and she swung the gun quickly toward him and then back toward Leon.

Connor still hadn't moved.

"No." Her voice shook, with fear, with anger. "We're going to settle this thing now."

"Just give me—" Barr said.

"*Shut up.*" Marcia swung the gun toward him again, but then focused on Leon. "You have this phone?" When Barr didn't answer, she nearly shouted, "You have the *phone*?"

"Yeah, I got the phone."

"Give it to him."

"What? You know what this thing is worth?"

Now she pointed the gun at Barr. "Get the phone out. Now."

Barr unzipped his coat and reached inside. He took the cell phone out.

"Connor," she said. "Take the phone and give it to Leon."

"You've got to be shittin' me." Barr watched Connor come toward him. After a moment, he gave him the phone.

Connor walked over to Leon and handed him the phone, and then backed away.

"I knew you were a smart girl," Leon said.

She trained the gun on him again. "You got what you came for, right?"

"That's all I need," Leon said. "Just let me pick up my knife, and I'm out of this tundra."

"Don't let him touch that knife," Barr said.

Marcia seemed now uncertain. Still she pointed the revolver at Leon, though her arms appeared to be getting tired. "You threaten my baby," she said. "You pick up that knife and walk out of here. Otherwise, I will pull this trigger until it's empty, and we'll bury you out here where they'll never find you."

Leon stared at her, then at Barr.

"Tundra," Barr said. "Lots of tundra."

Leon gazed about at the woods. "Guess so." He looked at Marcia. "Of the three of you, Sweetheart, you're the only one with the guts to pull that trigger." He smiled. "Sure, we're all cool here."

He stepped forward, leaned over, and thrust his hand into snow. Almost miraculously, he came up with his knife, and as he straightened up, he wiped the blade along the thigh of his jeans and then slid it back in its sheath on his belt.

"You got what you came for?" Marcia said. When Leon nodded, she said, "So this is done."

"Damn, I'll miss you," he said. "Look me up if you ever want to give civilization a try."

"Just walk out of here," she said, "and don't look around."

"Anything you say."

Leon did as he was told, walking out of the woods, though halfway across the field he said, "Marcia, it's a shame, really. You're wasted on Sasquatch and Dumbo. That baby is one lucky kid to have a momma like you."

No one spoke as Leon continued across the field, got in his car, and drove out of the parking lot.

"I want to know what you think you're doing," Barr said.

"You want, you want," Marcia said. "It's always what *you* want. Fuck what you want."

"Well, you could lower that gun," he said. "You could give it back to me."

"No. And I'm going to tell you what I want. I want to sit down. I want something to drink, water or maybe a cup of tea. I want my belly to stop this nervous ache. I want someone—a medical professional—to assure me that my baby hasn't been affected by all this." She lowered the gun, holding it at her side, clearly prepared to aim it again, if necessary. "What I want is to sit in a quiet room while my baby sleeps in my arms. Can you understand any of that?"

"I understand that that phone was mine," Barr said, "and you gave it away."

"He threatened my baby," she said.

"And *that's* mine," Barr said.

At first she didn't know what he was talking about, but then she looked at his gun in her hand. Barr took a step toward her, and she backed up. Connor moved to intercept Barr. He didn't do anything threatening but just stood in Barr's way.

"Dumbo. It fits, you know?" Barr said. "Listen, I want that gun back."

Marcia looked at Connor. "I don't want it."

Connor came to Marcia and took the gun. Calmly. No drama. He opened the cylinder and shook out the bullets. The way he stared at them in his palm he might have been considering eating them like candy, and then he flung them out into the woods. He walked over to Barr and handed him the gun. "You brought this shit on. Now take this and go."

"Just go," Marcia said. "Just leave us alone."

Barr stood there, staring at her, though it was too dark to really see her face. Then he walked out of the woods and across the white plain of the snowbound field.

Del was reluctant to look at Essi. He didn't know why. She'd eaten just a little bit of soup and now appeared to be asleep, lying on her back before the fireplace, covered by the blanket he usually kept at the foot of his bed. But though her eyes were closed, he sensed that she was alert, not watching everything, just receiving it. She didn't observe, so much as absorb.

A strong gust of wind caused the house to shudder, pushing it so that the timbers overhead creaked and groaned.

"It requires strength and give," Essi said. She opened her eyes and stared up at the rafters and beams. "A difficult combination."

"It is," he said. "These mortise and tenon joints have survived more than a century."

"You like old things."

"They tend to be reliable. How are you feeling?"

"Seems people have been asking me that my entire life. I nearly died when I was a girl. Some infection. Then I was in two car accidents while I was in high school. Kids died in both. After the second crash I was in traction for months. When I was thirty-one I was on a ferryboat going from Helsinki to Tallinn that capsized during a storm. People drowned. A few years ago I was in New Mexico and a rattlesnake bit me." She held up her right hand. "My index finger lost all sensation. But I'm feeling all right. My back's sore, which I think is a good sign—I can feel it. My legs, my arms, they're coming back. I was pretty bound up, out in that cold." Looking at him, she said, "Maybe I can borrow your cane to get into the bathroom?"

Del got to his feet and, keeping one hand on the cane, reached out and offered her his right hand. When she took hold of it, he leaned back carefully and helped her up off the floor. It reminded him of a dance routine, the kind that was extremely athletic, with the man twirling his partner above his head and then deftly swinging her down to the floor. But this was neither athletic nor deft—it took all of his concentration and balance to help her up off the floor. He could feel that her index finger had no sensation, no strength, yet her grip was strong. Somehow holding her hand embarrassed him, but he didn't let go immediately, and then he did as he guided her fingers to the smooth wood handle of the cane.

"Being immobile is hard," she said.

"It is."

"It used to just suck, but now people call it a challenge." Essi put her weight on the cane, testing it. "But immobility offers a different perspective, one we seldom have when we're busy doing things. During your recovery have you found that your mind tends to roam?"

"Far and wide."

"That's a good place. No map."

"No, no map."

"It's so seldom that we can see our destination." She began to work her way into the kitchen. "This is getting the blood moving in my limbs." Just before closing the bathroom door, she said, "My mortise and tenon joints, they're loosening up. Still very reliable."

Del eased himself down on the stool again. A penetrating warmth came off the stones behind him. He closed his eyes, and the combination of medication and alcohol provided the faintest sense of drifting, making him think of a rowboat on a glassy lake. For the first time in a good while he felt unburdened.

A sound.

Marcia opened her eyes. A pounding—another fist pounding on the door.

She must have dozed off on the couch next to Connor. Del was sitting on the stool by the fireplace. Essi came out of the bathroom, and though she was using Del's cane she was walking much better. When she turned toward the front door, Marcia threw off the blanket and pushed herself up off the couch, and said, "Let me get it."

She went around the couch to the door. Even closed, the wood gave off a penetrating cold that made her sweatshirt feel insufficient. Reluctantly, she lifted the latch and yanked the door open. Barr stood on the porch, snow covering his head and shoulders. She stepped back as he came inside and shut the door hard.

"Well, isn't this cozy?" he said.

"Come closer to the fire," Essi said. "You must be cold."

Barr gave her that smile. Like he could eat her. "Yeah, I'm half frozen."

Essi said, "We'll get you something hot to drink."

"A drink drink? That would be better."

Marcia looked at Del, who nodded, and she went into the kitchen and got the bottle of Irish whiskey from the cabinet.

"Sit here by the fire." Essi's voice was calm, reassuring, generous, but Marcia was certain she already understood that there was something going on here, some element of threat. "Your face—"

"What about my face?" Barr said.

"You have Caravaggio skin."

"What's that?" Barr said.

"Beautiful. Pale."

"What's your name?"

"Essi."

"So, you're not the missus?"

"Um, no."

"Your accent. It's . . ."

"Finnish."

"I see," Barr said. "We have all these Finns in the U.P., but you're like the real deal. Live here or just passing through?"

"I haven't decided."

"Really?"

"That it matters."

Barr gazed at Essi, not sure how to take this. Marcia had seen it before—when he was baffled he would either turn nasty or pretend nothing had happened.

She left the kitchen and handed him the glass of whiskey. He looked away from her dismissively and sat next to Connor, pushing the blanket aside. He drank the glass of whiskey down and then took a revolver from his coat pocket and pressed the barrel into Connor's thigh. "Hey, Dumbo." Everything got quiet. "I'm not so easy to get rid of, eh?"

Barr held his empty glass up and said, "That helped. I'll have another."

Marcia took the glass from his hand and went into the kitchen. Essi worked her way around to the fireplace, where she handed the cane to the guy, Del Maki, no doubt, and then she leaned back against the stone chimney.

Del Maki rested his hands on the top of the cane and stared back at Barr.

"And what's your problem?" Barr asked.

"My problem is that you've come into my house with a gun."

"Christ. You're not one of those gun-control assholes?"

The man didn't say anything. Behind those glasses he had steady, patient eyes. Eyes connected to a brain that was always working.

"Let's avoid politics," Barr said pleasantly. "I don't want to wreck the party." He lifted the revolver from Connor's thigh and held it in his lap.

The man's expression didn't change.

"So we have the geriatric Del over there," Barr said, and then glancing at Connor, "and what happened to you, Dumbo? You look like you got beat up and left in the snow."

Connor looked down at his hands, wrapped in a damp towel.

Essi said, "I had an accident down the road, and he brought me here, on foot."

"Ah," Barr said. "I saw that. Your car, his truck." Marcia, back from the kitchen, handed him a second glass of whiskey. "And over here we have the maternity ward. Jesus, what a crowd. And my skin is what?"

"Caravaggio," Essi said.

"That a disease? Some vitamin deficiency?"

"He was an Italian painter."

"A painter." Barr drank down half of the whiskey and put the glass on the block of wood that served as a coffee table. Looking up at Marcia, he said, "Take a load off. There's plenty of room here on the couch." She only stared at him, disgusted. "Think of the baby," he said.

She turned and walked away from him, going to the counter that separated the kitchen from the living room. With effort she climbed up onto one of the stools, faced him, and folded her arms.

"Even with the excess baggage, I'd recognize that ass anywhere," Barr said. He looked at Essi and the Maki guy. "She's so porked up you wonder if she's going to pop twins. Now that would be something." He elbowed Connor. "One for you, one for me. 'Course, if that was the case they're probably in there trying to kill each other, you know like those brothers." He looked at Connor. "You remember their names?" Connor shook his head. "Cain and Abel. Their names were Cain and Abel, Dumbo." Turning to Essi and the guy, he said, "I can't remember, which brother won that bout?" They both stared at him. "Well, come on, you know about this Caravaggio guy. You must remember who the killer brother was."

Maki said, "Cain."

"Right," Barr said. "Cain. Of course. Am I my brother's keeper? Something like that."

The guy nodded.

Barr picked up the glass of whiskey and raised it in a toast. "Well, Del Maki, you got some house out here, and this is one hell of a blizzard."

Del's shotgun was in the closet by the front door. No chance of getting to it.

The only pistol in the house had belonged to Liesl. Years ago, the first morning after they'd spent the night together, Del made a curious discovery: she kept a revolver under her pillow. She explained that in her early twenties she went to California and spent a year in San Francisco waiting tables, that sort of thing. While she was living in an apartment in Noe Valley she was mugged. One night while walking back to her apartment a strung-out-looking guy appeared from behind a bush and jabbed a pistol into her ribs. All he said was *Just give me the bag and everything's cool.* She removed her denim bag from her shoulder and handed it to him. He walked away with her keys, her driver's license, and twenty-eight dollars in tips.

She called her mother in Michigan, who sent her three hundred dollars to get her through. A portion of that money went to the purchase of a second-hand revolver. When Liesl told Del about this they were lying in bed, looking at the pistol between them. She had removed the bullets and laid them on the sheet next to the gun.

You sleep with this every night?

Every night.

Guess I better mind my Ps and Qs.

Liesl picked up the revolver and the bullets and placed them on her nightstand. When she laid down next to him she put her leg over his thigh. That was more than twenty years ago, a spring morning.

Over time, the pistol moved from under a pillow to the drawer in her nightstand, and eventually, after they were married, it was tucked behind a stack of towels on a shelf in the bathroom linen closet.

Marcia sat at the kitchen counter, her arms folded over the steep rise of her belly. Her fingers were shaking, and she didn't want to reveal the fact that she was so nervous. Or frightened. She wasn't sure which—wasn't sure it mattered.

Essi said to Barr, "So what are you going to do?"

"Do?"

"You're here. You've got a gun. Now what?"

"Maybe you'll just have to wait to find out."

A gust of wind seemed to caress the roof, and Marcia glanced up at the ceiling.

"I see," Essi said. "And after you do what you're going to do, what do you do then?"

"What is this," Barr said, "your idea of a philosophical inquiry?"

"In a way, yes."

"You want to know if I've thought this through, if I've considered the consequences."

Essi gave it a moment. "You think that might be worthwhile?"

"Ah." Barr was enjoying this. He liked it when things got edgy. He liked uncertainty and chaos. Marcia was convinced this was what drew her to him in the first place. There was something fearless about him. "First thing, you have to understand," he said to Essi, "is I'm a guy who got the shit kicked out of him a few hours ago and was left for dead in the snow out on Presque Isle. Second time this winter. Stuff like that changes your perspective. I've had enough."

"You brought this on," Marcia said. She couldn't control the quiver in her voice.

Barr considered her, trying to make it seem like he was surprised she was even in the room. "What? First, there's this business with your friend from Chicago, and then you sick Dumbo on me—and it's *my* fault?"

"That guy Leon from Chicago," Marcia said. "He wasn't my *friend*, he came here because of *you*. And ever since then you've been threatening me."

"Threatening?"

"Threatening." Marcia's voice was still quivering but it was stronger. "You call me several times a day. You drive by my place constantly. You follow me when I go to the store. The spookiest thing was the other night when I got home from work. I walk into the kitchen and find a bunch of glasses on the counter, when I know I didn't leave them out. I go in the bathroom, same thing. The tube of toothpaste is on the left side of the sink, and the shampoo bottle in the shower isn't upside down, the way I always leave it. Little things. You got in the apartment somehow—you don't have a key, but not having a key has never kept you from getting into places you don't belong."

"That is really sick, shampoo bottles and glasses," Barr said. "I see why it would get to you."

Marcia was wound up now. In some ways it was a relief. "I wasn't going to tell Connor you'd been bugging me until you broke into the apartment. I thought you'd just, I don't know, you'd just give up, you'd eventually figure it out and leave me alone. But that did it. I'm having a baby, and I don't need to be afraid in my own house."

"So you told Connor to kill me."

"No, I did not."

"And you set it up. You called me and said you wanted to meet me. I said anywhere, and you said Presque Isle. All right, I said, I'll meet you at Presque Isle. You should have heard your voice on the phone. It was almost like it used to be. You know that voice, Connor. A bit needy and a bit bossy, because she's talking just to you. That is a voice you'll do anything for, even if it means driving out to Presque fucking Isle during a blizzard."

"I did call you, Barr," Marcia said. "And I did want to talk to you. I thought of Presque Isle because it means something to us, to you and me."

"To you and Connor, too."

"All right. But I asked you—just *you*—to meet me there. I thought if we just talked we could set things straight. We used to be able to do that, remember? You'd do your usual dodge and weave, but eventually you'd come to the point where you'd be straight with me."

Barr stared down at the revolver in his lap. He almost seemed surprised to see it there. He looked up at the ceiling as another gust of wind caused the timbers to crackle. "Jesus, all we need is Jerry Springer to host this thing." At the other end of the couch, Connor swung his head toward Barr. "What?" Barr said.

"Who's Jerry Springer?"

With the palm of his free hand, Barr slapped his forehead. Looking at Essi and Del, he said, "See what I'm dealing with here?" Then, turning back to Connor, he said, "Are you shitting me?"

"No."

Barr turned to Essi and Del again as he pointed at Marcia, "That bitch lured me out to Presque Isle so this idiot could beat the crap out of me.

They left me for dead." He waited, as though he expected them to come back with a verdict.

Del shifted on the stool—Marcia realized it was a milking stool, and for some reason the fact that he had it made her like him even more. "This all has to do with a cell phone, correct?" Del asked.

Barr's expression was hard to read. He was impressed? Insulted? Disturbed? "She's been here how long and she's filled in all the blanks for you, huh?"

Del said, "I only know that this phone was in your possession and you thought it was worth something, and when you lost it, you felt that she and Connor were responsible."

Barr appeared to settle on playing along. "So, what's your point?"

"You seek a solution."

"A solution?"

"Yes, you resolve your differences."

Barr held up the pistol in his hand, not in a threatening fashion but as evidence. "I have the solution. I have all the resolve I need. Don't you get it? I'm supposed to be turning into a block of ice out there in the snow. This isn't a question of *differences*."

"Most everything is a question of differences," Del said.

Barr now seemed to be speechless. Del had been a constable and a probation officer. He'd dealt with people like Barr for years.

Finally, Barr whispered, "Motherfucker." It was not directed toward anyone in particular but just an all-purpose statement on the condition of things.

They all sat, listening to the wind. Marcia could feel a faint shudder in the floor joists and a wave of nausea swelled up into her throat. Her cheeks were hot, and her forehead felt clammy.

Barr was holding out his empty glass. "Again, if you please."

She climbed down off the stool. It seemed a long way to the couch, but she retrieved the glass—without looking him in the eye—and made her way into the kitchen. The bottle of whiskey was on the counter.

Quickly, she leaned over the sink as bile burned its way up her esophagus and out of her mouth. She turned on the kitchen faucet and the mustard yellow puddle was mercifully diluted as it washed down the drain. She closed her eyes as more bile rose swiftly up out of the vast, abysmal depths of her, out of a place that seemed so foreign that she imagined that she was harboring some alien life form in her womb.

Barr listened to Marcia at the sink.

He couldn't see her because of the kitchen counter. He said to Essi, "She's puking?"

"I think so."

"This isn't a giving birth thing?"

Essi stood up. "I'll see."

As she started into the kitchen, Barr said, "Shouldn't you ask permission to leave the room?"

Essi walked around the counter.

"See, Del?" Barr said. "This is why we have problems like this." Del was studying him, that brain working quietly, efficiently. "What are you staring at?"

"Your jaw," Del said.

"I know, it's killing me. My nose, too."

"Think something's broken?"

"Connor may not know who Jerry Springer is, but when it comes to kicking ass he's a genius. Everything hurts. My face, my nose, my ribs." Barr extended his arm until he tapped Connor's crotch with the revolver, causing him to sit straight up. "At least you didn't kick me in the balls, *hombre*. Otherwise, I guarantee you I would have already sent your *cojones* to kingdom come." He smiled, though it hurt, particularly the left side of his jaw just beneath his ear.

Things had gone quiet in the kitchen.

"Everything all right in there?" he asked.

Neither Essi nor Marcia said anything.

Barr pushed himself up from the couch. He was a bit unsteady on his feet, but he managed to get over to the counter, where he slid a haunch on to one of the stools. Essi was wiping Marcia's face with a damp dishtowel. "A little late for morning sickness, isn't it?" he said.

"Shut up," Marcia said weakly.

Barr laid the pistol on the wood counter. The house was creaking and groaning, and there was something rattling overhead in the wind. "In the movies, this is where somebody begins tearing up bedsheets and shouting 'Boil water!'"

"Just *shut up.*"

"I suspect it's nerves," Essi said.

"You do," Barr said.

He couldn't help himself, though he knew that he was playing this all wrong. The baby. He'd thought about the baby a good deal, and it pulled him in every imaginable direction. He wanted to kill Connor. Sometimes he wanted to kill Marcia. Just obliterate the both of them. But when he considered the possibility that *he* might be the father, this other thing began to surface, and he didn't like it, didn't know what to do with it. His father had been such a prick, and he assumed that, if he ever did have his own kid, he'd just naturally go down that path. But with Marcia there had been times, before all this crap happened, when she led him to believe that something else was possible, that he could be the kind of man she said she saw in him, that she even said she loved. And he wanted to be that man, even though he really had no idea what that meant. A man who was good to a woman, who knew how to be a father? What is that? Where does that come from? Trickle down through the gene pool? Or is it an acquired skill?

Marcia was standing sideways to him while Essi continued to wipe her face with the cloth. Her belly was huge. He had to admit that there was some kind of a natural miracle at work here. He knew her body. He remembered how she had been—her stomach flat, her thighs and ass firm—and now she'd morphed into this soft fleshy being. For a moment Barr had a devious sensation that felt like sympathy. "Essi," he said, "If it's not too much trouble, reach me that bottle."

Del was torn between a weary numbness and an undefined curiosity. A weight behind his eyes made him want to curl up on the floor and go to sleep. But there were all these strangers in his house. They'd brought their lives, their problems through this blizzard, come in the door, stamped and shook the snow off, and everyone was on the brink of disaster. Yet Del felt a peculiar distance, a membrane between himself and the tension in the room—probably because of the pills he'd washed down with Irish whiskey. Only a few hours ago he'd been here, alone in a Cello State. Bach and Yo-Yo Ma. How did it give way to this? He felt spread out. Thin. Diluted. One moment uncontrollable panic percolated beneath his skin. His mind tended to short circuit, and he caught himself staring blankly at a knot in the pine floorboards. The next moment he was overwhelmed with calculations. A house full of strangers and this guy with a revolver.

Essi helped Marcia back into the living room, where she eased down on the couch as only a pregnant woman can. Since vomiting in the kitchen sink, her face had developed a pale, waxy sheen. At the opposite end of the couch, Connor looked half out of it. Only Essi, this woman who had been dragged into the house in a litter, seemed now to be alert. She'd recovered quickly; she possessed strength that was not merely physical but was driven by a resilience of spirit, and she was invigorated by the simple act of helping someone. Once Marcia was settled on the couch Essi covered her with the blanket. The room was lit only by a throbbing glow from the fireplace and two storm lamps.

Del said to Barr, "The power's been out for several hours." He pointed toward the top of the bookshelves that lined the east wall of the living room. "Mind if we light a few more of those storm lanterns?"

Barr merely shrugged.

Essi wasn't tall enough, so Connor stood up and got the other two lanterns down from the bookshelf. Liesl had bought them at a yard sale years ago, and they'd been used often, particularly in winter. Del kept them filled with kerosene. Connor brought the lanterns to the counter, placing one next to Barr. Essi removed the glass and, using matchsticks from the tin dispenser by the fireplace, lit each wick. The room was now cast in a buttery, flickering light.

Sometimes, when Liesl was ill, she'd ask Del to turn off the lights and use the lamps while she lay on the couch beneath a blanket. Once, while staring at the shadows dancing on the walls, she said that she was certain that in a previous life she'd lived out on the frontier. She was intrigued by the notion of reincarnation. *Maybe I was one of those mail-order brides that end up in Nebraska or Colorado. I'm certain that I've known this light a long time.* The soothing glow from the lanterns made everyone quiet while the wind moaned and sang. There was an enormity to the sound of the trees, a rising and cresting ferocity that reminded Del of waves breaking on the shore of Lake Superior.

Barr poured himself another glass of whiskey. His breathing was shallow, possibly because he had broken ribs, and the left side of his jaw was swollen.

"That helping the pain?" Del asked.

Barr held his glass up to the lantern light on the counter. "Ain't hurtin'."

"If you want, I have something stronger," Del said.

Barr's eyes were suspicious but his smile was curious. "Do you now?"

"Meds they gave me after my surgery."

Barr considered the bottle on the counter, which was about a third full. "I'll consult with my physician," he said. "But thanks. You'd love to get me whacked out. What you got, something like Percocet?"

"And Darvon," Del said.

"Way I feel I could use some morphine."

"When my wife was sick, toward the end I gave her morphine."

Barr looked more than curious.

"It's gone," Del said. "The night she died the nurse who came out stood where you are and injected all of it into a can of coffee grounds."

"Such a waste. You ever wonder why we want our little taste? All in pursuit of your escape of choice. Everybody must get stoned." Barr probed his swollen jaw with light fingertips. "Imagine what Starbucks could do with morphine-injected lattes."

Essi sat on the floor in front of the fireplace again. "That's the solution for so many things. Finding an escape." She looked up at Barr, "Your solution include an escape?"

Barr was poker-faced, disinterested.

"Do you have a solution?" Essi asked.

Barr nodded. "Connor had his chance this afternoon. Now it's my turn. See, Connor, you're not only stupid, you're weak. I mean you're locked and loaded in the muscle department, but you have deltoids for a brain and don't have that thing that you need to finish it. You know, the old killer instinct. Must be a flaw in your DNA."

"I didn't know what I was doing," Connor said. "Really, I just got so pissed off, and then when I realized what I'd done I took off. It's like Marcia said, we didn't plan it that way."

"Sure, sure, sure," Barr said.

"I mean it," Connor pleaded. "She told me she was going to talk to you, but she didn't say where. So I followed her this afternoon, and when she drove out to Presque Isle, I knew that's where she said for you to meet her." He turned to Marcia, who was lying back on the opposite end of the couch. "I was angry at you, thinking that you and he were—you know."

"Getting back together?" Barr drank some whiskey. "That's nice, really nice, Connor."

"It's true," Marcia said. "You know it is. You know Connor."

"Yeah, I do," Barr said. With one finger he twirled the revolver around on the countertop, slowly, until the gun was aimed at Connor. "He's got this self-confidence thing."

"So, what's your solution?" Essi said. "You shoot him or whatever. What about the rest of us? You going to shoot all of us? Or you just going to leave us here? You don't think you'd get caught? You don't think there'd be enough evidence here to convict you? That's no solution, and it's no escape. And you know it. *You* are not stupid."

"Thank you for that," Barr said. "Of course, if I did shoot you, all of you, I'd at least shut *you* the fuck up. The world would be a better place. Quiet. Peaceful."

Essi got up from the couch and walked over to Barr. "We're all going to be here in this house until the storm passes. You're not going to shoot anyone."

Del realized that part of his concern, his fear, was this woman Essi. He didn't know her, but he could feel her. She had an unpredictable boldness that operated on a rare plane. She didn't give a damn yet she was rational and empathetic. She could go straight at a guy like Barr. She might get through to him, or she might get people killed. The concept of a second thought wasn't in her emotional or intellectual vocabulary. She possessed no regret.

Barr studied her, and he also seemed impressed, if a bit uneasy. "Don't be so sure, Essi." He was holding the gun in his lap now. With his free hand he took a box of cartridges from his coat pocket and smacked it down on the counter. "I got options."

The pain was outrunning the whiskey. His jaw felt as big as a basketball. His spine ached, and his ribs seemed to have dug into his left lung. He listened to himself sucking air through his mouth—his nose might be broken. "You mentioned pills," Barr said.

Del looked up from the floor.

"Where are they?"

He seemed to consider this question too carefully. "In the bathroom."

"You don't seem so sure."

"I had to think for a moment. Sometimes I keep them in the kitchen or the bedroom."

Barr pocketed the revolver and box of shells as he slid off the stool. "Show me."

Del placed his hands on the cane and hauled himself up off the stool. He worked his way around the couch and Barr followed him into the kitchen. He wasn't overweight. One of these old guys that keeps fit. "What exactly's wrong with you?"

"Old hockey player. Hip replacement."

Del made his way into the bathroom, which was dark except for pale light that came through the window. Barr stood in the doorway and watched as Del opened the medicine cabinet. He handed him two plastic vials.

"She mentioned a solution." Del spoke quietly. "I wonder if I might suggest one."

"What's that?"

"This has to do with a cell phone, right?"

"It's the tip of the iceberg, so to speak."

"I realize that, but you placed a certain value on that phone."

"Marcia has this habit of talking to strangers," Barr said. "Yeah, it was worth something."

"How much?"

"That depends. To these guys in Chicago it must have been worth a lot."

"What was it worth to you?"

"They offered five grand, but once I got hold of the thing I realized it was worth more."

"How much?"

"Twenty. I'd have asked twenty-five and let them talk me down."

"Twenty thousand for a cell phone, for the information on it."

"Yeah."

"If I said I'd give you twenty thousand, would you walk away from this?" When Barr didn't say anything, Del said, "Twenty-five. I'll make it twenty-five, so you get what they originally offered, plus what you thought it was really worth."

"You got that kind of money?"

"I can get it."

"It's under your mattress?"

"No, as soon as we can get out of here we can go to the bank and I'll withdraw it."

"Like in the morning."

"First thing."

"You got that kind of money—liquid, as they say? What you do for a living?"

"I did a number of things."

"Then one day you discover you're old. And your hips are shot. I don't need your résumé but give me a for instance."

"In recent years I was a parole officer."

"Bingo. A man familiar with the criminal element. Did pretty well, huh?"

"No, but we had some life insurance."

"Like how much."

"I'm offering twenty-five."

"Uh-huh. Not fifty."

"Not fifty."

"I see. We go to the bank, you withdraw the cash. You give it to me and I go."

"Right."

"Then you go to the police."

"Not if you walk away."

With the pale light from the window behind Del, it was difficult to see his face. His voice was raspy. In the near dark he sounded fatigued. But it was an honest voice, a sincere voice. "I suspect you mean every word you say."

"I do."

"You're that kind of guy. You keep your word."

"I try."

"The parolees—what did you call them? Clients?"

"Cases. They were cases, but I called them by their names."

"I'll bet you were straight with them. Even when you were tough, they respected you for it."

"I don't know. Depended on the case, I suppose."

"You were like those teachers we had in school. The ones that were tough but kids begrudgingly agreed were fair. I hated that shit."

"Why's that?"

"'Cause you're really talking about rules, about limits. There is no fair. Only rules. That's what you guys are really talking about."

"I'm talking about twenty-five thousand dollars."

"And you expect the rest of the world to play by the same rules. But it doesn't. I don't."

"Is that a no?"

"That's an I'll think about it."

"All right, think about it," Del said. "Mind if I use the bathroom?"

"Take a leak? No."

"Can I have a little privacy?"

Barr looked at the vials in his hand. He couldn't read the labels. "Just don't take forever." He went out to the kitchen counter, put the revolver down, and then held the vials close to the lantern so he could read the labels. "Which do you prefer, Percocet or Darvon? Or is that a Ford-Chevy question?"

The bathroom door closed.

Marcia had her eyes closed, but somehow she knew that Connor was staring at her from the other end of the couch. She opened her eyes and turned to him.

"You all right?" He glanced down at her belly as a means of making clear what he was asking. It was Connor. Nothing subtle.

She shrugged. "I threw up. Pregnant women do."

"How do you feel?"

"Pregnant. Very pregnant." She looked at Barr, who was sitting on the stool at the counter again. "My belly hurts. Pregnancy and guns don't mix."

Barr smiled. "There's a shotgun joke here somewhere."

"Don't bother," she said. "We're past that."

"Yeah," Barr said, glancing at Connor. "We ought to count our blessings, eh, Bro? If she had a daddy he'd need both barrels. One of us would get Swiss-cheesed, and the other would march down the aisle."

Marcia and Connor exchanged a look. She regretted it immediately.

"What?" Barr said. "Wait. You shittin' me?"

Marcia closed her eyes, fighting back the nausea.

"We've talked about it," Connor said.

Marcia kept her eyes shut, which only made her more aware of how bad she felt. She wasn't sure which was worse: her anger at Connor for opening his mouth or her fear of how Barr might react. Explanations were pointless. With Barr, explanations only made things worse. And explain what? That she and Connor had discussed getting married? That's such a crime? She was pregnant. She was considering it. She wasn't even certain. She asked herself if she would be doing this for the baby or for herself. Or would it be for Connor, herself, and the baby? The fact that she couldn't make up her mind kept her awake at night. She did love Connor. She already loved the baby. So why the hesitation? Why the doubt?

"Well, isn't that nice?" Barr said.

She opened her eyes. He was pouring more whiskey into his glass. He looked pleased—he looked *I'm-so-fucked-I-might-as-well-be-pleased*. He raised the glass in a toast, and as he did so he gazed right into her eyes to be sure she saw all of it: the pissed off hurt, the thing that was there inside him that she both loved and feared, the thing that she didn't have a word or a name for, the thing that made him dangerous. The thing that made him Barr.

"Let me be the first to congratulate you," he said, and then he drained his glass.

After Del flushed the toilet,

he opened the linen closet door. He reached in behind the stack of folded bath towels and felt for the athletic sock. Liesl had kept the revolver in the same sock since she'd bought it in San Francisco. After being kept under her pillow, it resided in her nightstand drawer for a number of years, but finally she came to a decision, one that she never really discussed with him, but one he believed he understood. She didn't like guns. She didn't like the idea of them. Tacitly, she accepted that they were part of living out. But she didn't want to live a life that required having a pistol in hand. So, the .38 just disappeared. He thought at first that she might have gotten rid of it—how, he didn't know, and he never asked. He realized now that much of their life together had been defined by what they didn't tell each other, because they didn't need to. What was important was that the gun was gone, from beneath her pillow, from her nightstand. But not long after they'd moved out here to the house, he was looking for a towel after a shower, and when he reached into the linen closet his hand pushed the stack of towels back on the shelf, causing something to knock against the wall. Something hard. He imagined it might be a tool left there from installing the shelves—or maybe a piece of hardware—but when he reached around behind the stack of towels his fingers touched the sock, and he knew immediately. He never mentioned it to her; he didn't need to. Now, as he removed the revolver from the sock, he was again impressed by its compact heft. He shook it gently, bullets rattling in their chambers.

Barr washed two Percocet down with Irish. Anything to kill the pain. What the hell, he had the gun. But something was nagging at him, something this woman Essi said. *What're you going to do?* She wanted to know his plan. He never really worked with a plan. He read the play. He rolled with it. He made it up on the fly. It wasn't just a question of style. It was a matter of philosophy.

Marcia used to get that about him. She saw inside him—not all the way, because that was also part of his deal, you can't really get too close—but she saw that embedded in there was something rare and strong. And honest. She told him that. It was the second night he'd spent with her. *You're honest.* They were lying on her bed, the room lit by candle flame that guttered in the breeze that came through the open window. They'd exhausted each other, and she was drowsy. She closed her eyes and smiled. *You're honest, and that means more than anything to me.*

Now she looked distressed. And in pain. She could handle pain. She was like that. He could see it in her face, the strain about the eyes. It wasn't just how she was feeling at the moment, but it was concern about what it meant for the baby.

And Connor. Sitting there looking like he was waiting outside the principal's office. Like he was in deep shit and he didn't have a clue how or why this always happened to him. But on Presque Isle he just appeared out of the snow. Marcia said something to him—*Wait*, she said, *Wait*—but he kept coming. Didn't say a word. Didn't even seem to really stare at Barr. He just came up to him, pulling off his gloves, and swung with his right, the punch sending Barr down into the snow. Below his left ear his jaw felt unhinged. He hoped that would be the end of it. He heard Connor say something to Marcia. They seemed to argue, but for once there was something in his voice that was unapologetic, that wouldn't take no for an answer. Barr rolled on to his side, trying to get up, and he saw Marcia walking back down to the plowed road, where they had left their cars. She was fleeing. It was then that Barr knew it wasn't over. This wasn't a warning, this wasn't one cheap shot to the head. Barr must have gotten to his knees because the next time Connor swung it was an uppercut that caused pain to blossom throughout his skull. Then it was boots, and if anything, they were worse than the fists as they pummeled his back and found his ribs, knocking the wind out of him. Barr curled up, but Connor kept circling him in search of the exposed places. Barr was reduced to gasping for air through his own blood while his hands protected his nuts.

The next thing he knew he was lying alone, covered in snow, listening to a phone ring.

And now he had them. No, he didn't have a plan. But he found them. It was the trapper in him. Way out here in the storm, he found his prey.

So now what?

The whiskey and the Percocet were working, giving him a sense of distance from the pain.

He felt insulated.

He felt clear.

Not knowing what he was going to do wasn't a problem. Don't need a plan. Figure it out as you go. Read the play.

That was his style. It had gotten him this far.

Marcia watched Del come out of the bathroom and work his way back to the stool next to the fireplace. Before sitting down, he tugged on his sweater with his free hand, a bulky wool sweater that she guessed his wife had knitted for him. Forest green, with a simple cable pattern on the front. A sweater for a winter's day, each stitch an act of love. When he lowered himself to the stool he eased his back against the chimney stones. He seemed preoccupied, but then he looked at Marcia.

Resting both hands on the top of his cane, he asked, "How you doing?"

"I've been better."

"Can we get you anything? Something to drink? Another blanket?"

Marcia shook her head. "You would have made a great father." He seemed surprised. "You're thoughtful. Very considerate." And then, she said, "I love your sweater. Your wife knitted it, I'll bet."

"She did."

"You're the kind of man a woman—a wife, a mother—would knit a sweater for."

She didn't understand his expression. It was worried, regretful. Perhaps the mention of the sweater and his wife wasn't a good idea. He gazed down at the floor a moment and then looked back at her. There was something in his eyes now, something he was trying to tell her without doing so.

She tilted her head slightly, as if to say, *What? I don't get it.*

He just lowered his head and stared at the floor, as if to say, *Don't. Don't ask.*

The gun felt like a rock against the small of Del's back. It wasn't smooth and rounded like the stones in the chimney but had edges that dug into his skin. Tucked inside his pants, it made his belt uncomfortably tight.

He wondered if the bulge had been visible as he returned to the stool by the fireplace. Marcia seemed to notice, but Barr had been preoccupied, staring off at the bookshelves. Del knew that stare: the Percocet gaze. He'd taken two pills a couple of hours ago. The stuff was subtle. You're aware of it as much as you're not aware of it. It didn't eliminate pain but pushed it away. It made it tolerable. It created a dreamy, drowsy calm. Del found that he could read on Percocet, though later he had trouble recalling what he'd read. He preferred listening to music. Lying on the couch, staring at the ceiling beams and letting Mozart or Bach or maybe some early Stones drift over him.

When he'd come out of the bathroom, he saw Barr take two pills. With the amount of whiskey he'd consumed, they should take effect soon. As Del sat on the stool by the chimney, Barr was occupied with refilling his glass. In the movies the guy is always tucking the gun inside his belt and acting like it was no big deal, but in fact you couldn't help being keenly aware of the weight of it, the bulk of it. Perhaps there was a bulge, and that's what Marcia saw. Perhaps she had figured it out and was trying to tell him so with her comment about his sweater. Perhaps she was saying the bulge was too obvious.

Perhaps she was saying, *If you've got a gun, why don't you do something with it?*

Del looked at Barr. He was sitting on the stool, his revolver lying next to his glass of whiskey. He was gazing toward the bookcase, his head tilted and squinting slightly—he was reading the titles on the spines of the books.

Del tried to imagine this: He slowly reaches behind him, raises his sweater, and pulls the gun from his belt. As he stretches out his arm, aiming the gun, Barr turns and sees what's coming—he moves quickly, trying to slide off the stool, reaching for his own gun, but Del pulls the trigger. Repeatedly. All five chambers. Barr is a heap on the floor. The sound of the shots is overwhelming. Blood everywhere.

Or this: he aims the gun at Barr and says, *Don't move.* And when Barr complies, he says, *Now stand up and step away from the counter.* And then he would ask Essi to get up off the floor, get the revolver, and bring it to him. It would be over.

But Del didn't do anything.

He sat on the stool, watching Barr stare at the bookshelves.

———————————

"You read all those?" Barr asked.

"Most of them," Del said. "Some were my wife's."

As Barr got off the stool at the counter, everyone seemed to stiffen. The attention pleased him, the power of it, how they studied his every gesture. He held his gun easily at his side. Even better: no one dared move. He walked around the back of the couch to the bookshelf, which spanned the entire wall. "What, three hundred? Four?"

"I never counted them," Del said.

"What I don't get is why people keep them. Or do you read them again?"

"Some, yes. But a lot of them, no. They just become part of the house, part of you."

"Just showing off your brains." He pulled a book off the top shelf. "I heard of this one." It was an old hardback, thick, with a brown dust jacket. A tear at one corner had been taped—and the tape was yellowed and curled. "*The Brothers*—how you pronounce this?"

"Karamazov," Del said.

"Right." Barr walked back to the counter. "Those Russians. Wrote some big suckers, eh? Must be their winters." Barr slid back onto the stool and opened the book, tilting it toward the lantern. He flipped through to the last page. "Look at this, eight hundred and twenty-two pages. I guess that Dostoyevsky had a lot to say." There were Post-It notes throughout the book, and many passages were underlined or highlighted. Notes were written in the margins in a tight controlled script. "Besides parole officer, you were a teacher?"

"No," Del said. "My wife was. Taught pottery at the alternative school."

"So why all the notes?"

"Habit."

"You read it, too?"

"Years ago, yes. Then we read it again, together."

"Together? And you'd discuss it."

Del didn't answer.

Barr looked up from the book. Del was staring at the floor. It was hard to tell if he was insulted or not. Barr suspected that Del resented his old book being handled. "If I asked what it's about, you'd probably say something like shit happens to the Karamazov brothers, because you think I'm too stupid to understand it."

Del continued to stare at the floor. "I don't think that, no."

"Let's see." Barr flipped through the book and stopped at a page where there was a Post-It note and an underlined passage. "A man who lies to himself and listens to his own lie comes to a point where he does not discern any truth either in himself or anywhere around him, and thus falls into disrespect toward himself and others. Not respecting anyone, he ceases to love, and having no love, he gives himself up to passions and coarse pleasures, in order to occupy and amuse himself, and in his vices reaches complete bestiality, and it all comes from lying continually to others and to himself."

Barr looked up and considered each of them. No one was watching him now. They were afraid to, it seemed. He slammed the book shut, causing Marcia to flinch. When she glanced at him, her eyes angry and fearful, he said, "But you're laughing inside, aren't you? You think that's—how to put it, how would Del say it?—it's *ironic* that I should read that part, right?"

"No, I'm not laughing," she said.

"You're not? Del's not resentful, and you're not laughing."

"No. I'm just sad."

"And why is that, Marcia?"

"Because it's true."

"About me?"

"But it doesn't have to be."

Barr felt the slightest spark of anger. She could do that to him. He decided it was best to ignore her. "Del," he said. "Is this the one about the guy who kills someone, his landlady or something?"

"No, that's *Crime and Punishment*."

"Of course."

"She was a pawnbroker," Del said. "And her stepsister was in the apartment, too, so Raskolnikov murdered her as well."

"Right, that guy. Raskolnikov. How's he do it?"

"With an axe."

"An axe. Where?"

"Split their skulls."

"That's messier than a gun. Well, I suppose it depends on the gun." For some reason Barr got the sense that Del thought this was humorous, that he was trying not to smile. Essi, sitting on the floor next to him, was absolutely still and staring straight ahead. She might have been meditating. "An axe requires a lot of effort," Barr said. "Real commitment." He picked his revolver up off the counter. "With these, you aim and pull the trigger. Just takes one finger. What, they didn't have guns in Russia back then?"

"They did," Del said. "But Raskolnikov was poor, a poor student."

Barr nodded. "See? This is what makes America great. A true democracy. Anybody can have guns. Rich or poor, everyone can have these." They were all looking at him now. "Cuts down on the axe murders." He laughed, though no one else did. "That's progress for ya." He laid the revolver on top of the book. "So, what happens to these Karamazov guys?"

Del tried to get more comfortable against the chimney rocks. "Like you said, shit happens. There were three brothers and their father."

Essi turned and glanced up at Del. "And there was the father's epileptic servant. I forget his name but he was the son of Lizaveta, the village idiot. There's always a village idiot."

"Still is," Barr said. "Check out Dumbo here."

Connor didn't move, didn't say anything.

Essi turned to Barr. "Everyone assumed Fyodor had fathered this child, and eventually he takes him in as his servant."

"So there are four brothers." Barr moved the handle of the revolver so he could look at the cover of the book. "Fyodor—is this Dostoyevsky?"

Essi shook her head. "Fyodor Karamazov is fictional. Russian names can be confusing."

"I guess," Barr said. "So. Shit happens. Money?"

Essi nodded.

"Women?"

She nodded.

"Nice. The brothers, the father, they're all after the same one."

"I think there were two in particular," Essi said.

Barr smiled at Marcia. "And you think you got family issues?"

Marcia only stared at him.

Barr said to Essi, "Murder?"

Essi nodded.

"Courtroom drama?"

"Yes."

"Who got murdered?"

"The father," Del said.

"Good call. And who did it?" Barr asked. "The butler—the idiot servant?"

Both Del and Essi seemed confused, uncertain.

"No, he hanged himself," Essi said. "You know, I don't remember how it all worked out."

"I don't either," Del said. "After the trial one of them was sent to Siberia."

"No guillotine?" Barr said. "I guess that's a French thing."

Del said, "Ivan—no, Dmitri is sent to Siberia."

Essi glanced at him. "Yes, and the other one, the religious one, Alyosha, went with him."

Barr shook his head. "Siberia. That's like Russia's version of the U.P."

"Worse," Essi said.

"You been there?"

"I've been to a lot of places," she said, "but not Siberia."

Barr could have put his head down on the counter and gone right to sleep. It was those pills, plus the whiskey. "Siberian winters got nothing on this. This isn't fiction. It's real. All we need is Jerry fucking Springer. Imagine what Dostoyevsky could do with *him*."

———————————————

Marcia could feel it: something else was going on here.

They were talking about one of those books she'd heard of but knew she'd probably never read. But that wasn't what was really going on. Del was different. She didn't quite know how, but he was alert in a way he hadn't been earlier. He'd taken some pain pills and had whiskey earlier, but that was hours ago now. Maybe he was coming out of it. She'd seen this too often in her clients. After surgery they fall into this medicated state, they become lethargic, and it's difficult to get them to do the simplest exercises. They just want to lie there. Del hadn't been that bad—his mind was still working away. But when it had been just the two of them on the couch, she could sense how his body had settled into itself. But now he was different, she was certain of it.

Perhaps it was simply the fact that Barr was fading. He was medicated with pills and whiskey, numb to the pain Connor had inflicted that afternoon on Presque Isle. She should never have fled. She knew that. She'd never seen Connor like that, in a kind of animal state. She was frightened, so frightened she just wanted to get away from him—from both of them. She wanted to flee the whole thing, these two men who had come into her dull, messed-up life and made it worse. She wanted to walk through the snow and driving wind, bearing the substance and heft of the child in her womb, and escape. She wanted to get to a place she'd never been. People called it normal, a normal life. Others had it. She'd never had anything normal, probably never would. There was just the slightest hope, the chance that she might get there. Marry Connor, have the baby. On the surface it looked plenty normal, but she knew that even then she wouldn't have it right. This was her deepest fear, that she'd never get it right. One day she'd be old like her clients and she'd know it was too late.

Looking at Barr's swollen, bruised face was sufficient confirmation. No normal. Never. His face was her life. At the bottom of it, this is what was so distressing, this was what caused the ache above her vagina. She hated Barr. She hated the blunt brutality of him. It wasn't physical; it wasn't animal, like Connor had been this afternoon. It was just *there*, in Barr, in his presence. She hated it but she loved it, too. She needed it. The reason was too deep down to reach, though she feared she already knew what it was: the baby might be his. She didn't know how she knew, but she sensed it, she felt it. This being growing inside of her, it was a part of him, too. Someday, she supposed, this could be proven with DNA tests or whatever, but it didn't really matter. She already suspected this to be true. Barr was the father of her child. If that were the case, no matter what Barr was, the child would need him, the child would want him. And this was why Connor beat him, beat him so mercilessly, because somehow he also suspected that Barr was the father. Connor had acted out of necessity, animal necessity. He had to kill the father.

She watched Barr, one haunch on the stool, both arms leaning heavily on the counter. He was not all there. The gun, the book, he stared at them as if he wasn't sure what to make of them. She wondered if what had changed Del was the realization that it was only a matter of time, enough time for Barr to settle down into sleep. So he could be disarmed. So they'd all be safe again, protected in this house from the blizzard.

And then what?

Essi looked up at Del but didn't say anything. She didn't have to. He could see that she knew it was just a matter of time and they only needed to wait.

The thing to do was not to seem to be waiting, so Del said, "You're good with the Russian names."

Essi's means of taking a compliment was to look disinterested. "I grew up in Helsinki and read it in Suomi, Finnish. Though we border Russia, two very different languages. But many names are the same in both languages. In my twenties I read the Russians: Tolstoy, Dostoyevsky, Turgenev, Chekhov. The names weren't difficult. I've forgotten a lot of the characters—there were so many—but some of it stays with you, like Lizaveta in *Brothers* or Anna Karenina." She touched her forehead. "I can remember where I was when I read certain passages. You remember where you were when Anna steps in front of the train?"

Del shook his head.

"I was a student at the university. It was summer, and I had taken the ferry out to Suomenlinna, which is an ancient fort on a series of islands off Helsinki. I was sitting in the grass that grows along the fortress walls, reading about Anna Karenina and that train. I remember looking out at the sea, wanting to speak to her, there on that platform, wanting to shout to her to stay off the tracks. Tell her to stop this jealousy bit with Vronsky. Do anything, move out, whatever, but keep clear of that train. This was very disconcerting, sitting in the August sun."

"I imagine it was," Del said. "I imagine a lot of people have wanted to warn Anna."

"But you can't stop her," Essi said. "You know she's going to do something irreversible."

"No, you can't stop her any more than you can stop that train." Del looked at Barr, whose head was resting on his arms on the counter. The revolver lay on the book next to his right elbow.

"Thank God for Russian literature," Essi said quietly. "You think it's time?"

On the couch, both Connor and Marcia seemed afraid to move. A baby might have been asleep in the room. "I think so," Del said.

Before he could move, Essi said, "Let me do it."

Del looked at the cane in front of him. He would need it to get to the counter. There was no way of doing so quietly. He tilted his head and raised an eyebrow to say, *I don't know. It's risky.*

"I can do it," Essi said.

Del leaned forward and put his arm behind his back. He raised up his sweater until he could get his hand around the grip of the gun. Somehow he was reluctant to draw it out, to show it to the others, though he suspected that Marcia might have guessed he had it. Still, what was the point of being armed if you don't use it? He pulled the revolver from under his belt, held it on his thigh. "All right."

Essi looked at the gun. "You're a man with options. Sometimes the best one is to do nothing."

She got up off the floor without making a sound, remarkable considering the condition she'd been in when she'd first come in out of the storm. She moved like a woman who had studied dance when she was young, who now did yoga or Tai Chi. She was in her stocking feet so there was only a whisper of sound as she walked over to the counter.

She stood next to Barr and remained still. This reminded Del of moments in the woods, when he would encounter an animal, deer usually, though a bear once. You stand still and pretend not to be there. No, you become part of what was there. Essi was part of the air in the house, lit by lantern light and warmed by the crackling logs. Slowly, she reached out and picked up the revolver. When Barr didn't move, she also picked up the bottle of whiskey. She walked back and stood in front of the fireplace.

Still, Barr didn't move, didn't stir. Neither did Marcia or Connor, sitting on the couch.

Essi placed the bottle on the floor and handed Barr's gun to Del.

He was disappointed and couldn't understand why, until he realized that he wished she'd also retrieved the book.

Marcia thought it was strange

the way they all remained still, as though waiting. After Essi had given Barr's revolver to Del, he held a gun on each thigh. How long he'd had his own gun Marcia didn't know, but she suspected he'd gotten it while he was in the bathroom—that was what she couldn't read in his expression after he returned to the living room.

Essi sat on the floor in front of the fireplace, and no one moved; no one said a word. They listened to the pop and hiss of the burning logs and the wind raking the house.

Barr began to snore, drawing in long, rattling drafts of air, a sound she was all too familiar with. In bed, she would just have to say "Roll over," and without waking he would obey and there'd be silence. It was the one command he heeded. She was afraid to say "Roll over" now. He might somehow fall off the stool. But she was more afraid of revealing such intimacy. Strange, being this pregnant and there was still the urge to conceal any recognition that she'd had sex with Barr—to Del and Essi, certainly, but especially to Connor.

"How are you feeling?" Essi asked.

"Better." Marcia's belly still hurt, but the nausea had been replaced by a dull ache. "Not great but better. I'm going to need—" She looked toward the bathroom. Essi began to get up off the floor. "I can make it myself, I think. Thanks." When Essi settled back on the floor, Marcia glanced at Barr, who had not stirred, and asked, "What now?"

"We wait," Del said. "We can't do anything until this storm lets up."

Connor took his cell phone from his pocket, and after poking at the screen, he said, "Nothing."

"Reception is spotty out here, even in good weather," Del said. "I often have to go outside the house because I get cut off in the middle of a call. Sometimes there's a hot spot halfway down the drive."

"I'll go see if I can get a signal," Connor said. Then hesitant, embarrassed: "Who do I call?"

"Try the county sheriff's office," Del said. "See if any plows can make it out here."

Connor got to his feet and zipped up his coat. He looked eager to do something—anything but sit there on the couch. "I don't have any gloves," he said. "Left them on Presque Isle."

"Look in that basket on the bookshelf," Del said. "I keep hats, gloves, scarves there."

As Connor sorted through the basket, he said, "I don't know what happened to me out on Presque Isle. I could have killed him." He turned to Marcia, as though he expected her support. "I'm not like that, am I?"

There had been a moment, when Marcia saw what Connor was doing to Barr, that she was relieved. Not just relieved, thrilled. She watched Connor's arms and legs, the force of them as he drove Barr down into the snow. But then she pleaded with him to stop, and when he didn't she panicked and plodded through the snow, awkward and slow with the weight of her child, until she was far enough away from them, from all of it, and there was only the sound of the wind in the trees.

She couldn't help the tears that overflowed her eyes and ran down her cheeks. "No, you're not like that."

He was pulling his wool cap down over his hair, and when he saw that she was crying, he left his hands on his head, a mock expression of shock and awe. But unintentional. He wasn't capable of sarcasm. "I mean I just lost it."

Marcia wiped her cheeks with the palm of her hand. "It was my doing as much as yours. I couldn't have stopped you, but you wouldn't have done it if—I wanted it and you knew it. That's why I ran. I wanted it. Just for a moment, I wanted you to put an end to it, but I couldn't bear to watch."

Connor looked as though he were ready to lunge toward her, sit on the couch, and take her in his arms, which was the last thing she needed at that moment.

"No," she said, her voice quivering. She held up a palm, a wet palm. "Go outside and see if you can get a signal."

"All right, and I'll take the litter out." Connor said it as though it were something he held dear. And then she understood: he'd made it with his bare hands, out there in the storm. Reluctant but obedient, he gathered up the litter and went to the door.

As he let himself out a cold blast of air embraced her back and shoulders. After he pulled the door closed, she said to Del, "Twice. Twice since I came here this afternoon. Enough tears."

Connor stood on the porch, his legs braced against the wind, and when he descended the steps, he held the litter across in his arms, using it for balance like a tightrope walker as he began to wade through the snow. The driveway was a landscape of sculpted ridges, cliffs, and cresting waves. The wind sent towering ghosts swirling up into the darkness. Tree trunks were pocked with driven snow, while their limbs, scaly and reptilian, clattered overhead.

Halfway down to the road he dropped the litter in the snow and took his cell phone from his coat pocket. The illumination of the screen seemed artificial, an illusion. There were no bars in the upper corner: no service.

Something in him wanted to keep walking. Years ago he'd seen a movie—he couldn't recall its name—that concluded with a character wandering off in a blizzard. What Connor remembered was that the film made the snow and the wind beautiful, and it was clear that the man wanted to die, wanted to wade out into the woods until he froze to death. At the time Connor thought it was bullshit. In Michigan's Upper Peninsula you could freeze to death—stranded motorists and fall-down drunks—but it was not some romantic choice.

Now, Connor wondered if he might be able to take that walk, just continue on through the woods until he was too far from the house, too far to turn back. This was his fault, all because he'd lost it on Presque Isle. He remembered the last moment in the film, the next day when the storm had passed and the man was seen from a distance, sitting upright in the snow, with tree-covered hills behind him, which gave way to a close-up, so you saw that he had frozen to death. His beard was covered in ice, his skin was blue-white, and his eyes were wide open, staring straight ahead in wonder—startled eyes that possessed some wisdom that is beyond this life.

Connor reached the road, which was a broad swath in the dark woods, a scar. There was no service here either, and he tucked the phone in his pocket. Even if he got a signal, what would anyone be able to do?

No one was getting out here tonight.

Barr was snoring so deeply now that Del wondered if it was necessary to hold the guns, if he might just put them on the floor next to his cane.

"You're not just a man with options," Essi said. "You have your surprises."

He suspected she was rarely ever surprised. She seemed to see it coming, whatever it was. "The real surprise," he said, "is how they're nearly identical. Both Smith & Wesson .38s, his with brown grips, mine with black."

"You had that pistol tucked in your belt all this time?"

"No. It was in the bathroom linen closet."

"Someone else might have come out shooting."

"Maybe."

"You didn't. That's what's surprising." Essi glanced over her shoulder at Barr. "We should restrain him before he comes around. What could we use?"

"Check the kitchen drawers. You might find something there."

Essi got to her feet. Del didn't want to watch her walk into the kitchen. He was afraid to look at her, to look too hard at her, to see her. He found that he could only take her in in small doses, small increments. It was a matter of absorption. So he stared at the floor, at the knots in the wide boards, until he realized she wasn't moving, but just standing there next to him. He raised his head. "I know," she said. There was a quality to her voice he couldn't quite identify. "I know it's hard."

She could mean anything, though he knew, despite resisting it, he knew what she meant. She was talking about them, about herself and him, about how she felt something from him as well, and that she understood that this was a difficult thing for him to acknowledge, let alone accept.

"Where were you going when Connor found you?"

She reached out and touched the side of his face, her fingers lightly invading his whiskers, seeking his skin. "Here, obviously."

She removed her hand and went into the kitchen. The warm imprint of her fingertips remained on his cheek. He heard her open drawers and move things about. Then a drawer was closed with finality and she came back around the counter, a roll of duct tape in her hand. Barr was sleeping soundly. Del knew that sleep; since his surgery he often sought such total oblivion through a combination of pills and Irish. It stopped the world from turning. Essi got to her knees behind the stool and pulled tape off the roll, a sound like no other, a hollow, sucking sound, as distinct as the ping of a basketball. As she began wrapping Barr's ankles to the legs of the stool, he didn't stir. When she finished the first ankle, she leaned over and tore the tape off with her teeth. Del was taken by its practical intimacy.

In the bathroom, Marcia had thrown up again. After washing her face and hands, she stood at the window with a towel. Outside, she could see the tailgate of Del's truck, the tendrils of branches clutching the wheel wells. The trees overhead seemed alive in the wind. Not tossed, thrashed. When she heard the crack, a spike of pain shot through her womb. Instinctively, she backed away from the glass as the tree trunk came toward the house.

The tree trunk snapped with the impact of an explosion, and Connor fell to his knees in the snow. There was a moment of disconnect, of suspension, before the tree began its tilt and swift descent. As it came down on the roof of the house there was a deafening series of pops and crackles, branches shattering, hurling shards of wood skyward. At first it appeared that the tree would slice clean through the house and burrow in the ground beneath it with the heft and determination of an axe, but the roof, a trestle of timbers, managed to support the weight of the massive trunk.

Del lay face down to the floor. He knew what had happened. The Norway maple—*the* maple he'd been concerned about for months—had fallen on the roof, sending a tremor through the house, which knocked him off the stool. He had been aware of this old maple, the height of the tree, the angle of the trunk, its proximity to the house. His concern about the damage it might cause had been as persistent as a toothache, but he became too preoccupied with other fall chores in anticipation of his second hip replacement. So, he didn't deal with the tree, thinking, *It can wait until spring.* And now the fallen tree had cleaved the roof ridge, its branches clawing at the shingles as though they were the talons of some mythical beast.

He felt snow on his neck—snow drifting down through the broken roof—yet the fireplace, which was only a few feet behind him, still gave off heat. It seemed he was indoors, but with the cold breeze and the smell of tree, he was also outdoors. For some reason his mind latched on to the peculiarity of the word: *outdoors.* And *out of doors.* This was not the time to dwell on linguistics.

There was no sound in the room, though overhead the wind howled around the trunk that was lodged in the broken skein of joists, struts, purlins, and rafters. Turning his head, he could see the couch, covered with bark, and one cushion, impaled by a broken limb, looking like a crooked javelin. He recalled that Marcia had been sitting there before going into the bathroom. And Connor had been on the couch, too, but he had gone outside—*outdoors*—to try and get a signal on his cell phone.

With effort, Del looked over his left shoulder. He could not see Essi, and Barr was no longer sitting on the stool, his head resting on his arms as he slept. Del suspected they were both also lying somewhere on the floor.

He wondered about his hips. He moved his legs, just to prove to himself that he could do so. Under the circumstances, his legs felt no worse than before the tree had come down on the house. But he became aware of a tightness in his right wrist, the jammed sensation one gets having broken a fall with a hand. The ache in his wrist was persistent, but he could move it. A sprain, most likely.

And then he realized that his hand was empty. Both his hands, in fact, were empty. Hadn't he been sitting on the stool, his back to the stone chimney, with a revolver in each hand? Or were they resting on his thighs? No matter, the pistols were gone. Looking about as best he could, he couldn't see either gun amid the branches and twigs and curled pieces of bark that littered the floor.

Barr walks down a corridor that is fluorescent-lit, a harsh flood of light that casts no shadows, and there are just numbers on all the doors, no signs. At the end of the corridor, he stops before an open elevator. A cell phone lies on the metal floor, but before he can step inside, the elevator door slides closed. The floor numbers diminish as the elevator descends to the first floor. He wants that phone. Doesn't know why, but it's important. Repeatedly he pushes the button until the elevator begins to ascend. When the doors open there are two men inside, both with shaved heads and leather jackets. They are from Chicago. One of them appears to be Leon. The other looks like Connor, with a polished forehead. Barr steps inside the elevator but can't see the phone on the floor. As the elevator door closes behind him, Leon extends his arm, the phone in his palm, and says, *Looking for this?* When Barr nods, Connor says, *What's on it?* Barr hears himself say *I don't know.* Leon closes his fist over the phone and nods. A signal, an order. As Connor pulls back his arm Barr prepares for the punch, which sinks deep into his left side. He's buckled over but still standing, and the pain is incredible. He tries to think what is on that side—the spleen? Connor has his arm cocked again, ready to deliver a second punch, when Leon says, *I said, what's on it?* Barr considers making something up. He might say, *Let me show you,* but he can only tell the truth, and because he's had the wind knocked out of him he can only whisper, *I don't know.* Just as Connor is about to throw the next punch, Barr opens his eyes, feeling a painful weight pressing on his left side, where he thinks his spleen might be.

It was the woman's head, her hair tangled about her face. Essi.

"What do you mean?" she asked.

"I don't know what's on the phone."

"The phone?" she said. "Doesn't Connor have it? Didn't he go out to try to get a signal?"

Barr didn't understand where he was, thinking this was somehow connected to the elevator at the end of the corridor. At least he wasn't going to get punched again. At least the pain in his side was only the weight of her head.

He was lying on his back and directly above he could see that several limbs of the tree had broken through the roof. Their branches reminded him of long, spiny fingers, something out of a horror movie. They clutched and squeezed the life out of people, they impaled others, thrusting through chests and abdomens. He wondered if he'd seen a movie like that. When he was small, his father used to play this joke on him. At the kitchen table, he'd be drinking beer while Barr ate his dinner, and he'd talk about growing up in Detroit, about how he once went to a horror movie in a theater that had wired seats so that at the scariest moments during the film a small electric charge would make the seat vibrate, and as he explained this, his hand came up behind Barr and suddenly the chair shook, causing Barr to scream. Barr recalled that he wasn't really frightened, that he knew his father was going to grab the back of the chair, but he screamed because that's what his father expected. And because Barr liked to scream. It got their attention. Sometimes one of them would slap his skull, and he didn't like that. As he got older he discovered the advantage of being quiet. It was safer that way, it didn't draw attention to him, particularly when his father was on a bender. Then it was best to hide, to keep clear of his parents, to avoid getting slapped. It was smarter to remain silent and out of the way. When people forgot about you, that was when you could get away with stuff. His father's billfold often sat on top of his bureau next to a brass dish filled with coins—the dish said *Pocket Change*, which were two of the first words he learned to read. While his father was in the kitchen or the living room, giving his mother hell, Barr would slip into their bedroom. Usually he just took some coins, a dime or a quarter, just enough to buy a candy bar or a pack of gum. But sometimes, particularly when his father was hollering, Barr would slide a dollar out of the billfold. Once he took two dollars, and his father never caught on. Barr thought he could steal more from his father's bureau. He believed he'd discovered this secret that made him different from everybody else. *If you want something, take it.*

But the branches overhead weren't fingers, and Barr wasn't sure where he was—some house in the woods. Then it came to him: Connor, Marcia, Presque Isle. She'd set him up, and Connor had beaten the crap out of him. That's why he was out here. And there was this woman whose head was resting on his side, and another guy, a guy with a cane. Del, his name was Del. They'd been in the bathroom, and Del had offered him money. Twenty-five grand to leave Connor and Marcia alone. Twenty-five thousand dollars. Cash. Not from his billfold, from his bank.

But the tree—it wasn't a dream, it was a tree that had come through the roof, its thick trunk caught in the rafters, just waiting to crash to the floor and kill them all. Fucking A.

———————

As Marcia had backed away from the window next to the toilet, she could see the trunk of the tree come toward the house and when it hit the roof the glass exploded, shards raining down on her as a limb drove into the bathroom. She fell into the claw-foot bathtub, the back of her skull first hitting the tile wall and then the rim of the tub, causing a soft bell tone that coincided with enough pain that for a moment she wasn't sure if she was going to throw up again. The weight of her belly seemed to press her down in the tub, her legs splayed over the outside rim. The branches filling the bathroom seemed alive—wood snapped, buckled, and scraped at the ceiling, sounding worse than fingernails on chalkboard. The limb, at least as big around as a football, was about three feet above her. It smelled of bark and gave off cold, the deep cold that trees endure throughout winter. The tangle of branches coming off the trunk filled the bathroom, pinning her down in the tub. Sharp fingers clutched at her breasts and thighs, determined to pierce her skin or part her legs and invade her vagina.

The maple tree was at least

a hundred feet tall. The trunk lay at an angle across the roof peak, reminding Connor of the old fedora his Uncle Roger wore. His custom was to absentmindedly take the hat off and fiddle with the crown, shaping the divot that ran down its center with the edge of his hand. The trunk of the maple had settled down in the buckled roof, branches reaching skyward, nodding in the breeze like tufts of hair.

A portion of the porch roof had collapsed, making access to the front door difficult, so Connor waded through the snow down the left side of the house, where he was somewhat protected from the wind. He could not see in any of the windows because the curtains were closed. Behind the house there were several cords of stacked wood. He climbed a set of wooden steps to the kitchen door and looked through the window. It was dark inside, except for the flickering light cast from the fireplace. The doorknob was locked, so he went back to the firewood and selected a log from the top of the stack. He returned to the kitchen door and rammed the log through the glass so he could reach through the window and turn the latch.

Once in the kitchen, he said, "Marcia?" There was no answer. He walked toward the counter, where Barr had been sitting. It was covered with branches. The floor was strewn with twigs that snagged on his jeans and bark crackled beneath his boots. Louder, he said, "Where are you?"

"Here."

It was Essi's voice. She was lying on the floor, perpendicular to Barr, her head propped up on his stomach.

"Where's Marcia?"

"She was in the bathroom."

Connor turned the knob but the bathroom door wouldn't budge.

"Marcia," he called. "Are you all right in there?"

There was no answer.

"*Marcia!*" he shouted.

"I'm stuck," she said, her voice weak, sleepy.

"I can't open the door. Can you?"

"It's the tree." She now sounded more alert. "A limb came through the window and it's jammed up against the door. The room is filled with branches, and I can't get out of the tub."

Connor turned the knob and threw his shoulder against the door, but it didn't give.

"You can't push it in," Marcia said. "Believe me."

"Are you hurt?"

"I don't know. Banged my head."

"Stay there," Connor said.

"That's good advice," Barr said.

Connor looked at Barr, lying on the floor with Essi amid a tangle of branches. "Shut up." Putting his face up to the edge of the door, he said, "I'm going outside to see if I can get in through the window."

"Connor," Del said. He was somewhere under the branches, too, over near the fireplace. "You may need something to cut the tree with. I keep a bow saw and an axe out back, hanging on the wall by the firewood."

"What you need," Barr said, "is a chain saw."

"Don't have one," Del said.

"Everyone out here has a chain saw," Barr said. "But no, not you."

"I don't believe in them."

After a moment, Barr said, "Of course you don't. Jesus, what was I thinking?"

"Is anyone hurt?" Connor asked.

Del said, "I don't think so."

"Same here," Essi said, as she pushed branches aside so she could get to her feet.

Connor leaned closer to the door, "Marcia, I'll get in through the bathroom window."

Barr laughed, sort of. "Funny, the Beatles never thought of that one."

Connor went out the back door.

"Unfuckingbelievable," Barr said. "Wasn't I just sitting at the counter with a bottle of whiskey, that Russian book, and my gun?" He turned his head and saw the book open, face down on the floor. "Now all I've got is reading material."

Essi was helping Del get up off the floor.

"I mean do you believe this, Del?" Barr was aware of something restraining him but he wasn't certain what it was—his legs felt anchored. "Look at this place. Bark and branches and roofing crap all over the place, and that trunk could come down on us at any moment. What are the odds?"

"Trees fall in the woods," Del said.

"Yeah, but on your house?"

"Pretty good odds, actually," Del said. "I've been concerned about that tree for some time."

"That so?" Barr turned his head the other way but could see neither the bottle of whiskey nor the revolver. "I guess you find this interesting, philosophically speaking. You know, in a one-hand-clapping sort of way.

If a tree falls in the woods and nobody's there to witness it, does it actually happen? You know, something theoretical."

Long moment. Too long. "When it falls on your house," Del said finally, "it might be considered empirical evidence that the tree has indeed fallen."

"Empirical?" Barr said. "Must have skipped school that day."

"Observation based on experience."

"Ah. Like proof."

"Correct."

"So we can't just pretend this never happened."

"That would be difficult."

"Had I taken your offer of twenty-five thousand, you think this would still have happened?"

"Likely."

"I was afraid of that."

Barr tried to turn on his side so he could get up, but something was gripping him by the ankles. He had to admit he was a bit spaced out, and there was a temptation to just remain horizontal, but he was the only one lying on the floor now and it was affecting his sense of stature. Prone and pistol-less. He bent his knees, confirming that there was true resistance. "What's with my legs?"

"I imagine it's the stool you were sitting on," Del said. "You're taped to it."

"Taped?"

"Duct tape," Essi said.

"Whose bright idea was *that*?" When they didn't answer, Barr said, "No, don't tell me."

Del managed to sit up on the floor, resting his back against the chimney stones. Bark and branches covered everything. Books had cascaded off the shelves and spilled across the floor. Only one of the storm lanterns still flickered. Essi sorted through the debris, picking up smaller twigs and tossing them on the fire. Keeping the fire going would be essential if they were to make it through the night. Not twelve feet away, Barr lay on his side, scanning the floor.

They were looking for the same thing.

Something glinted dully in the firelight, lying next to the far end of the couch. After a moment Del realized that it was the whiskey bottle.

He recalled the moment of impact, the way the floor jounced when the trunk broke through the roof—he'd been sitting on the stool, holding a revolver on each thigh. He went down hard, sharp pain jolting through his leg, causing him to think of the scar, the stitch marks on the side of his butt still raw. His right wrist ached but nothing broken. He must have let go of the pistols in an effort to break his fall with his hands. Both revolvers had to be concealed beneath the wood that littered the floor.

When Barr began to move, crawling across the floor, dragging the stool after him, Del's attention shifted to where the floor ran beneath the counter: a revolver lying beneath a skein of branches. Del rolled on to his side until he was on all fours and began to baby-crawl toward the counter.

Barr got there first, shoved aside the branches, and picked up the revolver. He was exhausted but ecstatic, the winner of the prize. Propped up on one elbow, he pointed the gun at Del. "You're barking up the wrong tree, pard."

Del stretched out a hand, as though it might actually stop a bullet. "All right."

Essi perched herself on the armrest of the couch. They both stared at Barr, who, apparently satisfied that they weren't going to rush him, lowered the revolver, resting his arm on the floor.

"Now," Barr said, looking at Essi. "First, we're going to deal with this stool you taped to my feet." When Essi didn't move, he said, "You may approach, on your hands and knees. If you please."

Essi got down on all fours and crawled toward him, pushing branches aside, ducking beneath others. When she reached him, Barr said, "You unwrap me." He touched the muzzle of the revolver to her thigh. "Careful. I am not shittin' you."

The grips. Del leaned forward slightly. It was difficult to tell by firelight, but the grips on the revolver appeared to be black. They were brown on Barr's gun, black on Liesl's. Yes, they were black. He remembered the logo stamped on them: *Bianchi Gunleather* inside a circle placed inside a six-point star.

For the moment, Barr didn't seem to notice.

In order to see Marcia, Connor had to straddle the limb that had rammed through the window. Inside the bathroom, the branches were like tentacles crammed against everything—the toilet, sink, linen closet, bathroom door. She lay on her back in the bathtub, her legs angled over the rim.

"You all right?"

She stared up at him through branches. "They're pinning me down."

"I'll get you out of there as soon as I can."

There were several branches that obstructed his way. Two smaller ones, close to him, he chipped away with the axe, allowing him to shinny farther up the thick branch. With one swing he sank the axe into the wall of the house and took off the bow saw that was slung over his shoulder. He began working on the nearest branch, sawdust drifting back in his face.

"I don't feel so good, Connor."

"Just hang on."

He'd always had great faith in tools. The bow saw's rhythm was reassuring, the teeth working through the first branch easily, until it gave of its own weight, and with one hand he broke it off and dropped it in the snow piled against the foundation of the house. The next branch was thicker, and setting the blade was difficult because it was hard against the windowsill. He took shorter strokes. The pitch of the steel rose as the blade worked deeper into the limb.

"Will you listen to that Eagle Scout?" Barr said. He was sitting up now, his back against the counter. He had the fifth of whiskey perched on his thigh. With his other hand he worked the cap off the vial of Del's pills. "Connor should have grown up to be a Mountie. My mother used to watch this cartoon show that had a lot of jokes I didn't get, and when I'd ask her she'd say I'll explain it to you when you grow up. But there was this Mountie . . ."

Del didn't bother looking up from the floor. "Dudley Do-Right."

"That's the one." Barr took a nip straight from the bottle. "Always saving the damsel in distress from that villain."

"Nell," Essi said. "And Snidely Whiplash."

"You could watch it in Finland?" Del asked.

"Are you kidding, a cartoon about a flying squirrel and a moose?" Essi nodded. "When I was a girl, I visited relatives here. Boris and Natasha were a stitch. Two bumbling Russian spies. But then it was not just funny. Finland and Russia, it's a complicated history. We hate them, even fear them." She glanced at Del. "But love their literature."

"So chummy," Barr said. "Like a couple of old classmates. Guess you all watched it when you weren't reading Dostoyevsky. Jesus, what kind of a childhood is that? We just had this one little TV. After the old man died, my mother watched it all the time. She talked back to it. She ate in front of it, slept in front of it." Barr tipped the vial up to his mouth and deposited a capsule on his tongue, which he washed down with a swig of whiskey. Del was looking at him. Essi was looking at him. "That's three," he said as he snapped the lid back on the vial. He rotated his right shoulder, which was stiff and sore. "Between Presque Isle and falling off that stool, I smart all over. I can handle three. Trust me, I can handle three." He placed the bottle on the floor and picked up the revolver. He studied it a moment. It felt different somehow. When he looked up, Del and Essi were still there. And Connor was still sawing away in the bathroom. "Don't look at me like that."

"Like what?" Essi asked.

"Like I can't handle three. It's not a problem. It runs in the family. She could pop all her pills without even taking her hand off the TV remote."

Again, Barr stared at the gun in his hand.

Marcia unbuttoned her jeans and yanked down the zipper, bringing some relief.

Connor was inside the window now but still sawing branches. Though he had one foot in the sink, he seemed miles away. She couldn't believe his energy, he just kept pushing and pulling on the saw. When he cut away one branch, he started on the next, until he stopped and looked down at her jeans. His eyes went from frightened to terrified. "What's that?"

The denim was soaking wet and her thighs were cold.

"Listen," Connor hollered from the bathroom. "We need some help in here."

Del said, "What is it?"

"She says her water's broke."

Essi got off the armrest of the couch. Barr looked at her curiously. She ignored him, and tree bark crackled beneath her feet as she walked to the bathroom door. "Can you open the door?"

"No way," Connor said. "I still can't get to Marcia. She's in the tub."

Essi looked at Del, then at Barr. "I've got to go out and around."

Barr nodded. "Is it time to boil water?"

"I could use blankets," she said to Del.

"There are some in the linen closet in there and also in the bedroom."

"Connor," she said, leaning close to the door. "Can you get in the linen closet?"

"Not yet, but I'm close."

"I'll come around," Essi said. "Marcia, how you doing?"

"I'm very wet. And cold."

"I'll be right there." Essi found her coat and boots by the fireplace and began to put them on.

Barr asked, "You ever deliver a baby?"

"Deliver? I've had two."

"I guess that counts." Barr laughed.

Del got to his feet and made his way to the couch. "Anything I can do?"

"Entertain our friend here. And I suppose you could heat up some water, in case we manage to get that bathroom door opened." She went into the bedroom and came out with two blankets slung over her shoulder, and then left by the back door.

Barr gazed at Del as though they were comrades. "Mothers."

Sawdust. Marcia kept her eyes closed much of the time, and though she frequently brushed sawdust from her face, it clung to her eyelashes.

When Essi arrived, Connor stopped sawing. She climbed up on the limb and passed two blankets through the window. He handed them down to Marcia, who covered as much of herself as possible. The backs of her knees were sore from hanging over the tub and she couldn't feel her feet—she wasn't sure if they had fallen asleep or had gone numb with the cold. Oddly, the bloated middle of her felt warm and her heart rate was accelerating. She was sweating so that she imagined herself melting in the tub.

Connor helped Essi climb into the bathroom, and she managed to get her feet down on to the rim of the tub. "Looks like we sprung a leak."

"I'm awful hot, till I get these cold chills."

"You keep the blankets over you," Essi said. "We're going to cut away these last few branches so I can get down there with you."

Connor went to work again on the limb, Marcia closed her eyes against the sawdust. She'd once asked her mother about having her, what it was like. She said there was nothing to it. She was real scared at first, but then your body just sort of takes over. *Does it hurt?* Here her mother hesitated, seemingly adrift in a flood of remembrance. *Well, sure it does*, she concluded, *but that's not what you remember, though this may have been due to the circumstances. You were born on a boat.* Marcia must have been six or seven, and at the time she thought this was the single most important thing she'd ever learned about herself. She was born on a boat, her mother assured her, and there was that smile that was difficult to read. Now, her own water broken, Marcia wondered how much, if any of it, was true. But why would her mother make up such an elaborate lie? *Your father and I had driven over to Munising. It was late August, and you weren't due for another few weeks. I was tired of lying around the apartment, getting bigger by the hour it seemed. So, we drove to Munising on a warm, sunny afternoon—a Sunday—and took the tour boat that went out to Pictured Rocks, those natural arches carved by time out of the cliffs overlooking Lake Superior. It was several miles from the harbor to the rocks, and the channel inside of Grand Island was calm. The boat had a diesel engine that caused everything to throb and vibrate, which I found somehow soothing. Dan bought me a Vernors, and he had a beer. The captain periodically spoke to the passengers over a loudspeaker, describing the scenery. I didn't pay much attention, except that he noted that they would be arriving off Pictured Rocks at about five-thirty, when the sunlight would best bring out the colors in the stone. When the boat came out of the protection of Grand Island, there was a chilly north wind on the lake, and the waves were running three to four feet. A lot of passengers went inside where it was warm, but we stayed up on the deck. By the time the boat reached Pictured Rocks, people were throwing up everywhere. But the rocks were beautiful, streaked with various shades of red and gold, and colors I wasn't sure I could name. The worst part was while the boat drifted several hundred yards off the rocks. Passengers tried to take photographs, though the boat was pitching violently, and more and more people were seasick. Finally, I said we needed to go down below and sit inside for the return trip. It was just as we reached the cabin. The diesel engine engaged again, and the boat headed back toward Munising. That's when I felt it. My water broke.*

Marcia didn't understand what this meant, and she thought it had to do with Lake Superior. She imagined enormous waves crashing over the bow of the tour boat. She wondered if she might have been tossed up by the waves, flopping around on the deck like a landed walleye. But her mother said that before she knew it she was lying on the floor, which was tilting and rolling every which way, holding on to the legs of the benches that were bolted to the floor, and from somewhere a man, a nice man with a full gray beard, knelt over her and said he was Dr. Lahti. Her mother paused then and seemed reluctant to go on until Marcia insisted. *Well, that engine vibrated and the metal floor clattered loudly, and you were born right there on the cabin floor in that boat. It didn't take long, fortunately. You were quite small, because you came early. And after you were delivered the passengers, most of them sitting in the benches farther forward to give us some privacy, they applauded when Dr. Lahti announced that you were a girl. They didn't just applaud, they cheered your arrival. Your father was more nervous than I was, though when the boat was about to tie up at the dock he joked that he hoped they wouldn't charge him an extra fare.* It was one of the few times her mother mentioned her father. Otherwise, it was like he had hardly existed.

Marcia opened her eyes because Connor had cut away the last branch. "I was born on a boat."

Essi was able to step down into the tub now. "You were born on the water? Sounds like a sacred ritual." She moved the blankets aside and began to loosen Marcia's clothing.

"No, on a boat on Lake Superior. My mother said I would always have an affinity for water."

Essi smiled as she worked Marcia's jeans off and looked at things down below.

"But I've never been sure that she didn't make it all up. Think someday I should tell my baby about being born in a bathtub?"

"Why not?" Essi said. "Maybe the child will develop an affinity for cleanliness."

Marcia gazed up at Connor, who was sitting on the limb, trying not to look directly at what was going on. "You look scared out of your wits."

"That's because I am," he said. "Am I supposed to leave?"

"Too late," Essi said. "You stay right where you are. Best you witness this."

"What do you want me to do?" he asked.

"Help me get her legs in the tub, and then cut that branch so you can open the linen closet. We'll need towels, and—" She looked down at Marcia with a gaze that said this is important, and it's not going to be easy. "And, honey, you're never going to be able to have that baby in this bathtub like this."

"Like what?"

"On your back," Essi said. "You think you can turn over? You need to do this on your hands and knees."

Del got on his hands and knees

and began crawling toward the couch.

"Looking for something?" Barr asked.

"My cane." He lowered himself until his cheek was touching the floor. The bottom half of his cane was under the couch, and Barr's .38 was under there, too, toward the back. He slid the cane out and, gripping the edge of the coffee table, managed to stand up. That afternoon Marcia had put him through his exercises, and it was difficult lifting his leg onto the bed. He felt stronger now. It must be adrenaline. "I'm going over to the bathroom door to see how they're doing in there."

"Fine. I'm the one with a lethal weapon in my hand, but nobody asks me anything."

"What would you like to be asked?"

"Asking my permission would be nice."

"Well, it's still my house."

Barr gestured toward the door with a grand sweep of his arm, gun in hand. "Be my guest."

Del concentrated on each step, nudging bark and twigs out of his way, working his way around Barr, who was still on the floor, sitting with his back against the counter. When he reached the bathroom, he turned the knob but the door wouldn't budge. "Awful quiet in there. How's it going?"

"I think we're going to have a baby." Essi sounded preoccupied but rather pleased about the prospect. "That door is jammed by this limb that crashed through the window. If Connor could cut it, relieving the pressure, we might get the door opened. How's that water coming?"

"Oh, right. Hot water."

"And, Del. We'll need scissors. Sterile. Boil them in the water."

"Got it."

As the sawing resumed on the other side of the door, Del turned and worked his way along the kitchen counter to the stove. First, he found a pair of scissors in a drawer, and then opened a cabinet and took down the pot he used for cooking pasta. He put the scissors in the pot, which he filled with water at the sink. The stove burner flamed up immediately— the line from the propane tank hadn't been damaged.

Barr got to his feet and tucked Liesl's revolver in the front of his jeans as he came into the kitchen. They both stood before the stove, holding their hands close to the heat from the burner. "This for real? She's going to have the baby in the bathroom?"

"Apparently so," Del said.

"Apparently. That supposed to be some kind of pun?"

"It didn't occur to me."

"I thought everything occurred to you."

"Hardly."

Barr turned his hands, warming both front and back. "You were me, what would you do?"

"If I were you I would never have come out here."

"Yeah. But I did. I'm here. What would be your plan now?"

They were both staring down into the large pot of water, where the first bubbles were beginning to rise off the heated bottom. "If I were you, I would take my offer," Del said. "As soon as we can get out of here, we'd go to the bank so I could withdraw the money."

"And then what?" There was the faintest slippage in his voice. Not yet a slur, but a kind of sliding between syllables. "I take off?"

"Sure," Del said.

"Head for some place—south, where my fingers aren't brittle as chalk. Then what?"

Del couldn't help but look at him.

"See? That's the problem." Barr kept his eyes on the water, which was beginning to send up steam. "I can see it up to a point. I can see getting the money. I can see taking it and getting out of here. I can see going a long way, really. But I can't see where I stop. I can't see why I stop. I can't see what I would do other than just the going. You can only go so long. Even twenty-five grand won't last forever. And when it runs out, then where am I?"

The steam from the pot was beginning to create the slightest sheen of moisture on Del's cheeks and forehead. "You might consider finding a job. You could work, and you could put some of that twenty-five aside. Save it. Add to it even."

"Right. And I could register to vote."

"It's what people do."

"Most people."

"All right."

"Not people like me."

"I get your point."

"Do you?"

Del gave it a moment, leaning forward slightly so the steam drifted up into his face. "What I'm thinking of is Friedrich Nietzsche."

"The philosopher guy?"

"Right."

"I can be above the law," Barr said. "Above everything."

"That's it."

"I really believe that, you know. It's the way I live."

"Why is that?"

"The rest of it is just bullshit, is why," Barr said. "You think that's really possible?"

"For most people, no."

"Yeah, most people need the bullshit. The God, country, family, decent job, mortgage, car payments bullshit. They say they don't, but they do. Otherwise, they don't know who they are."

The water was now coming to a boil, causing the scissors to rattle in the bottom of the pot.

"But there are exceptions," Del said.

"I am the exception."

"That's who you are."

"Apparently." Barr continued to stare down into the pot. "That's not a pun."

Connor concentrated on the limb, on each stroke of the saw. When there was something he didn't understand, something that bothered him, something that he thought he should avoid, his response had always been to *do* something. Anything. Work. The harder the work, the more physical the labor, the better. One night Marcia had asked him what he believed in. He thought she was talking about religion and God. He didn't know what to say, and he found himself talking about all the stuff he needed to do the next day. It made her laugh, and he apologized, saying something about not knowing what to think when it came to religion and stuff like that. And then she said, *It's all right. You just need to believe in something, and you believe in work, tomorrow's work.*

He'd cleared the smaller branches from the limb so that he could open the linen closet enough to pull out several towels and hand them down to Essi, who was now in the bathtub with Marcia. She had managed to get Marcia's blue jeans and panties off, and then she'd helped Marcia turn over until she was on all fours in the tub. Though they sometimes made love kneeling, it didn't seem right to look at her bare bottom and legs. Her jeans were rolled up, serving as a pillow between her knees and the porcelain tub. Essi had taken off her coat and draped it over Marcia's back. But he couldn't help taking glances: her entire body seemed positioned not to receive but to thrust, to expel, and Connor was afraid to look too long or too hard. It was indecent. It frightened him. It made him feel cowardly. He wanted to apologize, but he was afraid to do so because he knew Marcia would chastise him for it, saying, *What are you apologizing for?* And he wasn't sure—for the fact that she was pregnant and he might, just might, have something to do with it? Or because no matter how hard he worked, no matter what he did it was never adequate, never enough? Or was he sorry because he didn't even have the guts to look at her?

So he worked on the limb. She was right: he believed in work. He pushed and pulled on the bow saw, watching the blade descend through the limb, knowing what was going to happen—he could feel it with each stroke, which became increasingly difficult until the blade was stuck.

Marcia turned her head, curious. "Why'd you stop?"

"It bound up," he said. "I knew it would." He pulled on the saw but it wouldn't budge. "I can't even get it out."

Essi remained calm. Of course she did. He was convinced that nothing phased her, or if it did she had the poise not to reveal it. It was remarkable how small and compact she could make herself, squatting in the end of the bathtub. She had Marcia's bare ankles in her hands, somehow making Connor think of a wheelbarrow, and she said, "You'll figure something out, Connor, because we need to get that door open."

He ventured to look at Marcia again, who was gazing down at her hands braced against the bottom of the tub, breathing as Essi had instructed, taking in long, deep drafts of air and then exhaling slowly.

Though she didn't say anything, he thought he knew what she was thinking: *Work with me. Help us. Work with us on this.*

Connor gave the bow saw one more pull, but it wouldn't move. As he'd cut down through the limb the wood had pinched together, trapping the blade three inches down—not even halfway through the wood.

"I'll be back." He stepped up on the lid of the toilet and climbed onto the limb. He began to shinny out the window.

Barr leaned against the bathroom door. He could hear Essi speaking in a soft voice. He could hear Marcia breathing. He recognized that sound coming from her lungs, the same hoarse burst of air rising up through her core when she worked toward an orgasm.

He turned and looked at Del, standing by the stove, "Something's happening in there." Then he knocked on the door and said loudly, "What's going on?" They didn't answer. "Where's Connor? Why's he stopped sawing?"

"Ask her if they need the water and scissors?" Del said.

"You need this pot of water?" Barr hollered.

"Not yet," Essi said.

He stepped back from the door. "Good, 'cause I'm not delivering it. I'm not taking that pot outside." He went back to the counter, where he'd left the bottle of Irish whiskey. He put the revolver down on the counter and picked up the bottle and said, "No way."

As he took a pull on the bottle, he gazed up at the roof, where a cold blast of air caused the branches engulfing the beams to scrape against the ceiling. Twenty-five grand. Not a bad idea. Take the money and run. Some place warm, like Anna Maria Island, with the Gulf of Mexico on one side and Sarasota Bay on the other. Sun year round. Buildings overlooking the Gulf painted soft pastel colors. Cars that aren't rusted out from salted roads. No blizzards. A place where you don't need an overcoat to go outside, just a good pair of shades.

"What would I be leaving behind?" he said. "Even if I moved Connor out of the picture, you're talking diapers and breast milk and 3 a.m. feedings." He put the bottle of Irish on the counter. "Fuck that shit."

Del didn't say anything.

"Your plan," Barr said. "I like it. You give me the money, and I'm gone."

Del nodded.

There was a sound from the bathroom and they both looked at the door. Connor had begun sawing again, the blade driving back and forth through the limb, its pitch rising as the teeth moved down through wood.

"That's kinda sexy," Barr said. "Maybe Connor's good in the sack? I never asked her."

"Shut up," Del said.

"What?"

"Shut up."

Connor had yanked the axe out of the side of the house and climbed back in through the bathroom window. He stood the handle on end in the sink, and then wedged the axe head under the tree limb, pushing it toward the bow saw, until it relieved the pressure on the blade. Marcia was having contractions, and from her breathing, it was clear that they were coming closer together. When he resumed work on the limb, he tried not to look down at what was happening in the tub. His stomach had gone sour, and he could feel tremors in his shoulders and arms. He was afraid that he might throw up. When he was about halfway through the limb the blade began to tighten up again, so he stopped and moved back toward the sink, where he carefully tapped the axe head with the outside of his fist, hoping to nudge it a bit lower on the limb, without knocking it loose. It wouldn't budge. He gave the axe head a couple of firmer taps and it moved an inch, lifting the limb slightly. A few more taps, until the axe head was against a knot. He went back to the bow saw and found that the pressure was reduced enough that with each stroke the blade drove through the wood.

As he pushed and pulled he listened to Marcia's deep gasps—the sounds now coming from her were foreign, desperate, bestial, like nothing he'd ever heard before—and despite his need to concentrate on the bow saw his gaze occasionally drifted down to the tub. But he continued to work, putting his back and shoulders into it, hoping that the limb wouldn't bind up the blade again, because he needed the sawing, he needed the sound of steel tearing through wood. What was happening down there now was heaving, spastic movement, Marcia's body clenching and releasing in an effort to push this thing out, its head now appearing between her legs, and Essi's blood-slick hands not exactly pulling but coaxing—she might have been performing some magic trick where she would make something appear out of nothing.

Connor couldn't look away now. It was coming, with each push, each clench, Marcia was forcing it out of her—he could see its elongated skull. He stopped sawing and squatted down on the floor so he could pass an arm beneath the limb, and he placed his hand on the back of her neck, which was slick with sweat. As he began to massage the tense cords that rose out of her shoulders, a new sound came up out of her, a plaintiff wail as the baby surged from the center of her, arms and legs and feet glistening in the near dark, cradled in Essi's waiting hands.

When Barr aimed the revolver at him,

Del stood perfectly still. Barr's eyes: wide, stressed, exhausted. But mostly pissed off. Percocet combined with whiskey had clearly taken him well down the road to don't give a shit.

As soon as Del had told him to shut up he knew it was a mistake, knew that this was the last thing Barr needed to hear. You don't tell a guy like Barr to shut up without some response. In this case, the gun. Pointed at Del's chest. Not ten feet away. An easy target, despite his condition.

Perhaps this was the way out. The accumulation of pills in the medicine cabinet seemed too deliberate, too methodical. Too slow. How many times over the past few weeks had Del made his clumsy way into the bathroom and simply stared at the bottles on the shelf. The decision to do it always seemed to be derailed by a simple recognition: *it* would be too slow. After so much Irish, he could take the pills, all of them. He knew he could get them down with the aid of a glass of water, but it was the wait that put him off. After taking them, feeling them fill his stomach, he'd make his way back to the couch, or perhaps into the bedroom—somewhere to lie down. Lie down and wait. How long, he didn't know. Minutes? Five? Fifteen? A half hour? He assumed it was a matter of going to sleep, an irreversible descent into nothingness. Not unpleasant, really. Not like poison—no Shakespearean tremors and spasms, no death throes, in the final moments. Just dreamless sleep.

But it was those minutes, the waiting minutes that always gave him pause as he stood before the medicine cabinet. It would be the knowing that he had done *it* and that it was irreversible, the knowing that he had finally given in, that he was ready to give up, to quit. That's what stopped him. More than any fear of death, it was those minutes that he would have to endure, minutes during which he would have to accept his decision: knowing that he had quit, knowing that Liesl never would have done. Never.

So this, a revolver pointed at his chest, seemed what? An option. A viable option.

"What did you say?" Barr said.

"I said shut up."

Barr was looking him in the eye. Looking for something. Defiance? Fear? A plea, for reason? For mercy?

"Dumbo said that to me before he went in there to do his Eagle Scout thing."

"That's right, he did."

"And now you. People been telling me to shut up my whole life," Barr said. "Not anymore."

"Really?"

"Yeah, really." He wiggled his gun hand, a kind of testament. "See, I have this."

If anything his aim now was truer, the stout barrel of the .38 seemingly trained on the very center of Del's sternum. There would be pain, he assumed, a brief moment of searing pain. That was all. He'd probably be dead before he hit the floor. No waiting. *Bang, you're dead.* That fast.

The thing you can lose sight of is that death is painless. Dying, maybe not; but death takes you out of the pain for good. Best painkiller there is.

Del decided to say nothing. Let Barr make his own decision. He'd done this countless times with parolees, talked with them about the conditions laid out by the court, often why they weren't getting with the program. And at some point Del would just stop, just be silent. It usually made them nervous. Your parole officer was supposed to do the talking. But he'd be silent, and often he'd see them getting it: it was their decision. Now, there wasn't silence, though—there was the sound of the wind in the branches overhead. Connor's bow saw, he realized, had stopped working in the bathroom, had stopped measuring time in strokes, and that silence, that lack of sound, its gnawing rhythm that was a sound unto itself, had become an unsound. The sound coming from the bathroom was hideous but all too human—a huffing intake of breath, hoarse, desperate, and pleading. The baby must be coming now.

And in the sound and the unsound, he could tell that Barr was trying to decide, about the gun, about pulling the trigger.

Del would die listening to the wind overhead, while a new life was beginning. Think of it not as being dead but as being beyond time. *Timeless.*

A curiosity entered Barr's expression. Not confusion, not doubt. Curiosity. "You don't seem, you know, impressed."

"I'm not."

"Really?"

"Really. People who are about to die aren't easily impressed."

"Why's that?"

"Not sure. Maybe it's because they're waiting."

"Waiting?"

"Waiting. Not to die but to become timeless."

"Timeless."

"I've been waiting a long time, Barr. You want to end the wait, it's up to you."

Now Barr seemed at a loss. He glanced to his left at the bottle of Irish, as if consulting it, then back at Del. "You don't think I can do it?"

"I have no idea."

"It would give me satisfaction. And it would shut *you* the fuck up."

"True." Del eased his right hip against the kitchen counter. All this waiting, all this standing, it was making him tired. "And you'd be out twenty-five thousand."

"Ah. Still thinking. Wheels still turning."

"It's just that dead men don't make withdrawals."

Barr considered this a moment. "True. But pulling this trigger might be worth it."

"A twenty-five-thousand-dollar shot. Really?"

"Really."

Marcia felt the grip of Connor's hand ease on her neck, though he kept it there, kneading the muscles and tendons. *Trapezius. Rhomboid major and minor. Splenius capitis.* And the one impossible to pronounce: *sternocleidomastoid.* She wanted his hand to never stop, to never let go. She was exhausted. She wanted to sleep forever, sleep through the pain below, she wanted sleep that would allow her to drift away from the new and sudden void within her.

The porcelain was hard on her knees, so she lowered herself down until she was lying on her left side, curled up in the bathtub. Essi was holding the baby, matted hair, puffy eyes shut, and draped over her hands was the umbilical cord, pale blue in the dim light. "It's a girl," she whispered.

"I know. I think I've known that for some time now."

"Can you get on your back?" Essi asked.

Marcia became aware of the wool—there seemed to be two blankets in the tub—and with one hand she managed to spread it out on the bottom of the tub. Carefully she turned, lowering her shoulder until she could roll onto her back.

"Good," Essi said. "Now, raise that sweater and let's open your shirt."

Marcia understood. She pulled the sweater up, first allowing it to bunch under her chin, but then she lifted it over her head. It was difficult and awkward, but she got it off, and Connor helped her stuff it behind her head, a pillow protecting the back of her skull from the cold hardness of the porcelain. He undid the buttons of her flannel shirt, and then there was the thermal shirt, which he pulled up so she could get a hand behind her back and unfasten her bra. He looked mystified, maybe even horrified. She wanted to say something that would distract him, perhaps even make him laugh. The bra loosened, she pushed it out of the way, bearing her breasts. "Don't you remember," she said to him. "This is how it all got started?"

Staring at her breasts, he seemed alarmed, confused. Then a shy nod.

Essi leaned forward and laid the baby on Marcia's chest. She seemed pleased with the way things were going now. "As I recall," she whispered, "it helps if you rub your nipples—she'll smell the milk."

"It's not milk yet," Marcia said. "It takes a few days. I read about it once I started leaking." Marcia held the baby with one hand, her skin warm, so warm, while she rubbed her left nipple. "It's called colostrum."

Essi smiled. "I forgot, yes. It's been a while, you know." She unfolded the other blanket, the gray one, and covered Marcia and the baby with it, tucking it in under her. "We must keep you warm." She slid her arms under the blanket, and her hands gently kneaded Marcia's abdomen. "The rest needs to come out. They used to do this—it might help."

Marcia glanced over at Connor, who was afraid to ask. "No, not another baby," she said. "The placenta."

"And they're still connected," Essi said to him. "Once we get some hot water and the scissors in here, we'll deal with the umbilical cord. Can you get that medicine cabinet open?"

In order to reach the cabinet above the sink, Connor had to climb up on the tree limb. "What am I looking for?"

"Dental floss, and maybe some kind of alcohol, something antiseptic."

He opened the cabinet door and took out a bottle and a small white plastic case. "Dental floss?"

"I know," Essi said, deadpan, "and the baby isn't even teething yet." And then she laughed. "Before we cut the umbilical cord, we need to tie it off to reduce the bleeding."

"Oh." He leaned over the limb and placed the floss and alcohol on the edge of the tub.

"Parenting starts at ground zero," Marcia said.

Connor said to Essi, "She read that somewhere."

"Instinct sustained by moments of winging it," Essi said.

"Or the other way around, depending on the day?" Connor said.

"See, Marcia, he's getting it."

For a moment Marcia put her fingers on the top of the child's skull, its slick heat. The baby's head moved, and with her hand she guided her mouth to the left nipple.

There was a sound, a crack, above her, which caused her heart to bulge achingly in her rib cage. Connor, who had been leaning against the limb, looked uncertain, and then there was a second crack, louder than the first. The limb shifted beneath his weight, then it snapped, and he fell to the tile floor, the section of timber that had been lodged against the door coming down with him.

He didn't move. Sawdust swirled in the air like snow. Marcia covered the baby's head with the blanket.

Outside the door there was another crack, this one the report of a gun, she was sure of it. Essi stood up in the back of the tub. Behind the sounds, behind the tree and the gun there was a new sound coming from the kitchen. A constant, forceful sound.

"What just happened?" Marcia asked. "That was a gunshot."

Connor, lying on the floor, raised himself up on his arms until he could look over the rim of the tub at her. "I think so."

Still, the sound came from the kitchen, relentless, persistent.

Connor got up off the floor and yanked on the bathroom door—it opened perhaps a foot and a half before banging into the remaining section of the tree limb. He thought he could squeeze through sideways, but it was too tight. Essi was behind and above him, standing on the rim of the tub. It was incredibly close—the limb and tangle of branches, the angled door, Essi, the dark, and that smell—the baby smell.

"No, you stay here," Essi said.

Connor tugged on the knob, but the door wouldn't open any farther.

She took hold of his sleeve and pulled him back from the door. "No, Connor. They need you here, to help keep warm. You get in the tub with them." She slid by him and, turning sideways, managed to slip through the opening to the kitchen, pulling the door closed behind her.

Marcia was staring up at him, worried, perhaps even frightened. "What?"

"Them," he said. "Seems funny. She said *them.*"

Carefully, he stepped over the rim of the tub and eased himself down, the porcelain meeting his knees and hip, an unforgiving hardness. Marcia turned on her side, trying to make room, and he lay down beside her. He got his right arm beneath Marcia's head, and with his other arm he pulled her to him, the baby between them.

Yes, *them.*

He brushed damp hair away from Marcia's cheek, and then his hand sought the baby's head, the delicate soft spot there beneath his calloused fingers.

Del thought it sounded like some guy taking a leak on the floor.

The impact of the bullet had driven the pot off the stove and several feet down the counter toward the back door. An arc of water streamed out of a gaping hole near the bottom of the pot, forming a puddle on the pinewood floor.

His legs were weak and he needed to sit down.

The bathroom door opened slightly, something blocking it from opening wider. Essi, turned sideways, managed to sidle through and into the kitchen.

Barr also looked like he needed to sit down. He was staring at the revolver in his hand, seemingly incredulous that he'd actually pulled the trigger. "This isn't mine," his voice softened by disbelief, then he insisted, "This isn't *my* gun." He looked up, startled by Essi's appearance in the kitchen, as though she had materialized out of thin air.

"It's a girl," Essi said. "In case you're interested."

She was angry, but Barr was too distracted to notice as he inspected the gun in his hand.

Before the hip surgery, Del might have rushed Barr, knocked him down, and taken the revolver out of his hand. But he knew he couldn't move quickly enough.

Barr nodded toward the stream of water spreading across the floor. "We'll need to boil more water, I guess." He seemed to find this funny.

It was Essi who moved. She walked over to Barr, and somehow Del knew what was going to happen next. He knew by the way she moved—not hurried, but determined, purposeful. Del thought he should do something to stop her, to intervene, but it was too late. Essi raised her arm and slapped Barr's face. It caused Barr to take a step backward, and he almost lost his balance until he grabbed the counter with his free hand. He didn't drop the revolver. Del expected him to do something with it. But he didn't. Barr just stood there, leaning on the counter, looking spaced out in a sleepy kind of way, and then his face gathered around an annoyance: the baby had begun to cry in the bathroom.

And then a phone rang.

There were streaks in Barr's vision, white shooting streaks, and the left side of his face, which was already swollen, throbbed from Essi's slap. His balance was an issue and he kept his free hand on the counter, listening to the wind overhead, to the water pouring out on the kitchen floor, to the phone ringing, to the wailing baby. "What is that kid, all lungs?"

Essi was staring fiercely up at him. Couldn't she hear him? Maybe not with all this racket. Or maybe he didn't speak out loud. Maybe he just thought he did. So he said to her: "First thing you admire in a baby is its lungs."

He expected her to slap him again. But instead she said, "Aren't you going to answer it?"

"What?"

"The phone. It's ringing."

So it was. He put the gun down on the counter, reached into his right-hand coat pocket, and removed a phone. His phone. It wasn't ringing, and the ringing continued—in his other pocket. With his left hand he removed the other phone, Marcia's phone, which was ringing, sounding like some old telephone from back before there were cell phones, back when the phone was this heavy object that was connected to a wall outlet by a cord. Barr wondered why it had all come to this. Too many phones. Too many guns. Apparently.

"Answer it," Essi said.

Barr looked down at the phone's screen, which read *Lindy PT Dispatch*. He felt he should know who Lindy was, but it wasn't coming to him. "It's somebody named Lindy."

"What matters is the phone's working," Essi said. "Answer it and tell Lindy that we need help out here."

Barr nodded as he stared down at the phone. He understood her point. But this would complicate things, wouldn't it? He was no longer sure.

"If you won't answer the phone, I will," Essi said.

Barr picked up the gun from the counter. He waved it with a limp wrist, indicating that she needed to back away from him. She hesitated but then took a step back, staring at him with hard, glossy eyes. "All right, just don't, you know, push me," he whispered as he pressed the button on the screen and raised the phone to his ear. "Yeah?"

"I'm trying to reach Marcia." He recognized her voice: Lindy. It was one of those matter-of-fact, no-nonsense voices, the perfect voice for a woman who worked as a phone dispatcher.

"So am I," he said.

There was a pause, and then Lindy said, "Did I speak with you earlier?"

"I don't know, did you?"

"Maybe not. Where are you?"

"Here."

"Where's *here*?"

"I don't know exactly."

"Have you seen Marcia?"

"Yes."

"Where is she?"

"In the bathroom."

"I need to talk to her." This Lindy sounded like she was ready to slap him, too.

"That's not possible at the moment."

"Why not? Why isn't that possible?"

"Don't get so pissy."

"*What?* Why can't I talk to Marcia?"

"She's just had a baby."

"Oh, Christ."

"No, it's a girl."

"Who *is* this?"

"Call me Joe, as in Joseph."

Essi cocked her head. He tried to make a face to indicate that he was just kidding, but she wasn't buying. She and Lindy, they both needed to lighten up.

"It's late, very late," he said into the phone. "You're still at work, Lindy?"

"It's so late you might say it's early. I work from home—"

"That's convenient."

"Don't interrupt me."

"*Sor*ry."

"So late my day's already begun. I tried to reach Marcia several times last night and finally crapped out. When I got up I thought I'd find a message from her, but nothing. But then I found myself wondering why she didn't let me know she got home all right. It's not like her."

"I know what you mean," Barr said.

Lindy didn't speak, long enough that he wondered if they had been cut off.

"So you're with her." Her voice sounded cautious now. "Is she all right?"

"She's fine. The kid's got a great pair of lungs, so I guess everything's normal."

"*That's* what I hear—the baby."

"We're fine. The baby, the mother, everybody's *fine*."

Again, Lindy didn't speak for a long moment, and Essi and Del were staring at him. This was getting to be too much. It was all getting away from him. Everybody needed to lighten the fuck up. Yet he was the one with the gun. He looked at the gun in his other hand. He was sure now. "It's not mine," he said.

"The baby?" Lindy said.

"No," Barr said. "The gun."

"What gun?"

"Never mind. Yes, the baby's not mine. I mean, we don't really know for sure."

Lindy's silence now gave Barr the feeling that she could see right through the phone connection, that she knew the score. Essi and Del, they were in on it, too. The water had drained out of the pot, which was a relief. "And we need another pot," he said by way of ending the conversation. "We need to boil more water."

"*Wait*," Lindy said.

"As I said, Marcia's fine," he said. "I'll tell her you called."

Barr pressed the screen, ending the call. The phone began to ring almost immediately, and he pressed the off button until the screen went dark.

––––––––––––

Marcia might have been asleep when Connor said, "Are you warm enough?"

"I'm fine."

His arms encircled her and the baby, and his hands kneaded her shoulders. He had arranged the blankets about her so that she felt as though she were in a cocoon—a cocoon in an egg, the shell being the curvature of the bathtub.

"Did you hear that?"

"What?" she asked.

"The phone. It rang. That means we're connected, and maybe someone will come out here so we can get you into town."

"I'm fine here." She rested her chin on the top of the baby's skull. It was warm. Marcia thought she could sleep forever. "I've been thinking about names for her."

"What have you come up with?"

"Nothing that seems to fit yet. You have any ideas?" When he didn't speak, she opened her eyes and looked at him. He was tearing up, and she realized she'd never seen him cry. "I don't think her name should be anything, you know, weird or strange, nothing that she'll have to defend in the schoolyard." As she watched his eyes brim over, she said, "You are pathetic."

He nodded. "All these months, I've really only thought of her as your baby. I mean, I—we—don't even know if she's mine. But that doesn't matter, I've told you that."

"Then you can start by helping me with her name. I feel like she has one already, and we just need to find it." Despite his tears, he found this funny. Or maybe he was just embarrassed. "I can see you as her father. You'll be tender and soon she'll be Daddy's little girl. At times you won't know what to do—neither of us will—so we'll just have to figure it out as we go."

"I don't know. I guess I've never really thought that far ahead." He lowered his face until he could kiss the back of the baby's head. "Guess I'd better start." He kept his nose pressed against her skull. "She's going to have your hair, don't you think?" As he glanced up toward the door, he said, "If I can get that opened more, we could get you out by the fireplace. It'll be warmer. Want to give it a try?"

"You go ahead, and ask Essi to come back in here. I'm going to need some help first."

Del had gotten another pot from the cabinet, filled it with water, and put it on the stove when Connor shoved the bathroom door open just enough that he could slide out into the kitchen. The way Barr stared at Connor he seemed to be trying to recall where he had seen him before, which caused Del to glance at Essi. She saw it, too. Barr was nearing a point, a tipping point: between the whiskey and the pills, he was so gone he might just pass out. Or he might do something desperate, something rash. Something wounded-animal unpredictable. He faced Connor, not quite pointing the revolver at him. He seemed to be trying to identify its function and purpose.

"So, Papa," Barr said, "congratulations are in order. What, no cee-gar?"

Connor decided to ignore Barr. Looking at Essi, he said, "She wants to come out and be near the fire, but she needs your help in there first."

"All right." Essi went to the stove and, using a dish towel, removed a pair of scissors from the empty pot on the stove. She went to the bathroom door and slipped inside.

Barr seemed to be perturbed. He stared at the revolver in his hand as though it held the key to the riddle. "So whose is this?"

"What do you mean?" Connor said.

"This isn't mine."

Connor looked at Del, who just shook his head. Turning back to Barr, he said, "It must be."

"Nope, I don't think so." He considered Connor for a moment. "It's not yours, is it?"

"No."

"Well," Barr said, "It's not mine. He raised his arm and aimed the gun at Connor. "You don't have mine, do you?"

"Not me," Connor said.

Barr swung the gun and his attention to Del, standing by the pot of water heating on the stove. Del only shook his head. When Barr didn't appear to be convinced, Del said, "It doesn't belong to me."

"No chain saw, no gun." Barr took a long moment, the barrel of the revolver again aimed at Del's chest. "I don't believe you."

"I don't own a handgun," Del said.

"Well, it's not mine," Barr said and he glanced at the floor, strewn with branches and bark. "So mine must be around here somewhere."

There was a sound from the bathroom. Barr looked toward the door, and then slowly lowered the revolver to his side.

Essi leaned out through the open door and said to Del, "We could use that hot water now."

Del moved slowly, carrying the pot by its handles to the bathroom door, where he gave it to Essi. After she took a step backward, she said, "If you'd just," and he pulled the door closed.

———————————

Del and Connor and Barr stood in the kitchen. No one moved, no one spoke. They didn't exactly look at each other. They could hear two women in the bathroom, indistinct murmurings, punctuated by the sound of water sloshing and dripping. Once there was the faintest laughter, conspiratorial and joyous, and the baby, which had stopped howling, gave off playful sounds, gurgles, yelps, and an occasional shriek.

———————————

After Essi had helped Marcia deal with the placenta, they tied off the umbilical cord with dental floss and cut it with the scissors. Then they both washed with hot water from the pot, using several towels.

"I never thought I'd feel clean again," Marcia said. "And I have to get out of this bathroom."

Slowly, she got to her feet and stepped out of the tub. The baby was in her arms, nearly lost in the blanket that covered her shoulders. She managed to squeeze between the door and the jamb, and when she stepped into the kitchen Barr stared at her in disbelief. As she walked toward the fireplace she ignored him, working her way around the counter, stepping over branches, until she could stand in front of the wood-strewn couch. The fire was low, mostly embers, but it gave off heat. She knew that Barr had turned, that he was leaning on the counter staring at her. She did not look away from the fire.

Essi came into the living room. She cleared brush and bark off the couch and put them in the fireplace, where the pine needles hissed and crackled. "Here," she said as she brushed the cushions with her hands. "Sit. Or would you rather lie down?"

Marcia eased herself down on the couch. "After the tub, this is fine. Thanks." She continued to stare at the fire as Barr came toward her. He held his gun at his side, and he sat down on the wood block facing her. She refused to return his stare. "You're blocking the heat," she said.

After a moment, he slid to his right, and she could feel the heat coming off the fire, which Essi was building with more logs from the pile next to the fireplace.

"Can I see her?" Barr asked. His voice was slow, the result of all the pills and whiskey. She knew that when he got this way, he could either fall asleep suddenly, or he'd resist it and do something, anything to keep awake. She ventured a look at him, his damaged eyes. "Can I see her face?"

Marcia took hold of the blanket where it lay against her throat and drew it down, revealing the baby's scalp, its suggestion of dark hair. The child didn't weigh more than five or six pounds, Marcia guessed, and the moving, struggling mass of her already felt familiar. Carefully, she turned the baby until Barr could see her face.

Ordinarily, he maintained expressions that registered various degrees of indifference. It was what had drawn her to him at first. He was detached, untouchable. It wasn't just being cool. With Barr, it was an act of survival. Marcia studied his face. His lower lip hung open slightly. She couldn't read his eyes. Assessing, yes. But they were admitting something she'd not seen in him before. There was, she believed, uncertainty and even fear. For a moment she thought he might actually tear up.

"Nope," he said abruptly. "Definitely not mine."

Her suspicions that he was the father seemed to have dissolved since giving birth. Now it just didn't seem to matter. "No, she's not," she said. As if to confirm the fact, she covered the baby's head with the blanket, denying him a second opinion. "What was that sound?" she asked.

"What sound?" A kind of quiet terror seemed to enlarge his pupils.

"Didn't I hear a phone ring?"

In the kitchen, Del shuffled over to the counter. "You did." He placed his free hand on the counter for support. "Show her," he said to Barr. "Show her both phones."

Barr closed his eyes a moment and shook his head in disbelief as if to say, *It's come to this?* But then he stared at her, some of the familiar cold steel returning to his eyes, as he put the gun down next to him on the block of wood. He reached into his coat pockets and produced two cell phones. Hers was in his left hand.

"Which one rang?" she asked, but she didn't wait. She knew. "It was Lindy. Lindy would wonder why she hadn't heard from me." She reached out for the phone, but he drew his arm back. "Call her back."

"Why?"

"We've got to get someone out here."

"Do we?"

"Give me the phone. Barr. Give me. The phone."

There was a moment of indecision. He was struggling with it, she could tell, but then he made up his mind, and she knew what he was going to do before he did it because with Barr it was better to make the wrong decision than no decision at all. Without looking, he tossed her phone over his shoulder, and it landed in the fireplace.

Connor went for it. He rushed to the fireplace and fell to his knees before the crackling logs, almost in a posture of worship. Marcia thought he was going to thrust his hand into the flames, and there was a state of suspension among the others, suggesting that they thought so, too. But she knew Connor, knew what he was capable of; she knew that when he set himself to a task, to a job, his attention became riveted, his focus unwavering. As he knelt and bent toward the burning logs, his back held the same tension you see when a dog digs a hole in the ground. Though he was wearing a sweatshirt, Connor's musculature was still evident. She loved his back. She loved to watch it as he sat up on the edge of the bed and bent over to pick up a boot or a sock. She had massaged countless backs, and she knew every muscle group, their purpose and function. She understood the complexity of performing the simplest motion. Deltoid, trapezius, latissimus dorsi, levator scapulae, teres major and minor, gluteus maximus—muscles sounding like the names of Roman emperors, like clusters of celestial bodies, like gods from Greek mythology. Muscles that worked together to accomplish the task, and Connor's had been honed and chiseled from routine exertion. It was a back that was used. And now he leaned forward and stretched his arm toward the flames, seemingly unaware of the heat.

"Hey, Dumbo," Barr said. He had turned on the wood block coffee table to marvel at some valiant but hopeless enterprise and he seemed faintly amused. "You want to let it go."

Connor tilted his head, annoyed at the distraction, but then he reconsidered the fire and sat back on his haunches. Even in a state of rest, his shoulders and back seemed flexed, prepared to uncoil. Extending his right arm to the floor, he picked up a stick, and he began prodding the logs.

"Hello?" Barr said, his voice now incredulous and a tad concerned.

Connor ignored him. Rather, he didn't seem to hear him. There was only the phone, the fire. He poked at the logs and with remarkable delicacy managed to separate the phone from the embers. Carefully, he drew the phone out to the front of the fireplace. It was smoking.

"All right, Dumbo," Barr said. "Leave it be."

Connor continued to pull the phone out of the fire with the stick, so Barr extended his arm and tapped him on the right side of the head with the muzzle of the pistol. Once, then twice.

When Barr tapped the side

of Connor's skull with the revolver the second time, Del thought he heard something outside, but then it happened very swiftly: with instinct, animal instinct, Connor turned and swung his arm back until the stick in his hand struck Barr in the ribs beneath his extended arm. Maybe it was intentional, maybe it was simply the impact of the blow to his ribs, but the gun went off, and Connor fell on the floor, his right shoulder within inches of the burning logs.

The report affected Del's hearing, so Marcia's scream and the baby's crying seemed muffled. Essi went to Connor and, falling to her knees, pulled him back from the fire. Barr, hunched over on the coffee table, gasped for air as he clutched at his rib cage. Essi, still kneeling, put her hands to her mouth, and Del saw it: a pool of blood, black as tar in the firelight, spreading out from beneath Connor's head, channeling in the gaps between the hearth bricks. On the couch, Marcia had rolled on her side, holding the baby to her chest. She might have been moaning, but

Del couldn't be sure because of his hearing—it could have been the wind outside, he just wasn't sure. At least the baby was only whimpering now. Barr said something, his voice husky, out of breath. He said it again, and Del thought it was, *This isn't my fault.*

And there were other sounds, new sounds that Del couldn't sort out. They seemed to be coming from beyond the front door, from out on the porch. It wasn't just the wind in the trees; it sounded as though the damaged porch was being moved, shifted by some mysterious force—and then the door was shoved open, causing snow to swirl into the room. Through these strangely festive, pointillist wind patterns Del first saw a gloved hand on the door latch, and then a man stepped into the room. A wavering yellow light came from outside, beyond the sagging porch roof. Del thought it had to be the rotating light on a truck with a snowplow, most likely, and this light, coupled with the glow from the fireplace, gave the man both an ethereal and monstrous bearing. He was well over six feet, with broad shoulders and a substantial girth. Even his untrimmed gray beard was massive. He wore a snowsuit and a Day-Glo orange vest trimmed with white reflector strips that seemed to flash strobe-like in the flickering light.

After closing the door, he studied the devastated room and the branches entwined in the beams. Nodding, he said, "I like what you've done with the place."

"Paavo." Del couldn't remember his last name—something Finnish, certainly. Everyone just referred to him as Paavo. He lived farther out. Did odd jobs, hauled stuff in his pickup, ran a backhoe, and plowed the winter long. Del remembered something years ago about a run-in with the law over hunting out of season, or maybe it was poaching on the private reserve in the Huron Mountain Club.

Paavo stepped over and around branches until he stood behind the sofa. He looked at Marcia and the baby, then at the pool of blood on the hearth. "The tree do that to him?"

"No," Barr said, lifting the gun off his thigh. "This did."

"Ah. That's what I heard." Completely unfazed. "So we've got issues here." His gaze could pass for that of an idiot's, or a savant's. "He dead?"

"No," Essi said. As if to confirm her assessment, Connor moved his legs slightly. She leaned down close to his head. "It hard to tell but he seems to have lost a good portion of his ear."

"I hear that can be painful." Paavo smiled as his eyes, lit by the fire, settled on Barr. He appeared disappointed that no one laughed at his joke. "Really, was that necessary?"

"Fuck you," Barr said.

"So," Paavo said. "It's like that."

"You don't know anything."

"Agreed," Paavo said.

"You got a truck out there?"

"I thought so. But I don't know anything, so I'm not sure."

"Okay," Barr said.

"Okay, what?" Paavo said.

"Okay, asshole, my ride's here."

"Just you?" Paavo asked.

Barr only stared at him.

"Where am I taking you?"

"We're going to the bank." Barr glanced at Del and nodded. "Me and him."

"Now?" Paavo said. "It's six-something in the morning. Still dark out. Nothing'll be open yet." He waited and, when Barr didn't respond, said, "But if you want to make a deposit they got an all-night drop box."

"A fucking comedian," Barr said. "How 'bout I make a lead deposit between your ears?"

Connor turned on his side, his hands covered in horrific slickness, warm blood, his blood. More alarming was the absence of sound, his head wrapped in a dense, eerie muteness except for the slightest murmur in his left ear. It felt as though his skull had been ripped open on the right side and ice was being injected directly into his brain.

Looking toward the sofa, he saw Marcia clutching the baby and blanket to her chest. Above and behind them—perpendicular, because Connor was lying on the floor—stood an enormous man with a gray rodent clutching the lower portion of his face. His mouth moved, he seemed to be speaking to Barr, but Connor couldn't hear what he was saying.

The pain made Connor nauseous. Throwing up might help. Dogs ate grass to make themselves vomit, and he had this notion that he should eat grass, though there was nothing but branches and twigs strewn on the floor. He kept his eyes on the man in the snowsuit, trying to understand how he got here. Connor didn't know what was happening, what had happened. Fragments. Barr calling him Dumbo. The bow saw cutting through the tree limb, showering Marcia in the bathtub with sawdust. The baby coming out amid the slimy mess. He remembered cuddling with them, the heat of the baby's skull against his lips, and the smell of birth in the damp hair matted against Marcia's forehead. His child, their child? He was a father. Maybe? Did it matter?

He rolled onto his back and stared up at the branches that were entangled in the roof rafters. Essi leaned over him, and though her face was close to his and her lips moved, he had no idea what she was saying. With Essi it didn't matter. He never really understood her anyway, but in another way he did, even if the words didn't make sense. So he closed his eyes and felt as though he were falling backward off of some great height, a cliff or out of a tree, and he realized that he had a new appreciation for trees, for falling trees, for falling, and the nausea now forced everything to burn as it worked its way up his throat to the back of his mouth. He opened his eyes, which helped the nausea, but the pain was now a spike driving down into his neck and forcing his eyeballs out of his head.

Essi stopped speaking, and she seemed in awe. Yet there was a kindness in her face, assuring him that this pain, this incredible hurt, would soon disappear completely, as though it had never existed. She seemed to be saying, *It's all right, just let go.* As he closed his eyes, he believed her. The important thing now, the only thing now, was to let go.

———————————

The gunshot had drawn Barr out of a don't-give-a-shit haze. Plus, this jovial monstrosity walks in the door. *Paavo.* Day-Glo stripes and jokes about night bank deposits.

Looking at Connor, Paavo said, "Gunshot?"

Reluctantly, Barr turned on the coffee table to look toward the fireplace. His ribs were killing him. First, Connor's boots on Presque Isle and now this. The slightest movement caused a stabbing pain in his right side.

"Yes." Essi bent down until her face was within inches of Connor's, like she was about to kiss him. "He's alive. It's his ear."

"You mind?" Paavo was speaking to Barr, apparently. He made a gesture with his head, requesting permission.

"Mind, what?"

"If I take a look at him. Up close." When Barr didn't answer immediately, he said, "I was a medic in the army. Two tours in Nam. Gunshot wounds were my bread and butter, my métier."

"Your métier. Right. I'll bet you've read Dostoyevsky, too."

Paavo cocked his head, a dog getting a mixed signal from his master. "Sure." Sounding unsure. "Or was it Tolstoy? Long time ago."

"Well," Barr said. "Nice to see somebody here has some manners and, you know, asks me," Barr said. "By all means. Just what we need here, a medicine man."

Paavo made his way around the sofa and lowered his girth carefully until he was kneeling beside Connor. He placed his stout fingers on the side of Connor's neck. "Heartbeat is good," he said to Essi. "We have to stop the bleeding. Towels, we'll need towels—something to wrap his head in."

"Bedsheets," Essi said as she got to her feet and went into the kitchen, stepping over tree debris. Del shuffled after her into the bedroom.

"Jesus," Barr said, "We've already done the boil water for the birth routine."

Paavo looked past Barr at Marcia, lying on the sofa. "The baby, you just had it? Here?"

"Yes," she said, glancing up at the branches overhead. "Not here. In the bathroom."

Now something like blissful surprise registered on Paavo's face. "Boy or girl?"

"Girl."

"You have a name yet?"

"Not yet."

"Give it time. It'll come to you." Paavo's voice was gentle, almost cooing.

Barr raised his free hand and clutched his forehead. "Maybe I shot the wrong guy."

———

In the bedroom, Essi whispered, "What's this about going to the bank?"

Del was reaching up to the closet shelf, pulling down bedsheets and towels. "I made him an offer earlier. I would give him enough money to get out of here and start elsewhere. He didn't seem interested, but now maybe he realizes he needs an exit strategy."

In the near dark he could barely see her face, but he knew what she was thinking: now that he's shot Connor, he couldn't just walk away from all this. "I know," Del said. "Maybe it's too late for an exit strategy."

"Connor's got to make it. That girl and the baby would be better off. You should have seen him sawing away at that tree." She took one of the bedsheets and a couple of towels and led him out to the kitchen. Using her hands and teeth she began tearing a bedsheet into long, foot-wide strips. "There are no exit strategies." Her voice was muffled because she had the sheet in her mouth. "Just exits."

———

Marcia had been watching Paavo and Essi work on Connor. They used towels, which at first became soaked with blood quickly. But eventually—Del had been asked to get more towels—they managed to hold a folded towel in place and there was little sign of blood. Then, using a long strip of bedsheet, they wrapped his head, Essi gently lifting his skull each time Paavo made a pass around the back. When they were finished, Connor lay still, most of his face concealed in bedsheet and the wad of folded towel strapped to the right side of his head.

While Marcia observed this improvised procedure, the baby was insistent, clutching at her breasts as though she were hiding something in there, as though she knew something Marcia needed to understand. She made little gurgling, sucking sounds, and at one point, Marcia pressed her pinky against the child's soft, moist mouth, and immediately her fingertip was drawn in with desperate urgency. She shifted her weight on the sofa and, rearranging the blanket and clothes, freed her left breast.

Barr watched, fascinated. Her nipples would never be the same, now that they had arrived at this new purpose, and she was determined to deny him a peak. He seemed to enjoy this, a little game he thought they were playing. When the baby's warm mouth consumed her nipple, Marcia winced, and then she stared at Barr, hard, until he finally turned his head away. Game over.

"They can get cracked and chaffed," Paavo said. "But there are ointments that'll help. And there's the danger of infection or Raynaud's syndrome."

"That a fact?" Barr said. "You're a wet nurse, too?"

As Paavo got to his feet, he had to grasp some of the chimney stones to hoist himself up. "I am a registered nurse," he said, out of breath, "but I haven't worked the floors in years, since I went on disability. Arthritis, curvature of the spine, bad feet, you name it." As if to prove his point, he hobbled around the coffee table and lowered himself onto the sofa's armrest by Marcia's feet. "How's she doing?"

"She's hungry," Marcia said.

"The best remedy is tea bags," Paavo said.

"Tea bags?" Barr said.

"After they've been used, while they're still warm, place them on your nipples."

"While they're still warm," Barr said. "You learned this in nursing school?"

"No, my mother had eight kids. She drank tea all the time."

"Lipton?" Barr said in utter defeat. "Or Tetley?"

"Red Rose."

"Ah."

Marcia closed her eyes. She wanted to block it all out. She wanted to absorb the heat coming from the fire, to store it so she would radiate warmth. She wanted only to feel this new sensation, this moist mouth sucking on her engorged nipple. The baby's cheeks and forehead were hot and clammy against her breast, her tiny fingers prodding its swollen fullness, and it wasn't pain so much as a sweet ache, and she wanted this colostrum to turn to milk immediately, wanted her breasts to fill up like balloons, grow lighter, lighter than air, causing her to levitate from this sofa, rising up through the branches and rent shingles and into the winter night's sky, her newborn daughter, attached to her nipple, escaping with her, leaving all that is fearsome and vile on the frozen earth below.

Darkness.

Darkness, worse than the silence. Connor might have passed out, might have slept. He might have slipped into a state of exhaustion, which led to this floating sensation. All was darkness and silence, as familiar and foreign as emersion in a watery womb. The pain in his head was not receding so much as drifting away, becoming distant, and when it was gone he would be dead. The baby, *their* baby—he had come to believe this was so, had to believe it—had been immersed in Marcia's womb, growing toward life. She emerged into light, into sound, into cold. The first thing she knew of this world was pain. The last thing he would know was pain. A rebirth, born again. There was no effort, no work. All his life, it seemed, he had worked. His hands, his arms, his back, every day there was effort and release, the given of work. Now he couldn't see, couldn't hear, his body inert, a vessel passing from here to there. When you pause you wonder where *there* is, and you simply don't know, you can't know. People who believe they know are either fools, or they are lying and untrustworthy. Even when he was a boy, attending mass on Sundays, Connor couldn't really pay attention to descriptions of heaven and hell and purgatory and that place where unbaptized babies go, limbo. How can anyone know this? Who has been there? Who has charted the life beyond this life? Jesus Christ? He may have been the Son of God, he may have died for our sins, but did he draw a map and say, *This is heaven and this is hell?* Essi was right: the only thing that is certain is the storm. If he was dying, at least he would escape the storm.

Barr didn't catch that. "What?"

Paavo had this look of saintly patience. "I said, we need to get him to the hospital."

Barr considered the man, the bulk of him. It might take several bullets to drop him, stop him clean. Barr tipped the bottle up to his mouth and drank the last of the Irish. "He's not bleeding now?"

"We've slowed it," Paavo said. "His ear's pretty much gone. He's going to require medical attention. The sooner the better. And she and the baby should see a doctor, too."

Marcia lay on the sofa, her eyes closed. She wasn't sleeping, Barr knew, she was enduring. She was good at endurance, had it down cold. She could block it all out while the baby, wrapped in a heap of blanket, sucked away.

Barr placed the empty bottle on the floor. "So, we all drive to Marquette in your truck?"

"We can all fit," Paavo said. "King cab."

"Nice."

Del said, "We get them to the hospital, and then when the bank opens up—"

"We'll what?" Barr said. "We'll all go up to the teller while you make a withdrawal? And the whole time, I'll just keep this gun—wherever this one came from—in hand? I don't think that would go down too well at the bank. They might think it was, you know, a robbery, a freaking heist."

Del leaned a shoulder against the chimney stones. "All right. What do you propose?"

"Propose? I propose we find a liquor store first." Barr laughed, but no one else did.

He got up off the coffee table and walked around behind the sofa, where he could take them all in. Marcia on the sofa and Paavo on the armrest. Essi sitting on the floor next to Dumbo. Del standing next to Essi, leaning against the chimney. A family portrait, almost.

What did Del call it? An exit strategy. He needed an exit strategy. How could he get the money and get out of town? On the road south through new snow. On the road to where? In what? He went to the window by the front door and drew back the curtain. Paavo's pickup was still running, a yellow light rotating on the roof. It had a plow, a cap over the bed, and, yes, a king fucking cab.

"She in good shape?"

"Had her for years," Paavo said. "Some rocker panel rust, but runs fine."

"You couldn't really get all of us in that thing."

"It'd be cozy."

Barr dropped the curtain. "So we all drive in to Marquette, a family outing." He walked back to the sofa. Marcia was now lying on her back, staring up at him. The baby's skull rested under her chin. Like it belonged there. "This all started with you," he said. She turned her head away, closing her eyes. "That's right," he said. "Endure. Endure all of this. Do it for your kid."

Without opening her eyes, Marcia said, "Shut up, Barr. Just shut up."

He grinned at the rest of them, as if to say, *See what I've had to put up with?* "I have another idea. An exit strategy. Why don't Del and I take the truck into town and go to the bank."

"You heard Paavo," Essi said. "Connor needs a doctor, and Marcia and the baby need—"

Barr raised his hand and, to his surprise, she shut up. He was suddenly very tired, exhausted. What he needed was a half hour lie down where he could close his eyes and didn't have to deal with this shit. What he needed was another bottle of Irish. What he needed to get out of here was a hostage. That was how desperate it had become, and that was not where he wanted things to go. But what do you do? When he'd break into a house, he'd instinctively look for alternative exits. This one didn't have enough doors and windows.

"Need? *Need?*" he said to Essi. "You got to realize something. Earlier today I was left for dead by that guy lying next to you, and I'm going to give two shits about his ear? About whether he makes it or not? Did *he*, when he left me lying in the snow?" Glancing down at Marcia, he added, "Did *she*, when she ran off while Dumbo there tried to finish the job? What you have to understand is we are not having a conversation here. We are not talking about everyone's *needs*. We're not weighing our options and taking a vote." This was better. Pissed off was better. He could see it in their eyes, all of them alert, wary. "This isn't a question of the common good. This is about one thing: me getting out. You understand what I'm saying? Me, out."

No one spoke. No one moved.

"Good," he said. "I have your attention, and we are all on the same page, as passive-aggressive fuckers like to say. Now here it is, the revised forecast. You—" he nodded at Del—"are going with me, and she and her tit-sucking offspring are coming along."

They still didn't move, as though they hadn't heard a thing he'd said.

"*Now!*" he shouted.

As Del took his overcoat down from the peg by the front door, he looked at Barr's leather jacket and said, "I got an extra overcoat here. You want it?"

This seemed to worry Barr. With his free hand, he pulled the curtain back from the front window and stared outside. He looked exhausted but edgy, his eyes straining to keep track of everything all at once. Del suspected he was more unpredictable, more dangerous than he'd been since he'd come into the house.

"It's just that it's cold out there," Del said.

Releasing the curtain, Barr said, "The truck's heated." Louder, he said, "Right?"

Paavo said, "Heater works fine, yes."

"Your concern for me is touching," Barr said. "But fuck the cold."

Essi held the baby in the blanket while Marcia pulled on her boots, and then she helped her into her coat.

"All right, lead the way," Barr said. "You're driving, and she and the kid in back."

Essi came over and held Del's cane while he pulled on his gloves and wool hat. After he took the cane from her, she leaned into him, placing her arms around his waist. She held him for a moment, and then, stepping back offered him a smile, something brave.

"You'll be fine here," Del said.

Paavo got up off the arm of the sofa, and for a moment he looked confused, perhaps angry, as though he'd just realized that he was being left behind. But he held his ground and said, "It's in four-wheel drive. Just take it slow."

Del looked at Essi and her eyes agreed: no goodbyes. "There's plenty of firewood," he said to her. "Make something to eat. There's plenty of soup."

Heat. The air in the cab of Paavo's truck felt like it was ninety degrees and smelled faintly of motor oil. Once she was settled in the cramped back seat, Marcia could feel the tension begin to release in her shoulders and back. Remarkably, the baby had slept during the short, difficult walk from the damaged porch to the truck. The snow was at least two feet deep, and a drift at the bottom of the steps was deeper. She followed the trough Del made in the snow, leaning on his cane.

When he worked the clutch, Del winced—Marcia knew it was because of his hip—but the truck began to creep forward, the plow rumbling as it pushed snow aside. The yellow light on the roof created a strobe effect on the snow as they descended the driveway. He turned on to the road, following the path that the truck had made coming from Marquette. In the headlight beams the snow was horizontal, an absurd playful galaxy of reflected light.

"What are you thinking?" Del asked when he had the truck in third gear. "Drop Marcia at the hospital and then we go to the bank?"

Barr was seated sideways with his right shoulder wedged against the door so he could see both Del and Marcia. "What am I thinking? What are *you* thinking? You thinking I'm that stupid?"

"Not at all."

"Un-huh. Just drop her off at the hospital, where she can call the police and tell them we're on the way to the bank. No. No, she's going with me. She and the baby."

Marcia was afraid of this. She knew he wasn't going to just let her go, just walk away from her and the baby. She wanted to plead, even beg, but she knew that would only make him more resolute. "The three of us," she said.

"Just one happy family." His eyes were shadows, black holes, while his nose and jawline were faintly illuminated by the dashboard lights. "We used to talk about getting out of here, remember? Putting the U.P. and these endless winters behind us." His smile was more a leer, and there was the slightest slur in his voice. "Del's going to make that all possible."

"And what about him?" she asked. "He's going to come along, too."

"That would be a bit crowded. Let's not worry about Del."

Better to move away from it for the time being. No fear, no panic. "So. We get this money—what, twenty-five thousand?—and then we keep going. In this? In Paavo's snowplow?"

For a moment, Barr considered the plow, grinding down the center of the road, heaping a massive wall of snow along his side the truck. "Can you think of a better way to get out of here?"

"You know that soon the police will be looking for you, for this truck. Maybe not till later today or even tomorrow, but soon."

"Marcia, what you lack is imagination. You have to adapt as things change. The truck is just a step, the first step."

"In other words, you don't have a plan," she said. "What did you call it, an exit strategy?"

"Plan?" He laughed briefly, as though this was the stupidest thing he'd ever heard.

"All right," she said. "Twenty-five thousand is a lot of money. It can get you a long way." She studied the side of Del's face for a moment. He was concentrating on the road, on keeping the truck on where he thought the road might be. "You take me and the baby along and your money's not going to go as far." She detected the faintest dip in Del's head, as though he agreed with the argument she was presenting, the logic of it. "I mean we all have to eat. You do plan on letting me have something to eat? And the baby—you have any idea what she's going to cost? We'll need diapers, clothing, you name it—it's going to add up."

"Like I say, no imagination, because you're too practical." Now he spoke directly to Del. "I'm the only thing she's ever done that wasn't practical. She just went on impulse, you know? She just did it. And she really let loose. At first, believe me, she was something. Know what I mean? It was like she was trying to escape herself. She just needs a little incentive, the right persuasion." And looking into the back seat, his face in complete shadow, he added, "One day you'll thank me for rescuing you from yourself."

"Barr. You can't even rescue yourself."

"That so?"

"I'll be your prisoner. *We* will be your prisoners. You'll have to keep watch all the time."

"Not if you come around."

"Come *around*?"

"You did it before, you can do it again," he said. He said it like he meant it, like he believed it.

"You'll kill us, all of us," she whispered. "That's what you'll do."

"Maybe." He turned his head and stared out the windshield. "Then we'll be free."

————————————

Connor knew this: some of them had left the house. He felt the rush of cold air when they'd opened the front door. Now the floor beneath him shuddered slightly as those who remained walked about, but he didn't know who they were—then someone knelt by his right side and took his hand. From its size, he knew it was Essi.

Her breath, her voice, close to his left ear: "How are you doing in there?"

"All right," he whispered into the towel that was wrapped about his head, bound tight with a strip of bedsheet.

"Can I get you anything? Something to eat? Water?"

"No."

"Your hearing in this ear better?"

"A little."

"Good."

She started to let go of his hand and he could feel that she was gathering herself to get up off the floor, but he held her hand tightly.

"It's all right," she said. "I'm here. Paavo's here."

"Paavo?" He wasn't sure who that was. What that was. *Paavo.* But seemingly in response, he felt the floor jounce as heavier footsteps approached the fireplace. Someone sat down on his right side. Somehow he found this new presence reassuring.

"Do you have a cell phone?" Connor whispered.

"No." Paavo's voice came from the damaged side, muffled and distant. "Don't believe in them. No texting, no email for me. *Hombre,* I don't even have a Facebook page. I'm virtually invisible, out here off the grid, as they say. By choice, you understand."

"No cell? Then how'd you know we were out here?"

"Essentials. I have a two-way radio in my truck. Strictly business for plowing and hauling. I plow the lot where Marcia works, and I've known the dispatcher for years. Lindy knows I live out this way and called my truck."

"They've gone with Barr," Connor said. Neither Essi nor Paavo answered, a silent confirmation. "Where's he taking them?" He waited, certain that they were looking at each other trying to decide what to say. It was like dealing with parents, who often consult each other before answering a child's question. "You don't know," he said finally. "Okay. If you don't know, you don't have to make something up."

There was only the sound of the wind, the sound of the logs in the fireplace. Connor felt as though he were floating. Floating in a sea of helplessness. He'd never been so helpless before. He was frightened, but he also knew that there was nothing he could do about it. At least Essi didn't let go of his hand. He wanted to say something to her, tell her he was beginning to understand. They were in the storm. That's what she'd said. Earlier, she said it so playfully. But now he understood that she'd been serious, and whatever humor had been in her voice was an attempt to contain her fear. She believed in confronting that fear. He wanted to tell her that she was right. But he kept quiet, there in the dark, his dark storm.

––––––––––––––––––––

They passed Connor's truck, then a few minutes later Essi's car, both encased in snow, soft rounded contours that mimicked the shape of each vehicle.

"They look good enough to eat," Barr said. "What was the name of those things, covered with white coconut?"

"Sno Balls," Del said.

"Right."

Del glanced over at Barr, who was staring hard at the road. "You liked Sno Balls, as a kid?"

Barr gave this a moment of consideration. "Not really. Too spongy."

"And sometimes they were pink."

"Jesus, yes," Barr said. "Pink coconut. Who came up with that?"

They were entering the outskirts of Marquette. It was first light now, shades of gray rising in the forest. This time of year sunrise wasn't until about nine. During the winter months most people drove to and from work in the dark. When they passed a house with its lights on, Del looked up in the rearview mirror and said, "They've got power here."

Marcia gazed at him, the baby's head nestled beneath her chin. "They might have power at your house now."

"Maybe." Del depressed the clutch with his left leg and downshifted as they began to descend a slow curve. Each time he worked the clutch a spike of pain ran from his left hip down into his thigh.

"How's your leg?" she asked.

"It's all right."

"Sure it is."

"Thanks for asking."

"I could have driven," Barr said, "but it's difficult with a gun in your hand, you know?" He snorted. "It's already gone off once by accident."

"An accident?" Marcia asked.

"Of course it was. I didn't mean to shoot him."

"Of course you didn't."

"Well, not in the ear. If I'm going to shoot him, it won't be his fucking ear. I mean, how stupid can he be? I'm holding the gun against the side of his head, and he decides to take a swing at me. Come on."

"It's called a knee-jerk reaction," she said.

"Well, my finger-jerk reaction blew his ear off." He pounded his left fist on the dashboard. "*Bang!*"

"You're unbelievable," Marcia said.

"Yeah, I am. Because I survived. He didn't finish me off out at Presque Isle, so he's suffering the consequences. I am unbelievable, no shit."

But Barr's voice was weary. It was the heat in the cab, the monotony of the white road winding through the dark woods. Del looked up in the rearview mirror again. Marcia's eyes said she saw it, too. Barr's head lolled forward, his chin on his chest. A moment later he snapped his head up, his eyes wild, desperately alert.

"Must be about eight now. What, your bank opens at nine?"

"Most banks do," Del said.

"We've got time to kill," Barr said. "I'm hungry. Anybody?" He didn't wait for a response. "Let's hit McDonald's. Get a sausage and egg thing. And coffee. Liquor store won't be open for a while, so coffee'll have to do."

In Marquette, they went to the drive-through at McDonald's. Then they drove farther downtown and parked next to Del's bank. They sat in the truck eating McMuffins, the cab filled with the smell of processed sausage and coffee, and the sound of crinkling wrapping paper. In the early morning light downtown Marquette could have been a still life. There was only an occasional car or a pass by one of the city plows.

"How do you want to do this?" Del asked.

"We'll walk in there—all of us—and you're going to ask the teller for your money," Barr said. "They might think it's a lot, but you just say you're buying a used car or a truck and you want to pay cash."

"It's a lot of cash," Del said.

"Look at this place, it's like a vault. It's a bank. They'll have it."

They ate and sipped from their cups in silence. Every time Del looked in the rearview mirror Marcia was staring back at him. She was trying not to look like she was panicking, but it was there in her eyes, a startled gaze.

"I don't know how you can drink that stuff," Barr said.

Del looked at his cup of tea, its heat penetrating his leather glove and warming his fingers. "I don't drink coffee," he said. "Haven't for years. But this isn't very interesting."

"Must be the kind of tea Paavo's mother liked." Barr looked in the back seat, where Marcia had her coat unzipped while she nursed the baby. "If you're nipples are getting sore, Del might loan you his tea bag."

"Why don't you just—"

The bank's tall windows suddenly lit up, casting oblongs of light on the snow in Washington Street.

First, there was a cello, a solitary cello.

Then Connor felt it, but he didn't understand what was happening. He feared the house was collapsing. He raised a hand to try and lift the towel off his face, but something hard struck his forearm, pinning it to his chest. Then there was the sound of breaking branches as, Connor assumed, the tree shifted and settled deeper into the roof rafters. The floor shuddered beneath him.

"It's coming down?" Connor placed his other hand on the weight across his chest—a branch, the bark ice cold.

"Trying to," Essi said.

The explosion came from the kitchen, followed by popping noises.

"There goes the electrical system," Paavo said as though he had been anticipating it.

Connor smelled smoke, not the pleasant scent that came from the fireplace but the odor of burnt rubber. He could hear it, a hissing sound as fire rushed up what he assumed to be the back wall of the kitchen, igniting branches overhead.

Paavo got to his feet. Calmly, he said, "Guess it's time for us to go."

Connor was taken by each arm, Paavo on his right, Essi on his left, and they lifted him off the floor and began to walk him toward the front door, telling him to step around the sofa and over fallen branches. Behind them the fire in the kitchen began to roar, and he could feel its heat press against his back and shoulders, so hot that he expected his clothes might burst into flames. When the front door was opened, there was a blast of wind, his body caught between intense heat and cold. And then, blind, he was guided out into the storm.

Marcia sat on a leather couch in the bank's vast lobby, and she could feel it in her fingers and in her neck, her adrenaline surging with fear that bordered on terror. She kept looking up at the imposingly ornate ceiling, which must have been at least thirty feet overhead. Such vast space made people look small. Marcia felt invisible, and she wished it were true.

Del was standing at a teller's window, with Barr next to him, leaning an elbow on the black marble counter. Marcia couldn't hear what they were saying, but from head gestures she guessed that Del had said something about buying a vehicle from Barr. The teller, a large woman who was about Marcia's age, was desperately, awkwardly pleasant though somewhat baffled.

Marcia was amazed at how quickly the baby had become a part of her. She moved, she turned in her arms, but when she wasn't feeding she just slept, occasionally making small gurgling sounds. The soft, compact bulk of her wasn't heavy, but Marcia's forearms were getting tired, and she would love to stretch them out and relax her muscles. She also wanted a bath, a real bath. And she wanted to sleep in a bed beneath the weight of wool blankets.

If she got up off the couch and walked out of the bank, she wondered what Barr would do. Behind her there was a revolving door, the frame made of brass. She loved revolving doors and as a kid used to insist on going round and round in them until her mother said enough. She could go through that revolving door to the icy sidewalk and walk away. She could carry her baby through the snow, leaning into the wind. What could Barr do? Shoot her? With the child held to her chest? He wouldn't panic and do something stupid right there in the bank. But she wasn't sure. She'd never seen him like this. If she did something unexpected, he might do something sudden and irreversible. Like shoot Connor's ear off.

She remained seated on the couch, and while the conversation at the teller's window continued Barr glanced back at Marcia then and gave her a little reassuring nod. He was going to get his money, and they were going to leave the bank together, get back in Paavo's truck, and drive out of town.

And then what? With Barr you could never be certain. He had a plan, he didn't have a plan, you just never knew. *The best thing to do is to do what you're supposed to do?* But what is that? What do you do *now*? It wasn't a matter of right or wrong now, but of necessity, of survival. Marcia kissed the top of the baby's head, the skin warm and smooth, and her eyes welled up because she had to admit that she only wanted to see Barr, a man she'd once thought she'd loved, dead.

––––––––––

They stood in the wind and snow, perhaps fifty yards from the burning house. The light from the fire was visible through the towel that was wrapped around Connor's head, and the heat and noise seemed more overwhelming because he couldn't see anything.

When he had tried to remove the towel, Paavo took hold of his hands. "Bad idea."

Connor stuffed his hands in his coat pockets. "I can't believe how fast it went up."

"Electrical fire and a gusting wind like this," Paavo said, "there's nothing to stop it."

"It's really beautiful, in its own way," Essi said. "He's losing everything." Her voice reminded Connor of when they had been in his truck together, when she said things that didn't make sense, but saying them in a way that caused him to think she really meant something that he didn't get: snow ghosts and being in the storm. And those chocolate raisins. Like they were not just candy but some priceless, exotic experience. Or a kind of medicine. Or even a sacrificial offering. Del was *losing everything*, but she made it sound like a rare opportunity, something that would bring unexpected benefits.

"Why?" Connor asked. "Why is losing everything such a beautiful thing?"

Essi was still holding his upper arm, and she pressed herself even closer to him, as if to say, *We're really on the same side.* "It's preparation for the next thing."

"What next thing?"

"Who knows?"

She said something in Finnish, her voice raised as though she were speaking not only to him but to the fire, to the wind and snow.

"Is that another proverb?"

"Yes: *Se mikä on ollutta, on mennyttä.* What has been is gone."

"And that's beautiful?"

"*Parempi karvas totuus kuin makea valhe.* Better a bitter truth than a sweet lie. My mother, she always had a proverb for anything."

"So the way you talk, you got it from her."

"The way I talk?" Essi laughed. "I hope so. Her favorite was *Kyllä routa porsaan kotiin ajaa.* Frost drives the pig home."

"And that means?"

"I was never sure. But what mattered is that when she said it I believed her."

The young teller had a name plaque on the counter that read *Alison*. Del assumed that she was in training and, as instructed, was being pathetically friendly. She had been doing fine up to the point where she asked how much he wanted to withdraw and he said twenty-five thousand. He almost expected her to say "Dollars?"

"There are sufficient funds in the account, I believe," he offered.

She gazed desperately at her computer screen. "Yes, there's enough. It's just that, um, we don't usually get a request for that amount of cash, and I—" She looked over her shoulder toward a woman seated at the desk. It appeared that they were the only members of the staff on the floor, possibly because of the blizzard. "Um, Gwenn?"

The other woman got up from the desk and came to the counter. She was stout, perhaps mid-fifties, and everything from her short haircut to her black pants suit said no nonsense. Her demeanor reminded Del of probation officers he'd worked with over the years. They were people you didn't want to cross, and it was clear that Alison was afraid of Gwenn.

After listening to Alison *um* and *ah* for a moment, Gwenn looked out the teller window at Del. She was familiar to him, and he wondered—hoped—that he was familiar to her, as he'd done his banking there for years. "You want twenty-five thousand. In cash."

"That's right."

She merely stared at him. He didn't owe her an explanation—what he would do with the money was his business—but when she glanced at Barr he saw the nature of her suspicions change.

"I'm buying his truck," Del said. "Truck and plow. And we agreed I'd pay him cash."

Gwenn's eyes lingered on Barr a moment longer, and then, as Alison retreated from the counter, she stepped up to the computer.

"There isn't a question about the funds in my checking account, is there?" Del asked.

A moment of scrutiny as she stabbed the screen with her finger, the aggressive click of her polished nail as dogged as a time bomb. "No, that's not an issue."

"I realize," he said, "that this is a considerable sum, particularly first thing in the morning and with the blizzard and all. Would you need some time?"

Gwenn had flat lips, the lips of a woman who had fretted throughout much of her adult life. "That's not an issue, Mr. Maki, but it will take us a few minutes to put everything together."

Del glanced at Barr. He had pulled his hood up to conceal his swollen jaw. Leaning on the counter but looking away, he was trying to appear to be a disinterested party in all of this.

Turning back to Gwenn, Del said, "We're in no hurry." When she looked away from the screen, he thought he saw something there, some recognition in her eyes. "No rush at all. We're fine."

"I'll go down to the road," Paavo said. "Now that it's getting light out, someone will eventually drive through this way."

Essi didn't say anything. Connor didn't know what worried him more, when she said something or when she was silent.

"You've both been cold already," Paavo said. Connor heard his legs pushing the snow, each step a struggle as he made his way to the road. "You stay here and keep warm by the fire, so to speak." A house burning down, and he still sounded like he was making a joke.

"Turn, Connor," Essi said. "Let's turn around and warm our backs for a minute."

Her hand on his arm, she guided him around, and he could no longer see the firelight through the towel. Turning blindfolded was difficult. He felt dizzy, weightless, oddly detached from the earth. Just standing held a threat, a yawning sense of treachery, as though he were on the edge of something, a cliff or a ledge. Without her guidance he was sure he would lose his balance and not just fall into the snow but descend into thin, cold air, a gut-hollowing plummet until he hit rocks. The impact would kill him. Instantly, but not instantly enough. There would still be the moment, the split-second of pain before something was broken, his neck, his back, something that would shut his life off. Off, like a bullet in the brain.

He didn't like to trust people. He never had, and it was trust that got him here now. He had trusted Marcia, though he knew it was dangerous. But he couldn't help it because he loved her in a way that was even more dangerous. He knew that now, knew that he was weak and that he loved Marcia and this baby who had just come into the world, and it was all dangerous and he was going to have to find a way to be trustful. He just couldn't do it by himself. So he had to trust Essi and Paavo to get him away from this burning house in the midst of a blizzard.

Essi was guiding him around, until he was facing the heat from the fire again.

"So this is it?" he said. "We just turn?"

"That's right," she said. "Keep moving. If we stop, we get really cold."

"We rotate, here," he said as they continued to turn, and he surprised himself, the way he said it, with some kind of joy that he didn't know he was capable of. "Sort of a walk of life thing, like the song. Here, in the storm."

"Exactly."

"My balance, it's terrible."

"You're fine, Connor."

"I'll be fine when I find them. Do you understand? I need to find them."

She held his arm, turning him slowly between the heat and the cold.

"What's that?"

"What's what?"

"*That*."

They both listened to the wind, to the crackle and hiss of the burning house.

"Wait," Essi said. "I think I hear it."

It was an engine, with a bad muffler. It got louder and then slowed down and stopped at the bottom of the drive.

Gwenn came back to the teller's booth with a wad of bills and an envelope. She put the envelope on the counter, and then began counting the bills. It reminded Barr of someone dealing cards. She'd handled large sums of cash every day for years. Her hands had that confidence. He watched the bills on the counter pile up. New bills. Not crumpled or creased. Maybe she was onto this whole thing. Maybe she was giving them bills that would make it easy for the police to track him down as soon as he started to spend the money. He looked at her face. He guessed she had kids. Kids in college. Maybe kids who were married. Maybe she was already a grandmother. She had a life. She didn't give a damn—though she wouldn't even say *damn*—about any of them and the twenty-five thousand dollars. This was just what she did at work every day, and she counted the bills, as though she were dealing cards in a game of bridge. The way her lips moved while she counted she might have been praying.

When she was finished, she looked out at Del and said, "You want to count it yourself?"

"No, you got it right," he said.

There was no satisfaction in her face. Nothing. A compliment, an accusation—didn't matter to her. She just counted the money. That was her job. She picked up the bills and, like she would with a deck of playing cards, she repeatedly tapped the long edge of the stack on the marble counter until the bills were perfectly aligned, making it look like one thick, substantial bill. Finally, she slid the wad of bills in the envelope.

But then something happened: she didn't hand the envelope to Del. She held it in both hands and said, "All you have to do now is sign."

Barr wanted to ask, *Sign what?* But he didn't. He watched Gwenn's face. All routine.

As if on cue, Alison looked under the counter and produced a piece of paper, a form, which she slid across the marble counter.

"Just fill it out and sign and we're all set," Gwenn said.

Barr looked back at Marcia, sitting on the sofa with the baby in her arms. A form. Del had to sign a form.

There was always one more damn thing.

———————————

There was a glass jar filled with ballpoint pens on the counter. As he selected one, Del saw Barr out of the corner of his eye. He had shifted his weight, and he was staring across the lobby at Marcia, who was sitting on the sofa with the baby. Del assumed that he was trying not to appear anxious, not tremendously interested in this transaction, because it was supposed to be nothing more than the sale of a truck.

Del looked down at the form on the counter and said, "What's the date?"

"The twelfth," Alison said, glad to be of assistance.

"Ah, right."

Barr turned his head so he was looking down at the form.

Del hesitated and then wrote the date in the box at the top of the form. There were a couple of sentences that he didn't bother to read—something about sufficient funds. On the bottom of the form, next to *Name* he wrote, *Delbert Maki.*

As he pushed the form across the counter toward Gwenn, he said, "It's a lot of money, but it's a good truck. So don't look so surprised, okay?" Offhand. In jest.

Gwenn turned the form around on the marble counter and stared at it for a long moment, so long he wondered if she was unable to read his handwriting. But Gwenn only looked up at him, her lips not only flat but grim. "Will there be anything else?"

He gazed back at her. Her eyes were fiercely concentrated. He smiled as he picked up the envelope. "No. Thank you."

And then he turned and walked away from the teller's booth. This seemed the most difficult thing: to walk out of the bank, his cane tapping on the marble floor. To make it look natural. To walk out into the faint blue light of a bitterly cold winter morning. He wanted to stay inside, where it was warm and brightly lit. He wanted to hand the envelope to Barr and say, *Go, take the money, and leave me and Marcia and the baby here.* But that wasn't going to happen. They would walk out through the revolving door and get back in the truck.

Marcia got up off the sofa as they walked toward her. Del had an envelope in his free hand. Barr was right behind him, and beyond them the two women stared out through the teller's booth. There was nothing wrong except that it all seemed too normal. Her heart was racing, and for a moment she wasn't sure if she could do it, just leave the bank, push through that revolving brass door.

But she did. She fell in stride next to Barr and went through the door after Del. The cold gusts coming up from Lake Superior were a shock. As she climbed into the back seat of the truck, she held the baby tightly to her chest.

After starting the engine, Del said, "Now what?"

Barr reached over and took the envelope from Del. "Just drive."

They hadn't gone a half mile when the heater began to work, and Barr said, "Is that shit?"

Marcia opened the blanket, releasing the smell. "It is," she said.

"Damn."

"It's what babies do," she said. "Now before we go anywhere we've got to stop some place where I can get diapers."

"Suddenly you're an expert."

"You ever change a diaper, Barr?"

"No. Have you?"

"I have." They were headed out of Marquette. Marcia figured that they would take 644 because Barr wanted to get south and west to Wisconsin, rather than go south and east to the Mackinac Bridge and Michigan's Lower Peninsula. She was afraid of the woods, what Barr might do once they got out there. "There's that gas station, Fast Break, at the crossroads," she said. "They sell a little of everything. We could pick up what I need there."

Barr was hunched forward, deep in thought. She knew how it went: *Baby poop, now I have to deal with baby poop.* She almost wanted to smile, but she also knew that his spring was loaded too tightly. He had the envelope with twenty-five thousand in his pocket, and he felt close— close to this mythical escape he'd been seeking his entire life—and now all that was in his way was a load of baby poop. With Connor she could make a joke, she could ease him through this transition, call it *Parenting 101, Lesson One: Diapers.* But with Barr she had to be cautious. No jokes.

"Only way to get rid of this smell is to change her," she said.

Barr shook his head, unable to decide.

"I'm telling you," she said, "you'd be better off if you just take the money and the truck and leave us. Otherwise, it's going to be diapers and baby powder and 3 a.m. feedings. And my tits you're so fond of? They're going to be sore, tea-bag sore, and swollen and lactating. You won't like that smell any more than the smell of shit."

"Shut up. You've made your point." To Del, he said, "Okay, pull in at Fast Break. We all go in. You get what you need, and then we walk out."

Marcia leaned forward until her face was near his left shoulder. "What's the matter with you? He just had a hip replaced. He's walked enough already."

The morning light had turned everything the faintest, palest blue, and the snow was a soft music drifting across the windshield. Barr looked back at her. He hadn't shaved in a day or two, and his jaw was blue. "You think I'm going to leave him out here in the truck?" He sounded fed up and, worse, desperate. "Jesus, that smell."

"We're low on gas," Del said. "I can fill up the tank while you're inside."

"Right," Barr said. "Just leave you out here with the truck."

Del turned the truck in to Fast Break. There were no other vehicles at the pumps. Through the large plateglass windows Marcia could see rows of fluorescent lights above the aisles.

Del shut off the engine and held the keys out to Barr. "Take these. Go in the store with her, and while she gets what she needs, you can stand there near the register and watch me pump gas, if you want. I'm not about to run away on you."

Barr watched the station a moment, nodding his head. He opened his door, allowing a rush of cold air and snow to blow into the cab of the truck. "Think this place sells booze?"

The truck belonged

to a woman named Beryl. She and Paavo had been distant neighbors for years. Beryl was big. Maybe as big as Paavo, Connor couldn't be sure. Her laugh was big, her voice booming above the noise from the muffler. The cab of the truck reeked of exhaust mixed with the sweet tang of motor oil.

With Paavo sitting in the middle, Connor was squeezed against the passenger-side door. Essi sat on top, her weight more or less equally distributed on both men. Beryl thought all of them crammed in the cab was such a hoot. That was her word, *hoot!* Every time she worked the gear shift she hollered. Second and fourth gears were the best. "Here it comes, Paavie, second gear!" as she yanked the stick back into what Connor imagined was the vicinity of Paavo's crotch. "Fourth gear, coming up—balls to the wall!"

"Still working at the hospital?" Paavo asked.

"I'll die there!" Beryl hooted.

"Perfect," he said. "You can drop us at the ER."

"What do you do at the hospital?" Essi asked.

"I deal in blood, honey. Phlebotomy technician. Dozens of times a day I'm the one who says *poke* just before slipping the needle in your vein. People say I've got the touch. They don't even feel the steel piercing their skin." She drove as though they were being chased. "I could see the smoke way down the road," she hollered. "Shoulda known you'd have something to do with it, Paavie."

"Del Maki's place," Paavo said.

"Poor fucker!" Beryl shouted. "After losing his wife, and didn't I hear he recently had surgery at MGH? Open-heart, was it? Triple bypass?"

"Hip replacement," Essi said.

"Whatever!" Beryl downshifted as she took the truck into a tight bend in the road. "Paavie, sloppy seconds comin' at cha!" As she accelerated out of the turn, she said, "What's with the towel, honey? Fashion statement?"

"No," Connor said. "I think I've lost my ear."

"*What?*" Like she herself was deaf. She hooted. "How'd you lose your ear?" Before he could answer she hooted again. "Guess you don't hear so good!"

"They've had quite a night," Paavo said. "A tree fell on Maki's roof. A baby was born. And when the power came back on, we heard this incredible cello, until the electrical wires shorted out. That house is toast."

"And people say nothing happens out here."

"You have a cell phone?" Essi's elbow was boring into the left side of Connor's rib cage.

"I do," Beryl shouted. "But the freakin' thing won't work this far out. Gotta wait till we get closer to town."

As Marcia led Barr into the station, Del got out and kept one hand on the truck for balance as he made his way back to the gas pump, while getting his debit card from his wallet. Barr waited by the checkout counter, watching Del through the plateglass window. Marcia had disappeared down one of the aisles. She was right, the place sold a little of everything: liquor, groceries, and there was a Sub Base shop at the back of the store. A hefty man wearing a Packers sweatshirt stood behind the cash register, paying no attention to Barr—to him, they were just a young couple with a baby, the guy obediently waiting while the mother shopped. Barr kept his hands in the pockets of his jacket, one containing Liesl's revolver, the other the envelope stuffed with twenty-five thousand dollars in new bills.

Something about Barr's posture changed—he seemed to straighten up a bit—and then Del turned and saw it: a police cruiser had entered the parking lot and stopped in front of the station. Through the plateglass Del could see that Barr had not moved, and Marcia was still out of sight down one of the aisles.

As he pumped gas, Del watched the cruiser. On the side of the car were large black and gold letters that read *Marquette County Sheriff*. The officer took his time, just sitting behind the steering wheel, gazing down at something in his lap. Del recognized him but didn't know his name. He was in his mid-thirties and seemed totally absorbed, and then Del realized that he must be texting or doing something with his phone. Too often now you saw that intense preoccupation that made people oblivious to everything around them.

Del glanced at Barr, staring out the plateglass window, and then he watched the officer get out of the cruiser. He had a double chin and the kind of moustache that required a daily trim, a neat black line attempting to give character to a long, noncommittal face. Glancing toward the truck, he gave one curt nod. Del returned the gesture, a slight dip of the head.

But maybe the officer had been contacted by the dispatch at the sheriff's office and had been told about a call from the bank manager Gwenn. Maybe he knew about the twenty-five thousand dollars and understood the situation—the older man gassing up the truck, while the young mother was in the store with the guy who was armed. Maybe he was playing it cool, playing it safe. Perhaps he had texted a request for backup.

He walked around the front of the cruiser, leaning into the snow. His hands were in the pockets of his jacket, which had a fur collar that matched his black ushanka. No, he had no idea what was going on here—he was just thinking about getting inside the store, out of the frigid wind. He probably just got a text from his wife, telling him to pick something up on the way home from his night shift. Del imagined that they had several kids. They all had colds or the flu and they were staying home from school today, lying around in their pajamas, watching TV, and the officer, who was exhausted after working all night, was wondering if he might not be coming down with something himself. With the kids home for the day, he wasn't going to get much sleep.

Marcia walked down the aisle, the baby, a bulky package of disposable diapers, and a plastic bottle of talcum powder clutched to her chest. She was heading toward the restrooms at the back of the station, but stopped when a woman's voice said *Awwww* in that way that people do when they see puppies, kittens, and infants. The woman came to the counter and purred, "Lemme see the little darlin'."

Marcia obliged, thankful to set the package and the bottle of powder on the counter for a moment. The woman made soft cooing sounds as she gently unfolded the blanket, revealing the baby's head. She was at least in her fifties, and Marcia suspected that she was married to the man who was behind the counter at the front of the station. They both wore Green Bay Packers sweatshirts.

"Oh, isn't she cute," the woman said. "*She*, right?"

"Yes."

The woman's stubby fingers caressed the baby's skull. "I can never get over the feel, you know, of this soft spot here. My, she's a real little newbie."

"You might say that."

The woman looked like she was going to tear up. "Oh, they grow so fast. Before you know it, they're runnin' out the door and not tellin' when they'll be back. And then one day they don't come back. They just go away like they don't belong to you no more."

Marcia heard footsteps behind her and turned, expecting to see Barr, but it was a police officer, coming down an aisle lined with canned goods. He wore one of those Russian hats that looked like a furry animal was curled up asleep on his head.

"Mornin', Travis. Coffee?"

"Annie, thanks."

Barr appeared at the far end of the aisle, staring at Marcia.

"Well," she said to Annie, "we have business to attend to."

"*Ohhh*, yes," the woman said, reluctantly taking her hand away from the baby's head. "But thank you, sweetheart. Your little darlin' just made my day."

Marcia smiled at the woman, then ventured to look up at the police officer, who was now standing next to her. He seemed tired, desperate for a cup of coffee. She glanced back up the aisle at Barr, and then went into the restroom.

It was clean. Often Marcia hated to use public bathrooms because they were so filthy, but this one looked okay and smelled of disinfectant. She suspected that Annie and her husband at the counter owned the station, and they could no more imagine not keeping the bathrooms clean than missing a Packers game on TV.

On the wall was a Koala Kare table, difficult to fold down with her arms full. After she managed to put the baby, the diapers package, and the bottle on the table, she realized that her hands were shaking. She'd lied to Barr. She'd made it sound like she was an expert at changing diapers. That wasn't true. She had done it years ago, a few times while babysitting. As she unwrapped the blanket, she could barely control her hands. The baby's face began to bunch up, and she let out a cry, so Marcia started to sing. She wasn't sure what the tune was, and it didn't matter because her voice seemed to calm the baby. But her hands still shook, and the salt she tasted on her upper lip was from the tears that were streaming down her cheeks.

Barr kept his hands in his coat pockets. The revolver felt heavy and, he feared, obvious. After Marcia went into the bathroom, the cop remained standing with his back to the front of the store while he talked to Annie, the butterball working the Sub Base counter. Barr's other hand gripped the envelope filled with bills. The immediate problem was paying his way out of here. He couldn't remember how much money he had in the front pocket of his jeans.

The cop leaned on the counter as he settled into a conversation with Annie, who had begun slicing tomatoes.

Best to keep out of his line of sight. Barr went back to the plateglass window and checked on Del, dutifully gassing up the truck. He must have used a debit card at the pump, so Barr would only have to pay for what Marcia needed for the baby, but he didn't want to take the envelope out of his coat pocket and pay with a brand new bill—with a cop nearby. He removed his hand from the envelope and jammed it into the front pocket of his jeans. The folded bills there felt thin, creased. He took them out and saw that he had a twenty, a ten, and three ones. Better than he'd thought. He looked to his right, at the man behind the cash register. Behind him the shelves were stocked with bottles—vodka, whiskey, rum, you name it.

The man behind the counter was reading a newspaper spread open on the Formica, one hand idly stroking his droopy mustache. He glanced up from the newspaper and, though it was difficult to tell beneath that mustache, he seemed to smile. On his Packers sweatshirt was a name tag: Ron. "Get you something?"

Barr glanced down at the bills in his hand, and then at the shelves, squinting slightly, as though he were undecided, though he knew exactly what he wanted. "Let's see, Ron, you got . . . umm, you got schnapps, a pint of schnapps?"

"Sure do. All kinds of flavors."

"Just peppermint's fine. Built-in mouthwash."

Ron seemed accustomed to the desperation of early morning humor. As he walked down along the shelves, Barr glanced out the plateglass window. Del had finished filling up the tank and was getting back in the cab slowly—from the way he grabbed on to the open door as he eased himself down behind the wheel, he was feeling that new hip. Sometimes you just got to show mercy and put an old dog down. Won't be long now. Get out of here, drive maybe a half hour out into the woods, and pull over where there's nothing but trees. Say he needed to pee, and Del needed to go with him. Ol' Del would understand. Wasn't much Del didn't understand. Barr would take him by the arm and walk him away from the truck, somewhere out of Marcia's sight, behind some trees or maybe a bush. She'd know what's up. He didn't want her to see it, though there's no way she wouldn't hear it. Just a little pop, muffled by the snowy woods. She'd be crying when Barr got back in the truck, behind the steering wheel. There'd be that, her crying, but then she'd know he meant it, meant it all. It would break her. He realized his problem was he didn't push hard enough and break her earlier. Months ago. And that was why they were in this shit now. He should have done it back when he had the chance.

"That's nine ninety-seven," Ron said as he placed the pint of schnapps on the counter.

"Fine. I'm just waiting, you know, she'll have a few more things to ring up." He watched Ron slide the pint bottle into a paper bag. In the worst way, he wanted to grab it from him, twist off the cap, and take a long refreshing pull. "I'll pay for this now," he said, placing the ten spot on the counter, "and we'll settle on the other stuff whenever she gets up here."

"Okeydokey." Ron rang him up, handed back three pennies. Barr, doing his good citizen routine, dropped them in the Karma Pennies tray on the counter and picked up the bottle in the paper bag.

It was entirely too crowded in here. Seeking protection, he went around a display rack full of potato chips and popcorn to a small cluster of high tables and stools. He sat down where he could monitor everything. He could look over the display of Doritos at Ron standing behind the counter reading his paper. Because of the aisle shelves, stacked with canned goods, he could only see the back of the cop's furry black hat as he stood at the Sub Base counter, but beyond that he had a clear view of the bathroom door at the back of the store.

Marcia was taking an eternity to wipe the baby's butt.

And no one was paying him any mind. Invisible was good. He leaned forward on his stool, so Ron couldn't see him through the Doritos. After peeling down the paper bag, Barr unscrewed the cap, and raised the bottle to his lips. The cold peppermint rush was a shock to his sore mouth, and the schnapps burned his throat all the way down, but then there was that luminous moment, that slight acceleration in his swelling chest, and he snuck another pull before screwing the cap back on the bottle. Fuck it, she can take her sweet time with the baby.

The cop walked up an aisle, pausing along the way, and when he reached the counter Ron rang up a box of Eggos and a bottle of maple syrup. The real thing, not some Aunt Jemima corn syrup. Because of the snow it was a no-school day, the cop explained, and his wife had said the kids all wanted waffles for breakfast. He was the kind of yo-yo who loved to provide for his brood, bringing back the Eggos and maple syrup, as caveman virtuous as if he'd gone out and slain wild boar. Ron knew him, of course, and called him Travis. Fucking Travis, with a houseful of kids on a no-school day. Here's to you, pal. Barr opened the bottle, hunkered down, and took another pull. He just needed for Travis to clear out so he could have Ron tally up whatever crap Marcia needed. Barr would pay up, they'd get back in the truck, and disappear forever into the great white woods.

Barr was considering one more pull on his schnapps when Marcia finally emerged from the bathroom. Though her arms were full, she paused at the Sub Base counter to say something to the woman who was now sliding trays of bread loaves into the oven. Barr couldn't hear what she said, but the woman's voice boomed, "That's okay, honey. Now you take care of that gorgeous little one of yours."

Barr thought about taking a piss, but going into the bathroom now was out of the question. He'd have to remain vigilant and hold his position, which meant he'd have to hold it until they got out in the woods. By the time he told Del to pull over, he'd really have to go. Do you go before or after you do it? Maybe it was a matter of comfort? Piss first, then shoot. Or a matter of respect, shoot first, then take a leak. It all comes down to how bad you got to go.

"My phone really sucks but I usually get reception by the time I reach Fast Break." Beryl's hoot was a form of punctuation. "Depends on the weather and what I had for dinner and how the stars are aligned, y'know?" Hoot. "Really, do you think God ever intended for there to be so many phones in the world?" Hoot. "Remember how we used to hate Ma Bell? You had one phone line to your house unless you were filthy rich and had a bunch of teenagers." Long hoot. "And when you were out somewhere and needed to make a call you'd find a *public* phone booth, drop a dime in the slot, and dial a number, a number you keep in your head because that's how you knew who was important to you. I mean, Ma Bell was the Virgin Mary, the mother of communication." Hoot. "They broke her up, and she spawned a gazillion little smartphones jamming up the atmosphere. Now everybody walks around with a Bluetooth glommed on to the sides of their heads, and you never get away from the freakin' chatter." Double hoot. "And when you're out here in the woods and can't get a signal, it's the dark side of the moon." Hoot. "Use to be you were just in the woods, you were out there, and it felt so complete. And that's a good thing, usually. Though maybe not if you have, you know, issues with your ear, like it's gone missing. Know what I mean, Connor?" No hoot but a sympathetic *Mmmm* that rose in pitch at the end.

As if to prove her point, Connor could hear tapping—phone screen tapping. After a moment, Essi said, "Not yet. I'm getting one, two bars, and then they disappear."

"Is that your phone?" he asked.

"No, it's yours," she said. "I don't have a cell phone."

"You picked my pocket? When?"

"While we were doing that turning thing outside the burning house," she said. "When I was a teenager I used to hang around the train and bus stations in Helsinki. I got pretty good. But I'm not getting a signal."

"Wait for the hill a mile or so after Fast Break," Beryl said. "We get to the top of that and you got a clear shot at civilization." She hooted and then shouted, "*Baaack on the griiiid!*"

The rear end fishtailed slightly as the truck went into a bend in the road, forcing Connor to lean into Paavo, while Essi's elbow dug into his rib cage.

"I'm about out of gas and need to stop at Fast Break," Beryl said. "You be okay with that, honey?" *Mmmm.*

Connor liked that Beryl called him honey, part maternal, part tease. "I'm fine."

"Sure. You're just a standup guy, I can tell. Soon as we gas up I'm going to get you right into ER so they see what's left of your ear. If you're lucky, they'll have me draw your blood." Double hoot. "Won't feel a thing. *Poke!*"

Del sat behind the steering wheel, his window rolled down. He watched the police officer at the cash register while Barr sat at a table in the opposite corner, doing the same: watching. He had taken a few nips from a bottle in a paper bag. When he stared out at Del, he seemed to be daring him. *Try something with the cop and see what happens.*

The policeman left the counter, pushed open the glass door, and stepped out into the horizontal snow. He wasn't fifteen yards from Del, but as he walked to his cruiser he never turned his head in his direction. Barr, sitting behind the plateglass, remained perfectly still, poised, watching Del. The officer got into his car, pulled away from the building, and passed slowly in front of the truck. His tires creaked in the snow as he turned out into the road.

Del looked back at Barr, who was standing now. Marcia was coming up the aisle from the back of the store, the baby wrapped in the blanket that she held in her arms, along with a bundle of diapers and a bottle, and she gave some of them to Barr. He wasn't pleased about it, clearly, but he took the items to the cash register and placed them on the counter.

The transaction all seemed perfectly normal. The man behind the counter rang everything up and put them in a plastic bag. When they came outside, Marcia had a stony expression, and she refused to look at Del. Barr walked a pace behind her, the plastic bag dangling from one fist.

When they were all in the truck, Del drove to the entrance to the road and stopped. "Now what?"

"Go to the intersection and turn right."

"I know what you're thinking, Barr," Marcia said from the back seat.

Barr didn't bother to answer.

"We're taking 644 west," she said. "We're going to Wisconsin."

After a moment, Barr said, "Have you ever noticed how you can't go north from here, unless you want to swim across Lake Superior to Canada? And that's, what, a couple hundred miles?" It seemed like a concession that he had to explain his plan at all. "So, yeah, we're heading to Wisconsin."

"Then why can't we leave him here?" she said.

He didn't answer.

"Barr, just leave him and we go."

There was something in Marcia's voice that Del didn't understand. It was desperate, yes, but it wasn't timid, not like it had been earlier. She was almost making a demand, as though this was her last offer.

Del was certain Barr had heard it, too, but he only stared out the windshield as he unscrewed the cap on his pint bottle and took a pull. The smell of peppermint schnapps filled the warm cab. He turned to Del and said, "Just drive."

At the intersection, Del turned on to 644 heading away from Yellow Dog Township. Though it was nearly whiteout conditions, a snowplow had made a pass, leaving high banks of new snow on both sides of the road. Years ago, it was along this stretch where he'd first encountered Liesl. He didn't think of it as when they'd first met—that came later; it was where he encountered her, a woman lying on her back in the snow, injured from a fall from a ledge. He wanted to explain what this road and these woods meant to him. He wanted to say something to Barr that would matter, that would change all this. He wanted to say, *If you're going to kill me, do it here.*

Occasionally he glanced in the rearview mirror. Marcia tried not to look at him, and the few times she did he thought she was about to lose it.

About five miles down

County Road 644, Del stopped the truck.

"The fuck are you doing?" Barr said.

Del stared straight ahead and seemed interested in something out there, but the road was nothing but a deep white furrow of snow running straight through the woods. "This is it for me," he said. "You have your exit strategy, Barr. You have the truck, you have the money, so I'm getting off here."

"I'll tell you when you're getting off."

"I can barely walk, so you don't have to worry about me getting back to Fast Break."

"I said drive the truck."

Now Del looked at him. "If you're going to shoot me, then do it. Do it here."

"What?"

"I'm not driving any farther."

"Really?"

"Whatever happens it happens here. I'm not dying in Wisconsin."

Barr took the revolver out of his right pocket. "This says you're driving."

"No, it doesn't." Del was still staring at him, those eyes behind his glasses steady. "I'm getting out of the truck now, Barr."

He yanked on the handle and pushed open the door. It took considerable effort to climb up out of the truck. He had to use both hands, clutching the top of the door and hoisting himself to his feet. Once he was standing, he dug his cane out from behind the driver's seat and then shut the door.

Barr watched Del cross the road, where he climbed partially up the snowbank. Exhausted from the effort, he turned and sat down in the snow. He gazed back at the truck and didn't move.

Barr reached into his left pocket for the pint of schnapps. He unscrewed the cap with the hand that still held the pistol and took a long swallow, then turned and looked in the back seat. Marcia hugged the bundled baby to her chest.

"You believe this?" he said.

"Just go."

"I'm going to get out and shoot him right where he sits."

"Barr. Get behind the wheel and drive."

"The way this shit's coming down he'd be covered in no time. So this is preferable to Wisconsin. This is where he wants it. You have to admire that."

"You got what you want. Just leave him."

Barr took another warming pull on the schnapps.

"Barr, shooting him isn't going to make whatever you do any easier."

"I should go over there and shoot him. Once in the kneecap, just to let him know I don't take kindly to defiance. There's a lack of respect here. Let him know that and then put him away."

Marcia didn't say anything.

"I mean, look at him, sitting there already half covered in snow. He's an old dog, and he wants to be put down. He's pathetic."

"You're the one who's pathetic."

"That so?"

"That's so. Even when you get what you want, you don't get it."

"I don't get it? *I* don't get it?"

"That's what I said."

He turned his head away from her in disgust. Staring out the windshield at the snow, he took another slug, peppermint heat descending.

The towel wrapped around Connor's head was white and admitted a grayish light that was broken into stripes by the pattern in the fabric. He couldn't stand not being able to see anything any longer, and he began to tug on the duct tape.

"I'd leave that," Essi said. "You might start bleeding again."

"I don't care. I've got to see. I need to find them."

"All right. Hold still. Let me do it."

He leaned forward so she could get her hands on his head. Peeling the tape away from the cloth caused a painful pulling on his wounded ear, probably due to dried blood. Then she adjusted the towel so he could see out of his left eye.

"How 'bout if I leave it like that? I don't think removing the towel is a good idea."

"Yeah, honey, I'd leave that thing on." Beryl said as she turned the truck into the parking lot at Fast Break. "Soon as I gas up, we'll get you to the hospital." No hoots. She might have been speaking to a child.

Connor didn't mind. He hoped if they needed to draw his blood she'd be the one to insert the needle. "This is better," he said, though the ear ached even more now.

When Beryl pulled up to the gas pumps, she said, "Anybody got to pee, do it now. In this stuff it might be another half hour before we get to the hospital."

They all got out of the truck. Beryl led them inside, explaining that she paid only in cash since she'd cut up her credit cards.

Connor was glad to just be walking without someone holding him by the arm. The snow was quickly building up on the towel around his right eye, but through the plateglass storefront he could see a large man in a Packers sweatshirt behind the counter. He held a telephone to his ear.

Walking next to him, Essi was toying with the cell phone. "Still no reception here," she said.

"They have a landline," Connor said. "Maybe they'll let us use it."

Essi said, "With one eye, you're pretty good."

"You were really a pickpocket?"

"I've been a lot of things, Connor." Essi said this in a playful way, the way she'd been when they were in his truck. Chocolate raisins and snow ghosts. And old songs while wandering around out there in the storm.

They entered the store, its warm, still air a relief after the numbing cold wind. As the man behind the counter hung up the phone, he looked confused, or even afraid.

Beryl laid a twenty dollar bill on the counter and said, "I want regular, Ron."

"And we'd like to use your telephone," Essi said. "We need to call the police."

Ron opened his mouth but didn't say anything. He seemed so preoccupied, so spooked that he didn't notice—or didn't care—that he was looking at someone whose head was wrapped in a towel.

"Well, I'm going first." Paavo started down an aisle toward the back of the store.

Finally, Ron managed to say to Beryl, "I already called 'em."

"Who?"

"The police. And when I explained they said they'd send a squad car and also have an ambulance sent out, too."

"Why?" Beryl asked. Looking around, she said, "Annie, where's Annie?" When Ron didn't answer, she said, "Honey, what's going on?" *Mmmm.*

"I can't," he said. He put both hands on the counter for support. "I can't—it goes back a long way, you know. My wife's been . . ." He gave up then.

"She's been what?" Beryl said.

"She's been carrying this a long time."

"Carrying what, honey?"

"This hurt. You know she says she's moved on, but every day I know it's still there. It's in her eyes. Sometimes I hear it in her voice. Doesn't matter what she's talking about—even when she's laughing, it's still there, just underneath everything, you know?"

From the back of the store there came a pounding. Connor took a step backward so he could see with his left eye down an aisle stocked with canned goods. He had no depth perception. The sign that said, *Sale—Van Camp's Pork and Beans—2 for $3* partially blocked his view of Paavo, who was standing before a door down a corridor beyond the Sub Base counter. Though Paavo was big, the sign was almost bigger. Connor could only see his raised arm. As he pounded his fist on the door, he said, "What do you mean you aren't coming out? Other people got to use the bathroom, you know." He listened for a moment and then said, "Annie, please. It's me, Paavo, a big guy with a tiny bladder."

Paavo listened for a moment, shaking his head, then he turned and looked up the aisle toward the front counter. He held his arms out and clapped them against the sides of his snowsuit, a comical gesture of frustration offset by the look of someone with an urgent need to pee.

Marcia felt electric. A current ran through her veins, making her quiver. It was fear.

"*This,*" Barr said as he screwed the cap on the bottle of schnapps—the smell of mint reminding her of the industrial disinfectant in the bathroom at Fast Break. "This is what he wants, this is what he gets. He *wants* this—you know that, don't you? He wants me to do this. That's the thing, isn't it? That's what it is about this guy. Well, fine, here it comes."

As he reached for the door handle, Marcia dropped the blanket, releasing several rolls of toilet paper—Barr watched them bounce and tumble to the floor of the truck, one unraveling as only a roll of toilet paper can. He whispered, "What the hell?"

Her arms came up, and she clutched his head. He tried to lean back out of her reach but one hand grabbed his hair as her fingernails gouged his right eye, its tenderness akin to a soft-boiled egg, until blood ran out over her fingers. His hands came up, and he grabbed her forearms, first getting the hand away from his eye. When he pulled her other hand from the top of his head she yanked a clump of hair from his scalp. There was a moment when he simply held her wrists, so hard she feared the bones would break. They both were breathing heavily, plumes of vapor pouring into the air between them, and then he released her left arm and punched her face. The pain in her nose and sinuses seemed to spike into the back of her skull. He punched her again and again—she didn't know how many times, three times, maybe more. Perhaps she'd blacked out, but she was now lying against the back of the bench seat, the warmth of her own blood running down her face and neck, thickening in the back of her throat.

Barr turned his head so he could stare down at her with his good eye. She thought he might hit her again, but he cupped his right eye in his other hand, blood seeping out between his fingers. "Jesus, you fuck," he whispered. "What, you leave her back at the station?"

"Whatever you do, you'll never get her. *Never.*"

He reached over and shut the engine off and pulled the keys out of the ignition. "All right. First things first."

———————————

While Paavo stood out in the snow, finishing a very long pee, a police cruiser pulled up in front of the store. The officer got out and came inside, with Paavo behind him.

"I hope you didn't call because Paavo is making yellow snow," the cop said.

"Sorry, Travis," Ron said. "I know your shift's ended, but we got a situation here."

Travis looked at Beryl and Essi, and then at Connor. "What kind of a situation?"

Before Connor could answer, Essi said, "Hurt his ear."

"So that's dried blood." Travis seemed exhausted. Not exactly upset but not fully engaged, as though he might just decide the hell with it, get back in his cruiser, and take a nap. "Dispatch called me—something about a baby?"

"It's Annie." Ron made it sound like there were issues that he and Travis were both all too familiar with, as if to say, *We've seen this before and I don't know what else I can do.* "She's in the bathroom. Found a baby in there."

"With the baby," Travis said.

"I've talked to her. Paavo's talked to her. But she ain't coming out."

"Whose baby?"

No one spoke immediately. "It's my baby," Connor said.

"Yours?" the officer said.

"Yes, sir."

"Father of the baby, okay. And your name is?"

"Connor."

"Connor. This have any connection to how you hurt your ear, Connor?"

"I guess it does, sir."

"They said they'd send an ambulance," Ron offered.

Travis nodded while he still considered Connor, his head wrapped in a bloody a towel. Sweetly, he asked, "What's the baby's name?"

"We haven't decided yet. She was only born last night."

"We. Who's we?"

Connor hesitated. "Me and her mother."

"Her mother and I," Travis said.

"That's what I said."

"In a manner of speaking. I should have been an English teacher. They don't work nights."

"Excuse me, sir?" Connor said.

"Never mind," the officer said. "Have you decided on the mother's name?"

Connor wasn't sure if he was being sarcastic or trying to make him more at ease with a little joke. He also wasn't sure if identifying Marcia was a good idea.

Patiently, Travis asked, "Who left the baby in the bathroom?" When Connor didn't answer, the officer said, "The mother or was it one of you?"

"We don't know for certain," Essi said. "We just got here."

"I know Beryl and Paavo—they both live out." Travis turned to Essi. "Who are you?"

"My name's Essi."

"Essi. Connor. Nobody has last names anymore?" He tried not to appear to be looking her over while he looked her over. "May I presume that you are not the mother?"

"No, I delivered the baby."

"I see. Essi, you delivered the baby. And you, Connor, you're the father."

"Yes, sir," Connor said.

"Travis," Paavo said. "They've had quite a night."

"Have they really? Well, I did, too. A blizzard like this, the calls never stop all night long. Three domestics, a bar fight, and a burst water main. I was on my way home, when I get this one." He turned to Ron. "So how is it that Annie's in the bathroom with the baby? The lock won't work?"

"I kinda doubt that," Ron said. "She locked herself in."

Travis looked around and settled on Beryl. "Why would she do that?"

"I think," Beryl said, "she probably wants the baby?" *Mmmm.* "Doesn't want to give it up."

"That's right," Ron said. "I tell you, this goes a long way back. Annie lost a little one soon after it was born, and she ain't never gotten over it." Then he added, "She won't hurt it or nothing."

"Anything," Travis said.

"That too," Ron said.

"Okay. Let's see what we've got." Travis placed his hands on his hips and then began walking down one of the aisles toward the back of the store. When the others began to follow, he turned, causing them all to stop. "Just wait here, please." Then, having a second thought, he said to Connor, "If you're the father—are you really the father?"

"I think I am."

"You think you are. Why, because it was dark?"

"Excuse me, sir?"

"Never mind. You're the father. That'll have to do. You come with me."

Connor followed the officer down the aisle. He was embarrassed because he realized that he was so hungry he was tempted to grab something off the shelves, pull open this damn towel, and stuff his mouth. Doritos. White cheddar popcorn. Jars of salsa and guacamole dip. And straight ahead was the Sub Base, with menu boards hanging from the water-stained ceiling featuring large photographs of foot-long sub sandwiches. Ham and cheese. Meatball. Teriyaki chicken. Italian cold cuts with provolone cheese. Connor felt light-headed and thought he might faint.

The officer had said something over his shoulder which Connor didn't understand. "I'm sorry, sir, what did you say?"

"Was this baby left in the bathroom?"

"I believe so."

"By whom?"

Whom. There were two kinds of people in the world. Those who knew when to say who or whom, and those who didn't. Connor suspected that the officer was using the word correctly, though he wasn't sure. It had something to do with what he said about being an English teacher. Connor never liked being around people who could talk that way, figuring that he was missing something that later might turn out to be important.

"Whom?" he said. "You mean who left the baby in the bathroom?"

The officer stopped and turned around. "That's what I said."

They were right in front of the glass Sub Base counter. Beyond the officer, Connor could see aluminum bins filled with ham, cheese, pepperoni, salami, cheese, lettuce, tomato—and on the counter there were several pans lined with loaves of bread. He could smell them and assumed they'd only recently been taken out of the oven.

"Did the mother leave the baby in the bathroom, Connor?"

"I don't know for certain, sir. But I suspect she might have."

"Do you suspect it was, you know, an oversight on her part?"

"You mean by accident?"

"Yeah, did she leave the baby behind by accident?"

"I can't say for certain."

"Is she forgetful? Or perhaps she had too much to drink? Or maybe she's on some kind of medication that might impair her memory."

"I doubt that."

"Then what would induce her to do such a thing?"

Induce. Connor was helpless. He wanted to reach right through the glass case and grab a fistful of sliced ham. Or turkey. Or both, and a little of that Swiss cheese. Anything. Anything but the green olives with that red stuff jammed in the pit hole—pimento. He hated those. "I honestly don't know, sir," he said.

"I didn't catch the mother's name."

"Her name? It's Marcia." Connor felt ashamed, as though he had given up information that might be useful to the enemy. In his defense, he said, "We're engaged."

"Congratulations."

"I mean while she was pregnant we talked about getting married, and now, now that the baby's here, that's what we're going to do."

"I see," Travis said. "Marriage is an honorable institution, Connor, particularly when children are involved, so, if you don't mind my saying so, I think you're both making a wise choice. But I don't see what would compel her to leave her child in the bathroom."

Compel. "I don't know, sir." And then it poured in, thickening his confusion. Marcia and Del, driving off with Barr in Paavo's truck, driving to the bank. "There's a lot going on, a lot has happened, sir. As Essi said, it's been quite a night. I think we're all a little stressed out."

"Essi, who delivered the baby." Then something occurred to Travis, some disturbing thought. "In the bathroom?"

"Yes." Connor could see something in the officer's face recoil, as though this piece of information changed everything. "Oh, no, sir. Not *here.* The baby wasn't born in *this* bathroom. But she was born in a bathroom—in the bathtub, actually. I was there with Essi when she delivered the baby."

"You witnessed the birth."

"Yes."

"In a bathroom, but not this bathroom."

"That's correct, sir."

"That's a relief. No pun intended."

"Pun?"

"Pretty messy, huh?"

"Yes, it was, sir. But they got the baby cleaned up all right, once we could get the door open."

"The door? It was locked, too?"

"No, not locked. But yes, the bathroom door wouldn't open." The officer was looking more than a little skeptical. "I know it seems like a weird coincidence, sir, but it just happened that this other bathroom was, well, when the tree came down on the house this branch—a sizeable limb, it was—came through the bathroom window and jammed the door shut."

"It came in through the bathroom window." Connor detected the faintest smile. "But you, Connor, you got the door open."

"Yes, sir. I sawed the limb till we could open the door just enough to slide into the kitchen, where they had been boiling water until—" Connor stopped, realizing it might not be a good idea to mention that a bullet hole had drained the first pot, requiring them to boil more water. "We boiled water so the baby could be washed."

Travis nodded appreciatively as though he now fully understood the circumstances, until his face clouded with a new concern. "Your ear. You cut it before or after the birth." When Connor didn't answer immediately, the officer said, "Or did it happen while you were sawing the limb?"

"Is that intended to be a pun?"

"Connor, you're sharper than you look."

Barr stood outside the truck, and he knew for sure. His right eye, pooled with blood, was out of kilter in its socket, and the damage made it feel like the eyeball was a grotesque orb the size of his fist. The swelling of the right side of his face stung, the skin feeling clawed and shredded. He could only look out of his left eye, which itself was swimming in goo. Tears. Not crying tears but a release of fluid that made everything appear to float and slide and shift as though under water. The pain was a revelation. It provided clarity.

He slammed the door shut, took his revolver from his pocket, and tapped the muzzle on the window glass. "Don't. You. Move. Hear me?"

Marcia was lying on her side in the back seat, her hands raised to her bloodied face. Connor loses an ear. He might lose an eye. And everybody was going to lose blood.

He was past threats. There was only blood now.

He aimed the good eye toward the opposite side of the road. Snow-flakes ticked against his face, points of cold that were distracting but also soothing. The cane lay abandoned in the snow, but Del was not where he had been, and there was a break in the ridge of the snowbank, evidence of his struggle to climb, perhaps crawl, up and over and into the deep unbroken snow that led into the woods.

"All right," Barr said, pocketing the gun.

He walked around the front of the truck, crossed the road, and climbed up the snowbank to the passage that Del had made. This was what hunters did, tracked down their prey. They liked to talk of it as something sacred, the relationship between hunter and quarry. His father and all his drunk pals, smelling of beer and bourbon and cigarettes, talked about it like it was religion. Like it was the reason for being put on this earth, to chase an animal down and kill it. As though a man wasn't a man until he got his deer, downed his bear, his moose, his elk. Shot it clean. And if not clean, then stalked through the woods—sometimes taking hours (these were often their favorite stories, how they waded through muck and mire in pursuit)—to finish the deed. Gutted it while the entrails and organs were still hot, steaming on the cold ground. Because man was in essence a hunter. It was law; it was written. They talked of the rituals of the hunt, the spirit of the animal, the completeness of life and death. There was nothing else, not drink, not money, not women, that brought you to that secret place, that sanctuary. To kill was to survive.

This was something else. It wasn't an animal. It was a man. A man that was meant to die, and until that end was achieved there was nothing else. That was the sole purpose. And it was good that this man was trying to run away—not run but crawl. Barr could see it in the snow leading from the back side of the snowbank: a wide disturbance in the pure, smooth whiteness. Del might be on all fours, or he might have fallen here and there, but the path was there, winding back into the shadows of the woods. And then Barr aimed his distorted vision at this, too: the path led to a house, a shack, really, in a clearing some eighty yards from the road. One slant of roof had caved in and another sagging swayback as though the weight of the air above might cause its collapse at any moment. Window sash framed black air and a weathered door stood ajar, clinging to its uprightness by a lose hinge.

Yesterday all of them, all of these fuckers, wanted him dead. And they missed. He eased himself down the back of the snowbank and began to follow the path left by his quarry.

There was just the one bathroom

at Fast Break. Its door, painted white, had a halo of hand grime encircling the knob. The sign at eye level read *Restroom*, and beneath that was a handwritten message adhered with curled, yellowing tape: *Customers Only.*

Travis took one hand off his hip and rapped on the door. After a moment, he said, "Annie." A slight nod, as though it was just as he expected. "Annie," he said, louder, though his voice remained calm and even friendly. Connor was beginning to believe that Travis really did regret not having become a teacher, though the business about teaching English was puzzling. "Listen, Annie, I'm out here with the baby's father. His name is Connor, and we'd like to talk this over."

He waited, longer this time, gazing at the sign on the door as though it were itself a person or at least a portal through which he could see inside the bathroom, or even inside the heart and mind of a woman who would lock herself away with a baby.

"Okay," he said, and if anything his voice seemed more agreeable than before. "Maybe you'll talk to Connor here. He'd like to know how his little girl is doing." Leaning toward Connor, he whispered, "Go ahead now. Talk to Annie."

Connor didn't know what to say. His brain did this; it just froze up—it happened often when he was expected to speak. One of the reasons he hated school was because there were times when the teacher asked him to stand before the entire class and speak. Nothing was more intimidating than staring back at a room full of classmates, all of them confident that he was about to make a fool of himself.

Travis made a little dipping motion with his head, urging Connor to say something.

He cleared his throat, and in doing so he realized that the towel would muffle his voice. "Hello. Annie." It was almost a shout, and he was both startled and embarrassed. He leaned closer to the door and said quietly, "I just want to know if she's all right."

He glanced at Travis, who mouthed, *Use. Her. Name.*

"Annie. How is she, Annie?"

Somehow this gave Connor a shot of confidence. He was speaking not to a locked door but to the woman behind it. And with Travis perhaps he was in the hands of a true professional, someone trained to handle hostage negotiations. Travis understood the psychology behind all this, and he was shaping their tactics so that Annie wouldn't feel threatened or intimidated. The idea was to gain her trust.

"How's she doing, Annie? Is she sleeping?"

Travis nodded vigorously.

Connor's stomach felt hollow. He wished he had something in it. A hot ham and Swiss sub. Or one of those twelve-inch meatball grinders with melted provolone. He recognized that this was a dangerous situation—potentially life-threatening. This woman had locked herself in the bathroom with the baby, and it was very possible that she wanted to do the child harm. There was total silence in there. She may have already strangled or suffocated the baby. Or even committed murder and then killed herself, a homicide-suicide case, one of those unfathomable stories reported so often by the media that they seemed to be a routine solution to life's problems. Maybe he and the officer shouldn't be so la-de-dah; maybe they should pound on the door and shout, and if that didn't work then they'd find a way to open the door. A crowbar. Or, like in the movies, he could pull out his gun and shoot the doorknob and unlock the door. Or they might kick it in, though the door seemed far too substantial, not one of these cheap hollow plywood jobs you get on sale at Menards. But Travis's hand, which had been resting easily on his gun holster, floated up into the air, and he gestured toward the door, encouraging Connor to continue. He might have been conducting a symphony, telling the oboes to come in softly.

"Listen, Annie. The baby was born just hours ago. We haven't even decided on her name yet." He glanced at Travis and, as he feared, there was some consternation in his expression. Somehow this wasn't the strategy a trained professional would employ. But Connor didn't know where else to go, what alternate tack to follow, so he said, "She's so tiny. And so helpless." Travis shrugged: this was better, or he was at least accepting that Connor was developing a logical and consistent approach. "I have to tell you, Annie, we've had quite a night. I won't take you through all of it, but I have to say that the birth was really awesome." Travis appeared to be insulted, and he closed his eyes as though that might help him endure it, whatever it was that Connor did or did not say or do. "She was born in a bathtub, you know. I mean so far my little girl, my daughter, has spent most of her life in a bathroom."

Travis opened his eyes and cocked his head, as if to say, *What?* He seemed not to know what to make of it. Pursing his lips and puffing his cheeks, he blew air from his mouth.

At that moment, they heard the faintest voice say, "What?"

Connor wondered if it was a trick, if Travis was practiced in the art of ventriloquism. The way he mouthed the word *What*, followed by this distant uttering of the word, Connor wondered if he was actually capable of throwing his voice through the door and giving it a faint but majestic echo. A police officer who had considered a teaching career, who made puns, unintended or not, who knew when it was appropriate to say *whom*, there might be no limit to the man's abilities.

But with his one good eye Connor could see that Travis was startled, genuinely so, and as a result he seemed quite buoyant, encouraged even. "What was that, Annie?" he said, not too loud, maintaining a conversational tone. "We didn't quite catch all of that."

True. There was an echo, the reverberation that one gets in a tiled bathroom, and Connor realized that she might have said more than *What?*

"What bathroom?" Annie said. Slow, a bit testy. "The baby was born in what bathroom?"

Travis now squared himself to Connor, and there was no question that he expected a full reply. Annie had spoken. They had piqued her interest. This was a breakthrough.

Now Connor was confronted with so many considerations his head, which still ached terribly, was in danger of seizing up. An officer of the law was standing next to him, and if there's one thing Connor understood about himself it was that he had always harbored an intense fear of authority. Even Travis, potential school teacher and ventriloquist, represented a form of judgment that was severe and final. Connor saw himself in Presque Isle the previous afternoon, kicking the shit out of Barr. Killing him—he had wanted to kill at that moment. That was his intention. He had failed, but still there was the intention. There were things he should and should not divulge in the presence of an officer of the law. And Travis was waiting, his eyes urging Connor to respond to Annie—say something, say anything, but just keep her talking. The baby's life may depend upon it.

"It was out past Yellow Dog Township," Connor said. "Del Maki's house."

He and Travis both leaned closer to the door and waited.

Nothing.

Finally, Travis said, his tone pleasantly offhand, "Oh sure, out 644."

Again, they waited.

"I know the house," Annie said. "I know Del. He lost his wife a while back." Her voice had a touch of phlegm in it, the kind of gravel that results from years of smoking. She had to be at least in her fifties, quite possibly older. Though she was curious, there was an underlying dullness to her voice, suggesting that she was tired, worn out from the tedious bombardment of daily life. And then it came to him: she worked the counter at Sub Base. Of course, what else would she be doing back here? Marcia had gone into the bathroom, and for whatever reason she decided that it would be better to leave the baby here rather than to take her wherever they were going with Barr and Del. Marcia must have seen this woman, Annie, behind the counter, preparing for the day's business. Maybe they spoke, maybe they didn't, but in desperation Marcia made a decision: it was better to abandon the baby so that Annie would find her. But Marcia couldn't have known, wouldn't ever have expected, that Annie was someone who would decide to lock herself in the bathroom with the baby instead of doing the normal thing and calling the police. Yet she knows Del Maki, at least well enough to know that his wife had died. How does that square with a person who keeps an infant locked in the bathroom with her?

"We were at his house through the night, stranded by the storm," Connor said, "So, you met Marcia, the baby's mother?"

Annie didn't respond immediately. The baby made a small, constricted gurgling sound. Connor was encouraged, as was Travis, who nodded. "Why would she abandon this child?" Annie asked.

"That's hard to answer," Connor said. "It's complicated."

"It's always complicated. You say you and she have talked about getting married, so this is a case where she's knocked up." There was a pause. They could no longer hear the baby, but there was some movement, and Connor suspected that Annie was shifting the child in her arms. "At least she had her. So often you kids get in trouble and you just get rid of it."

"That was never going to happen," Connor said. "Not with Marcia."

"So she just leaves her here?" Annie's voice was trembling and angry. "I'm surprised she didn't throw her in the dumpster out back. You see it on the TV news, that's what they do. If she wanted to have the baby, then why'd she abandon it?"

Travis was staring at him as if to say it was a legitimate question. Maybe he should spell it all out, tell this woman in the bathroom and this police officer what these complications were—but once he went down that road, he'd have to admit too that he wasn't even certain that he was the father, and he'd have to bring Barr into it, explaining how *he* might be the father, and yesterday he had been left for dead in the snow.

Connor leaned closer to the door. "She did it, Annie, because she's afraid."

"Yes, I could see that, though I didn't realize it at the time."

"So you did meet her."

"Just for a moment. But now I realize she was, yes, she was troubled."

"That's why she did this, Annie," Connor said. "That's why she left the baby here—because of you. Because she knew you'd make sure our little girl was safe."

"We all got troubles. There's only one end to them." Something had crept into Annie's voice, some anger or resentment. "But that don't mean we lay them on the children. You hear me? You don't put your troubles on the children."

The one-room cabin creaked and rattled in the wind. Snow drifted down from the opening in the collapsed roof. Amid the shingles strewn on the floorboards, empty bottles and cans glinted in the near dark. Beneath one window facing the road lay a pile of charred wood, most likely left by kids who came here to hangout. Having crawled much of the way from the road, Del was exhausted, and he sat on the floor, resting his back against plaster and lath wall. Through the window, he watched Barr following his path from the snowbank into the woods.

This was the best he could do: lure Barr away from the truck. While he was here in the woods, out of sight of the truck, Marcia might escape. Run, leaving a trail of her own in the snow, but getting a good head start. Better still, she might flag down a passing vehicle for a ride out. There was no plan, no exit strategy. Del would just sit here and wait for Barr. At least the baby was safe—there was that. They had driven several miles out 644 when Del realized that Marcia seemed different. When she came out of Fast Break, with Barr following behind, she didn't look directly at Del. The baby in her arms was completely bundled in the blanket. Once they were underway in the truck and had made the turn at the intersection, Del frequently glanced in the rearview mirror, and still Marcia wouldn't return his gaze. At first, he thought that Barr must have said or done something while they were in the store that caused her to shut down—her face was remorseful, her averted eyes defeated. He kept glancing in the mirror hoping to get a response from her but there was nothing. Not once did she pull back the blanket to reveal the baby's head. She didn't move at all, as she'd done before, giggling and rocking the baby, her movements mysteriously in sync with the needs of the little body struggling in her arms. She just sat still in the back seat.

Then he got it. He didn't know how or why, but he understood that the baby wasn't in the blanket. Something was there in her arms, but it wasn't a baby. There was something else swaddled in the blanket and that's why she'd avoided looking back at Del, in the rearview mirror, believing that one look might give her secret away. She'd left the baby in Fast Break. How, he didn't know. At this point, it didn't matter. The baby was safe, and now it was just the three of them out here on 644.

It was nearly whiteout conditions. It would probably be that way for hours as they made their way through the woods of the western Upper Peninsula, until they reached Wisconsin. But Del understood that once they were in Wisconsin, once they were on a real highway, say, south of Oconto, on the highway to Green Bay and Milwaukee, they would make good time. At that point, Del would no longer be necessary. Once they were across the Wisconsin border, still in the woods, that's where Barr would tell him to pull over. He'd make up an excuse for them to get out of the truck, and he'd probably not want Marcia to see him do it.

So why wait? Del's chances were the same here as there. And here at least Marcia knew where she was, had a sense of which way to go. If he could get Barr out of the truck, hopefully out of sight of the truck, maybe she could get out and make a run for it. Not great odds. Even if Del managed to get Barr away from the truck, there was the possibility that Marcia wouldn't run, that she would remain in the back seat, frightened, traumatized, unable to move.

Del remembered this cabin, which he'd been driving past for years. A landmark, of sorts. When he gave directions to someone who'd never been out to the house, he'd say, *You'll pass a cabin falling down on itself.*

When Barr was about thirty yards from the cabin, Del realized there was something different about him. Something dark ran down from one eye and from his scalp. Every step he took toward the cabin it became clearer that his head was covered with blood.

Until he stopped. Barr turned and gazed back toward the road, and Del wondered if Marcia was dead or injured—something happened back there in the truck. If she could, Marcia might indeed attempt to flee, might run into the woods on the other side of the road and work her way back to Fast Break. Barr raised his head, as though sniffing a scent or gauging the direction of the wind, then as he turned he yanked down the zipper of his jeans. There was a sense of urgency in his fumbling, but uncharacteristic embarrassment, too, as he repeatedly glanced back toward the road, in the fear that someone passing by could actually see his stream of urine, arcing and carrying with the wind at his back, steaming as it bore deep into untrodden snow.

———————————

Marcia wasn't sure if she could open her eyes or if she was afraid to open them. Her face had exploded inward, a black hole of pain. Her nose, which felt as big as a fist, now seemed centered over her right cheekbone, and a throbbing ache spread to where her jaw was hinged beneath her left ear. Everything about her face was swollen, fat, plump to bursting, especially her left eye.

She lay still in the back seat of the truck. It was getting cold in the cab and she could hear the wind-driven snow raking the side of the truck. She was listening for something else, what she couldn't remember, and somehow she was convinced there was nothing more she could do. Just listen. The baby was gone. Connor was gone. The only thing, the only place for her to be was here, consumed by pain, a very different thing from the pain of giving birth. That was south, this was north.

She kept her eyes closed, listened to the wind, and tried not to think about any of it.

———————————

Travis made a circling motion with his hand, indicating that he wanted Connor to keep talking, then he pointed toward a black woman who was entering the store, followed by a large white man. They wore identical black parkas, and at first, Connor thought they were police, but they had *EMS* in reflective yellow letters on their sleeves, and beyond them an ambulance was backed up to the plateglass window. Travis walked up the aisle, the holster and a radio giving his hips a bovine lilt.

Connor turned his good ear toward the door. Silence. "Annie," he said. "It's just me now. The policeman's left us alone."

"So."

"So talk to me."

"Why?"

He hesitated. "Because the baby's mine. Ours."

"You gave it up."

"It's not that simple. There were circumstances. Marcia had to—"

"I'm tired of people and their circumstances. Want me to tell you about circumstances? I have two children, both grown and gone now. I miss them, but they have their own lives. But there was a third, a girl. She would be seventeen next month. I didn't think I could have any more kids, and there she was and I was so thankful, you have no idea. I was in my forties and carrying her was difficult. Eight and a half months, it near killed me. She was born early, a tiny thing, didn't weigh four pounds. There were complications. Or circumstances, if you want. Her lungs were underdeveloped. She had jaundice, which made her skin yellow. And they suspected that there might be some sort of brain damage, though they wouldn't be able to tell right off. They mentioned the possibility of cerebral palsy. They kept her in the hospital on a ventilator. I rarely got to see her, hold her in my arms. You never saw anything so tiny, a small life. Have you looked at this little baby's hands, her fingernails, how delicate, how perfect they are? Well, they're huge compared to my little girl's. We named her April, after my mother. It was Ron's idea. He knew I was depressed. I was feeling poorly afterward and that helped, giving the baby the name April. But they wouldn't let either of us out of the hospital. It was days, and then we were into the second week, and it seemed like an eternity. I saw her mostly to breastfeed her and when I asked when we could go home they wouldn't give me a straight answer. Very cheerful but I knew something wasn't right. Ron's a good man but meek, and he couldn't get anything out of the doctors. Then one day they come into my room and tell me she'd died during the night. Like it was a foregone conclusion, like she never had a chance. Considering the complications she faced, they made it sound like it was for the best. Better for the baby, better for us because we wouldn't have to deal with so many difficulties. Her lungs gave out, they said, but if she had lived she wouldn't have been normal. What is that, normal? You don't carry a baby for eight months and then love it just because it's *normal.* You love it because it's alive, because it became a life inside you. I wanted to see her. They were reluctant. For once Ron was insistent. They took us to a room, I don't know, I guess it was the morgue. They kept her in a drawer. She'd turned from yellow to this pale blue because her lungs failed and she suffocated. I've never stopped thinking about how she must have struggled to breathe. They finally released me from the hospital, and we buried her next to her grandmother, April and April."

"I'm sorry, Annie."

"Everybody's sorry. I've been sorry every day of my life since then. You have no idea."

"True, I don't. But I do know what it took for Marcia to do what she did."

Silence. He needed to hear something from the baby, some movement, something from her lips.

"She didn't want this child," Annie said finally. "So she's mine. I'll take good care of her."

"I know you would, Annie, but—"

"No," she said, her voice ringing off the ceramic tiles. "You're not taking her away from me. What's mine is mine. You—you and Marcia—you had your chance. If I can't keep her, nobody can."

"Annie."

"You go away and leave us be. You gave her up and—"

"Marcia was protecting her, don't you see?"

"Leaving her here, how is that protecting her?"

"She and the baby, they were in danger. Marcia still is." He waited. Silence. "There's another man, and he thinks he's the father, so he took Marcia and the baby and—"

"They ran off together?"

"He took her, against her will."

"She's mine," Annie said. Her voice was higher, and it trembled, making her sound like a child who was pleading. "You can't take her from me, you hear?"

Connor turned his head until he could see up the aisle, where Travis was talking with the EMS staff. "Annie, an ambulance is here for her."

"They want to take her to the hospital?"

"I think that's the best—"

"She's not going to any hospital."

"Listen, Annie."

"*No.* I won't let them take us. I won't let that happen. I have a knife, from the cutting board. I keep it very sharp. If she goes, I go. We'll go here, not let them do it there." Annie's voice was breaking, and she began to sob. "Oh, God. I don't want this, but we can't go back there."

"Annie, please, be reasonable."

"This is beyond reason."

"What's the point of threatening a baby when you love her?"

Annie was crying uncontrollably now. "You just, just leave us alone. Hear?"

Connor looked up the aisle again, where Travis and the paramedics seemed to have come to some decision.

"They'll be here in a minute, Annie. I don't know, they might want to break the door down or something. I just don't know."

"They can't have her." Her voice was high, quaking. "*No hospital.*"

"All right, just let me in."

"What?"

"Let me see the baby, that's all."

"Let you *in*?"

"Yes."

"You think I'm stupid?"

"No, I think you're frightened. I am too, Annie. Let me in. Please."

Connor looked toward the front of the store, and with his one good eye he saw Travis and the black woman starting down the aisle. He wanted to hold his hands up, to indicate to them that they should keep away, keep their distance. He wanted to shout to them that Annie had a knife, that there was no knowing what she might do, and that having police and EMS paramedics outside the bathroom might be too much for her. He wanted to know where Marcia was right now. If she were here, she'd know what to say, what to do.

There came a soft click, and he tilted his head until he could see the doorknob.

Barr followed Del's path, leaning into the snow. When he reached the cabin he pushed the door open and climbed in out of the wind. As he crossed the room his boots sent asphalt shingles and empty beer cans and bottles skittering across the floor. In the dim light he saw Del sitting with his back against the busted plaster wall.

"Marcia do that to you?"

Barr's eye was a crater of pain, his face frozen numb beneath the blood. "No quit in that girl, I'll give her that."

Del shifted uncomfortably.

"Can't believe you got this far. It was hard enough getting here on two good legs. If you were smart, you would have just waited in the snowbank and saved yourself the grief. If I was smart I would have gotten you to withdraw more dineros from the bank. You have more, right?"

"Not enough to really make a difference. Doesn't matter now. You won't get far."

"Farther than you."

Del raised his head to stare at the gaping open space in the roof. "This is far enough."

"That so."

"I met my wife near here. It was during a blizzard like this. She was lying in the snow. She'd taken a fall and injured her back."

"And then you both lived happily ever after."

"For a time."

"Well, time's up. Nobody's going to save you."

Del nodded. "Could be a while before anyone finds me."

"Probably be some kids, come here to drink and screw around. Maybe coyote or something will drag you off, barely leave a trace."

"That would be all right."

"You know I believe it would. I came to understand that about you. You want this. You've been looking for a way out. I suppose it has to do with that wife of yours? Something in you doesn't want to keep going, but you don't quite have it in you to do it yourself. But you want an end to it." He felt the slightest disappointment that Del wouldn't bother to look at him. He was transfixed on the light coming through the roof. "You've been preparing."

"There's something to be said for it. Think you'll ever be prepared, Barr?"

"I was born prepared. Prepared to survive. They tried to kill me yesterday. But here I be."

Barr took the revolver out of his coat pocket, his fingers so cold he could barely feel the grip in his hand. "I just don't get this. It must be yours."

Del shook his head slowly.

"Then whose is it?"

"Yours now."

Barr looked at the revolver in his hand. The man was right. This was his. Everything. If you can take this, you can take anything. He cocked the hammer as he raised his arm and pulled the trigger. Overhead, crows flushed from the trees as the report came back off the woods, soft, muted, as though someone else was out there doing the deed.

That sound.

Marcia opened her eyes. The sharp abrupt report, muffled by snow.

She struggled to sit up in the back seat of the truck. The blizzard was a total whiteout now, but that sound split the wind, and in response irate crows protested in the sky.

It was an effort to open the door and climb out, but once she was standing in cold air she knew she could walk, and that she only had a few minutes. A branch lay in the snowbank, and she picked it up—straight, about four feet long, it would make a good walking stick. If she got out into the woods this side of 644, Barr wouldn't be able to see her, and she could make her way back toward the intersection and Fast Break. It was miles; she didn't know how many. He would give up, eventually. He'd follow her path, but soon he'd realize that his only option was to return to the truck. He'd get in the truck and go. It would be a matter of self-preservation.

And her daughter, she might still be there in the bathroom. More likely that Sub Base woman Annie would have found her. They'd call the police. She'd find the baby, and they'd call the police.

Five miles. At least five.

Marcia would have to keep moving, to keep warm. To keep ahead of Barr.

But she just stood there, gazing into the white.

―――――――――――――――

Annie was sitting on the toilet lid, with the baby asleep in her lap, wrapped in a green and gold Packers sweatshirt. One hand cradled the infant's head, while the other held a kitchen knife, the kind with a long honed edge that would slice a ripe tomato effortlessly.

"Now lock it," she said.

Connor turned the latch on the doorknob.

"Sit down."

He lowered himself to the floor, the tiles against his back cool. But clean, everything really clean—there was the smell of pine disinfectant. This had to be Annie's doing. There were no windows, just white floor and wall tiles and a fluorescent light in the ceiling. Light that flickered slightly, making everything a faint pulsating blue.

Annie wore jeans, taut over bulging thighs, and a denim shirt with a patch on the breast pocket that read *Fast Break*. But her eyes, the skin beneath them not just dark but purple, the eyes of someone who hadn't had a decent night's sleep in years. The baby was sound asleep, lying on her back. Annie held the knife across the sweatshirt.

"Annie, please be careful with that."

"I am careful."

"I know that."

"Just stay where you are."

"I will."

"I'm tired of being careful. All day I make subs. My hands always smell like onions."

"Thank you for letting me in."

"You seem like a nice boy, like someone who can understand." Her smile was crooked, her lips turned up on one side, as though only half of her face was capable of joy, while the other was constantly dejected. Depressed. Deranged.

She took no notice that his head was wrapped in a towel.

He thought of Essi when she'd first gotten into his truck. She talked about snow ghosts and the storm and chocolate-covered raisins as though these were the most important things in the world, spiritual things. And there was that business about the song she couldn't remember, how she wouldn't let it go until it got in his head, too. Connor thought she was nuts. Outwardly nuts. Maybe this woman was gone in the other direction. Inwardly nuts. She was staring right at him, but he suspected she was barely seeing him. Like this bathroom, her brain had no windows and the door was locked. She couldn't see out, she couldn't get out. And somehow, because she'd lost a child years ago, she believed she deserved this baby she'd found in her disinfected bathroom, and if she couldn't have the child then nobody would—this wasn't a reason, it was something else. Something else like when Connor was hitting and kicking Barr in the snow on Presque Isle the day before. He was beyond reason. He knew what that was, he knew where that was—not where it came from, but where it took you. Annie was beyond reason, and she clung to it for dear life. Once you get there, you don't have any choice.

Outside the door, he could hear their footsteps, the knock of heavy winter boots. Somewhere in the distance—the front of the store, probably—there was static and an incomprehensible voice on someone's two-way radio.

Connor couldn't tell if Annie heard any of it, anything beyond the bathroom door. He had an uncle, Uncle Roger, who, according to Connor's mother, heard voices. That was how she explained him: *My brother has been hearing voices since we were little.* Connor liked Uncle Roger. He was funny. He farted at the dinner table. He would say things, speaking loudly, things that seemed totally out of the blue. When Connor was about nine, Uncle Roger came and lived with the family one winter. He was given the room on the third floor, and he didn't come down often except for meals and sometimes to shovel the driveway and front walk—he was obsessed with keeping them clear. Though Connor's mother said it was best to leave Uncle Roger alone upstairs—he needed to rest because he wasn't feeling well—Connor would sometimes go up after dinner, when he was supposed to be doing homework. Uncle Roger had a TV, an old wooden thing he called a console. It was so old the pictures had no color. But he rarely watched it. Most of the time he had a bedsheet draped over it so the screen was covered. Once Connor took the corner of the sheet and began to raise it, but Uncle Roger said, "Don't do that!" Frightened, Connor let go of the sheet and backed away. Then Uncle Roger, who was in the creaky wicker chair in the corner, smiled and said, "Don't want them to see us, do you?" Connor shook his head. "Good." It was like their little secret. When Uncle Roger wasn't there in the house one day in the spring, Connor couldn't get a straight answer from his mother, who was more annoyed than usual. This went on for days. *Where's Uncle Roger?*, and all she'd say was that he had to go somewhere for some help. It was in June, after school was out, when Connor helped his father clear out Uncle Roger's room. They took most of the stuff, including the wicker rocker, which was coming apart, to the dump. His father said getting that console down all those stairs was going to be a problem, and then Connor said, "Can I have it?" His father asked what he would want that old thing for, but Connor said he wanted it, and he wanted to move into the room on the third floor. His father and mother discussed it, and at dinner they said he could move up there. Connor asked, "So Uncle Roger's not coming back?" His mother teared up while she dished out casserole, and his father shook his head and said that no, Uncle Roger wouldn't be coming back.

There was a knock on the bathroom door. "Connor? Annie? What's going on?"

"Travis is back," Connor said pleasantly.

"I gather that," Annie said.

"The ambulance has arrived," Connor said. "One of the paramedics is with him."

"Hey," Travis said, not trying to sound alarmed. "Want to tell me what's going on in there?"

"Keep it down," Connor said, leaning toward the door so he wouldn't have to raise his voice. "The baby's sleeping."

Annie smiled. A half smile.

––––––––––

Barr left the cabin and started back through the woods toward the snowbank that lined CR 644. The only thing to do was finish it. Finish it and get himself out of this shit. Get so far away from this fucking snow that there would be nothing but sun and warm air, so far away nobody would recognize him. Not only leave them behind but leave himself behind. What was it called? *Molt.* Shed this skin for a new one.

He'd shot things before, deer, small animals. He believed in the notion that you—your soul or whatever—was joined with your prey. He believed that hunters formed a sacred bond with them, that you gained strength from killing them. You had to admire what you defeated, you had to take from it. He had to admit in some way he admired Del Maki. Not based on a desire to be like him—that was not possible—but by learning what he could from him. There was something clean about Del Maki. Something clear. Like running water in a shallow stream, where you could look down and see the rocks and pebbles, see the streaming moss, see a rainbow trout hovering in the lee of a fallen tree trunk. The man was clear, clear through. He took it well. Barr had tracked him down, seen what he was about, knew that he had long wanted this to end. But the man wasn't trapped; he wasn't cornered. There was dignity in that. He sat there in the light and snow coming down through that roof and looked at it straight on. He accepted it. That's what you take from this. Acceptance. Not acquiescence. Not giving up or giving in. But recognition of the truth of it. Time. It had to do with time. Del understood time. For all the books he and his dead wife had read, for all the days of his life he kept sight of time, its perpetual dominance over everything, he knew you don't beat time. You live yours, and you take everything you can in it, and then you accept the result. You believe in the end of time.

When Barr reached the snowbank, he climbed up to the crest and stared at the truck. It would be slow going in this snow, but he would get south, get down through Wisconsin, then Illinois, then wherever the highway took him, as long as it left the snow—and this northern skin—behind.

But here, it wasn't finished. Del Maki was the easy part. Marcia had brought this on; she'd earned it. He descended the snowbank and crossed the road toward the truck, his determination tempered by something he didn't want to recognize. But it was there, all the same. Sorrow.

Marcia had started to climb up the snowbank, but then she stopped and turned around, and in doing so lost her footing and fell, rolling and sliding down through the snow until she hit her shoulder against the rear tire of the truck. She wanted to cry, but that would only elicit more pain from the broken bones that were her face. She wanted to scream, to plead. But there was just the snow, the constant wind-driven snow, and crying out wasn't going to make it stop. And five miles might as well have been five . hundred miles. How had it come to this? There was no running away, no escape. She lay there on her side, hurting.

Until she heard it, some movement, something pushing through the snow on the other side of the truck. She propped herself up on one elbow and listened. It had to be Barr, crossing the road and coming around the plow attached to the front of the truck. She turned until she was on all fours and crawled until she was around the rear fender.

"Okay," Travis said, his voice close to the other side of the door. "Okay." He sounded like he was trying to calm himself down, convince himself that everything was all right. "Just tell me what the situation is in there."

"The situation," Connor said, "is the baby's having a nap. She's fine."

"Then why don't you open the door? Annie let you in, why don't you let—"

"Officer," Connor said, keeping his one eye on Annie, who seemed appreciative that he was taking control of what had become a situation. "Right now, we need you—you and the paramedic—to back off. Just give us some room."

"Listen, Connor," Travis began, but then he seemed to think better of it. He knew the difference between who and whom, and he understood that the situation had reached a delicate phase, one that required tact and diplomacy. "What you're saying is you want us to move away from the door, give you some space."

"That's what I'm saying."

There was a moment, a silence in which Connor imagined Travis and the paramedic exchanging glances, determining their options, coming to an agreement about what to do. "All right," Travis said. "The baby is okay; she's sleeping. So Yvonne and I are going to give it a little time. But not too much time. Do you understand?"

"I understand," Connor said. Names. Use names. "Now, Officer, you and Yvonne go back up front with the others."

Again, silence, but then he heard those boots, those heavy insulated boots, knock on the linoleum floor as they walked past the Sub Base counter and up the aisle to the front of the store.

Annie seemed relieved, but at the same time there was something totally immobile about her, reminding Connor of the way a cat would be still: as though to become invisible, capable of evading detection. But also ready to pounce. The thing about animals was they often avoided looking right at each other. Connor had seen this in cats, in dogs, and he imagined it was something that you'd find when two animals encountered each other in the woods. To look right at Annie might seem aggressive, a challenge. He lowered his one seeing eye, his revealed eye, and turned his head toward the sink next to Annie. The plumbing pipes beneath the sink were chrome, and there was a small tag hanging from one of the two valve spigots in the wall, which read: *Hot Water Shut Off TIGHT! You'll Need a Wrench.* It must have been written by Annie, or maybe Ron, up at the front counter. People who understood work, understood the need for the proper tool, people who planned ahead.

"I had this uncle," Connor said. "Uncle Roger. He lived with us one winter when I was a kid. I didn't learn until much later that when he suddenly disappeared he had been taken away, maybe to a hospital, but I think probably some kind of institution, and it wasn't long before he died. He left this old TV up in his room. A console."

"I remember those," Annie said.

"It was a black and white TV."

"Everybody had black and white when I was little. And there was no such thing as a remote."

"I know. He used to ask me to go over and turn the dial to change the channels. But he seldom watched the TV, though once, when I was home sick from school, he let me watch an old movie with him."

"What was it?"

"I don't remember the name. Cowboys, Indians, a wagon train. Westerns, he called them. He said they'd been his favorite when he was my age. I would never have watched this movie on my own, but with Uncle Roger it was kind of neat. He wrapped me up in a blanket on the floor with his pillow under my head, and at one point he went down to the kitchen and made us popcorn. In the end, the wagon train got through the mountain pass to California."

"In the movies, they always did," Annie said. "My mother was Ojibwa, and I remember when we got our first TV—with these rabbity ears for an antenna, which we wrapped in tinfoil for better reception—and my grandfather came over from Brimley, and he said it was a dangerous thing to have a TV in the house. Said it like evil spirits had invaded the house."

"You believe in spirits, Annie?"

"I do."

"I could tell."

"They're everywhere. The earth is filled with them. People who don't realize that, there's something they don't get, something about this place we inhabit that they don't appreciate. Understand what I mean?"

"I do," Connor said. "My uncle, he understood that, too. Know what he did?" He glanced at Annie, and she shook her head. "He kept this old bedsheet draped over the TV so you couldn't see the screen. When I asked him why, he said, 'Because of them. The people in the TV. They can see you.'"

"You betcha. TVs, cameras, don't trust 'em. But radios was okay."

"After he left, after Uncle Roger died, I moved into that room on the third floor, and I kept the TV. Took me a while to figure it out. I kept that sheet over it and only used the console like a table to keep stuff on. But then one day—I musta been eleven or twelve—I took the sheet off and turned the TV on and looked at the screen. The picture was lousy. The people looked out at me, particularly during the newscast, but I knew they couldn't see me." Connor laughed. He started, couldn't stop, and soon Annie joined him. "The meteorologist, I gave her the finger. Nothing. Then I stood up, pulled down my pants, and mooned her. Nothing. She kept talking about the weekend forecast."

Annie was in tears from laughing, so hard the baby stirred on her lap.

"But that doesn't mean there aren't spirits," he said.

"No," Annie said, looking down at the baby. "They're just not in your TV. They're here, with us. In the world, in our hearts. They're everywhere. Always."

Connor let his eye drift in her direction. "You think she might be getting hungry?"

She seemed perplexed. "Has she been breastfed?"

"Yes, but it's been some time ago now."

Annie nodded. Sad, remorseful. "I'm afraid I'm well beyond that."

"She's a little young for a meatball sub."

That didn't bring her out of it. She was staring at him now, as if for the first time. Something in her eyes, in her face had unlocked. "Why is your head wrapped in a towel?"

"Thought you'd never ask. Had an accident last night."

"What happened?"

"Well. A gun went off and I guess the bullet took part of my ear."

"An accident."

"Kinda. It was the guy who's taken Marcia away. He's why she left the baby here, to keep her away from this guy. His name is Barr. I've known him for years, but it's only been over the past year or so that I've really had to deal with him." She was nodding. He might have been speaking a foreign language, only a few words and phrases of which she understood, but it was enough that she could get the gist of what he meant. "You might say it's been difficult."

He raised his arms slowly, so she wouldn't think he was trying anything, and felt for the tape that held the towel in place. Carefully, he began to peel the tape away.

"That part over your ear," she said, "the blood looks dry."

As he unwrapped the towel there was a nasty pulling sensation on the side of his head, but as the cloth was unwound his skin welcomed the exposure to air. When he had the towel off, he touched his ear with a fingertip. "Still bleeding?"

"Just a little."

"It's good to be able to see with both eyes," he said. "That was the worst part of it, no depth perception."

"This guy, Barr, he did this? By accident?"

"I guess. But that's not all of it, to be truthful. Yesterday I tried to kill him. I didn't plan it. It was out on Presque Isle, just as the blizzard was ramping up. I thought he and Marcia were meeting out there, and it's like something switched inside me. I was beyond all reason, know what I mean? I beat him; I kicked him when he was down. I left him for dead in the snow. I wanted him dead, Annie. I wanted no more trouble from him. If I had killed him, we wouldn't be here now. I don't know where I'd be. But it wasn't the right thing to do. I was beyond all reason, that's all, and I shouldn't have done it. I'm responsible for all of this, the baby being left here, Barr taking off with Marcia. Everything."

Her mouth was working, and she hadn't taken her eyes off of him. From the front of the store, they could hear boots knocking on the linoleum floor, getting closer.

"So I've got to make things right."

Nodding, she said, "I believe you, honey."

"For starters, Annie, I'd like you to hand me that knife."

At first, Barr couldn't see past his reflection in the truck window but leaning closer realized that she wasn't in the cab. He turned around and saw the deep prints that climbed up the snowbank, but they stopped before reaching the crest. The snow at his feet was tamped down, as though she had rolled around in it, and he thought of her on her hands and knees. In the end, Marcia would crawl.

He'd hit her pretty good, several jabs to the face, and there was some satisfaction in the knowledge that he may have really hurt her, so bad that she could only attempt to get away on all fours. This wasn't the same as with Del Maki. He wanted her to hurt first. He wanted her to see it coming, to have that moment of recognition. He wanted her to know that it was payback. What he'd wanted from her had been twisted into something dark and vile, and she had refused to go back to the way it had been, and at least at the end he wanted her to know that whatever hurt she'd caused him he was able to ride it out.

Del Maki had asked him if he was prepared.

He was prepared. That was how you survived.

She wasn't going to survive, and he wanted that knowledge to hurt. He wanted her to crawl and to be afraid. She owed him that much.

"Where'd you go?"

Marcia had found her walking stick lying next to her in the snow. She took hold of it in both hands as she got up into a crouch. Good heft, like a baseball bat. She heard Barr's boots in the snow next to the passenger side of the truck, and then there was nothing, only the wind in the trees overhead. There was a cap on the truck bed and, looking through the rear glass and the small side-window, she saw Barr. He had his back to the truck when he said, "Where'd you go?"

Rising up, she stepped out from behind the truck. As he turned around his right hand came out of his coat pocket holding the revolver. She swung the stick, hitting the side of his head and causing him to stagger backward. She swung again, this time lower, catching him under the ribs, doubling him over as he hoarsely inhaled air. He seemed mystified, as though he couldn't remember something important. He began to straighten up and raised the arm that still held the revolver. Marcia swung again, landing a blow on his forehead, knocking him back against the hood of the truck, and she kept hitting him as he went down, the pistol falling from his hand. At this point she may have been shouting, she wasn't sure, but she continued to club him until she was on her knees, out of breath.

The gun was partially buried in the blood-red snow, and she picked it up. Barr lay on his side, motionless. She got to her feet, aimed the gun at his head, and waited. He didn't move, and he didn't move, and when she couldn't wait any longer, when she was sure he wasn't ever going to move, she heaved the gun over the snowbank and into the woods. She didn't hear it land in the snow, as though it had been carried away on the wind in eternal flight.

There was a knock on the door. "We need to know what's going on in there." It was Yvonne. "Talk to us."

Connor continued to look at Annie now. "We're getting ready," Connor said.

"Ready?" Yvonne waited but only for a moment. "Ready, how?"

"Give us another minute," Connor said. "We're almost there."

Annie exhaled, and it was as though she'd been holding her breath for a very long time. Her hand, the hand holding the knife, came toward Connor, her arm extended, the fingers turning the knife until she was offering the handle to him. Her eyes didn't leave his until he leaned forward and took hold of the knife by the handle. For a moment they remained that way, both hands on the knife handle, their fingers touching, and then she let go.

"I wouldn't have hurt her."

"I know."

"You're going to be a good father."

"I hope so." Louder, he said, "All right, we're coming out." He got to his feet and wrapped the knife in the bloody towel, and then tucked it in his coat pocket. "Annie, can I hold her?"

She looked up at him, uncertain.

"I haven't even held her yet."

As Annie stood up, he placed one hand on her elbow. She seemed to appreciate the gesture. As she placed the baby in his arms, she took his left hand and guided it so that his palm was cradling the soft skin at the back of her skull. "I'm afraid I'll drop her."

"No, you've got it. You just want to make sure you support her head like that." Annie seemed relieved as she turned the latch and opened the door. Travis and the paramedic Yvonne, who had short bristling gray hair and one earring, both backed up as Annie led Connor out of the bathroom.

"So?" It was all Travis could say.

"She saved the baby," Connor said.

Yvonne looked skeptical, but then she looked like someone who had never believed anyone in her life. She pointed toward the knife handle sticking out of Connor's pocket. "What about that?"

"Annie was working at the counter when she heard the baby. She had the knife in her hand when she went into the bathroom."

"And locked the door," Yvonne said.

"Jammed," Connor said.

"Jammed." Yvonne seemed to suddenly realize there was something wrong with one of his ears.

"Yeah. The lock jammed. Annie got it open but after I went inside it jammed again."

Annie's eyes were welling up. She was wearing an apron about her waist, and she took up a corner of it and daubed at her face.

"So what's with your ear?" Yvonne asked.

"Long story," Connor said, looking down at the baby in his arms. "She's only a few hours old."

Travis reached toward Connor's coat and removed the knife. He unwound the towel carefully, as though expecting to find evidence. "This is your blood," he said.

"Yes," Connor said.

Travis inspected the knife blade. "And this?"

"Tomatoes," Annie said. "I was slicing tomatoes when I heard a baby crying in the bathroom."

Connor could see that Yvonne wasn't convinced, but Travis appeared undecided. "Well, I'm holding onto it for the time being," he said. "Yvonne, maybe we should get him and the baby in the ambulance?"

Yvonne nodded, and stepping forward she extended her arms. "I'll take her."

"No," Connor said. "I've got her. She's fine."

Yvonne clearly wasn't pleased about this, but then Annie said, "He's the father. He can take her."

For a moment Yvonne looked like she wanted to argue the point, but then she nodded—not approval but acceptance.

Marcia crossed the road and climbed to the crest of the snowbank, where she could see a cabin in the woods. She eased herself down the back side of the snowbank and followed the path through the snow. When she reached the open cabin door, she said, "Del?"

There was no response.

She was reluctant to enter the cabin, thinking of an appointment she had in Negaunee last spring. Her client was a woman in her nineties who, along with advanced osteoporosis, was beginning to show signs of dementia, yet she still managed to live alone. Marcia had found the front door unlocked—which was not unusual—but it was left ajar. After saying the woman's name, Elaine, several times, there was still no response. When Marcia shoved open the door and stepped into the living room, she found Elaine sitting in her recliner, her head back and her mouth open, reminding Marcia of the way newly hatched birds open their mouths expecting food. The television was on with the sound muted, and a red banner across the bottom of the screen read *Breaking News.* Marcia called Lindy, who said she'd have an ambulance sent out. Marcia turned the television off—it seemed disrespectful to leave it on—and sat in the rocking chair in the corner and waited. While pushing herself back and forth, she stared at Elaine, trying not to think about anything in particular. But now, standing outside the cabin door in the wind and snow, she realized she'd been thinking about death, how she had no idea what it was, other than the end to the here and now. It was all you really had, until it was gone, and it was gone for Elaine.

It wouldn't be anything like Elaine dying in her recliner while watching breaking news. Marcia was certain that Del had been shot. There would be blood. Though she'd just seen blood where Barr lay in the snow, and though she'd given birth only hours earlier, which in itself was a different sort of blood and gore, she didn't want to see it now. But she couldn't just leave him there.

She grabbed hold of the doorjambs and pulled herself inside the cabin. It was a relief to be out of the wind, and after a moment her eyes adjusted to the absence of light. Across the room she could see him slumped over on one side, his head against the wall. Snow fell through a gap in the roof, fine as sifted flour. His wool cap and coat were lined with snow, each crease edged in white, a reverse shadow. He'd been shot in the chest. She couldn't tell exactly where because there was so much blood.

She went to him and got down on her knees.

He raised his head.

Marcia was kneeling before him as snow drifted down from the faint light overhead. The pressure on his chest seemed to have made his mouth thick with blood.

Marcia whispered, "We need to get you out of here."

Del wasn't sure where *here* was.

"I'll carry you out to the road," she said, louder, more insistent, as though she expected an argument from him.

It came to him: he remembered Barr pointing the gun at him in the kitchen, but he didn't understand how he got here. This was the fall-down cabin in the woods on 644. The road home. He knew every turn, every tree. "You just had a baby," he whispered. "You can't carry me."

"Okay." A faint smile, dimpled, as though she realized the joke was on her. "I could build a litter, like Connor did, and drag you out to the road."

His throat was closing up, making it difficult to breathe. He wanted to say something, he wanted to tell her that he understood: she'd left the baby back at Fast Break. He didn't get it at first, the way she held the blanket when she got back in the truck. She wasn't cradling it as before but clutching it to her chest. But he wasn't sure. They went into the station, and somehow, without Barr knowing, she managed to leave the baby. Where? Where do you leave an infant in a gas station?

"I'll need—" she said, looking about the cabin. "I'll need to go out and find some branches to build a litter."

When she began to get up off her knees, he reached out and grabbed her forearm. It took most of his strength to hold on, until she gave in and sat back on her haunches. He managed to say, "Just stay. Here."

She took his hand. Resignation did not come easily to her eyes.

"Where's Barr?"

Blood covered their hands, warm between their palms. "I know why you came out here to the cabin," she said. "You wanted him to follow so I could run off into the woods."

"Why didn't you?"

"I couldn't," she said. "He's dead, he's gone."

"You killed him?"

She nodded once.

"Where is he?"

"In the road, by the truck."

"Someone will come by soon. They'll help you carry me out." He knew she understood what he was saying. "Listen. In his pocket, there's the bank envelope. It's for you, you and Connor and the baby." She shook her head, but stopped when he said, "Let's just wait. It won't be long now."

He raised his head and through the gap in the roof saw pines arching high above the cabin. Their branches, laden with snow, moved in the wind. There was a cadence to the gusts, which caused the trees to lean together, to give until the press of air eased, and then, stubborn and resolute, they righted themselves, as though preparing for the next blow. Snow drifted down on him, melting on his face, catching in his eyelashes, and he knew that this was the last thing, trees that will one day fall but today refused to yield.

Marcia felt the life go out of his hand. His eyes, gazing up at the light coming through the roof, were unseeing, still. She continued to hold his hand, waiting, though she knew he wasn't coming back. Everything she'd said to him he'd taken with him. Not lost. Safe.

Connor sat on the lowered gurney in the back of the ambulance, the baby in his arms. The double doors were open, and he could see Travis, sitting in his patrol car while he talked on his two-way radio. When he was finished, he got out of the car and spoke to Yvonne and the other EMS paramedic, a large man named James. They appeared undecided. When they came to an agreement, they walked toward the ambulance, and Connor was sure.

"They've been found," he said.

"A snowplow driver called in to the station," Travis said. "They're out on 644."

"Let's go," Connor said.

"You should go to the hospital," Yvonne said. "You and your little girl."

Connor shook his head.

Travis was about to speak, but then he looked at Yvonne, and they stepped away from the back of the ambulance to confer again. Essi, who had been standing by Beryl's truck, talking to Paavo and Beryl, came over to the ambulance.

"What is it?"

"They've found them," Connor said.

Travis and Yvonne returned to the ambulance, and Connor said, "You need the ambulance out there, don't you?" Neither of them said anything, which seemed sufficient confirmation. "Then we're going with you. We'll ride in back here, and you can do what you can with the baby and my ear. The baby is fine, though I think she's hungry. Let's go."

They only looked in at him.

Connor raised his free arm to salute Paavo and Beryl, and they waved back, like a couple about to send their kid off on his first day of school, proud, fearful, and trying to maintain brave faces for whatever was to come.

Travis and Yvonne still hadn't moved.

"I said, let's go." Connor didn't raise his voice. He didn't need to.

"When the police get here,

you're going to have some explaining to do."

"Everything I told you is the truth."

"Just tell it like you told me." He said his name was Bruce and his snowplow was a little ways up the road, idling. He might have been wearing his snowsuit since October, and the furry flaps of his hat stuck out sideways like stubby airplane wings. He pointed to the woods beyond the pickup truck. "You threw the gun out that-away?"

"Think I should go get it?"

"No. Then there will be tracks and who knows what they'll make of that. Let them find it. Let them see that you flung it out there." He had collapsed cheeks above a gray beard, and he surveyed the road until his seasoned gaze settled on the cabin.

"I couldn't carry him out," she said. "I wanted to try, but he said no. And then he was gone."

"Leave him be. Don't want the police to think you've tampered with their crime scene."

Marcia folded her arms. *Crime scene.* She hadn't felt cold until now, hadn't even thought about the cold. She looked at Barr, lying next to the pickup truck. Most of the blood had been covered with fresh snow.

Bruce raised his head, nodding. "Here they come."

Marcia turned and watched a police cruiser followed by an ambulance emerge from the snow, lights flashing. She closed her eyes, but the strobe effect still pulsated in the darkness, which only heightened her fatigue. Before Bruce's snowplow had arrived, she had struggled through the snow from the cabin back to the road, hoping to flag down a passing vehicle. But then she remembered her cell phone. Barr had it. She wanted to see if it might pick up a signal out here. She knelt beside his body and examined what she'd done—she couldn't remember it clearly, other than the exertion required to swing that stick. Long after he was down, she had continued to hit him, his face and hair covered in blood, his closed eyes swollen, his lips split. She thought she'd yelled, but she wasn't certain; it might have been the sounds made with the effort of each swing, something primal like when she was pushing the baby out, her body seeming to explode with the force of it. Eventually, she looked away from the damage she'd done and reached inside his coat pocket and found a cell phone. His, not her flip phone. No signal. She returned it to the pocket and took him by the shoulder and rolled him onto his back. Her phone was in the other pocket, its rounded casing familiar in her hand, but she also felt the edges of the envelope. Del's cash. Take it, he'd said, for her and Connor and the baby. It was an offering, an instruction. She removed the phone and jammed it into her coat pocket, and then put her hand back in Barr's pocket, the envelope containing the wad of bills thick and substantial in her cold fingers.

When she heard the car door shut, she opened her eyes and watched a policeman walk toward them.

"It's Sloane," Bruce said quietly. "Good. He's okay."

Sloane looked weary, like he'd also been up all night. "Bruce," he said cordially.

"Travis."

"And you must be the woman who left her baby at Fast Break. Marcia, is it?"

"Yes, sir. Marcia Fournier."

"Thank you for that."

"For what?"

"Your last name."

She didn't know what to say, so she said, "You're welcome."

He wore one of those Russian fur hats and slid a hand up under it to rub his forehead as he studied Barr's body lying next to the truck's snowplow. "How'd this happen?"

"I did it," she said.

"You did?"

"Yes, sir. With that stick. After he shot and killed the man in the cabin out there."

"What man?"

"Del Maki."

Looking toward the cabin, he said, "I know Del. Knew." Sloane considered Barr again. "You used that stick." She nodded. "Where's the gun?"

"I threw it," she said pointing to the woods on the opposite side of the road. "Over there."

Behind him someone got out of the ambulance, a black woman with graying hair that spiked out from beneath a wool cap. Sloane turned and raised his hand as though directing traffic. She thrust her hands in the pockets of her parka and waited by the ambulance.

Sloane faced Marcia, his eyes kindly but neutral. He stared at her long enough that she wanted to look away but didn't dare, fearing it might suggest guilt. "I'm going to have to call this in, get more people out here." He regarded the way she was hugging herself. "Cold?"

"I'm getting there."

"We may be here awhile," he said. "You can sit in my patrol car."

"What about my baby? And Connor? She's with him?"

"Yvonne will put you in my car where it's warm," he said. "She'll take a look at your nose. And then she'll bring the baby to you. But for the time being it's best we keep you and Connor separate. They'll want to take your statement." He said to Bruce, "Let's you and I have a look in that cabin."

My statement. Marcia said, "There's something else."

"What's that?"

"In Barr's pocket, there's an envelope with money in it. A lot of money. It belonged to Del Maki." She began walking toward the patrol car.

Yvonne climbed into the back of the ambulance, pulling the double doors closed behind her, shutting out the wind. "How's that ear?"

James, the paramedic, had been taping a gauze pad over Connor's ear. "What's left of it will make a nice conversation piece. Just tell 'em, 'Ear today, gone tomorrow.'"

"You people who deal with blood and needles, part of your job to be funny?" Connor asked.

James's fingers touched something that made Connor wince. "All in the name of medicine."

"Never been quick with jokes."

"You don't say."

Essi was sitting on the bench on the other side of the gurney, holding the baby in her arms. "Can you hear out of it?" she asked.

"Sort of. I'll have to learn how to . . ." Connor mouthed, *read lips.*

James laughed. "A real comedian. Only needs to work on his delivery."

"Scoot over." Yvonne sat down on the bench next to Essi. They were all close to each other, knees touching. She leaned forward, resting her elbows on her thighs. She was going to tell him why they were keeping him here in the ambulance. Connor watched her mouth, waiting.

"Marcia's all right, Connor, but you can't see her just yet. We're going to have to keep you in here until the police tell us it's okay."

"Why?"

"You're going to have to wait a bit longer." She had a slight sore in the corner of her bottom lip, the kind of thing that develops in cold weather. "There are procedures that have to be followed in such cases."

"In such cases?"

"A lot has happened here. I don't know exactly what myself. I can tell you that two men are dead. I don't know their names." Yvonne hesitated, glancing at Essi. "They were in a pickup truck with Marcia. Did you know them?"

Essi didn't answer immediately. She was very still, quite calm. "Yes," she said finally. "We knew them."

"One of them is Del Maki," Connor said. "And the other, his last name is Barr. Two Rs. I don't know his first name. He just went by Barr."

"You'll have to stay here till the police sort it out." Yvonne spoke slowly, and she seemed to be enunciating carefully for his benefit. "They're coming out from Marquette. Officer Sloane said he'd come and let you know when you could see Marcia." Yvonne considered the baby sleeping in Essi's arms. "She's asked to see the baby. I'd like to take her to her."

Connor held out his arms, and Essi placed the baby in them, so gently that she didn't wake up. When they'd gotten into the ambulance at Fast Break, James gave them a blanket to wrap the baby in. The wool was rough in Connor's fingers. "Why can't I take her to her mother?"

"I understand what you did back there in the bathroom," Yvonne said. "But, as I said—"

"I'm her father." Connor thought he might be speaking too loudly because of his loss of hearing. He said, more quietly, "Marcia's my fiancée." He'd never used the word before. He liked it.

Yvonne sucked in her lower lip, which seemed to suggest that there was a limit to her patience. She was accustomed to telling people what to do, not explaining why they had to do it.

"She must be hungry," Essi said. "If Yvonne takes her to Marcia, she can feed her."

Yvonne seemed grateful.

"Marcia," Connor said, "she's really all right?"

"I've looked after her, and she's okay," Yvonne said. "She's sitting in the back of a patrol car, keeping warm."

"Looked after her?"

"She has a broken nose, at least. Won't be certain till we get her to X-ray."

"Barr, he did it."

"I don't know, nothing's certain. But she's okay. I told you, she wants to feed the baby."

Connor patted the infant's back, small as a loaf of bread. "You have children, Yvonne?"

"Two grown and one teenager."

"You remember how to carry a baby?"

Her mouth smiled, and she said, "That stays with you, like riding a bicycle."

He handed the baby to her. "You let me know as soon as I can see them."

"I will," Yvonne said.

"Yvonne." Connor leaned toward her and made a point of whispering. "How did they die?"

"I'm not sure. That's what they're trying to determine." As Yvonne got to her feet, she seemed to reconsider. "I believe the man in the cabin, Del Maki, was shot." She looked at Essi. "Are you . . . are you related?"

Essi shook her head.

"We spent the night in his house," Connor said. "To get out of the storm."

James opened one of the two back doors, and Yvonne stepped down from the ambulance, being careful of the baby in her arms. As he pulled the door shut, James said, "Let me finish taping you up."

"I'm fine," Connor said.

"One last."

Connor nodded, and then he said to Essi, "Then we're going to wait outside. It's hot in here."

"Deal." James tore off another strip of white tape. "Wind's starting to let up. Storm's supposed to clear out by tonight. This one has been a beaut. Now hold your head still."

———

Everything seemed to take a long time. But it was warm in the patrol car, and Marcia sat with her back against the rear passenger-side door so she could stretch her legs out across the seat. *Crime scene.* The police kept arriving in cars and vans, uniformed officers and people who seemed to be technicians, toting cases with equipment and wearing white jumpsuits that made them resemble animated snowmen. They inspected the road, the snowbanks, the interior of Paavo's truck. The area around the truck had been cordoned off with bright yellow tape that shimmered and twisted in the wind. Photographs were taken. There was the frequent static and crackle of two-way radios, as though the air had become charged with electricity. One group of men climbed over the snowbank next to the pickup truck and returned with a plastic bag containing the pistol Marcia had thrown into the woods. Barr's body was placed in one of the vans, which immediately headed back down 644 toward Marquette. Another team, carrying a stretcher, set out for the cabin. An older man in a fedora was at the center of it all, giving instructions to the others.

First, a paramedic who said her name was Yvonne had gotten in the back seat with Marcia. She had a first aid kit and cleaned the dried blood from Marcia's face. Her nose felt enormous, and the pain radiated out into the bones around her eyes. "Broken, most likely," Yvonne said. "You'll have a couple of shiners for a while."

"What about my baby? Connor? Why can't I see them?"

"Sorry, not yet," Yvonne said.

After she left a police officer, a woman whose name Marcia didn't remember, got in the patrol car. Very officious. She asked questions, recording Marcia's answers on a notepad.

Once she was alone again, Marcia dozed until the man wearing the fedora opened the rear door of the cruiser. He said his name was Detective Sunderson, and he said it as though he didn't quite believe it himself. If she had seen him in a bar, sitting with a beer mug in front of him, he would not have looked out of place. His mouth was concealed by a gray mustache, the kind that would collect foam off the top of a beer. She pulled her legs up so he could sit next to her in the back seat and shut the door against the cold. The alignment of his eyes wasn't quite right—she suspected he could only see out of one, but she couldn't be sure which was the good eye. He seemed distracted, spending considerable time staring out the window at the others going about their business. When something came to him, he mentioned it as though he were just trying to make conversation.

"That was some beating you put on him."

It wasn't a question. Marcia said nothing. She wondered if the investigators would be able to determine that not all of Barr's injuries had been sustained today.

"You did it with the stick?"

"Yes."

"After he shot Maki."

"Yes."

"You saw him shoot him?"

"No. I was in the truck, but I heard the shot come from the cabin."

"I suppose you thought he might come back and shoot you."

"I didn't know what he'd do," she said. "He'd already done this to my face, and he had a gun."

Sunderson removed his hat and placed his forehead against the window glass. She thought he might nod off. If she closed her eyes, she was certain she'd fall asleep. She tried not to think about the ache that radiated from the bridge of her nose.

"Did you know Del Maki?" she asked finally. "He said he'd been in law enforcement, and then was a parole officer."

"Sure, I knew Del."

She waited, but he didn't say anything else. Not that he was holding anything back but as though they shared the same opinion of the man. As though it were a foregone conclusion.

"Del's money," she said. "You found the envelope in Barr's pocket?"

"Yes. We checked with the bank. It was as you said."

They didn't speak for some time. Sunderson didn't appear to be satisfied, but he wasn't particularly distressed or perturbed either. He seemed to be a man who had heard it all before but knew it would never be enough. She suspected he just wanted to remain in the car and keep warm.

After gazing out at the snow for several minutes, he said, "A good blizzard . . ."

She waited, but he seemed not to realize that he'd spoken. "What about it?"

"What?"

"A good blizzard, what?"

"Oh. They always make me hungry." His fingers stroked the little feather in his hat band. "But then so does a sunny day in July."

"My baby must be hungry. When will I get to see her? And Connor?"

"Of course, the baby—she's fine. Yvonne has gone to her ambulance, and she'll bring her to you. She says Connor did something brave at the gas station."

"What did he do?"

Sunderson fit the hat on his head and gave the brim a tug. "You'll see him soon. Why don't we let him explain it all to you?" He pulled the door handle but seemed reluctant to leave the car. "That was some beating, Marcia Fournier. You are one strong young woman."

Sunderson opened the door, admitting a brutal rush of cold air. He hoisted himself out of the car, and then waved to Yvonne, who stood next to the ambulance, carrying the baby wrapped in a wool blanket.

When James put his roll of tape away, Essi got up off the bench, opened one of the back doors, and led Connor outside. His loss of hearing affected his balance, and the earth seemed in danger of tilting. The road was now clogged with police vehicles. Groups of men and women inspected the area around Paavo's truck, which had been cordoned off with yellow tape. Connor listened to his blood surge inside his skull as he watched Officer Sloane walk toward the ambulance, followed by Yvonne, who must have delivered the baby to Marcia. When she reached the cab of the ambulance, she climbed up into the driver's seat.

Sloane came over to Connor and Essi, his hands jammed in the pockets of his coat. "We just received a call," he said. "They need the ambulance to go see about a fender bender on 41."

Connor felt the slightest pull of jealousy, realizing that these people in uniform lived from one emergency to another. It was hard work, good work. "I understand you have procedures to follow," he said.

"A matter of formalities. They're finished taking Marcia's statement. You can join her and the baby in my cruiser, and soon as I'm finished here I'll get you to the hospital."

Almost a welcome distraction, they moved to the side of the road as Yvonne turned the ambulance around so she could drive back toward Marquette. The spinning yellow lights and Day-Glo reflector stripes on the vehicle seemed alien amid the infinite degrees of white.

"My car and Connor's truck," Essi said. "They're back there on 644, several miles past the Fast Break intersection, on the way to Yellow Dog Township and Del's house, what's left of it. They'll need to be towed."

"I'll call to see if they can send wreckers out—storm like this, they're busy. It'll be awhile."

"And my dog's out there," she said. "She died when we went off the road."

Sloane seemed at a loss. He looked over his shoulder at the county snowplow that was farther up the road, idling like some great mechanical beast. "Bruce says he's heading that way. I'm sure he'll give you a lift." Sloane looked as though he needed to get something off his mind. "I'm really sorry about your dog."

He went back toward Paavo's truck, stooping to pass beneath the yellow tape.

"He told me he should have been an English teacher," Connor said.

"Or maybe a veterinarian."

Connor didn't know what else to say, didn't know if he should even try. "You all right?" It was all he could think of.

"I'm all right."

"I expected you to say something like 'What's all right?'"

"And what would you say?"

"I have no idea." He paused, looking at her. "I would say 'I have no idea.'"

"That's what I'd hope you'd say." She reached up and touched the bandage over his ear. "We should all learn to read lips. Helps you get to know people. You'll be good at it."

The four men who had gone out to the cabin appeared at the top of the snowbank carrying the stretcher with Del in a body bag. They were careful getting it down to the road and in the back of one of the vans.

"I don't think he was afraid of Barr," Connor said. "Barr expected you to fear him. Del wasn't afraid of anything. That's what you and he have in common. No fear."

Essi watched the van move down 644, slowly weaving around the other vehicles. "I wish that were true, Connor." She nodded as though she had just come to a decision. "I think I will see him again."

"Really?"

"Yes, soon." She seemed to like something about his face, his reaction, as though she were staring at a curious little boy. "In my dreams. Dead people often come to me in my dreams."

"Do they?"

"You probably don't take much stock in dreams."

"That's true. But I'm learning to."

"Good. Know what's interesting about these people?"

"The ones that come to you in your dreams?"

"Yeah. They don't know they're dead."

"They don't?"

"No, they're really kind of clueless."

This was getting to be like when they had been in his truck together. Then, he was baffled and a bit unnerved, but he now felt comfortably alert. "Maybe this is all a dream," he said. "Maybe it's one of your dreams?"

"Why do you think that?"

"I don't know. But then I'm kind of clueless."

"We all are," she said. "And that would explain a lot. We don't really know our purpose."

"No, I believe we do," he said.

Now it was she who looked surprised. Pleased.

"You and your dream," he said. "Like it's God, or something. Clueless but responsible for all this. All of us. The storm. Chocolate raisins. Everything. Even that song we couldn't remember the name of."

"You would think God would at least know *that*."

"You would think. When you see Del, you'll say hi for me?"

She didn't say anything but mouthed, *I will.*

The investigation teams had begun to pack their gear in the cars and vans, and the yellow tape was being rolled up. As Essi walked among them, no one took notice of her. She might have been invisible.

Not a ghost.

A spirit.

After she breastfed the baby, Marcia dozed again until there was a tap on the window. She looked out at Essi, who placed her gloved hand on the window for the briefest moment. She gazed through the window at the baby, and then nodded once and walked on down the road to the snowplow. After speaking to Bruce, she went around to the passenger door and climbed into the cab. Bruce deftly maneuvered the truck around the parked vehicles, and the massive vehicle disappeared in the snow, heading toward Yellow Dog Township.

Marcia stroked the fine hair on her child's head. "I remember my mother used to sometimes ask me if I was happy. She'd ask it when I came home from school. Sometimes when she put me to bed. It was one of the few times she ever seemed interested in what was going on with me. 'Were you happy today?' she'd ask. I don't ever remember telling her that I was—but I don't really remember what I said. I usually just nodded and let her draw her own conclusions. I don't know what happy is. I don't think I ever have. I'm not sure why. If you're not happy, does it mean you're unhappy? Why is it important to be happy? Is life a disappointment if you aren't? Really, I don't know many people who seem genuinely happy. And those who are, I either don't trust them, thinking they're hiding something, or I don't believe them. For some reason I don't envy them. But we all have this thing about being happy.

"I don't know if you will ever be happy. Not often, anyway. I would like you to be content. It's a deeper thing, a kind of satisfaction—don't ask me to explain it, but I know what it means. It comes from someplace else. Where, I'm not sure. Contentment, we often call it contentment, though that suggests that you're kind of sitting back and soaking it in and not doing anything. That's not it either. I want you to be doing whatever it is you want to do and find that it makes you content. I doubt I'll be able to explain this to you later, when you're older. I also doubt I'll be able to help you with anything that's important. I will try not to get in the way. Let you do it yourself, find it on your own. Whatever it is. Because I suppose that's the only way you might be content, by finding what it is on your own.

"Maybe someday I'll tell you about how you were born, about this night and morning. Maybe I won't; we'll have to see. Maybe I'll make something up and say you were born on a boat or in a hospital, like most babies. Something like that. But I hope I don't. I hope I don't feel it's necessary to lie to you. I think you'll know, or eventually you'll know, when you're being lied to, and there is nothing worse than that. You can't be lied to and be happy. Or content. You need the truth. You need to see something for what it is. In this moment. I'm seeing your hair and the skin on top of your head, and it's all the truth I need right now. You just have to keep looking at things and seeing them as they are. Before Del died, he was staring up at the trees, these very tall pine trees out there above the cabin. I don't know what he thought or felt at that moment, but he knew he was about to die. He knew it was coming. For some reason I think he might have been content to know that. And if you can live that way, all the better. Once you're dead, all this doesn't matter, I guess. I don't know, but I don't think he's out there somewhere looking down on us. That's the hard thing to accept, that this is all there is, and it's only important while we're here, and after that it isn't important at all. Which makes you wonder why we find it all so important anyway. But we do. While we're here, every day you live your life you have to see what's important. What's important to me is you. You, and your father, whose name is Connor. And that I knew someone like Del Maki. He gave me something, I can't even describe it other than that he listened. Maybe that's what I can give you. I can listen to you. That's what I will try to do. Promise."

Marcia closed her eyes and began to doze again, until she heard some of the police vehicles leaving. She looked out the rear window at the trees above the road. The wind had let up and snow fluttered out of the sky like confetti. She was thinking she could watch the snow forever when he emerged from the white, Connor, shoulders hunched against the cold.

Stopping next to the car, he stared through the glass at her and the baby. In that moment, everything lay before them, and then he reached out to open the door.
